Upon finishing Suzanne Kelly's poetic novel *Stolen Child* I marvel at how accurately and completely the author captures the complexities of the Irish-American experience. Every page sings with particulars—familiar customs, superstitions, song lyrics, dance steps, history, snippets of the Irish language, clan loyalty, upward mobility, and the fierce Catholicism that spawns the familiar wry humor on one hand and coexists with belief in the faeries on the other. The book is a remarkable read if one is looking for authentic cultural immersion.

Nine-year-old Lucy Fahey is sent to her paternal grandmother during the summer of 1960—as her mother endures a summer of hospitalization for a cancer we see only through Lucy's eyes—a mysterious force that disrupts the family and removes her from communication. Grandma Fahey is charged with teaching Lucy the catechism which the dreamy girl has failed to master during the school year and she seems a perfect choice—strict, straight-laced, devout to a tee, and armed with defenses that have removed her from her own roots in western Ireland's County Mayo. When Lucy observes Grandma Fahey speaking in Irish to the backyard faeries, her curiosity begs: is there something else besides the catechism to believe in? When circumstances bring Lucy and Grandma Fahey in close contact with Lucy's mother's family, an Irish family of a different sort—fun-loving, irreverent, musical and effusive—the resulting conflicts give rise to some very humorous and rewarding chapters.

This novel is a testament to extended family, especially elder members of the family, who provide the links to culture.

—Mary Minock, author of *The Way-Back Room: A Memoir of a Detroit Childhood*

Stolen Child

Suzanne Kelly

For Natasha —
a great and _irreverent_
Colleague.
Warmest regards,
Suzanne

HARMONY SERIES
BOTTOM DOG PRESS

HURON, OHIO

General Editor: Larry Smith
Editor: Susanna Sharp-Schwacke
Cover Design: Susanna Sharp-Schwacke
Cover Image: © Getty Images

Acknowledgments

I wish to thank my husband Dave and my late mother-in-law, Inez Bass Garrison, both relentless in their encouragement of my writing. In the long process of writing this book I have been spurred on by my siblings, Larry Kelly, Nancy Kelly Waters, Janet Kelly Thoma, and the memory of Gregory Mansfield Kelly and our parents, Mary Rose Keary Kelly and Lawrence J. Kelly. I have been cheered constantly by the next generation: "Big Sean," Michael Joseph, Annie Robin and Stephen Quinn Kelly, Ryan Joseph and Sean Mansfield Waters, Ellen Rose and Margaret O'Fallon Thoma.

Any resemblance between characters in this book and those you know is merely coincidental, unless of course, it isn't.

Many thanks to the generous fiction writers who provided support and insights: Molly Campbell, Ed Davis, Erin Flanagan, Nancy Jones, Katrina Kittle, Nancy Pinard; and to the members of the Greenville Poets who labored good-naturedly through the "long version" and provided useful direction through the thicket: Catherine Essinger, Lianne Spidel, Myrna Stone, and Belinda Rismiller.

I am glad to have a chance to thank two wonderful reasons to have majored in English, Professors John P. Farrell and Max K. Sutton.

This book would never have come to be without the dogged support of Editor Larry Smith and Associate Editor Susanna Sharp-Schwacke at Bottom Dog Press.

Come away, O human child!
To the waters and the wild
With a faery, hand in hand,
For the world's more full of weeping
than you can understand.
                    "The Stolen Child," W. B. Yeats

For my family, past, present and to come, and especially for my husband, Dave.

"Let fate do her worst, there are relics of joy. Bright scenes from the past that she cannot destroy."
—Thomas Moore

PROLOGUE

I was nine in the summer of 1960 when I first heard the faeries—who were known in Ireland to steal what you value most—being directly addressed in Gaelic, heard Senator John F. Kennedy's accent echo though an auditorium in my parish, and heard the click and stomp of a proud old woman's heel strike the floor as she danced her native step. This was also the summer I was sent away during my mother's surgery convalescence. The memory of that time seems as clear as my own name shouted across an open field. How can I not turn and look back?

CHAPTER 1: EXTREME JUNCTION

"Lucy Fahey! Do you hear me, Lucy?"

The classroom was warm for May. The school year couldn't be over too soon. My head rested in the crook of my arm. My geography workbook lay open to a map of the world where the continents and oceans waited for me, just as they had for Adam, to name them. Instead I had drawn shark fins up and down the Atlantic coast of North America, put a diving board off the end of Cape Cod, and in the middle of the ocean I was drawing the humped backs of breaching whales. So pleased with my whales, I thought they should have some splashy noises to accompany them on their journey.

Do whales have ears? What do they hear as they wander the ocean? I bet they played games like the one that my brother, Jackie, and I played at the swimming pool, where we would float just below the surface and call out words to each other. No matter how hard we tried to hear and no matter how loud anybody yelled, only garbled bubbles of sound would bring us laughing and sputtering to the surface.

"What were you yelling, Luce?"

"My name. *Lucee Faheee, Luceee Faheee.*"

Because Jackie at twelve had just been memorizing his altar boy Latin, he said it sounded more like *Agnus Dei, Agnus Dei.*

Nope. Not *Agnus Dei*, the Lamb of God. Just me. Lucy Fahey. But it's hard to make something as simple as your own name understood when you're under water. And lately it was becoming harder and harder to make myself understood in most places above water, too. At school for instance, I couldn't make Sister Mary Columba understand that there wasn't only one way to spell a word or only one exact answer to a *Baltimore Catechism* question. What she didn't understand wouldn't matter to me for long. This was one of our last days of school before summer vacation.

My drawings of whales were filling up the ocean like kids at the public pool where Jackie and I would soon be hanging out again. There were whales of all sizes smiling back at me as I made louder underwater noises, like what roars past my good ear when I push off from the bottom in the shallow end. Summer couldn't come too soon.

"Hey, Lucy. You're supposed to stop making those noises." Jimmy Dowling, the boy in the next seat was nudging me. "Sister's yelled at you twice already."

I raised my head and looked at him. I had lost most of the hearing in my left ear from an infection last winter. He pointed to Sister Mary Columba now rising from her desk like the angry Neptune with the three pointed spear I'd seen in Jackie's Classic Comics. She was sticking her words on a trident, getting ready to hurl them towards my desk, the last one in the first row. I ducked down and heard my name reverberating off the back wall where her trident struck.

"Lucy Fahey! What is all that commotion?"

I turned my good ear towards her.

"Lucy, can you hear me?"

"Yes, Sister."

"Please come here then."

As I stood in front of her, she peered over her rimless glasses and said, and not for the first time this year, "Lucy, I have a very important letter for your parents. Please see that they get it."

"Yes S'ster." Letters to parents never contained good news of any sort. Unless you were Jackie Fahey.

I quickly reached for the envelope with the green and gold Mary of Gaels School insignia on it, and as I did she pulled it back and said, "Lucy, I mean business this time." She began to tap the corner of the envelope on the palm of my open hand for emphasis, "You are woefully behind the class in catechism and nearly every other subject, young lady. How do you expect me to pass you on to the next grade with your classmates?"

I just stared at my palm where she was raising a small welt as red as I knew my face to be. The more she talked and tapped, the more I worried that this might be how those bloody stigmata get started. But they only spurted from the palms of very holy saints, not fourth graders like me.

At the final tap, she sighed, "We never had this trouble with Jack Fahey."

She didn't need to say that. I closed my stinging hand around the letter.

I didn't understand the sudden kindness in her voice when she asked, "Where will you be staying this summer while your mother is in the hospital?"

I was pretty sure I'd be staying at home and going to the pool every day with Jackie. Then I would leave for my regular summer visit, a few weeks with Mama's mom, Grandma Keary. She'd called last night to talk to Mama about my summer visit. I didn't answer Sister Mary Columba. What I did in summer time was beyond her reach anyway.

When she told the class to remember Mrs. Fahey in their prayers over the summer, I felt my cheeks turn hot and prickly. I didn't want anyone to know my mom was that sick, especially when it seemed like it had something to do with my not knowing my catechism.

"Go on now, Lucy, and take your seat."

I felt the envelope in my hand dampen as I walked back to my desk. My scalp tingled a little as sweat cooled down my shame. I didn't have to look around at anyone to know all eyes were on me. Jackie told me that I was too little to flunk completely out of school, but now I wasn't for sure. The letter was a pretty thick one, and that couldn't be a good sign, so I drew a few whales on it just for good luck when I got back to my desk.

Sister Mary Columba rang a little silver bell that she kept on her desk and announced that we'd discuss catechism next, the seven sacraments. Since the warm spring weather hit, it was hard for anyone to pay attention in class. Today a gusty wind dislodged a kickball that had been stuck in a drift of leaves since last winter, and a breeze now came through the open window like a friendly voice calling us out to the playground for a game of jacks, or anything that wasn't school. It was easy not to listen to Sister Mary Columba, who was, after all, talking about something I already knew, the final sacrament. The last rites, the extreme junction. Let her ask me that one, instead of old questions like "Why did God make you?" That had no real answer I could see.

But I'd heard my dad say those words, "extreme junction," on the phone to Grandma Fahey that day last fall when he came home from the hospital and cried. He sobbed so loud it scared me, but Jackie told me not to worry, that there was an ointment they can give you when things get extreme, and that it will make Mama better, or else why would they have given it to her.

"Really, Jackie?"

"Yeah, but the word is unction, Luce, not junction."

"Does it sting, Jackie?" I had cringed thinking of the ointment Mama used when I had bloodied both of my knees falling from Jackie's bike onto a gravel path.

"S'pect so. It has to be powerful to work."

Today Sister said we would not go all the way through the seven sacraments but would stop at confession. Did we have any questions about what might be sins to confess?

Ever since Mama's bad headaches started up, I wondered if it was a sin to believe that God played favorites or at least didn't hear any better than me. He never answered anybody's prayers. But before I could raise my hand to ask, Sister had called on Jimmy Dowling.

"Sister, what if a kid, who was out of baseball cards, clipped a plastic holy card into to the spokes of his bike, you know, with a clothes pin to make it sound like a motorcycle engine?"

Big deal. Jackie and I did this all the time because one really thick plastic-coated holy card slapping against your spokes outlasted a whole pack of baseball cards that the public school kids were stuck using. In fact, my bike parked in the schoolyard had a card of sour old Pope Pius that had been going strong all week. Jackie had come up with a sandwich of a couple of baseball cards in between two plastic-coated saints cards. His St. Francis of Assisi and St. Francis Xavier combo lasted all spring once, even in the rain. After that he took Francis as his confirmation name. Francis Xavier was our dad's name, too.

After Eggs Carney, who was sitting through fourth grade again, asked if it was a sin to baptize your dog if your big brothers gave you a dime, Sister sized up the number of raised hands, and reminded us that we would still have to stay after school for doing stuff that God might not have noticed as sins. Hands came down. I never asked my question about God's hearing loss.

The school day ended as it had begun, with prayers. Afterward we lined up single file to dip a finger in the little holy water font that hung on the wall by the door. We signed ourselves and headed for freedom. I was generous with the holy water when my turn came on this hot afternoon. The splash on my forehead felt like the promise of summer days at the swimming pool with Jackie. I walked with my classmates toward the open door and let the holy water run down my forehead to the tip of my nose. As I hit the outside air, I closed one eye and looked at the tip of my nose where the droplet was forming. With one quick puff that made my bangs stand up straight, I blew the holy water drop away in a little arc. I thought of the breaching whales in my drawing and wished I were there with them as they sounded in the blue depths.

Soon I was on my bike with the wind in my face and evaporating holy water cooling my forehead. I pedaled as fast as I could to put the school day behind me, the face of the old pope ticking steadily against my spokes. When I got to the footbridge over the creek, I hopped off my bike, peered into the clear water, caught my breath, and then reached for the envelope in my uniform pocket. My hands and face were hot and itchy again as I looked at the familiar handwriting on the thick envelope addressed to "Frank and Rose Fahey." My name was in parenthesis under theirs, so it was kind of addressed to me, too. Why shouldn't I open it before they do? They'd probably want me to go through it first, and take out anything that would upset them.

I turned page after mimeographed page of what had to be the longest homework assignment that anyone had ever been given. The letter to my folks said that I had to master all these assignments before she would recommend me for the next grade. I crammed every page back into the envelope. What if I never delivered it, how would anyone at home ever know? The thought confused me, but only for a second or two. I looked over the railing on the little bridge and studied the water flowing through the light and dark shadows on the surface. I tore the envelope in half, right between the "Frank and Rose Fahey," then in half again, and let the pieces of the paper questions fall and turn into a fleet of little boats on the eddying stream below. I watched the words, "Rose Fahey," sail swiftly under the bridge. I quickly moved to the other side to see my mom's name emerge on the stream briefly, the water dissolving the blue Scripto ink from Sister Mary Columba's fountain pen. I stared until the last bit of paper sank or disappeared among the cattails.

I got back on my bike and headed for home. When I reached our kitchen door, I saw Dad through the screen, sitting at the kitchen table, *The Kansas City Star* spread before him. A small glass on the table was half full of Jameson's whiskey, the same reddish brown color of his thinning hair. The tenor on the record player in the living room was singing the tomb scene from *Lucia di Lammermoor*. My dad was energetically whistling the tenor part, in between shots.

As I opened the door, he looked up and said, "Hey Luce, don't let that door ..." His last word was obliterated by the rifle shot noise of the slamming screen door.

"Lucy, how many times do I have to tell you not to let it slam like that ... you'll upset your mother. And don't be leaving your bike out in the yard for someone to steal. That's the last bike I'll pay for, by God."

"Yes sir." I turned to go back out and put the bike away when he said, "Go in and see your Mother now. She wants to talk to you about something, something important." I stood in the middle of the room, uncertain of which of his commands to follow when he exploded at the tenor repeating himself on the scratched record, "Damn it all to hell." He yelled like something really hurt him somewhere. "Doesn't anything around this place work right?"

My dad swore more the closer it got to the time Mama was supposed to leave. I raced off to my mother's bedside.

Mama was lying on her back with her eyes closed.

"That you, Lucy? I thought I heard you come in," she chuckled mildly.

"Sorry, Mama." I crawled up next to her on the bed as I hadn't since I was very small.

"I guess that door doesn't sound too loud to you, but it does disturb your Dad. Do try to be a little quieter."

"Yessum."

"Lucy, you know that as soon as school is out I'll be leaving to go to the hospital."

I said nothing but began to trace with my finger the pattern of the white chenille bedspread under which she lay.

"Your Dad and I are trying to decide what's best for you. You've got the entire summer before you with some catching up to do. We are trying to decide, well, where you should go."

I clutched the chenille with both hands. She was the one leaving home, not me.

"Luce, it's like this, everybody has to, well, pitch in and do their best now. You understand don't you? You are getting to be a big girl now."

"Couldn't I just go with you, Mama? I wouldn't get in the way at all." My voice was sounding as wobbly as Mama's.

"Hospitals are not places for little ones, Luce."

How could I be too little to go with her, but big enough to be left behind at the same time? I didn't much care for being nine, if anyone was asking.

Mama got out of bed, put on her robe and sat down at her dressing table. I scrunched in next to her on the bench. We looked at each other through our reflections in her mirror. Mama seemed taller to me now that she was getting thinner.

She silently combed my bangs a bit and smoothed the hair on the sides back behind my ears with her cool hands. After she powdered her face, I slapped some on my nose and cheeks to hide the freckles. Then I rooted around in her top drawer for the little silver basketball on a silver chain. This was her trophy for being the basketball free throw champion at Kansas City Power and Light during the war. I loved playing with it, and wanted one for my own. I wanted all of Mama's glamour for my own, her soft face powder, and her lipstick. I even envied the small pox vaccination mark on her upper arm. Once I tried to make a vaccine mark on my arm with the bristles of her hairbrush. It stung but was worth it to be like her.

~ 17 ~

"Lucy," she said so quickly that it startled me, "how would you like to spend an entire summer with your grandmother?"

I guessed going to Grandma Keary's would be almost like being at home and I was used to staying over with Mama's mom.

"Can I bring my bike to Grandma Keary's?"

She seemed too tired to hear my question.

"Your Grandmother Fahey will be able to help you with your school work this summer while I'm gone," she continued.

Grandma Fahey! I knew Mama had a lot on her mind these days, but I couldn't believe she was sending me to the wrong Grandma's house. My dad's mom had never even once asked me to stay overnight at her house. But I had learned to walk at Grandma Keary's, or so they told me. It was easy to imagine Mama launching me across the living room floor and my falling into Grandma's open arms and laughter. There was always something fun going on at Grandma Keary's little house, like learning to put my hand through Great Uncle Red's smoke rings. It was full of relatives of all kinds, loud, red faced, musical people. Great Uncle Red taught me to sing the best songs I knew at Grandma Keary's.

Things were much different at Grandma Fahey's Tudor house on the wide boulevard that was much bigger than Grandma Keary's, or maybe Grandma Fahey's house just seemed bigger because it kind of echoed. I'd never seen more than a few people in it at one time, ever.

"I'm sure Grandma Keary and Uncle Red will look in on you from time to time."

I could barely imagine them in the same room at the same time with Grandma Fahey, who would come for Sunday dinner at our house in the suburbs, but only if it was clear that none of the Quinns, or any of my mother's people had also been invited. This seemed to suit everyone—especially during this election year.

The last time I had seen both of my grandmothers together was at Jackie's Confirmation party. Grandma Fahey sat in the corner of our living room, away from the TV where Dad and Mama's brother Mickey were watching the Notre Dame game. Grandma Fahey looked like she was waiting for the bus.

When it came time for Jackie's gifts, she'd announced that she'd pay Jackie's tuition, if he studied hard and got into the Jesuit high school my dad and his brother went to. Grandma Keary gave Jackie two dollars in an envelope and her smile that told you right where you stood with her.

Grandma Keary was friendly to everyone and could talk to anyone about anything.

"Mrs. Fahey, I was wondering, did you see Bishop Sheen on the television last week?" she'd asked.

"I did, Mrs. Keary, and isn't he dead right about transubstantiation after all."

"He is indeed, Mrs. Fahey. Dead right," she'd replied while smiling at Mama.

That was about all Grandma Fahey said to anyone until she asked my dad to take her home. Mama hadn't served the cake yet and Notre Dame was on Army's 20-yard line, but Dad went for his keys.

"Does Jackie have to go to Grandma Fahey's, too?"

"Luce, Jackie needs to stay closer to home, to help Daddy with the yard work. And he's got his pitching season coming up. He'll be over at Uncle Mickey's most of the time on game days."

Uncle Mickey was Mama's favorite brother, who had no children of his own and had the best job anyone could imagine. He was a milkman who drove his own dairy truck, full of ice cream bars that Jackie would get first dibs on.

I wanted to yell, "How come? How come he gets to go there and I have to go someplace scary?" but I knew it would be like yelling under water. Even Mama wouldn't understand me if I told her I was afraid to go to Grandma Fahey's by myself. I always stuck close to Jackie whenever we were at her house. Jackie didn't much like it there either, except for when she fussed over his catechism medals and his grades, or when we got to roam around her terraced back yard with all the old elm and oak trees. But the inside of her house always smelled like furniture polish and starch. She made everyone, even Daddy, sit on her plastic upholstery covers, and that made him crankier than ever. I hated the way the plastic stuck to the backs of my legs in the summer when I wore shorts or culottes. And then there was the praying. There was bound to be plenty of that.

"Please, don't make me go there," I blurted, not caring whether anyone could hear me or not.

"Luce, it's like this. Grandma Fahey will know how to help you get caught up on your learning. You wouldn't want to be left behind when your class moves up next fall, would you."

Mama started to rub her forehead over the eye that was causing her trouble. I hoped she wasn't getting a bad headache again, but I felt kind of achy myself. I was surprised how big my own eyes seemed to me in the mirror. I'd be all alone at Grandma Fahey's all summer. I knew how to measure an entire summer in days at the pool but not in days at Grandma Fahey's.

"But what about Grandma Keary? She'll miss me at her birthday party, Mama," I told her quietly. "And Uncle Red needs me this summer, too. I already promised to help him register people to vote for Senator Kennedy."

Mama's hand came from her eye, "Is Uncle Red already planning for that?"

"Yessum. He says it'll be just like Jackie Robinson stealing home right under their noses, Mama." A brief smile came over her face like a bit of sunshine on a cloudy day, so I pressed the point. "Uncle Red says Senator Kennedy's grandparents are from Ireland, like mine, so he's counting on my help."

"Lucy, I don't think he'll need our help just yet."

"But Mama, Uncle Red does."

"Senator Kennedy is a long shot, Luce, a real long one. I don't think even Uncle Red thinks he can get the nomination, let alone win the election."

I wanted to tell her that he did believe in luck that strong and that Uncle Red said there were unseen forces at work that were about to turn a big page in a history book somewhere, but I knew she wasn't listening to me anymore.

"It is best, Luce, not to get your hopes too high." She was looking through the window to her garden as if something there gave her a pain that rubbing her forehead would not help.

"Your dad thinks, Luce, it would be best to go to Grandmother Fahey's, so you can really focus on catching up on your school work, especially your catechism and history."

I knew Dad was behind this and every other serious thing we ever had to do that was good for us.

Mama was looking at me directly now, not through her mirror.

"I don't want to go, Mama. I don't want to go anywhere. I don't want anybody to go anywhere."

She hugged me to let the warm tears spurt from my eyes.

"I'll talk to your dad, Luce. We'll see. His mind is made up though."

I wiped the little streams that my tears had made through the powder on my cheeks and squeezed the basketball charm to change my luck maybe.

"Lucy, are you really trying your hardest at school?"

"Yessum," I answered, not looking at her face.

"Can you hear Sister Mary Columba okay, Luce?"

I thought that the dead could hear her today as she made my failings public.

"Lucy, did you bring home some lists from school?"

"No'am." I looked up at her quickly.

"They called from school this afternoon about a letter sent home with you. Did you remember to bring it home?"

It was so close to summer vacation. Why was everyone making such a fuss over homework now?

"Lucy, can you bring me the letter? Is it in your school bag?"

"No'am."

Mama sighed wearily, but I was just protecting her from what they were saying about me. It would just hurt her feelings. She wouldn't want to know it if I was a dope.

"Does Dad know?"

"He answered the phone when Sister Mary Columba called."

I winced. He didn't much like talking to the nuns and priests even when there was good news from school. And Mama usually didn't bother him with school news about me. Now I felt like everything was spinning out of control, like I was riding one of the shreds of paper I'd made of the letter home, eddying right on down the creek.

CHAPTER 2: DINO DANCING

Dad hadn't said anything in a couple of days about my going to Grandma Fahey's, which I took as a very good sign that Mama had figured something out. She and Grandma Keary had spoken on the phone just this morning as usual. By the weekend, my family would be splitting up for the summer.

Dad had made breakfast this morning and the sight of him wearing an apron and the rubbery taste of the bacon made Jackie and me laugh behind his back. Mama had shushed us. With Dad serving her for a change, it looked like she was the head of the family and could make the final decision that I'd be going to Grandma Keary's. She might even decide that Jackie and I both needed to go to Grandma Keary's.

Or maybe, as happened a lot lately, Dad would just forget what he'd said before. Yesterday Jackie asked him to catch his practice pitches, and Dad pounded on the table and said how could anybody think about baseball at a time like this. Then after dinner he'd suddenly said, "Get your mitt, Jacko," as always. Something lucky like that was bound to happen to me, too. Mama would see to it that I didn't end up all alone in that big old house all summer. Anybody could see that I belonged at Grandma Keary's.

There I could unwind. There was always a kind of melody, an Irish one, in Grandma Keary's voice. It wasn't that she sang all the time, like her brothers, Uncle Red and Uncle Conny. It was that her quiet, steady way was like music. Uncle Red had music in the way he spoke, too, but he was noisier. He could fill her living room with his laugh. And Uncle Conny could shake her house with his politics and rebel songs. They were all Quinns, and Quinns loved their singing as much as they loved their own company. They also couldn't seem to resist slapping my dad on the back in a friendly way, but one that made him mutter under his breath. They told Mama that's the only reason they did it.

I'd find a place there to wait for Mama to come home again. Grandma Keary never lost sight of me, even when things started to change for Mama last fall. When I asked Grandma would everything be okay again soon, she'd taken me on her lap and rocked me. She'd held me close as she sang "The Vale of Avoca," about the cool, green place by a stream in her native home of Ireland, "Where our hearts like thy waters are mingled in peace." Thinking now of that stream in my mind made the creek where I'd gotten rid of the letter from school seem much farther away. Grandma Keary's songs always made more sense than whatever I worried about.

Grandma might announce the seasons with song. When a season changed, her song would too, like the liturgy at church. I sat in her kitchen one day last fall after Mama dropped me off on the way to the doctor's office. Mama was so nervous she hadn't even remembered to say goodbye to me, so Grandma Keary sang "Come, Little Leaves" as we baked green apple pies that afternoon. Although she sang "that summer is gone and the days grow cold" as she trimmed her pies, it didn't seem sad. The song was round like her pies, with the last verse folding into the first. It was an unbroken circle: it began with the wind calling to the leaves to "come over the meadow to play" and ended with the leaves "singing the sad little song they knew" about the wind inviting them to play.

If Dad drove Mama to the doctor, I'd be dropped off at his mother's. The rosary, not a baking pie, was the circle at Grandma Fahey's. We'd kneel on her floor and pray that the Blessed Mother would hear our prayers for Mama. Like most things about Grandma Fahey, the rosary was complicated and it was easy to get lost in all the Hail Marys, one repeating decade right after another in the Five Sorrowful, Five Glorious, and Five Joyful Mysteries. Once Grandma Fahey gave me one of her fanciest rosaries to help me keep track, but it didn't help. Its beads were blue cut glass that became little kaleidoscopes fracturing the light in the room about me.

There were at least three Grandma Faheys floating in air when I looked up at her through the largest bead. I was counting her images when she snapped, "Lucy, pay attention! You'll lose your way. We are in the second decade, move forward two beads past the first *Pater Noster* bead."

"Yessum."

After the rosary, I had to listen to stories from the lives of the saints while I tried to keep the backs of my legs from sticking to her sofa cover. I squirmed until she got to the story of Father Jacques Marquette exploring the Great Lakes and the Mississippi. That story held me like a boat upon the river. Waving the silver crucifix on her rosary for emphasis, she told me that this holy explorer brought the true faith to the Indian tribes along the banks and in his spare time discovered the river that ran right through Chicago, where she grew up. I thought only of the good luck of being on a raft and floating on the river all day long for an entire summer.

"Did he get to fish for catfish and hunt crawdads whenever he wanted, Grandma?"

"He most certainly did not, Lucy," she scolded. "Father Marquette was a very famous Jesuit on an important mission—not some Huckleberry Sawyer! Your Uncle Nat was a Jesuit too, you know, God rest his soul."

She always brought the talk around to my dad's dead brother. She sounded sadder than my dad when talking about Uncle Natty. Daddy was still upset, too, but it was more like he was mad but wasn't allowed to say at whom. But both Dad and Grandma shut a door on you like you weren't there whenever his name came up.

No, Grandma Keary's would suit me better. There were no lectures on anything and, except for the house rule that the losing party at Chinese checkers had to put the marbles away, no other rules or regulations came to mind. At Grandma Keary's, I could spend hours lying on the floor listening to her humming tunes to the steady rhythm of her Singer sewing machine and watching the motes of dust glide effortlessly through the sunlight, like small boats that appeared out of nowhere and sailed to the edge of the sunlight and then disappeared again.

"Where do they come from, Grandma? Where do they go?" I asked when I felt her watching me, the warmth of her gaze mixing with the warmth of the sunlight on my back.

"From God and to God, I suppose, Lucy. From silence into silence."

This morning while riding bikes with Jackie, I thought of how good things could come out of silence. For example, I took it as a good sign that neither Mom nor Dad had said anything more about the letter and homework assignments from Mary of Gaels. I told Jackie I thought they'd forgotten all about it, like it had been really washed downstream. But Jackie said that throwing the letter in the creek wouldn't stop anything because Sister Mary Columba would just put another copy in the mail. He said, "The only reason Dad didn't say anything was he was just too mad at what a chowder head you are."

Just the same, I turned off on my bike and rode to the bridge to look into the water and think in quiet about the shreds of the papers from school sunk there in the mud. Probably some old hard shelled crawdad like the kind Jackie and I would catch under rocks in the deepest pools in the creek was holding a bit of the mimeograph in its claw, maybe trying to make sense of it, too. I laughed at the thought.

As I stared at my reflection in the water below the bridge, I wasn't surprised that my face looked rippled like it was breaking up into streaks of silver and black. It was pretty much how I had felt for days, light headed from not knowing if I was going to laugh or cry. Sometimes when I thought I was going to cry, it came out as a laugh instead. And sometimes things that were funny made me tear up. Riding my bike back home I got to thinking that Jackie felt the same way, but he'd never say so. He'd wanted to play together more in the last couple of days than we had in a long time, probably because he knew we wouldn't get to for a while. Everything we said or did seemed funnier and sadder, as if we were in church or some other serious place.

When I got home, I stood in my brother's doorway watching him rummage around under his bed for the Sears football game he hadn't played with in months. He'd been going through all his old toys like there was no tomorrow. We could both hear Dad's voice rising up from downstairs.

"Lucy's in trouble at school, Rose. Do you really think any of your people would take that seriously?"

I couldn't hear what my mom said—her voice would get softer when she had an important point to make—but I'm sure she was just telling Dad that I would have a much better time at Grandma Keary's and that Grandma Fahey's house makes my nostrils burn from all the cleaning she does.

"We might as well let her drop out of school altogether as send her to your mom's for the summer, Rose."

I turned my good ear towards the hall to hear Mama's reassuring argument. "But Frank, Lucy and my mom get along so well. It would be more like home to her while I'm ... away."

Exactly. Who couldn't see that Grandma Keary and I were like pals?

Jackie looked up front his place on the floor, "Hey Luce, you want to play electronic football?"

"Sure." I closed the door behind me. Mama was holding her own.

Jackie's prized game was a particleboard football field about two feet long that sat over a motor that hummed and made the field vibrate. It came with two-inch high blue and red plastic football players with painted numbers on their jerseys. When you switched the board on, the players would shimmy and charge down the field at each other at whatever speed you wanted, high, medium or low. Jackie knew just how to set the men up so that the blue running back with the magnetized football on his metal base would be able to shudder his way to the goal, after the reds and the other blues got tied in a hopeless mess at the line of scrimmage.

Now when he opened the little pouch where he stored the players only a handful tumbled out.

"Lucy! You were messing with this, weren't you?"

What was the big deal? He never minded before. He was just cranky because he was grounded again. Dad grounded Jackie a lot now that Mama was getting ready to go to the hospital. I got grounded once just for being in the room when Jackie was getting grounded, but then Dad forgot the next day that he'd grounded either of us. We took off on our bikes and stayed away all afternoon just in case he thought about it again.

"Did you look in the dinosaur boxes?" I asked. "Maybe there are football guys in there. I think that's where I put them."

"Why did you mix up my dinos and my football players?" he huffed. "Why can't you be like other girls and just play with dolls or something? And why don't you just pay attention in school? It would be a whole lot easier for everybody. Nobody flunks catechism but you. Catechism isn't any harder than keeping track of a baseball season. It is all just rules, teams, and players. National League, American League. Angels, Archangels. You know baseball well enough."

As he opened two large boxes full of plastic dinosaurs he brought from his closet, he yelped like the world was coming to an end, "And this, what about this? You mixed my carnivores and herbivores like I told you never to do."

If the herbivores didn't mind being in with the carnivores, why should Jackie?

"So what?"

"So what nothing. It's my stuff. Stay out of it."

Whenever I tried to line up the football players with Jackie the same thing always happened. When the blue offensive ends, who were posed with their arms out in front, met the red defenders at midfield, they would stop playing football and start to dance, locking arms and spinning like a gang of jersey-wearing square dancers. Watching them all sway and dance was a better game anyway, except for one thing: the football players all had the exact same dumb, grim expression. Jackie's dinos, on the other hand, had more interesting faces, all growls and roars. They were just as determined as the football guys, but by their faces you could see they knew they were in a fight for their lives, not just a football game. It must have been pretty tough being a dinosaur. They might want to get out of Jackie's closet and go to a dance.

So, the last time I'd played with Jackie's game I'd taken my favorite of Jackie's two-legged dinosaurs, the duck-billed plant eater, and paired her up with another dino who, although his face was stuck mid-roar, looked pretty stable on his feet. I flipped the switch to high since the dinos were much larger than the football players. Just as I had hoped, when they came towards each other, the carnivorous Allosaurus with the scraggly arms linked up with the claw of the distracted duck-billed dino. Her slender claw that looked like it had been reaching for some tender green leaf to eat had clung to her dance partner, the fierce Allosaurus.

Now I figured if I showed Jackie my new invention —dinosaur dancing—he'd cool off about my playing with his stuff.

"Look, Jackie. Here's another game."

I again selected the Allosaurus and the duck-billed dino across from each other at the 40-yard line and flipped the switch.

"This isn't a fair fight, Luce. The Allosaurus'll eat the other guy alive."

"They aren't going to fight, Jackie. They are going to dance."

"Bet me," he laughed. "They are mortal enemies. Enemies don't dance. This'll be a fight to the finish. In this cornah, wearing gahreen trunks"—all the herbivores were made out of green plastic—"weighing 12 tons ..."

We giggled together like we hadn't since seventh grade girls had started calling the house for Jackie. He did a pretty good job of imitating the announcer on the Friday night fights on the television. Daddy might miss Sunday Mass but never Friday night fights. The two dinos waddled toward each other. When their arms got tangled, for all they could do about it, they pulled each other into a graceful dance, spinning slowly in a circle. The peaceful, duck-billed dino seemed to smile and the roaring Allosaurus now seemed to be throwing its head back as if to laugh. It was like watching something impossible that you wanted to believe could happen, like the elves and flying reindeer in Macy's window at Christmas. We knew they weren't real, but there they were in the biggest department store window downtown.

Our parents' voices were now loud enough for us to hear even through the closed door, especially my dad's.

"I can't do everything, Rose. Your mom will want to be helping you. My mother is the only one free and able to help Lucy with her school work."

"Frank, you know that Maeve won't want Lucy underfoot for any period of time. Are you forgetting how much she complained that the kids rattled her good china from the shelf running through her house the last time they were there? And that was only for a few hours."

Jackie and I looked at each other. We never knew she complained about both of us. Well, I didn't have any fun there either if anyone was asking. I didn't want to stay with her any more than she wanted me there.

"Lucy shouldn't be running in the house any-way ..."

Jackie shrugged and began to crowd the line of scrimmage with plant eaters and meat eaters, both four legged and two legged ones. "Here's a better game than dino dancing, Luce. Watch this. It's dinosaur football. Which side are you going to bet on? I'm going with the side with the most meat eaters."

There was the meanest looking line anyone could imagine, all these prehistoric faces frozen in their ferocity. It wasn't really football. It was just crashing and clashing of monsters at the line. The new rule was that you got points if any of your dinos made it to either end zone.

We quickly learned that whoever had the huge Brontosaurus with the long neck in the backfield always broke through the line first. Jackie dubbed him Bronto Nugurski after one of his favorite players. Bronto easily pushed aside plant eater and meat eater alike. But even after the Brontosaurus tore a hole in the line, your best players might not make it to the end zone for a couple of reasons. The big four-footed ones were slow. And the lighter two-leggers seemed to sprint by on their hind legs, but they couldn't go the distance. They would shake so violently on their haunches when we turned up the speed that they would just fall over and spin on their sides. We needed players who were both more lightweight than the big dinos and more stable than the two-legged sprinters.

This is where our glow-in-the-dark saint statues came in handy. Jackie had a bunch since he won practically every catechism and history contest at Mary of Gaels. I had only two that Grandma Fahey had given me as birthday presents. These guys never fell over even on high and they moved pretty evenly down the field. To determine who the fastest saints were, we ran qualifying heats. My St. Joseph the Carpenter against his St. Thomas Aquinas, my St. Anthony Patron of Lost Objects against his St. Ignatius Loyola. Jackie tried to put up his little metal statue of Duns Scotus, but I'd never heard of him. He didn't even glow in the dark, so I didn't think he was a real saint. Jackie said he was too a saint, he just couldn't play the night games.

I was soon out of saints, so he ran Duns Scotus against his own St. Thomas More.

In a race between his smart guy saints and my good guy saints, the good guys finished last. St. Thomas Aquinas was clearly the fastest of them all and Jackie said he was also the smartest guy who ever lived. He was sure smarter than any dinosaur that let himself get extinct. They are still naming schools for St. Thomas but you only see dinosaurs in toy stores. But could he get past Bronto Nugurski coming at him at midfield? We needed to know. I told myself that if Aquinas won, it would be good luck for me.

We were yelling so loud for Aquinas to make his end run around the Brontosaurus that we almost didn't hear Dad roaring like a wounded Tyrannosaurus from the doorway, "What the hell is all this racket? Your mother is trying to rest. Jack, I want you front and center in the yard, there's grass to be cut and hedges that need to be trimmed. And Lucy, it wouldn't hurt you to look over this schoolwork of yours."

He had some mimeographs in his hand that had come in the mail that morning just as Jackie said they would.

We scattered before we found out what was going to happen to St. Thomas Aquinas and the Brontosaurus in the big game. But when Dad left by himself to go to his mother's house after dinner that night, Jackie and I met up again in his room. The final battle was at hand. All of the glow-in-the-darks against the biggest dinos this time. I told myself if the saints won best out of seven games that would mean that Mama would win over Dad, and I'd get to go to Grandma Keary's. Holy glowing saints against extinct old dinos? No contest.

No matter how many play patterns I tried and no matter which glow-in-the-darks I used, the dinos won, six out of seven.

That night I couldn't get to sleep. My room was completely dark except for the greenish light from the still glowing St. Thomas Aquinas that I'd taken from the field of battle. I sat up when I heard my dad's car in the drive way. He was home from Grandma Fahey's and was calling out to Mama as soon as he opened the front door. I got out of bed and went down the hall. I was leaning over the banister by the time he said, "My mind's made up, Rose. It's for her own good. My mother has agreed to take Lucy."

Jackie's door opened now and he came into the hallway holding a Tyrannosaurus by its tail.

"My mother'll put some good old-fashioned Fahey starch in that kid."

Fahey starch didn't sound like a good thing to me.

I couldn't hear Mama's voice at all. Meat eaters versus the gentle plant eaters.

"Lucy hears well enough, Rose. That's not what's keeping her back in school. She's a daydreamer, and spending any more time with your people certainly won't help that. She has to face facts, learn to work at things."

"Looks like you're going to Grandma Fahey's," Jackie said from the shadows.

I sat down on the floor to keep from falling over.

"Sorry, Luce. Here, you want this one?" Jackie handed me his favorite and most fierce dino, but I didn't think that would help anything now. I wondered if gentle plant eaters went extinct before the meat eaters. Mama had lost our battle. Up until that moment I thought she could fix anything.

"Jackie, why is she even going to the hospital?"

"She needs to get a new eye, Luce. It will be just like her old one except she won't be able to see out of it."

I asked how she would be able to see us both at the same time. Jackie covered one eye, squinted and concluded that she'd have to look at us one at a time. I didn't like the sound of that one bit. I already felt in line behind Jackie in most things, especially in making sense of schoolwork. But my dad said he wasn't standing for me being behind at school and that after my time in his old parish this summer, I would learn to pay much better attention.

"I'm sorry, Rose, really I am. It has to be done this way. We can't let her grow up to be lazy. She's a Fahey and Faheys are not lazy."

I went back to bed and threw my head against my pillow. I'd never been called lazy before. Is that what I was? I wished I had something like Jackie had with his pitching that everyone agreed was important enough to keep him closer to home. I buried my good right ear in the pillow and muffled out the rest of the noise from the living room, but the word "lazy" kept going around in my head. If lazy meant wandering through half-heard words, allowing them to glance off each other without being concerned for meaning, then I guess that described me.

Lazy. But then I liked the word because of the buzz and vibration it made in my good ear. I repeated the word over and over, stressing the last syllable and stretching out the "z" sound. La*zee*. La*zee*. La*zee*.

The word, as I repeated it, reminded me of the chanting of the locusts in the trees at the end of last summer at Grandma Keary's. They sat high in the old trees that grew along her street. We'd sit at our place on her porch and I'd imitate their song, thinking they might be chanting my name. Lu*cee*. Lu*cee*. Lu*cee*.

Lazy sounded like hazy. "Looks like another hazy old night, Lucy darlin'," Grandma Keary would say as she brought out two ice-cold 7-Ups in small green bottles. The word itself brings to memory the kind of night in which the heat would rise like a mist off hot neighborhood streets and sidewalks into the cooler night air, and form prismed haloes around streetlights. The city on summer nights was always hazy. My hopes for going to Grandma Keary's were gone, faded into a haze.

CHAPTER 3: LIKE FAERY GIFTS FADING AWAY

It was Sunday night and I'd be leaving the next morning for Grandma Fahey's house for what might as well be the rest of my life. I couldn't sleep for the thought of leaving my own bed before I was ready to. An empty space around my heart was starting to grow a shell. I had never been away from home for more than a week except at Grandma Keary's, where she would sing me to sleep in the little bed she made up for me in her sewing room.

The lights were still on downstairs. No one had come to hear our prayers as on other nights. The screen door squeaked open and bumped closed. Dad had stepped outside to smoke a cigarette, the smell of his unfiltered Camel wafted up to my window along with his words, "Jesus, not asking why anymore, just how the hell we'll get through this." He said "Jesus" a lot when he was mad, but this was something between praying and wanting to start a fight. This took the place of anybody's prayers getting heard in our house this night.

My mom was playing soft chords on the piano, no song really, just chords that went from major to minor and back. The old upright that was a gift from Uncle Red never stayed in tune the way Mama's fine piano did. The tinny sound of Uncle Red's piano sounded hopeful and imperfect. It never made sense to me that Mama would suddenly decide last Thanksgiving to sell her baby grand that she polished so often the crystal vase full of flowers seemed to float on the shimmering mahogany surface. Jackie said they needed the money for doctors' bills.

I sat next to her on the bench while she waited for the men from Jenkins Music to take the piano away. She played arpeggios like she was trying to hit every single key, up and down the scales for the last time. My whole body was humming and light seemed to be everywhere in the room. I'd been surprised when she suddenly closed the keyboard and locked it with a fancy brass key that I never knew belonged with the piano. Jackie and I used it as our skeleton key when we played pirates.

After the movers had taken her piano, she'd tried to smile and said, as if she'd just thought of it, "There. That's much better. Gives us more room. Don't you think, Luce?" Mama's voice echoed off the walls in the corner where the piano had been. The house went silent when the piano went away. It made my dad's moodiness and my mom's edginess louder.

Now I tapped on the wall between Jackie's room and mine. Two taps meant, "I'm awake." Two taps back meant, "me, too." I tapped twice, and then again. I heard Jackie's sleepy voice through the wall, "Go to sleep, Luce. Don't worry about it. It's probably just for the summer."

"Just the summer? How could it be any longer than that?"

When Jackie didn't answer, I tapped twice again and didn't wait for him to tap back.

"Jackie, do you think I could get to Grandma Keary's house from Grandma Fahey's if I really needed to?"

"No way. Well, unless you had your bike—and you had a map with all the streets or something. But they won't let you take your bike to the city because of all the traffic, so forget it."

As I tried to think how to get through the summer, my brain felt like my bike the time the chain slipped off the teeth of the gear. I was pumping but going nowhere. I wondered if Uncle Red could save me from a summer at Grandma Fahey's if Mama couldn't do it. After all they didn't call him the great ward healer down at the Al Smith Room for nothing. Uncle Red might be able to turn things around as he had before. He'd saved us all from a chilly silence last Christmas.

Jackie had said we wouldn't be getting anything at all for Christmas because they couldn't afford it this year. Boy, was he wrong. Mama got a new piano. When Uncle Red showed up on Christmas Eve to bring Mama the old upright, it was like things were almost back to the way they were before she got sick.

Great Uncle Red hollered from our front hallway, "Hello, the House of Fahey!" as he always did when he came by on Christmas Eve with presents. Jackie and I both ran down the stairs to the front door where Dad stood, his hand against Uncle Red's chest, "I won't take charity from you, Red."

"Well then, Frank, it is a good thing I am not bringing it to you, isn't it?" Uncle Red laughed and waved to the two men hauling the piano across our front lawn to hurry in out of the cold.

"I can't afford this, and you know it," Dad said in a low tone so the men wouldn't hear him.

"Oh, it's not for sale, lad," he boomed. "It's sort of a, well, a loaner."

Uncle Red put his hand on Dad's chest and backed him out of the way of the men now lifting the piano over the threshold. "No, Frank," he continued, "This is what we'll call a temporary gift. It'll go back in time to its proper owner—the Ancient Order of Hibernians."

He winked at Mama who had just come to the front hallway, fussing with her hair.

"You took this from the AOH clubhouse?" Dad asked in disbelief.

"What did you think, Frank, the faeries from auld Galway left it on my door step? Where else would I find my niece, Rosie, a piano?"

Mom laughed like she hadn't in a long time. He began weaving some tale about how the Hibernians would never miss the piano, and even if they did, they'd have no right to complain, having pinched it themselves from the Holy Name Society for a sing-along during the years when Uncle Red himself was president. By the end of his story, a scuffed-up old upright stolen by the AOH from the Holy Name was in our living room. It still smelled faintly of cigarette smoke and beer even though it had come in from a long ride out to the suburbs on such a frosty night.

When Uncle Red lifted a packing blanket that had covered the keyboard, Jackie pointed out what was obvious to everyone, "Hey, it's got some teeth missing." Some keys were chipped and discolored with two ivories above middle C missing altogether, but the instrument seemed to smile a crooked Irish smile.

Mama watched as Dad rubbed his finger tip on a large burn in the wood, before she said, "It is wonderful, Uncle Red. Just wonderful."

Uncle Red pulled out the bench for Mama, pecked her on the cheek and whispered, "You look as beautiful as ever, Rosie."

"Oh, I don't really Uncle Red," Mama blushed a little while she used her thumbnail to scrape away some unknown substance from the F above middle C.

"C'mon, Rosie, play '*Adeste, Fideles*' or something else we all know," Uncle Red said looking at Dad, "and you sing, Frank lad, and we'll all join in on the '*Venite adoramus.*'"

Uncle Red didn't take any of Dad's excuses not to sing, and Mama played an introduction twice before he took his hands out of his pockets and began. There was no in-between singing for my dad. He either sang all out or not at all, and he almost quivered when he did sing, filling up the empty-room echo that the baby grand had left behind. *Cantet nunc Io. Chorus angelorum.*

"Red, can I get you a drink?"

"No my boy, I must be off. I've got those boys waiting in the truck, and I've only got it for a few hours."

"What's on the agenda, Red? You off to steal furniture from the Veterans of Foreign Wars?"

Uncle Red bent forward and laughed like he wished he'd thought of it first. "I could fence it to the Little Sisters of the Poor and give the proceeds to the Democrats. There's hope for you yet, Frank Fahey."

Dad didn't move quickly enough to avoid Uncle Red's slap on the back.

After Uncle Red had gone, Mama and Dad stood together before the battered piano. "Your uncle is a thief, Rose. And not a very good one."

Mama's laughter was as welcome as the music coming back to the house. They hunted through the old sheet music in the piano bench and found an old green book called *Moore's Irish Melodies.* Dad sang "Kathleen Mavourneen" while Mama played. Then he sang "Believe Me, If All Those Endearing Young Charms," the solo from his voice recital at St. Ignatius College. He sang it so often that we all knew the words by heart about faery gifts that fade away.

But no one sang the way Dad did, steadying himself with an arm on the piano, his eyes glistening. Then they played and sang "I'll Be With You in Apple Blossom Time" by heart because that's what Daddy had sung to Mama on the phone to ask her to marry him before he left for the war in France.

How I wished that Mama would play this music now and that Dad would come in from the porch where I heard him blowing his nose, and sing the old songs that would keep us all home tomorrow, that would keep us together as a family.

Chapter 4: The Map Home

I didn't think I could sleep that night until I had some plan to make it through the summer. As the glow-in-the-dark St. Thomas statue finally faded, I felt a sob rising up around my heart. If I left tomorrow for Grandma Fahey's, I'd miss Grandma Keary's birthday and the lilies of the valley. Summer always began when the lilies bloomed in Grandma's side yard. They were the only other guests to share her birthday every May since as far back as I could remember.

I was very small when I first went there for her birthday. We sat together in her rocker as she sang about a sally garden in which you were supposed to "take life easy as the leaves grow on the tree." I figured the sally garden was where the lilies grew wild as they did in every patch of shade in her yard. They showed up right on time every year. I'd pick some lilies as my gift to her and we ate my favorite ice cream, lemon crunch, from the dairy around the corner. Then we talked about how famous we would be when Grandma turned 100. She was born in 1880 so it was still a ways off, but she promised she would live at least that long. I could see the headline in *The Kansas City Star*, maybe with our pictures: "Girl's Grandma turns 100!"

Last year she put the overflow of lilies in her favorite white pottery vase in front of me on the table as I had seconds of lemon crunch. I'd seen this vase before. It had on it a hand painted scene of an empty boat tethered to the bank of a stream. A tree hung over the stream and underneath the scene was the legend in green, "The Vale of Avoca, County Wicklow, Ireland." Uncle Red had brought the vase to her the last time he went over because she liked that song so much: "Ah, sweet Vale of Avoca, how calm could I rest, in the valley of shade with the friends I love best." The bubbles of Elmer's Glue along an uneven edge reminded me of how awkward I'd felt when I broke it.

The vase sat on a shelf at the end of a long hallway that led to her front door. I had been practicing my slide into home by running through her carpeted parlor to build up momentum, then transferring my weight to a throw rug that would slide over the hardwood floor of the hallway. I wanted to see if I could make it all the way to the front door by sliding on my side on the rug. I pretended that I was at the Kansas City A's stadium and all eyes were on me as I prepared to steal home.

It seemed a good game until I jarred the vase from its place on the shelf. We had gathered all the pieces we could find, and Grandma glued them back together. I watched sheepishly later as she determined that the mended vase held water. She smiled "That's all a vase needs to do. Just hold a little water."

Lying in bed now, thinking about Grandma Keary, I could almost smell the lilies of the valley, as I could last summer when I decided that I'd like to nestle in among them. I sat down in the flowerbed and then lay back and watched the sun dappling the green leaves silver in the highest branches of the old elm. I lay there watching the tree branches sway when Grandma's face appeared over me.

"Grandma, look, an angel." I began to wave my arms and legs through the bed of white lilies, breaking stems and crushing little flowers, remembering how in winter Jackie and I made angels in fresh snow.

Grandma had said that I was her angel. I happily turned my good ear to the earth and listened to the swishing, leafy sound I was making. I sat up, proud of my ingenuity. Grandma Keary slowly stooped to pick up some broken lilies.

"They are like little bells, aren't they, Lucy."

I held one to my right ear and shook it.

"Does your ear still hurt you, darlin'?"

It didn't hurt like when I had the infection. It was like there was an empty place on the side of my head where my ear used to be. Sometimes I had to look in the mirror to make sure I still had an ear. Grandma's hands stroked both of my ears now.

I was shaking a stem of flowers and thinking about bells ringing. "How can they be bells if you can't hear them?"

She'd laughed. "There are bells you don't need ears to hear."

I liked the idea of bells that never rang but were bells nonetheless. I stood up and let Grandma gather flowers and sticky stems from my back. Turning around I saw in her pale blue eyes a look that I took as concern for the lost lilies. I looked at the crushed flowers in her hand.

"I'm sorry about the flowers, Grandma."

"Ah, but there's plenty left, Lucy." Then putting her hands to my cheeks, she'd said, "They come back every May ... and they always will." She kissed my forehead. I'd looked back at the impression I'd left on the lily bed and waved my arms in satisfaction.

And now for all my worries about having to leave it, my own bed began to comfort me, warmth and heaviness coming to my arms and legs. I was nearly asleep when I remembered the touch of Grandma Keary's hands as she held my face and smiled, "Did you know you have a map for a face, Lucy darlin'?"

"What kind of map?" It had seemed like a good thing judging by the way she looked at me.

"Why of Ireland, Lucy," she'd laughed and taken me to her mirror and said, "To find your way home, your dear little face is all you'll ever need. Wherever you end up in the world, look for other faces like yours and you'll know that's home."

My face was part Quinn and part Keary, as she'd told me many times with a pinch of my cheek. That suited me fine. It was good to belong without having to try—being Irish was just what we are. It might be an invisible quality to some people, but it was clear to them. Grandma Keary pointed on the globe to County Galway where they came from, the Quinns and the Kearys. It was a long way off. It took Uncle Red almost an entire day on TWA to reach the relatives in Loughrea as he did every few years. But right now it was the distance between my two grandmothers' houses here in America—all the way across St. Ignatius Loyola parish—that seemed farther apart than any ocean.

Grandma Fahey was pleased to be where she was and didn't ever need to cross the Atlantic again. Being American was the big thing with her.

"Remember, Lucy, that your Grandfather Fahey was born here in America, so you are third generation American. On your father's side, of course."

Being American didn't seem like that big of an accomplishment to me.

"Are you an American?" I asked her once.

"I am," she said with the zeal of a convert, "but I was born in County Mayo, so I know my place."

This seemed a little complicated to me. Grandma Keary's view was simpler. It had only to do with names and faces, and it didn't matter where you were born, in Ireland or Kansas City or Chicago, you were welcome at her house. My mom's family could tell a lot by a face or a name. And John Fitzgerald Kennedy, who was in the news almost every day now, had two fine names and a fine face to match. Uncle Red would pound something, the arm of a chair or table top, and shout "Atta' boy, Jack!" whenever Senator Kennedy was on the television.

I'd heard Grandma Fahey say that it wasn't wise to draw attention to being Irish or Catholic, either one. "That Kennedy boy should know his place and not stir things up for the rest of us. It is ridiculous, him acting like we all think he should be President someday."

How could both sides of my family be Irish and be so different? They were both from the same part of Ireland, the West. They looked to me like they all belonged together somehow.

I still didn't understand how a face could be a map, as Grandma Keary said, but I finally gave in to sleep, glad to have any kind of map this summer and with the scent of lilies of the valley in air.

Chapter 5: All Things, Seen and Unseen

My dad carried my little gray suitcase up the steps to Grandma Fahey's house the way he carried his brief case off to work in the morning. She was a slender but energetic woman with large eyes as dark blue as the cover of my *Baltimore Catechism*. She told me not to worry about my mother because it was all in God's hands now.

"Take your things upstairs now, child. You'll be staying in your Uncle Nat's old room. Top of the stairs on the right."

I looked to my dad for confirmation of this plan, but he had shoved his hands in his suit coat pockets and looked away as he almost always did when Grandma mentioned his dead brother. He began busying himself looking through a neat file of records, mostly RCA Red Labels, in the console under Grandma's record player. He was asking Grandma Fahey if she didn't have a collection of Donizetti arias, telling her that Jackie or I had managed to ruin his copy of *Lucia di Lammermoor*. Grandma said, "Oh, I do indeed, but it isn't leaving the house."

They both seemed suddenly aware of me standing there.

"Well, up the stairs with you now, child," ordered Grandma Fahey.

I struggled up the stairs, put my suitcase down on the bed and looked around. On the dressing table was a picture of my Uncle Natty smiling broadly from behind wire-framed glasses, just the way I remembered him the last time we drove to St. Louis to see him at the seminary. His teeth were as gleaming and straight as the Roman collar he wore. He reminded me of Jackie with a lock of straight dark hair falling on his forehead.

A metal plate in the wood frame was engraved: Ignatius Loyola Patrick Fahey, S.J. The "S.J." was important to have after your name, standing for the

Society of Jesus, the Jesuits. Mama said that looking for the letters after a priest's name was like looking for the brand label on clothes to see if it is quality. The old parish of St. Ignatius Loyola was much more important than our own Mary of Gaels, not just because it was twice the size and part of a college, but because all the priests had S.J. after their names.

Grandma Fahey had shown her loyalty to the Jesuits by naming Uncle Natty and Daddy after the two topmost Jesuits there were, Ignatius Loyola and Francis Xavier. Uncle Natty was named for the very first Jesuit, who might have been on friendly terms with Jesus Himself.

But my dad was not a Jesuit. After Uncle Natty died, I had asked Mama if he was.

"Of course your Daddy's not a Jesuit, Lucy. Why would you say such a thing?"

"I heard him tell you he was. I heard him last night."

My dad drank his Jameson's in the kitchen for weeks after Uncle Natty died because he said there's nothing sadder than a dead Jesuit. It was hard not to hear what he had on his mind at that time.

"Here's one to me then, the other son, Francis X. Fahey." His voice had risen. "Let's raise a glass to His Eminence, the Right Reverend Frank Fahey, S. J."

I'd heard the sound of Mama's voice but not her words, and then Dad continuing, "Did I say Right Reverend, Rose, I meant the Tight Reverend, Francis Xavier Fahey, Society of bloody Jesus. I can't take his place with her," he'd sobbed. "Jesuits aren't supposed to die, for Christ's sake."

Mama had quietly closed the windows and the door that night.

Now standing alone in my dead Jesuit uncle's room, I heard my dad's voice rising up again, from Grandma Fahey's living room.

"Lucy is on a provisional pass, Mother. They've given her a list of things to learn before they'll let her go on to the next grade. Catechism mostly."

"Catechism! You're not serious, Frank," she said sharply.

I thought I was the one in for it until I heard Grandma scold my daddy. I felt dizzy from wanting to laugh when she demanded, "Just how did this happen, Frank? Faheys have always been at the top of their class."

Grandma Fahey was so mad at the both of us that she sounded ready to change her mind about agreeing to take me in. Uncle Red always said being on thin ice made its own luck, probably because you are just one splash away from a change in a tense situation. I never imagined the good luck that not knowing my catechism would bring. Maybe I'd get sent to Grandma Keary's after all.

I picked up my suitcase and ran back to the top of the stairs and listened for my dad to call up and say that there was no room in the inn for the likes of me. Just like the baby Jesus, who got to be born in a stable surrounded by friendly animals and folks glad to see him—not to mention the wise men from the Orient who brought a nice Chinese checkers set to the Holy Family according to Uncle Red. I'd end up playing board games with him and Grandma Keary by the end of the day.

Dad was telling Grandma Fahey the reason for me failing, which I never understood before now was part of my luck, too.

"Rose thinks the problem is with Lucy's hearing."

"Then she needs to be led more carefully, Frank."

"Mother, this has not been an easy time for any of us."

"I know you've your troubles, Frank, but you can't just let Lucy grow up wild. That little girl will need her faith, you all will, if our prayers for Rose are not answered."

I hated the silence that always followed talk of asking God to help Mama. Either God could hear the prayers or He couldn't. Maybe He should listen better, as people were always telling me to do. I heard my dad blow his nose, and Grandma Fahey say, "You've done the right thing to bring Lucy here for the summer, Frank. Now, let me make you a nice cup of tea."

Oh, they *were* leaving me for the whole summer. My whole body felt suddenly sweaty, like I needed to escape, but where to. There was no place to go. I sat down heavily on the top stair and let my suitcase slam down next to me. Grandma Fahey and my dad both called out, "Lucy!" and Grandma told me to please begin unpacking my things. I didn't want to hear any more from my dad or Grandma Fahey. I left the suitcase where it was and wandered back down the hall to my uncle's room, passing the picture of Our Lady of Perpetual Help. Even she wasn't paying any attention. In the room that was to be my home for an entire summer, I turned up the switch on the lowly droning window fan and stood with my hands on its vibrating frame. The dull sound kept their voices from reaching me, but the fan was drawing air from the room and pulling it in a steady whoosh out the window. This machine with its whirring blades as invisible as God might be drawing something out of me too, maybe my soul or the rest of my life. At least the moving air on the back of my sweaty neck cooled me down. The fan hummed a note that I concentrated on matching as if the effort would keep the tears that stung my eyes from flowing down my cheek.

The fan chopped up and threw back any sounds I made into it. First I whistled, softly and then as loud as I could. Soon I was saying, "Hello. Hello. Hello. This is Lucy." I was yelling into the whirlwind "Is anybody out there?" when my dad startled me by tapping me on the shoulder. He turned down the fan.

"Here's your suitcase, Luce. I've gotta go now. Mind your Grandmother. Study hard. Keep your feet off her furniture and, uh, don't run in the house." He stood looking down at me for a moment. Both hands in the pockets of his tan gabardine suit, he was jangling his keys and some change. Twice he opened his mouth to speak but no words came out. Then he said, abruptly, "Well, whaddya' have to say to your old man, eh Luce?"

I wanted to say "Don't leave me here in this place," but instead asked if I finished my schoolwork, could I come home sooner.

"Well, it's just not that simple, Lucy."

Nothing ever was that summer.

That very first night with Grandma Fahey, on what would have been the beginning of the long nights of summer vacation, she seated me at the kitchen table and handed me a pencil and a Big Chief tablet saying, "Lucy, start copying the catechism at page one while I do the dinner dishes. You'll know the answers to every question on your list before you return home."

June bugs batted themselves senseless against the screen. They wanted in. I wanted out. I watched Grandma as she washed the dishes. I had never seen anyone put her hands in water that hot. It steamed up the windows next to the table, so I wrote "Lucy F" and then "P L E H" as I had seen Jackie do in the dirt on car windows. He said it would look like someone trapped inside wrote H E L P. It seemed much funnier writing this on parked cars on the way home from school with Jackie. I missed my brother and my own home already and I had only been away a few hours. I looked at the cover of my catechism book and thought about what Jackie had written in big block letters on his that got him a detention: "In Case of Fire, Please Throw In! Signed, Jack Fahey."

I was taking my pencil to the cover of my catechism when Grandma suddenly appeared over me with a tea towel scolding that she worked night and day to keep her kitchen and windows sparkling and she did not appreciate a "little Kilroy was here" putting her name everywhere. She cleaned the window until it squeaked underneath her towel. Looking at my all but blank page she said "Lucy!"

"Yessum?" I cringed.

"Who made you, Lucy?"

"Made me do what, Ma'am?"

"Your *Baltimore Catechism*. First question: who made you?"

"Oh, do you mean God, Grandma?"

"Well of course I mean God, child! Whom did you suspect?" she boomed. "Now, Lucy, why did God make you?"

I squirmed to keep from crying and said, "I don't know, Grandma."

"Now listen to the answer, Lucy, and try to remember this. It's important. 'God made you to love and serve Him in this world and be happy with Him in the next.' Did you hear all that, Lucy?"

"Yessum." I said but thought this God was pretty selfish if I had to wait to be happy until the next world.

"And don't run your words together like that, say 'Yes, Grandmother' not 'Yessum.' You don't want people looking down on you because of the way you talk, now do you, Lucy?"

"No'am," I said sincerely. This was something
new to worry about.

"Sit up straight. You'll think better." She
sharpened my pencil even though it didn't need it and
returned to her steaming sink.

"Lucy, it is important to learn your catechism.
People have suffered all kinds of things for hundreds of
years so that you'll have the chance to sit here tonight
and study your religion. Why in Ireland, in the penal
times when the English closed down the schools, the
school masters had to teach outside under the hedges
in all kinds of weather, just to keep the faith alive."

I'd like that school. Sounded like one long field
trip to me.

"Once you learn your religion, Lucy, there's
nobody that can steal it from you." She was shaking a
serving spoon that she'd just washed. Soapy water flew
from it like a priest's holy water censor at benediction.

I was more worried about losing something
valuable like my bike than my religion or my catechism
book. *In case of fire, throw in.*

The next day began as each day at Grandma
Fahey's—with 8:00 Mass. She was not one for calling a
taxi to take her to Mass each day when a good brisk
walk of 20 minutes would get you there just the same.
For in everything she did, Grandma Fahey always chose
the hardest, rockiest road.

Though in her seventies, Grandma was hard to
keep up with as we climbed the hill to Troost Avenue and
through the St. Ignatius College campus to the church.

"Come along, child. Quickly now," she called to
me. It was her practice to hear Mass, which was said
and never sung, by a certain Jesuit at a certain time
and she would not have us be late.

"Grandma! I've got to stop." If I lied saying I had
a rock in my shoe, she'd have to slow down.

"Do we have to go so fast? My feet hurt." I sat
down to take off my shoe.

"Come on, Lucy. It's not that far we are going.
When I was a girl in County Mayo, children younger
than you would climb to the very top of Croagh Patrick,
and some of them in their bare feet, mind you, and no
one heard a peep out of them. Not one peep."

I rubbed my little toe when I noticed that there really was a blister starting up. "What's Croagh Patrick, Grandma?"

"It's a very, very steep mountain. I could see it from my own grandmother's house. St. Patrick himself climbed it, Lucy! Now stand up, we need to keep moving."

"But why did kids do that, why did they climb a mountain in their bare feet?" I asked, soothing my bare foot by wiggling my toes through the dew on a clump of wild violets.

"Why indeed, Lucy. It was a pilgrimage to retrace the steps of our patron saint. At the Feast of *Lughnasa*, people came from all over the West of Ireland to climb Croagh Patrick. Many made the pilgrimage barefooted as a sacrifice they were offering up to the memory of St. Patrick, who made Ireland a Catholic country after all. Come along now, child."

"So what's the Feast of Lunacy, Grandma?"

"It is pronounced 'loon ah sah,' not 'lunacy.' *Lughnasa* is rather like a Holy Day of Obligation, Lucy."

When I told her that *Lughnasa* wasn't on the list of Holy Days of Obligation I was supposed to memorize for school, she chided, "Now when did you become such a scholar of church history? *Lughnasa* most certainly is a very holy day in County Mayo and has been so for a thousand years or more. That's all there is to that."

I learned not to argue with Grandma Fahey about Holy Days. Years later I realized that this extra Holy Day in Grandma Fahey's calendar honored the pagan Celtic god, Lugh. Grandma had simply grafted *Lughnasa* on to her personal liturgy, the way the worshippers of Lugh had entwined St. Patrick and his green symbols into their harvest celebration.

Grandma was looking down at my feet. "Those socks are the problem, Lucy. They're too flimsy. We'll take the bus downtown today and buy you some thicker ones. But you can certainly make it to Mass this morning. On your feet now."

This was not what I wanted to hear on a hot summer morning. When I thought of the sockless days last summer in my worn out Keds, walking to the pool with Jackie every day, I could have kicked myself for not paying more attention in school.

"Come along, child. Don't dawdle."

Back on my feet, I continued up our daily version of Croagh Patrick.

"Do we have to go to Mass every day, Grandma?"

"God gave you two legs for that express purpose, to carry you off to daily Mass. You should be thankful for your own two feet and your own two legs, though I must say, I've never seen a skinnier pair anywhere. Those long legs ought to make you a good dancer though, like my brother, Packy. You come from dancing stock, did you know that, Lucy? He danced on the stage in Chicago years ago. Packy Regan was known as the fastest runner and highest jumper in Mayo. Do you know he could jump out of a barrel?" She stopped, hiked up her skirt and made a bit of a jump step, then shook her head in admiration at the memory of her older brother.

"What kind of a barrel, Grandma?"

"What, Lucy? Well, whiskey, I imagine."

"What was he doing in the barrel, Grandma?"

"He wasn't in the barrel for any reason other than to jump out of it, Lucy, which he did from a standing position. Point is, he was agile and strong, and you'd be lucky to take after the Regans." She looked at me as if she might have been thinking that the good Sisters knew what they were doing trying to keep me back a grade.

On the way home from Mass, Grandma Fahey was always less anxious, but no less talkative. She taught me the names of the trees and flowers and how to identify birds by their whistles.

"Listen Lucy, there's a bobwhite."

"I don't hear anything, Grandma."

"Try harder, child. You'll hear them all if you know how to listen for them."

"Oh, now there's another song. Hear that, Lucy?" she asked, tilting her head and pointing off over her left shoulder. I still didn't hear anything but Grandma whistling her response to an unseen bird. I turned my good ear in the direction she pointed and listened as hard as I knew how. I began to hear something rhythmic and high pitched that reminded me of the squeaky *up and back* and *up and back* sound of the swing set in my backyard. I wondered if anyone was using my swing set on this clear warm morning. You didn't see too many swing sets in the city. I longed for my own backyard swing where I could feel the warm sun on my back and against my face and arms like a hug, as I pumped as high as I could. If I closed my eyes, it seemed like I could fly. Sometimes Jackie would dare me, "Bail out, Luce!" and I would let go of my grip as the swing reached the top of the arc and land in the clover.

"Do you hear the bird song, Lucy?"

"Is it a titwillow, Grandma?"

"A what, Lucy?"

"Titwillow. I think it is a titwillow."

"Well, think what you like, Lucy, it is a thrush. There's no such thing as a titwillow."

"But Jackie and I know a song about a bird called a titwillow. It can only sing one thing. Do you want to hear it?"

Without waiting for a reply I tucked my arms up to my shoulders like wings and sang: "On a tree by a river a little tomtit, sang 'oh, willow, titwillow, titwillow.' And I said to him, 'dickie bird, why do you sit singing 'willow, titwillow, titwillow?'"

"Lucy," she interrupted, "wherever did you learn that nonsense?"

"Uncle Red taught me. It is my party piece. Uncle Red brought Mama a whole book of funny songs by Gilbert and Sullivan. They are friends of his."

"I assure you Lucy, that is not the case."

What did she know about it? She didn't even understand how I had the best lines to the whole song. "See, Grandma, I get to play the birdie and Mama nods to me whenever they need to hear me sing 'Oh willow, titwillow, titwillow.' It's really a funny song. This bird just keeps singing the same thing no matter what questions people ask him about what's wrong, or why he is so sad. Jackie and Uncle Red know all the words, but I have the most important part.

"So, when Jackie sings, 'Now I'm sure as I'm sure that my name isn't ...' And everybody looks at me, do you know what I get to sing?"

"I'm sure I don't, Lucy."

"I sing 'Oh willow, titwillow, titwillow.' That's what I get to sing," I said impatiently. She'd been doing all the talking for weeks.

"Everybody laughs, Grandma. I even get to fall out of the tree at the end when the birdie dies of a broken heart. Like this." As I pitched myself forward onto the grass clutching my heart expecting her to finally get it, she said only "Enough of this silliness, Lucy. You'll get grass stains on that dress and I won't have you going around the parish looking like a street urchin."

It would be hard work making Grandma Fahey laugh. Jackie would have laughed to see me on the grass.

"Your grandfather, Will Fahey, God rest his soul, knew all there was about real music, Lucy. He taught me everything I know about music, even opera. I don't mean that Gilbert and Sullivan nonsense about titwillows and pirate kings from Cornwall either."

"Yessum," I said, feeling suddenly foolish sitting on the ground.

"Have you ever seen a titwillow, Lucy?"

I didn't have to answer.

"Well, I should think not."

The organized learning all took place at Grandma Fahey's kitchen table. Grandma was as serious about the bad grades on my report cards as she was the weeds in her garden. She didn't care for either. It was clear she was on a mission to the ignorant just like the old hedgerow schoolmasters in penal times had been. Night after night she would sit and read me catechism questions and then arch her eyebrow and quiz me about what she had just read, then she'd order me to copy out the answers, word for word, until I had mastered them.

When I told her that this wasn't the way my mom taught me catechism, she started to say something, but then said only, "Back to work now, Lucy." It was slow going until one night, quite by accident, I delighted her with my answer to her question about the nature of the sacraments.

"Is the answer 'An outward sign instituted by Christ to give grace,' Grandma?" I knew this answer, but wasn't exactly sure what question it went with.

"You are certainly right, Lucy." Grandma announced triumphantly that we would be going beyond the assigned questions on my list and that we would begin tomorrow with a very important question, "What are the Chief Truths that the Church teaches?"

Grandma told me that I reminded her of herself and that my eyes were the same shade of blue as all the Regans and McNamees of County Mayo. She brought me two vanilla wafers as a reward for looking like her people when I recited catechism, and happily watched me while I munched them.

I was pleased too. Now Jackie'd have nothing on me with his catechism gold medals two years running. Maybe I'd win one.

Chief Truths that the Church teaches. I liked the way those words bounced along with me as I repeated them climbing the stairs to bed that night. They made me laugh like when Uncle Red would ask, "Lucy, do you know what kind of a noise annoys an oyster?" This answer I knew cold. "A *noisy* noise annoys an oyster, Uncle Red."

The new questions she added to my list were not as much fun as I hoped they might be. They were just like the others, only longer like the Nicene Creed.

One windy night I sat copying each phrase of the Creed ten times as Grandma finished up the dinner dishes.

"We say the Creed in Latin at Mass, Lucy. Do you recognize it?"

"Ma'am?"

"It is the *Credo* in the Mass. *Credo in unum Deum patrem omnipotentem*—I believe in God the Father Almighty, don't you see. We say it in Latin today because people have believed it a very long time. Oh, it's a very old prayer indeed."

I didn't suppose they would stop believing it this summer just to lighten up my load.

"What else do we believe, Lucy? What are you up to in your copying?"

"I believe in, ah ... " I looked down at my tablet at the last phrase and read "all things, seen and unseen."

"Good," she said, "that's *visibilium et invisibilium* in the *Credo*. You must look carefully at the Latin. Do you see how the words 'visible' and 'invisible' spring right out of the Latin at you?"

"Yessum, I do. Visible. Invisible."

Even if Latin was the language that God liked us to pray in, it all sounded pretty much like "a noisy noise annoys an oyster" to me. Besides, the *Credo* didn't say exactly what those invisible things were that we should believe in. It would have been more useful that way, then I'd know for sure. Were there things more invisible than God and the angels that I was supposed to believe in? I tried to return to my copying, but every time a gust of wind whistled through the screen door, I had to look up. Something seen or unseen?

The summer storm brewing outside competed with Grandma's nightly whirlwind of scrubbing her pots and pans over her steamy sink and drying our dinner dishes until they squeaked. A sudden chilly breeze came through the door like a friendly neighbor announcing the rain was on its way. It made me shiver in the damp heat of the room, like drinking cold milk right after hot chicken noodle soup. When Grandma finished the last dish, she picked up the pan full of dish water, carried it the few steps to the back door, swung the door open with her hip as she did every night, but tonight she threw out a string of wild syllables with the dish water that wasn't English but didn't sound like Latin either: "*Sheachaint! Sheachaint ar an uisce.*"

"Grandma, who's out there?"

"Oh Lucy, no one really," she laughed and seemed a little shy that I was watching her so closely. "I was just giving the warning—to the faeries. I haven't done that since I don't know when. When you throw something out in the darkness like that, you should warn the faeries."

She wiped her hands and her forehead with a dishtowel. "When I was about your age, my Granny McNamee taught me to warn them just to be on the safe side."

"Do we say that at Mass too, Grandma?"

"No, child. It is Gaelic. It wouldn't do much good to warn the faeries in Latin, or English for that matter," she laughed and sat down at the table with me. She seemed surprised that I wouldn't recognize it. "Have you never heard the Irish spoken, Lucy?"

Although I realized that mentioning the Quinns was like waving the red flag in front of her, I answered anyway, "Is speaking Irish like when my Uncle Red says he was *t'inking* about *somt'ing* he never *t'ought* of before?"

"Indeed it isn't!" she shot back and eyed me like she was trying to decide if I were trying to get her goat. I didn't know for sure myself. I knew we were Irish, but I never knew we had our own language and that only Grandma Fahey, and apparently the faeries, bothered to speak it.

"The Gaelic. It is the language I spoke with my own grandmother when I was very young. It was all she spoke. My granny called me Maeve *og*. Maeve the young one, and she was *Maire sean*, Mary the old one, don't you see?"

I didn't.

"So now you are Lucy *og*, the little one, and I am Maeve *sean*, the old one, just as my granny was to me. Here, let me show you the Irish."

She took my pencil and wrote our names in the faery language on my tablet like we belonged right there in the middle of the creed. Floating somewhere between "all things, seen and unseen" and "the communion of saints, the forgiveness of sins and life of the world to come" were our names: "Lucy *og agus* Maeve *sean*."

When I repeated her Irish words Grandma had a light in her eyes like I had just gotten two catechism questions right in a row. I liked the attention. And just for saying a few nonsense words back to her.

"Now *Tir Na N'Og* means the Land of the Young in the Gaelic."

"Where's that place, Grandma?"

"Oh, off the Western seas of Ireland they say." She paused and tilted her head and seemed a bit sad. "I'll tell you about that sometime. Not now when we are in such a fine mood."

She felt it too.

"We'll add a little Gaelic to your list of lessons."

Didn't matter much to me. I didn't expect that the entire summer would be long enough to get through my homework anyway.

"Would you like that, Lucy? Maybe that would interest you?"

My curiosity only ran to those other Irish speakers in her backyard.

"Who are the faeries, Grandma?"

"Lucy, do you not know of the faeries, either?" she asked me earnestly.

"No, Ma'am," I answered.

Grandma, too, seemed to warm to the subject, and I wondered if we were talking seen or unseen.

"Well, the Church does not approve of the idea of them. But I'll tell you then what I know and what was taught to me. The faeries lurk there in the darkness, you see, and they would be annoyed to be hit by the water. They are easily annoyed, and oh, they are great ones for revenge, the *sidhe* are. You have to at least give them a 'Here goes!' don't you see, Lucy."

"Where are they, Grandma? I don't see anybody out there." I looked out the window and then back at Grandma.

"Very few people have ever seen them really, Lucy."

"Are they like the angels then, Grandma?" We were taught in school to believe in angels, although nobody has really seen one.

"No, child. They are the faeries."

This answer didn't help me much.

"Are they more important than the angels?"

"Oh, I don't think so, Lucy." Then she laughed as if describing a very clever but mischievous friend, "But you know, there's no ordinary angel that couldn't be outwitted by a Mayo faery. And that's the truth of it. But Lucy, remember that Mother Church does not approve of the idea and has given us saints and angels for our guidance. You finish your copying now."

"But Grandma, how do you know there are faeries if you can't see them?"

"By what they cause, Lucy. By their effect. Oh, they are there, Lucy. Take it from me, they have ways of making themselves known."

"But what do they do?" I went to the screen door where she had spoken to them.

"They cause things to happen, Lucy."

"Good things?" I questioned eagerly.

"Yes. And sometimes bad. You never know which it'll be."

I took three slow steps back from the doorway as Grandma continued her story. "Once, I believe they might have left me a single white rose on my door step to ease my sorrow when my poor dear boy, Nat, died. I found it there one day after Mass."

Then she added, darkly and suddenly as if she was talking of an old enemy, "But they can play tricks on you, hide things from you, confound you, and all just to get your attention. All they want sometimes is your attention. In Mayo, Lucy, they were known to steal cats and dogs—even children from their beds—if people took them lightly."

I checked to make sure that the screen door was latched. I wondered what Mama knew about the faeries.

"What happened to those who are stolen?"

"They become changelings, and they travel the earth for eternity, or so the story goes. Or I suppose, they might go to the Land of Faery."

I could only think of how homesick a faery changeling would be, never getting to go home again, and never getting to go to Heaven either. I didn't have to be able to see them to believe in them and feel really sorry for them.

"Where is that Faery Land place, Grandma? Is it at least near Heaven?"

"Closer to earth than Heaven. On *Samhain,* that's near Halloween, the *sidhe* come stealing around the earth, playing their pranks or rewarding kindnesses shown to them through the year. And on All Saints' and All Souls' Days, they tap the old ones who will die soon to let them know it is their time, if they know how to listen for the signal."

This was almost enough to put me off trick-or-treating altogether, yet it made sense to me that whatever was in the air on Halloween night had to be caused by something unseen. It might as well be the faeries.

"Lucy, have you ever seen the wind suddenly kick up through the fallen leaves? Well, pay attention when you do. Granny McNamee said that such a gust signals the coming of the faeries. It was one gusty fall night that she saw them for herself."

She picked up my tablet and began to review my work.

"But have *you* ever really seen them, Grandma?"

"I may have heard the faeries once, Lucy. From the hallway window upstairs."

I knew the one she meant. It was right outside my bedroom door.

"It was when my mother was still alive up in Chicago and I was down here in Kansas City," she continued. "I woke in the middle of the night because I heard a commotion at the hallway window, a high, keening sound. I didn't know who was there or what it meant. And don't you know, Lucy, it was on the next day I had a telegram that she had passed on the night before, my mother."

"Who was at the window? Did you see who was at the window, Grandma?"

I was standing next to her at eye level. This was serious. I wanted to know what to look for that might be bringing me news of my mother through this window.

"I blinked my eyes and she was gone, Lucy. It may have been what the very old ones in Mayo called the _Bean Si_, the White Faery Woman. The banshee as they call her here. I do believe there was something of my own mother about her. They say we all have a faery double, Lucy. I've often thought it could have been my mother's faery self coming to me after she died. I guess I'll never know for sure."

My thoughts went back to the window in the hallway where the faery woman had made herself known. On a table under the window was a picture of Our Lady of Perpetual Help, just like my mom had at home, and on the wall a framed photograph of a fierce looking old man that I took for some relative. He looked right at me every time I came out of my room. Now I imagined a third face, completing this new trinity, a faery woman at the window floating above the haloed icon of Mary and the old man. Which one had the most power of the three? I was sure hoping it was Our Lady Of Perpetual Help because just this very morning Grandma had me put fresh peonies in front of her picture; and because it was still the Holy Mother's month of May, she'd added a drop or two of holy water into the vase from the little wall font that hung next to her bedroom door. Now, I wished we'd sprinkled holy water all around the window for special protection from the White Faery Woman. I didn't want her showing up with any messages for me.

"Well, Lucy, let's get back to your catechism questions now." She was tapping her index finger on the page, but I had a few questions more important than the ones in my catechism.

"But Grandma, what did she look like, the White Faery lady?"

"I shouldn't have distracted you from your work, Lucy. Let's go back to the *Credo*. You need to master this," she said thumping her finger more insistently.

"Was she pretty or scary, Grandma? Is she good or bad? Do I have a faery double, too?" I refused to take my eyes off her until she answered. If I had a faery double she might be able to help me out, like a guardian angel or something. Maybe send a message to Mama to watch out.

"Oh, Lucy, I'm not even sure if I saw anything at all. And besides I'm sure that it is just as the catechism teaches that God and his angels wait for us after death. And not at all what I was told in Mayo when I was a little one. Back to your lessons now."

"But Grandma, you said your grandma saw them. Did they come to her window, too?"

Grandma Fahey looked me in the face like she had just found something she had lost so long ago she no longer missed it. She began slowly, "Well, Granny McNamee told me that she had once seen the faeries dancing. At the crossroad near her cottage, Lucy, she saw a troupe of the *sidhe* dancing in the road as bold as you please. She was very, very small when she saw them, but she knew they were having a high old time of it. She could hear their music and the click, click, click of their shoes."

"Did she ask them what they were doing there, Grandma?"

"Oh my, no, Lucy." She looked at me as if I lacked all sense. "They can steal you away if you engage them in conversation—or even stare at them for too long. If she had talked to them, why we'd both be faeries instead of Faheys today," she laughed.

It didn't seem a laughing matter to me.

"I imagine," she continued "that she wanted to know what they were doing so close to her house, but you can't risk getting too close without falling under their sway."

"Is that how they steal you?"

"Oh, there are many ways they can draw you in. Music is the most powerful. And she said their dance was enthralling as well. They can fill your senses with their music that is so sad and beautiful that it charms the soul right out of you."

"Just music can do that, Grandma?"

"Oh my yes, what is more entrancing than music? And if you begin to dance just one step of their faery dance, why that means they've won you over, completely. You may never stop or ever go back to your life before you crossed their path. They say faery music has the strongest charm. You are to hold your ears from it, like this," she said placing the palms of her hands over her ears.

With my bad ear I figured I was less vulnerable to the magic in their music. Grandma Fahey smoothed my bangs from my eyes saying "I haven't thought of that in years and years. Oh, such nonsense, but that is what she told me, my Granny McNamee back home in Mayo. Not what Holy Mother Church assures us of, certainly."

Grandma fell silent with a rare smile on her face. I waited motionless for more of the story, but she only sighed and said that lately childhood stories were easier to recall than what she had ordered from Wolferman's Grocery this morning.

"Time for you to get to bed, Lucy. I'll have to close this old place tight as drum tonight. That rain will be here before midnight, and thanks be to God for it. Terribly hot day," she said rising from the table.

Before she pushed the heavy wooden kitchen door closed for the night she gazed through the screen door and added idly, "A little warning doesn't hurt anyone, I suppose." She crossed herself as she did every night as she shut the back door. Turning to me she suddenly clapped her hands twice as a conjurer might to dispel an image and said, "Off to bed with you now, child. It's late."

Standing on the bottom step, the darkened stairs seemed much longer than they had before I knew of faery changelings and the White Faery Woman at the window. I sprinted up the stairs and went straight to the little holy water font outside Grandma's room. I crossed myself three times, once for Mama, once for Grandma Keary, and once for me. To keep from being seen by what might be out in Grandma Fahey's yard, I dropped to my hands and knees to keep well below the level of the window and scrambled as fast as I could, the carpet burning my knees, to my room and slammed the door behind me.

I exhaled as I switched on the light and was glad to see Uncle Natty still smiling from his picture. There was comfort in that friendly face behind the Roman collar until I began to wonder if he, too, heard the banshee give him the signal that he was going to die. Maybe from that window, this was his room after all. Everyone said he died before he was supposed to and that he was too young to die. The faeries may be quicker and more alert than God. Did the faeries steal Uncle Natty right from under His holy nose? God would not let one of His own Jesuits die young. I turned Uncle Natty's picture to the wall and tried to sleep, hoping that the holy water was strong enough magic to keep me safe until morning.

Chapter 6: Don't Look Back

I was glad for the sunlight flooding my room when Grandma got me up for Mass the next morning. My room, the hallway, everything looked different. She turned Uncle Nat's picture back around and before she could say anything about it, I asked, "Grandma, who is that old man in the picture in the hallway?"

"That gentleman, Lucy, is my old Da, and your great grandfather, Patrick Sarsfield Regan."

I liked his face much better in the daylight. There was a bit of a smile but only on half of his face, and his nose seemed to be pointing in a slightly different direction than his eyes were looking. But his eyes were looking right at you, like he was sizing you up. Grandma and my dad both had that same look, those same angles to their mouths and jaws. Familiar as he was, I still didn't want to linger in front of that particular window.

On the way up the hill to Mass that morning, I learned that Great Grandpa Regan discovered Chicago in 1892, and as soon as he set down his suitcase he went to work on the fine buildings and palaces of the World's Fair in Chicago on the shores of Lake Michigan. Today marked the beginning of Grandma's practice of telling me some of her best stories, not about the saints to whom we were not related—but about the mighty Regans of County Mayo and later, Cook County, Chicago.

"I was just a little girl, about your age with five older brothers who all worked building the Fair. Chicago was the new world, Lucy." She swept her hand in front of her like she could see it all again, just at the top of the hill to St. Ignatius. I'd never seen her slow down on her way to Mass for anybody or anything as she did now telling how her dad and brothers built the World's Fair singlehandedly. She came to a dead halt as she smoothed her hand in front of us to show how the mortar had to be applied just so. I didn't doubt that

Grandma could lay down mortar to build a wall of her own whenever she needed to.

"He was what they call a masonry man. And oh, but he carried the hod proudly, Lucy. Very proudly indeed."

I imagined that Great Grandpa Regan was like a king of some sort, carrying his hod like a royal scepter, instead of what it was, a pole across his back by which the cleverest of Regans carried the heaviest buckets of mortar and white plaster. When Grandma Fahey was my age, her da told them they were off to America where "even hod carriers live like kings." And Grandma, like some sort of princess herself, was getting to survey the White City and the World's Fair grounds before any other little girl in all of Chicago.

"I climbed the scaffold one Sunday with him. I was afraid down to the tips of my toes to climb up there, but I did, Lucy, I did. I saw it all. Everything my father saw, the wonderful white city with a huge rectangular pool in the center reflecting everything back at us. Just us and the sky above. Imagine that if you will, Lucy. It was grand. He was putting gleaming white plaster on the façade that day. But this was only on the temporary buildings that would disappear like the dream it all seemed when the Fair closed. Can you imagine it, Lucy?"

She fell silent for so long that I was wondering if she might have forgotten all about Mass when she started up with, "Do you know what he said to me that day? 'This is America, little Maeve. Don't ever look back.' I can still see the scuffs on his swollen knuckles and the freckles on the back of his hands."

She rubbed the back of her hand, then said, "It's good advice and that I'll pass on to you now, Lucy. Don't look back for anything. And sure, why would I have wanted to look back at all when I could sit by the edge of that reflecting pool and see my own face and the beautiful white buildings, and know America was my future."

Then laughing like something was tickling her from deep inside, she continued, "My brother, Packy, said he never would have worked so hard digging those canals if he had known it was going to make me so vain. Chicago seemed in those days a city built by Regans, for Regans. Ah, but that time is gone from me now."

The bells for the 8:00 began to toll. We were usually in our pew by this time. Grandma dropped her story like it was a heavy sack of groceries and picked up her pace. "Oh, see now, Lucy, see what comes from dwelling on the past. Come on, child."

As we barreled across the St. Nat's College campus, Grandma huffed, "The old stories just slow you down and keep you from doing what needs to be done now."

She was leading the pace right out of the past, walking faster than I knew how without breaking into a run. I don't think Grandma was ever late to Mass in her life. We just made it to an empty pew in the back, not our usual seats in the front left side near the Blessed Mother statue, as the eighth bell chimed.

She was still breathing hard as she turned the ribbon in her missal to the Prayers at the Foot of the Altar. "*Ad Deum qui laetificat juventutem meum*," she puffed her response with the others. As always, she pointed to the English alongside the Latin words for me to read silently, "I will go now to the altar of my God. The God who gives joy to my youth." I looked up at the sharp-edged profile of Grandma's stern face and was glad that she had a good time at the fair with her daddy. I wondered when I would see my daddy again.

I'd never seen St. Ignatius from the back of the church where we sat this morning. It had much more echo and color to it than Mary of Gaels. God seemed a little less complicated, maybe less like a showoff in our own small brick church at home. But St. Nat's was where Mama had been a schoolgirl and where she and Daddy had gotten married. Most days during Mass I tried to imagine her in her school uniform or even coming down the long aisle in her bride's dress. This morning I couldn't remember from the picture what her veil looked like, so I substituted the fanciest thing I owned, my own First Communion veil, the one with all the handsewn sequins that Grandma Keary had worked past midnight to finish. Grandma Keary hardly ever came to Mass during the week, and if she did, she would be late since Uncle Red would drive her. She said he kept Irish time. Today as every day, I kept alert for latecomers.

When the traffic noise shouted in at us for a second, I turned to see who was slipping in a side door when we were well into the *Confiteor*. It was just a lady with a scarf tied under her chin the way my mom and everybody's mom wore them at daily, but not Sunday, Mass. I always thought the ladies at weekday Mass looked like a flock of friendly mother birds the way their scarves smoothed the tops of their head and covered their necks. Behind this lady there was a boy about Jackie's size and another kid younger than me. I hurt when I thought that I could fit right in there between those two kids.

My eyes wandered up to the multicolored window we sat alongside of today. It reached nearly all the way to the high ceiling and came to an arched point, like the Vanguard rocket ship they kept trying to launch into space. This window was crowded with stories of haloed saints and soaring angels told in stained glass that broke the light falling on Grandma and me into blues and reds and greens and purples.

Mary of Gaels church didn't have windows that looked upon Heaven like this, but I knew every detail of what could be seen of the playground from its clear glass windows since Sister Mary Columba thought my spending time alone in the church during recess would help me think about why I hadn't done my homework.

Mary of Gaels and my own home seemed far away this morning, but sitting on the aisle near a window on a sunny day at St. Nat's wasn't that bad. I made a new game of moving my cupped hands through the colored light, to see how many colors I could hold at one time. I wanted to laugh at the way the colors were streaming over Grandma and me. When she bent forward at the *mea maxima culpa,* her silver hair moved through patches of green and blue and made her look like a bright tropical bird of some kind.

I untucked my white shirt from my navy skirt and held it out from my waist to catch more of the colors that flowed over me like water. Did Mama see all this when she was in school here? I wished I could ask her. Right here. Right now. I wondered did she sometimes forget little things about my face and my voice, like I did about hers. It was Grandma Fahey's face now that filled my days, not Mama's. And when my earaches came back, it was Grandma's voice that tugged me out of feverish sleep to give me my medicine each night, the silver in her disheveled hair glowing like a halo in the light from the hallway behind her so that I thought she might have been a sleepy angel.

I hoped Mama wasn't forgetting me. I wanted to close my hands around all this bright color and light and make it mine. Hold on to it forever, no matter what. I wanted to clutch at it like it was fabric, like Mama's dress, but the more I grabbed for something to fill my hands, the colder my fingers felt. I was inside of a place I'd never been before, and I felt something lunge and then tighten in my chest. What if Mama forgot more and more little things about me until at last she couldn't see *my* face when *she* went to sleep at night? It could happen. I knew. I saw other faces before sleep now besides hers, my dead Uncle Nat and Great Grandpa Regan in the hallway, and sometimes no matter how hard I tried not to, even the faery woman at the window.

That Mama could forget about me made me dizzy and feverish. The windows became ice, not glass, and I closed my eyes, certain that they were all about to shatter. I thought I might fall over until I heard Grandma Fahey's voice. "Lucy, Lucy, Lucy. This will never do."

I opened my eyes to her quickly tucking in my shirttail. Her face might have been red even without the stained light upon it. I was divided into blue and red, like part of me wanted to stay a different color than the rest of me. The red and blue cut Grandma in half, too. As if she were in between two worlds. Why would she say to never look back if the past was the only place where she was with her whole family, too?

That afternoon Grandma said I should just rest and we'd have no school lessons. I could play outside but must stay in the shade, as it might have been the heat that had upset me so at church. I sat in the grass under an elm, feeling sorry for myself, staring at the bark. Sometimes you can see faces in the bark if you stare for a whole minute. Something was looking back at me from out of the trunk that was all giant eyes and claws like in the monster movies. It was a perfect locust shell, the kind Jackie and I could have hunted high and low for and never found in our suburb where the shade trees were too puny for the locusts to leave their shells in. I plucked this one from the bark. It was a keeper by the size of it alone. I looked up and down the trunk for more. There were plenty of good ones just for the taking and down low at my level, not like at home where we had to climb the tree to get at them. Jackie'd flip if he saw some of these grinning little guys. I'd keep an eye out for them. I was staring back at one sad and spooky little face, thinking about where the green insect inside had gone to, when Grandma called from her bedroom window.

"Lucy, come up here a minute, please."

She was taking two shoeboxes from the back of her closet. Had she found out that I prowled around in all the closets upstairs when I was supposed to be studying in my room? I had never noticed these old shoes before. These weren't like Grandpa Fahey's dress shoes that she still kept in a Florsheim box. These looked like the shoes of a giant when she stood them on the floor, side by side. She looked at them herself like she didn't know what to make of them. Deep creases lay between the toes and the place where laces should have been, and these creases were filled up with what looked like cement.

"I kept these in the garage with his old trowel because Will Fahey didn't want them in the house. I didn't bring any of it inside until Will passed on."

These must be his mighty shoes, Great Grandpa Regan's shoes.

Grandma had all but disappeared again inside the closet.

I was looking at one of the empty shoe boxes, thinking it would be a good place to keep my locusts, when she yelled from deep inside her closet.

"Here it is."

Her voice was muffled by the hanging clothes that surrounded her. She was very pleased with herself when she emerged with a black-varnished walking stick worn smooth at the top. I could have told her, if she'd asked me, that it was back there.

"This, Lucy, was the old gentleman's too." Grandma had a funny smile, like a kid almost, and her hair was all out of place, like someone had just tousled it the way my dad always did when he got back home from a business trip. She was having so much fun that I thought she'd like to see what *I* had just found, and held out the two dried locust shells.

"Oh, my Lord, Lucy, leave those frightful things in the yard."

"Yessum," I said quickly.

Then she picked up the shoes, smiled and brushed off as much of the dust and cement as she could into the shoeboxes.

"Here, Lucy, take these boxes down to the alley for the trash man, will you please."

I took one box straight to my room, put in two locust shells, and slid it under my bed. Then I took the other box to the alley. When I came back upstairs, Great Grandpa Regan's shoes were under the table in the hallway and his stick was leaning against the wall under his portrait. I was glad about that, as I thought it might be useful in thumping any banshee that might try to get in the window. Later she began to use it on our hikes to Mass. It was something from the past she was supposed to forget but it helped her up our hill every morning. I realized quickly that when she carried it, anytime I wanted to sidetrack a catechism lesson all I had to do was to ask about her people, the Regans of Mayo. It didn't matter to me if the World's Fair of 1892 was held to celebrate the year that the Regans came to America, or to mark 400 years from Christopher Columbus's own discovery of it. She added both 1892 and 1492 to my list of important dates in history.

Sometimes, even without my asking, with a flat sweep of her Regan hand, Grandma would smoothly fill the silences in our days with stories of County Mayo and Chicago and long-dead relatives—the same way Grandma Keary would fill her house with noisy, living ones. I think we were both a little less lonely that way.

Chapter 7: Lord Nelson's Nose

The morning that Uncle Red called to invite Grandma Fahey and me to a Quinn family gathering while some of the Chicago relatives were in town, I happily accepted for the both of us.

"Oh, Lucy, you should have asked me first," Grandma said when I told her. "We'll have to call him back and tell him we can't make it. Hand me the phone book, if you please, Lucy."

I pulled at the phone book on the shelf above the extension in the kitchen like it weighed 300 pounds and began to bargain, "But Grandma, I'll study my lessons twice as hard tomorrow if we can go tonight." Grandma might have fun, too. They could all talk about Ireland and Chicago.

"There are so many Quinns in the directory. What is your great uncle's baptismal name? It can't be Red."

"I don't remember, Grandma," I lied.

"I know people like him. They romanticize everything, carrying on about dear old Ireland, singing those old songs at the drop of a hat. I've no use for that. None at all."

"Please can't we go, Grandma?"

"Here, this must be him on Forest Avenue. Your great uncles cannot be relied upon for the facts."

That only made me question the value of facts. Warm tears welled up in my eyes for the first time since I left home, and I threw myself on the couch. How could this door open up for me and Grandma not let me through?

"Oh, Lucy. It is not as bad as all that."

What did she know? Grandma Keary would be there and maybe even Jackie.

"Stop that sniffling, child," she said sternly, putting down the phone book.

I didn't even think I could stop. I'd been afraid of crying since I left home.

"Oh, I suppose we could stop by," she sighed, "but only for a short while. Mind you, I do not relish an entire evening with your mother's people, no, I do not, Lucy."

"Yessum."

"We'll leave here at 6:30."

"Uncle Red said he'd come by for us at 6:00."

"We will take a taxi, at 6:30," she said checking her coin purse. "I won't be beholden to the likes of Mr. Red Quinn."

Uncle Red lived on the first floor of a brownstone apartment building. When we arrived his little parlor was already full of Quinns, Chicago relatives, and pipe smoke. I immediately looked around for Grandma Keary but didn't see her. Grandma Fahey held my hand a little too tightly as I led her into the crowd to find my great uncle.

"Hiya, Uncle Red."

"Lucy, how's my best girl?" He pinched my cheek.

With one hand extended to Grandma Fahey and the other plucking a suspender, he said, "John Redmond Quinn at your service."

Things were off to a good start I thought.

Uncle Red was still holding Grandma's hand. "We've never formally met, Mrs. Fahey. I am Lucy's great uncle. Well, at least she thinks I'm a pretty great uncle." He winked at me.

Grandma recovered her gloved hand and nodded her head in my direction. "Mr. Quinn, will there be excessive drinking here tonight?"

"Only if you feel up to it, Mrs. Fahey. Don't feel under any obligation. No one will think any the less of you."

"Really now, Mr. Quinn, I have an obligation to my granddaughter."

"Please call me Red. Everyone does. It's Maeve, isn't it?

"It is," said Grandma Fahey. She clutched her pocket book with both hands as she did when we were among strangers downtown.

"A beautiful name. A name with history. Maeve was a Queen of Ireland, if I'm not mistaken," smiled Uncle Red.

Then said to me: "Did you not know, Lucy, that your Grandmother Fahey was named for a Queen?"

"No, sir." I warmed to the idea of royal relations.

"Oh, yes indeed, and a Warrior Queen at that. Maeve was Queen of all Connaught more than a thousand years ago. She waged one devil of a roaring battle against Conn, the High King of Ulster."

That sounded like something Grandma Fahey would know how to do.

Uncle Red tilted his head and smiled at Grandma. "A second Helen of Troy was Queen Maeve. Let me find the best seat in the house for you ladies," he said, surveying the room.

I looked hopefully at her now, too. I thought for sure she'd like to talk about being named for a Queen of Ireland, but she just kept a cold eye on Uncle Red as he continued, "Correct me if I'm wrong, Maeve, but it was Queen Maeve's desire to be the richest woman in the land that led to war against Conn of Ulster."

Turning to me he asked, "Do you know what she wanted that she couldn't have for love nor money, Lucy?"

"No, sir."

"Conn of Ulster had a bull that was the finest in all Ireland. She wanted that old bull something fierce and that's what began the famous ruckus about a thousand years ago."

Grandma squinted at Uncle Red as she would any tradesman at her back door presenting a bill for her approval and said, "These are just old stories, Lucy. I was named after Our Lady, and not Queen Maeve, I assure you, Mr. Quinn."

"Oh, of course, of course you were, Mrs. Fahey. It's a beautiful name nonetheless. May I call you Maeve?"

"You may call me what you like, Mr. Quinn."

Uncle Red laughed, then directed us towards a sofa just vacated by three silver-haired Chicago cousins off to listen to the A's game on a transistor radio.

As he sat down beside Grandma Fahey, Uncle Red asked, "What County are you from, Maeve? From Sligo perhaps. Or is it Leitrim?"

"Cook, I'm from Cook County, Illinois, Mr. Quinn," Grandma Fahey said firmly.

"Cork, is it?" smiled Uncle Red, pretending not to catch her drift. "We have people from Skibbereen in Cork, the Cavanaughs, do you know them?"

"I am from Chicago, Mr. Quinn. Cook County, Illinois."

"Ah, yes, I understand, that's where you landed. But where are you from, Maeve, *where are you from?*"

"Mayo. The Regans and the McNamees are all from County Mayo, Uncle Red," I piped up thinking that Grandma would be proud of my reporting that fact, but she just kept up her sidelong squint at Uncle Red.

"Well Mayo, of course," said Uncle Red tapping his ear. "There's the lovely sound of Connaught still in your voice. And I should have guessed Mayo. The most elegant women in the West of Ireland are from Mayo. Am I not right, Lucy?"

Grandma brought her pocket book flat against her chest.

"Yes sir, Uncle Red. And Great Grandpa Regan was a Mason."

"Well now. A Mason named Regan? That's a rare bird," laughed Uncle Red.

"He was in the masonry trade," Grandma corrected. "That is not the same thing as being a Mason, for Heaven's sake, Lucy."

I was glad to have that cleared up. It had worried me that he might have been a Mason because Uncle Red told me we had to cross to the other side in front of the DeMolay Masonic Temple downtown to keep from getting grabbed off the street and boiled for lunch.

"My father worked in the building trades in Chicago, Mr. Quinn. And he was, I assure you, as Catholic as the day is long."

"Now the McKee brothers are from Chicago, Maeve. They are all here today. Maybe you knocked into them there in Cook County at some time? No mind. They've graciously provided us with two fine kegs of stout. It's harder to come by down here in Missouri. Can I get you a glass, Maeve?"

"Thank you, no, Mr. Quinn."

"I know. I know what it is you are saying to yourself, that if it isn't the *potcheen* from Mayo, then I'll have no part of it. Am I right?"

"Not at all, Mr. Quinn. I never tasted *potcheen* in Ireland."

"Well, better late than never, eh Maeve?"

"If you insist, Mr. Quinn. I'll take a half glass of your stout, but no more. It has been a hot day, and it will remind me of my home—Chicago, Illinois."

"Half a glass it is," Uncle Red chuckled. He turned to go back to the kitchen but stopped suddenly and turned, "Lucy, would you like the other half of your Grandmother's glass?"

I wasn't sure if I was allowed to laugh at that, so I just shook my head.

"Are you sure now, Lucy?"

How could I not giggle with Uncle Red waiting for me to?

After Uncle Red headed for the kitchen, Grandma brushed some lint from the arm of the sofa, pulled out an ace of clubs that had somehow gotten wedged between two sofa cushions, and whispered, "We will not be staying long, Lucy. Don't get too comfortable."

I looked around at the assortment of loud and mostly ancient relatives. I'd never met most of the Chicago relatives, but I'd seen red and shiny faces like these before.

"Grandma, what's *the potcheen*?"

"Oh, Lucy, I knew it was a mistake to bring you here among these people. *Potcheen*, if you must know, is, well, an alcoholic beverage. It's distilled. They called it *potcheen* or moonshine ..."

Great Uncle Conny came over to our sofa and sat down heavily beside Grandma, mugging, "She's a little young to be taught about the *potcheen*, don't you think, Mrs. Fahey?"

"Oh, really now. I am having a private conversation with my granddaughter."

Grandma stood up as suddenly as she had the day a stranger sat too close to her on the downtown bus. We got off two stops early and had to wait for another bus to take us home. At the same moment, Uncle Red appeared with her stout, a lemonade for me, and a small plate of sandwiches on tray.

"Where are you two Mayo women going?" he asked. "I was looking forward to our visit. I see you've met my brother, Conn."

Uncle Conny smiled at Grandma and as soon as she nodded to him, someone from across the room, shouted, "Hey, Conny, get over here, we're laying odds those damn A's will finish in the cellar again," and Uncle Conny was off.

I was just as glad. Uncle Red was trying harder to get along with Grandma than Uncle Conny ever would.

"Please stay and enjoy yourself for a little while, Maeve. You work hard and deserve a little breather. We all appreciate what you're doing for Lucy with Rosie being away." Uncle Red placed our drinks on the coffee table. "Let Lucy enjoy her lemonade. And you ought to just taste this stout. It's the genuine article, Maeve," he beamed at her like he'd known her all his life.

I reached for my lemonade and Grandma put her pocket book on the floor and sat back on the sofa. She took off one of her white gloves since Uncle Red hadn't handed her a napkin and she took a sip.

"That's the ticket, Maeve." Uncle Red was watching her closely.

I don't think Grandma was even aware of the bit of a smile on her face. I thought of the time the grocery boy delivered an extra pork chop she hadn't ordered. She was ready to read somebody the Riot Act until she saw that she hadn't been charged. She was enjoying the stout the same way she had enjoyed that bonus chop.

"Well, now, we're set for the evening," Uncle Red said as he looked around the room at the trays of ham and butter sandwiches and pitchers of dark stout. "This is a fine gathering of Gaels."

An old woman, a Chicago relative, wagged the top of her cane from the corner of the room to get Uncle Red's attention.

"Red, we should begin with a prayer."

"Well, we can do that, too, Norrie," he said, then slowly sipped his stout. I knew that Grandma probably didn't like someone besides her calling for prayers, but this woman seemed much older than either of my grandmas or great uncles.

"A prayer then," he said putting down a half-finished glass, "yes, a prayer, now that everyone's here."

Everyone? What did he mean, everyone? "Where's Jackie, Uncle Red? Jackie's not here yet."

"No, he is pitching in a big game tonight. Your Uncle Mickey is with him. Not sure if they'll make it tonight. Conny, did you hear that Jack nearly pitched another no-hitter the other night?"

The lemonade that was caught in my throat began to burn. "And where's my grandma? She's not here yet." I felt Grandma Fahey shift on the couch next to me, but I didn't care that I hurt her feelings. I hadn't seen Grandma Keary since I left home.

Uncle Red put his hand on my head. "Your Grandma Keary is with your mom tonight. She is staying at the hospital in fact. Maggie's just a bit worn out herself from coming and going. I'm sure she'll be just fine, they both will."

I hated it when things were "just fine." I've heard it so many times since Mama got sick. It meant that no one really knew what was going on.

The old woman in the corner started shouting the beginning of a prayer we all knew by heart. "Hail, Holy Queen. Mother of mercy. Our life, our sweetness, and our hope." Although Grandma Fahey crossed herself and was on her knees before any of the other old people had made whatever move they were able to, I didn't see any need to pray. It wouldn't do any good if a pack of spiteful faeries were in charge of everything anyway. I didn't even join in when they got to the part of the prayer I knew the most about—"the poor banished children of Eve." But when Grandma's right hand shot out and pointed at the floor next to her, I slumped to my knees. "To Thee do we send up our sighs, mourning and weeping in this valley of tears."

After the prayer, everyone's glasses, including half of Grandma Fahey's, were refilled and Uncle Red quickly raised a toast to the Chicago McKee and O'Fallon cousins for stopping in. Then he took me by the hand and said to the group, "This is Rosie's little girl. This is Lucy Fahey. Many thanks to Mrs. Maeve Fahey who has brought her to us tonight."

Grandma nodded stiffly around the room to the Chicago relatives who smiled or raised their glasses in her direction. Uncle Red led me to where old Norrie O'Fallon sat huddled and nearly motionless under a black shawl. The Hail, Holy Queen had worn her out. I thought she must have been the oldest living person in the world. At least, I supposed she was still living. I wasn't sure I wanted to be this close.

Uncle Red was yelling to her, "Norrie, this is Lucy, Rose Keary's youngest." As I stood before her, she slowly pulled herself forward with both hands on her cane. She looked at me like she might have known me. I'm sure I would have remembered her face that was as lined and cracked as a clay creek bed gone dry in the summer. Her quick blue eyes studied my face, then she made me jump with a sudden laugh, "Doesn't she have the nose of the O'Fallons. And the brow too, for that matter."

Many O'Fallons agreed.

Then the one they called Old Ned McKee said the O'Fallons were all dead wrong and that I could be taken for a McKee any day of the week, "Look at her dark hair. She's a ringer for Ellie McKee back in Galway. Now there was a real looker. Ran off with a seminarian from Oughterard you know."

I was starting to like this game they were making out of my face.

I could hear Grandma Fahey's little tisking noise from clear across the room, but I ignored her. I hoped they'd all keep talking about me, but the McKees fell into a heated argument as to whether the seminarian was from Oughterard or from Nun's Island and whether he was only a choirmaster and not a seminarian after all.

When I wandered back over to sit with Grandma Fahey, she squeezed my hand and whispered, "If you look like anyone, it is my people, the Regans and McNamees of Westport and Killala in County Mayo, and that is that. I'll hear no more."

I wondered how I could look like so many different people and all of them old or goners. I must look a lot different to them than I do to myself. I was looking around for a mirror, when Old Ned called out, "Do you dance, little Fahey?"

"No, sir."

"You should learn. We'll have some music here at Maggie's when she's out of the hospital. That'll make her feel better. She's got the room for it. Not like your place, Red. What do you think? I brought the fiddle."

Old people are always confused. It was my mom not my grandma that was so sick in the hospital.

Uncle Red was still standing in the center of the circle of silver-headed relatives, when he turned to Uncle Conny and said, "Cornelius, another toast for us."

Uncle Conny wiped his mouth with the back of his hand, raised his glass and without hesitation shouted, "Up the rebels!"

The phrase echoed around the room before it was carried away by laughter because no one ever took Uncle Conny too seriously.

"The rebels?" Grandma asked, a little too loudly I thought.

"The Irish ones, Maeve," smiled Uncle Red. "My brother Conn is well known for his sympathies with the cause of a united Ireland.

Uncle Conny lifted his glass again, "To the martyrs of the Easter Uprising of 1916. To Connolly and Pearse and MacDonagh ..."

But Grandma Fahey cut short his familiar litany.

"I think it was blasphemous what Connolly and the others did in 1916, starting a rebellion during Easter Week when they all should have been at Mass."

The room tensed like a live grenade had just been rolled across the floor. She just might have been named for the Warrior Queen of Connaught after all.

"But, Maeve," Uncle Red said very patiently, "there'd be no Republic of Ireland today without the Uprising and the heroes of 1916."

"Oh, go on with you, Mr. Quinn. The Easter Uprising was nothing more than godless rascals running amok. Those men with Connolly were a pack of hooligans who blackened the eye of Ireland in the opinion of the civilized world. Carrying on that way, trying to take Dublin back from the British when they didn't stand a chance. Disgraceful."

There was such a sudden and complete silence in the room that I shook my head to make sure my good ear was still working. This was like being for the Redcoats and against the colonists who threw the tea into Boston harbor in another uprising. Why was Grandma putting her back against the wall like this in Uncle Red's parlor when she'd taught me in her own parlor that America was a great nation because the first thing we did was to send the English packing in 1776?

Norrie O'Fallon shouted, "What'd she say? What'd she say?"

Old Ned McKee yelled back the gist of what Grandma had said so that the words "disgraceful" and "hooligans" hung in the smoky air in Uncle Red's little parlor.

Norrie O'Fallon squinted long and slow at Grandma, "How are we related to her again?"

I was the only person in the room really related to Grandma Fahey. I wished they'd talk about something else besides politics and the rebels. Something like baseball. Grandma didn't have a real opinion on baseball other than that it was a waste of time and therefore nearly a mortal sin. The looks on the faces of Uncle Red and Uncle Conny made me squirm. I tried to draw attention away from Grandma Fahey by changing the topic, saying what Jackie always says that gets attention from my uncles and great uncles. "The A's will always be in the cellar. Our relief pitching stinks."

Precisely no one was interested in my opinion about baseball. Uncle Conny seemed the most anxious to set Grandma straight, "Our men in 1916, Connolly and Padraic Pearse were heroes as great as any Ireland ever had. Who was greater?"

"The old heroes, that's who! Patrick Sarsfield or Daniel O'Connell to name a few." Grandma answered Uncle Conny in the same tone she'd use to correct my catechism answer.

"I give you O'Connell," she went on, "the Great Liberator, who fought with words not with guns and bombs if you are looking for a hero, Mr. Quinn. As great as Abraham Lincoln. He freed the Catholics in Ireland and never fired a shot. There's his statue in Dublin on O'Connell Street put up for the world to see and admire. Was there ever such a statue to your upstarts, Connolly or Pearse?"

"You don't have to have a statue to be a hero, do you Maeve?" Uncle Red chuckled like he was trying hard to get the joke he wanted her to be making. "And if having a monument on O'Connell Street in Dublin makes you an Irish hero, what about Admiral Nelson's Pillar at the other end of the street? Does that make an English Lord an Irish hero?"

"Och," was all Grandma said.

"What about it, Mrs. Fahey? You wouldn't say that Admiral Horatio Nelson, an Englishman, is a hero to Ireland, would you?"

Grandma answered calmly, "Where England saw fit to honor a seafaring man as great Nelson is of no concern to me."

But she might have said that Admiral Nelson was a better man than Jesus of Nazareth, judging by the way Uncle Conny exploded, "What's the sense, what's the bloody sense of having a monument to the British Empire on Irish soil anyway? Where's the sense in that somebody tell me."

His face got redder and shinier. Grandma stared him down, until he shouted, "If that Pillar stands for England lording it over Ireland like just another one of her pitiful colonies, I say somebody ought to blow the damn thing up!"

Norrie O'Fallon wheezed out the most sinister laugh I had ever heard, then shouted back, "Ned, who is it that Conny wants to blow up now?"

Old Ned McKee shouted back, "Just some old English Lord's statue in Dublin."

She wheezed again in delight and then patted the corners of her wrinkled mouth with a hanky. "Oh, that boy. He's never been to Dublin, I'll wager."

But Grandma wasn't having any of it. I recognized the strained smile on her face. It was her A&P smile. It came over her like a veil on the rare occasions that we shopped at the A&P instead of having groceries sent from Mr. Wolferman's Grocery. It meant that she was just passing through and certainly didn't want to be taken for someone who shopped at the A&P regularly. Now she was trying to pass through this evening at Uncle Red's the same way, like she was a Queen Maeve in exile.

Uncle Red said seriously but not without kindness, "Maeve, the heroes of 1916 were principled men who died for the sake of the Republic. James Connolly was a labor leader. Padraic Pearse and MacDonagh were poets ..."

"Poets and unionists!" she interrupted. "That is exactly my point. Daydreamers, the lot of them!" Grandma was carefully putting her white glove back on her hand, having finished her half glass of stout.

Uncle Conny scrambled to his feet and boomed, "How can anyone from Mayo be so bullish on the Brits when they tried to take everything from us, our land, our language and even our music?" He stayed standing to better lock horns with Grandma Fahey. "Need I remind all here exactly what your civilized British Empire did to James Connolly?"

"C'mon, Conny sit back down now, we've heard it all," Uncle Red urged, but Uncle Conny went on, "They were afraid Connolly would die in the Uprising and spoil their fun. So, they tied him to a wheel chair, rushed him to the prison yard wall like a bunch of Keystone Cops, then shouted, 'Wake up, Jimmy boy!' And when he looked up—they shot him dead!"

"We know, Conny. Now sit down."

Uncle Conny returned to his chair like a prizefighter returning to his corner, with a smile that said he'd won this round. What could top that? Not much. I was surprised that Grandma couldn't see that, but not surprised that she refused to give up the fight. She never gave up on lost causes. She'd practically turned me into a walking catechism after all.

"You know," Grandma continued, "I've heard it said that they were followers of Karl Marx. Oh yes, I've heard it said more than once that James Connolly himself was a *socialist*."

Uncle Conny looked like he'd been punched in the gut. There was nothing lower to call a man than that, not in this parish anyway. Grandma pinned him with a cool stare and then deftly delivered her right cross. "I'm not bullish on the Brits as you say, Mr. Quinn, but I prefer the British to communists and atheists."

Norrie O'Fallon reared back and thumped her cane three times on the floor, "She's got you, Conny. Give up. You're beat. You're beat. You're beat."

Uncle Conny swallowed hard a mouth full of stout and sputtered something I couldn't make out. I think he had just run out of words to argue with Grandma Fahey. I sure knew that feeling. He turned his back on Grandma and raised his empty glass to the far side of the room.

"To James Connolly!"

"To all dead Irishmen!" Norrie O'Fallon called out with glee.

"And to those of us soon to be," Old Ned McKee shouted out of the rumble of laughter from his side of the parlor.

"Now sit down for crissakes, Conn," implored Uncle Red who was watching Grandma very closely.

"Not until I hear a song to that great man, Red."

Uncle Conny, started them off singing the one about James Connolly and the "bright spirit of freedom."

At the end of the first verse, Uncle Conny and some of the McKees shouted rather than sang Connolly's famous cry, "No Surrender!" And even though most of the relatives laughed, Uncle Conny acted like it had all happened yesterday and he had been there in the crowd outside of Kilmainham, the day they shot James Connolly.

I wanted to sing along, too, but I knew Grandma wouldn't stand for it. Connolly was no hero to her. He was no dashing Patrick Sarsfield at the walls of Limerick after all. Grandma and I were the only ones in the whole room not singing or keeping time, and I was supposed to not move a muscle, not even tap one toe. It was about as easy as trying not to laugh when you're being tickled.

I knew that once my great uncles got singing rebel songs there was no stopping them. Uncle Red told me once that rebel songs are like sardines in a tin. It's impossible to eat just one without digging out the rest of them. It made perfect sense to me that Irish heroes were like sardines. They all looked pretty much alike and one tasted just as salty as the next. They even seemed to be lined up in rows almost like soldiers waiting to be done in by the Brits, then turned into songs.

To me there was no difference between Uncle Conny's hero and Grandma's. It was the fight, never the outcome that made an Irish hero. I knew from the number of songs they sang there was an almost endless variety of ways to stand your ground against over-whelming odds.

Patrick Sarsfield, Grandma Fahey's approved hero, for example, did such a memorable job of outwitting the Redcoats all over Limerick and the West 300 years ago that Grandma often sang "down the glen rode Sarsfield's men, and they wore their jackets green" when she sent her best things to the dry cleaner. What still mattered was that he had worn his bright Irish color and a hat with a white feather on it so that the English knew exactly who was running them around in circles. But even Patrick Sarsfield, gallant and well dressed as he was, was overrun, simply outnumbered by the Redcoats. He fought until the last at the city walls of Limerick, like any great hero would. Just like my hero, Davy Crocket, at the walls of the Alamo. Jackie and I both coveted coonskin caps.

I wonder if the Irish were ever allowed to win anything for keeps. Uncle Conny and Grandma Fahey fought like Queen Maeve and Conn of Ulster over whose heroes were better, but I don't think any of my relatives would have traded an Irish victory for their proud songs of their brave Irish heroes dying young.

I was glad for Senator Kennedy that he didn't have to fight the English, only some guys named Estes Kefauver and Lyndon B. Johnson for the nomination, and then, if he got lucky, the Republicans.

Uncle Conn had listed off key, but Norrie O'Fallon was leaning forward keeping time with her cane although the song probably went on longer than it took to execute Connolly and the rebels in the Uprising in 1916. Grandma sat perfectly still. She had an expression that was a bit more than her A&P smile. Two beats after they ran out of verses, Grandma turned to Uncle Red, "Mr. Quinn, has the church canonized James Connolly and the rest and just not announced it?"

She said it loud enough for Norrie O'Fallon to hear because she started to cough her laugh. I never could tell which side she was on, unless it was just the underdog at the time.

"What's that, Maeve?" said Uncle Red taking a long thirsty draw on his stout.

"You make Connolly sound like a right old martyr—or Christ himself, Mr. Quinn."

"Did he not forgive the English soldiers who shot him, just as Christ forgave the Roman ones?" Uncle Red said, suddenly more seriously than he was about most church things.

"He did at that, Red," Uncle Conny joined in. "And the English, like the good thieves they are, stole his forgiveness—and then they killed him."

"Do you think, gentlemen, that such blasphemy is called for in front of an impressionable child," she chided.

I gulped when everyone looked at me like I had something to do with Grandma's opinions. Uncle Red gave me a once over to make sure I was still standing, and then added quietly "Maeve, James Connolly left this world saying that he forgave all men who did their duty according to their lights. Are those not the words of a great man?"

"Och. Och. Och," she said with three chops of her hand, and how could anyone argue with that? I couldn't because I didn't know what it meant, but it sounded final.

With her hands at last in her lap, Grandma said to the group, "Don't we have American heroes anyway? Aren't we, most of us in this room, American citizens? And besides, my granddaughter Lucy doesn't need to hear all these old tales. She is an American child after all."

"Aw c'mon now, Maevsie. She needs to know about our heroes," Uncle Red said teasing her like they were old friends. "Where's the harm in that?"

"She's an American child, Mr. Quinn, and she has her own heroes. American ones."

I did. I'd saved up more money for a coonskin cap than even Jackie.

Norrie O'Fallon proclaimed, "That child can't have that face and not know the old stories. And what about that new Kennedy lad? He'll make us all proud again before it's over." She wagged her cane at Grandma to show she'd been trumped. "Red, what's an old woman got to do to get a drink at your place?"

"Coming right up, Norrie." When he came back with a pitcher of foamy dark brown stout Uncle Red called, "Who's for another round?" He elevated a pitcher over the assembly as a priest would a chalice.

As Uncle Red came at last to Grandma, he looked her in the eyes and smiled, "Between you and me, Maeve, I'm glad Nelson's Pillar is where it is."

Grandma seemed to be taken so off guard that Uncle Red had poured her another half glass before she knew it.

"Yes, indeed. The way I heard it, before the Brits rounded them up that Easter, the rebels had been taking turns shooting at Lord Nelson's statue. One lucky lad shot the nose clear off of old Horatio. So you could say, the rebels did more than tweak the nose of the Empire—they shot the bloody thing off."

Someone yelled, "Red's making that up. Is he making that up?"

I'd never heard that part of the story either.

But Uncle Conny crowed, "It's true, what Red is saying. They blew the damn thing off."

"Thank you, Conny. So you might say that Nelson's Pillar, sans Horatio's proboscis, is the most fitting tribute to the Eastertide rebels. And the Brits were none the wiser." Uncle Red slapped his leg and his belly shook like no one on earth could have enjoyed his joke more than himself, except for Uncle Conny, of course, who was laughing so hard he could barely speak. Uncle Conny blew his nose, and said, "Oh Mrs. Fahey, Mrs. Fahey, let me revise my earlier toast to the rebels. Yes, oh yes, let me be more specific." Uncle Conny was back on his feet and with the back of his hand to his nose, he sniffed once more, then deadpanned, "Mrs. Fahey, I give you, Lord Nelson's nose."

"Nelson's nose!" intoned the old ones like they'd been waiting all evening for this very toast.

I wanted to laugh at the sight of them acting like kids on the playground teasing Grandma, who was telling me that we had worn out our welcome and would be leaving shortly. I wondered who had won that war between the other Queen Maeve and King Conny of Ulster. Probably neither. How could they? They were both Irish.

My summer had just gotten longer. I knew I wouldn't be seeing my great uncles any time soon after tonight.

Chapter 8: Uprisings

When the laughter died down Norrie O'Fallon, looking like a solemn little mouse in her corner, said, "These uprisings have their way and their day. They won't be denied."

"How's that, Norrie?" asked Uncle Red, still smiling and wiping a bit of moisture from the corner of his eye.

"All uprisings, I mean. When the English put bounties on our Irish harpers and rounded up the harps and threw then into the bogs like so many old shoes, we all know what happened." She smiled a grim smile that looked like it might hurt her wrinkled face.

"We do indeed, Norrie, we do indeed," said Old Ned McKee. "But damn it, Red, the stout's gone flat."

Uncle Red swirled what remained of the dark stout around in the pitcher to see for himself as Norrie O'Fallon continued, "These uprisings follow the one law of all nature, of all living things, do they not? I trust I have made my point." She leaned back in her chair, and her face became obscured by the long shadows that now cut across the room, which was as quiet as it had been all night. A pause like this around Uncle Red only meant another story was about to start, but Grandma put a stop to that by asking him could she use his phone to call a taxi.

"Oh, here now, Maeve, I'll see you and Lucy home, but you can't be leaving so early."

Grandma said that we must, but made no move herself to leave while there was stout left in her glass. I jumped to my feet, but not to leave. I needed to know what everyone else seemed to know in their bones, what happened to the harps they threw into the bogs. One of the things I hated most about my mom being sick was that I was always the only one in the room not to know what was going on. Jackie said sometimes it is better not to know everything.

What happened to the harps? Did they just sink and disappear from sight forever like the English wanted? This wasn't a story either of my Grandmas told. Not even Uncle Red told this one and he knew practically every good story there was. I felt pulled steadily across the room towards Norrie O'Fallon. I needed one true answer about the way things work.

I approached my ancient cousin like I was walking to the end of a dusty road, hoping that there was something, anything there for me. I stood before Norrie O'Fallon, holding my breath. Her eyes were closed and she seemed to have crumpled in upon herself for another nap. I reached for her hand but decided not to touch her. She might be cold like they say dead people are. I nudged her chair a little and I called softly "Cousin Norrie?"

She didn't budge.

I needed her to hear me, so I cupped my hands and said a little louder, "What happened to the harps that sank in the bogs, Cousin Norrie."

I wasn't even sure I knew what a bog was, except that it sounded like a very cold and dark and soggy place where the earth can swallow you for good because there is no bottom to it. Not the kind of place anybody would want to end up, or be made to throw their favorite things into. That was a mean trick. Worse than when a couple of the public school kids chased down a kid in Jackie's class, tied his Mary of Gaels tie in knots and then threw his book bag off the bridge over the stream between our schools. Next day Jackie helped throw some public kid's whole bike into the creek "for safe keeping."

I was surprised how clear and loud my voice sounded, not at all like I was shouting underwater to be heard, when I yelled, "Cousin Norrie! I don't know!"

"Oh, Lucy," Grandma Fahey sounded her reproof from across the room. She'd been arguing so much with Uncle Red about the taxi that she hadn't even noticed I'd slipped into the enemy camp. "Don't be so forward with your elders."

I was sure it was the sound of Grandma Fahey's voice, and not mine, that caused Cousin Norrie's clear blue eyes to spring to life. I was standing before her for the second time tonight, hoping that she'd remember again what she liked about me, that I looked like an O'Fallon. I blurted, "I don't know how the story ends."

Does it end like Sarsfield being overrun and defeated at the Walls of Limerick? Or Connolly shot in his wheel chair? Just done in and nobody could do anything about it but sing? I didn't want it to be another story with an Irish hero. I needed a story where things turned out well.

"Lucy, why are you bothering Mrs. O'Fallon like that?" Grandma called.

I didn't have time to answer. The answer I needed was as important to me as any catechism. Cousin Norrie's eyes moved quickly across the room to Grandma and then I felt them latch on to me and pull me closer.

"What is it you're asking, little one?"

"I don't know how the story ends."

"Which story would that be now?"

"The harps that got thrown away into the bogs. What happened to them? How does it end?"

"Oh, that. Like every true story." She coughed a laugh that rippled through her otherwise motionless body giving off a scent that made me think of a cedar chest.

I felt my heart sinking.

"What happened, little one," she said, pointing one gnarled hand at me that looked like it might have frozen a hundred years ago while playing a harp, "was that the harps rose again from the deepest part of those old bogs. Exactly three days and three nights after the English left them there, thinking they had taken our music from us. The harps rose to the surface of the bogs on the third day."

"Was it on an Easter Sunday?"

Springing out of something like a bog ought to happen on Easter, but Norrie wheezed that she believed it was on a Tuesday after tea.

"But, little one, didn't our harpers fish them out when they rose up again?"

"I don't know, did they?"

"They did, indeed," she confirmed as if she had been there to see this particular resurrection.

"What made them rise up like that?" I felt like something inside of me had pushed off the bottom of the deep end of the swimming pool, and was rising without effort to the surface.

"What made them rise? Why, it was our music. The music that still needed to be played that wouldn't let them sink. It was our music alone that wouldn't be denied."

Hearing this tale was almost like having Grandma Keary here to hold me and tell me to wait and see, that something good will happen. I began to miss her a little less as I listened to Norrie O'Fallon's story, but I still worried about one thing.

"Did all the harps make it out? It wasn't just the most important harps that made it back to the surface was it. There wasn't like one that got forgotten, was there?"

"Not a one was lost."

"Weren't they kind of soggy? Wouldn't they be ruined when they got them out?"

I left Mama's ukulele outside overnight once and it was never the same.

"Oh, not at all. They say that the greatest harper of them all, who was himself blind as Homer Hooley, could tell by the sound alone which harps had risen from the bogs and which had not. Those from the bogs had a sweeter, sadder sound to them than any others."

"Come along now, Lucy. Let's not trouble Mrs. O'Fallon any longer," Grandma called from across the room.

"It is never a trouble to tell a little fish how to swim, Missus," Cousin Norrie called back like she didn't really care if Grandma Fahey heard her or not.

I felt Norrie's eyes go over every inch of me and give a silent chuckle like she knew the answer to some riddle that had to do with our eyes having the same shade of blue in them. "Turn around let me take the size of ye."

I held out my arms and turned in a circle as I would before Grandma Keary to show off how well a dress she had made for me fit. "Oh, yes. Yes. Yes," said Norrie. "You'll do fine, little one. Haven't I seen this little shape and face all before? And tell your old Granny from Mayo that trouble only comes from little ones not hearing the old ways or the old ones forgetting where they came from."

This had been a noisy and confusing evening, not at all like what I hoped it would be. But I could leave it now if I had to, even without getting to see Jackie, because I knew something now I hadn't before, that nothing important will ever sink from sight, at least not forever. What matters most will come around again and again, like the lilies of the valley every May at Grandma Keary's. I believed in uprisings now, or wanted to.

CHAPTER 9: SAXONS IN THE WHISKEY

"Lucy, we are leaving." Grandma smoothed the folds on the front of her navy blue dress as she stood up. "Please thank your host and say your goodnights."

Uncle Red jumped up as quickly. "C'mon Maeve, let me give you Mayo women a lift home tonight? It's a dark night and this air has turned a little damp. I'll take you, Maeve. Save you a few dollars on the taxi."

Grandma crossed her arms and seemed uncertain what to do or say for the first time all night. Two dollars was two dollars.

I could see Uncle Red was smiling even though his teeth were clenched around his pipe. As he struck a match and held it over the tobacco, it reminded me of the Westerns Jackie and I watched where the Indian chief lights the peace pipe to end the war between the cavalry and his tribe.

"It's in fun, you know, all of it. No harm intended, Maeve," he said gently.

"I am beyond this form of high jinx, I assure you, Mr. Quinn," she answered, but checked to make sure her pocket book was still on the floor next to her where she had left it.

"Let me just find my keys," he said as he patted his trouser pockets. "Here, Lucy, why don't you take your Grandmother's glass into the kitchen. And I need to freshen this pitcher before we leave. Your relatives, Lucy, they drink like fishes."

I took my glass and Grandma's and followed Uncle Red down the hall towards his kitchen. He stopped short to drink from the pitcher, "Old Ned's right. It's gone flat. I'll have to pitch it." He opened a screen door and started to throw the stout in the yard.

"Wait, Uncle Red!" I yelled.

I didn't want to risk annoying the faeries now, especially since Cousin Norrie's story made everything seem simple again. Grandma said that they love nothing more than to cause confusion if you don't pay them their due, and that they were nothing if not spiteful.

"I know, I know it's an awful waste. Taste it yourself, Lucy," he kidded. "It's only good now for killing the weeds."

"No, Uncle Red, aren't you going to, you know, warn the faeries?"

"The faeries, Lucy?" Uncle Red bent over me with a quizzical look.

"You know, just for luck." He looked at me like I was making something up. But he believed in signs and luck even though he didn't talk much about it. Why else would he study his *Daily Racing Form* as carefully as Grandma Fahey studied her *St. Andrew's Daily Missal*, but end up betting on the horse with the funniest or most likeable name?

"You're supposed to holler to the faeries before you throw anything into the dark like that. Grandma told me the faeries would get very mad to be hit by the dishwater she throws out the kitchen door."

"Maeve says that?" He put down the pitcher. The slow smile that spread over my great uncle's puckish face made his eyes crinkle. "Are you sure you heard her right, Lucy?"

With my bad ear I was used to people asking me that, often several times a day at school. "Yes, sir, I am sure. She yells something to them in Irish."

"Oh, this is rich, too rich."

After tonight I wouldn't be seeing Uncle Red for a long time, so I figured I might as well get his take on how much control the faeries really have. And just how it is that they can steal real things from you if you can't even see them.

"Grandma says they only understand Irish. I don't know exactly what she says, because she says it so fast, but it sounds like 'chickens in the whiskey.'"

Did he know enough Irish to give them just a little warning? I knew he knew enough Latin to keep his luck running like a good horse. Uncle Red was still bending over me with his hand on my cheek when Grandma Fahey came into the hall to see what was holding us up now that she was ready to leave. He turned on his heel and looked up at her and laughed,

"The faeries, Maeve? The faeries in America?" He stood up straight to wait for her reply.

The way she looked at me made me instantly regret saying anything to Uncle Red. Riling Grandma Fahey might prove to be more unlucky than riling the faeries themselves.

"Are there many faeries in Missouri? More to the point, can I register them to vote? They're surely all Democrats."

"I'm sure I don't know what you are talking about, Mr. Quinn," Grandma said still squinting at me.

"I'm talking about delivering your ward in every election. We'd never have to worry about it again. It hasn't gone Democratic since Roosevelt's last term. You know, wasn't it another Maeve who was Queen of the Faeries? This is rare and grand, to be sure."

He seemed barely able to control his glee as he relit his pipe.

"I was just giving Lucy an example of the old language, of the old ways that everyone was lamenting the loss of a few minutes ago. That's all."

"Not very American, is it Maeve, talking to the faeries? Carrying on secret communication with, ah, foreign powers like that might border on sedition. You know, I'd be worried about the House Un-American Activities Committee finding out, if I were you." He stifled an all-out laugh by shoving his pipe in his mouth. "But don't worry, Maeve old girl, no one here in my end of the parish would be after turning you in to the HUAC just for speaking a little Irish."

Grandma suddenly looked behind her down the hall. Uncle Red followed her glance and said, "I don't think Conny would be as understanding about this as I am. No, my brother may believe in other illusions, like a united Ireland, but not the faeries. Your secret is safe with me though, Maeve."

"I need nothing from you, Mr. Quinn, but a ride home for my granddaughter and myself. Unless it's a hollow offer you've made."

"Oh, no indeed. No indeed." Uncle Red was clearly enjoying having the goods on Grandma, and seemed to be mentally pulling material from the bolt of comic possibilities. Because he was always kinder than he was comical, he said only, "It is just that I haven't heard Irish in years. My mother had the Irish, too, Maeve. Can you give me a few words?"

Grandma tried to ignore him. "Lucy, are you ready to go?"

"Maeve, it's just that I'd like to hear what it was you said to make such an impression on this child." He stood in the middle of the hall and wouldn't let her pass until she had said something in Irish.

"It was just an old habit I picked up I don't know where. *Sheachaint, ar an uisce* is all I said. Look out for the water. It means nothing."

"What a marvelous sound Gaelic is the way you speak it," he said, his face lighting up in a smile that grew as bright as the tobacco in the bowl of the pipe he puffed on. "Collect your things, ladies, and we'll head straight away for the house of Faery, ah, that is, Fahey."

"Make as much fun as you want, Mr. Quinn, but my only point tonight is that the Irish will never be respected for siding with hooligans. Never. No, the Irish will not be respected until ..."

"There's a Mick in the White House?! Is that what you were going to say, Maevsie?"

"Indeed, I wasn't. That Kennedy boy will make us all look like fools before it is over. Do you think he thinks of the shame he'll cause us all when he's beaten? Not for one minute. I won't be made a fool of. Lucy, I'll wait for you at the front door."

When she left, Uncle Red chuckled, "Lucy, it sounds like she's saying 'Saxons in the whiskey' to me. Now, by Christ, that would be a greater cause for alarm than some damn chickens. Those old boyos were after stealing everything from everybody."

I stepped out of the door of his apartment with Uncle Red, who yelled, "There may be Saxons in our whiskey!" as he swirled the stout into the darkness. "I guess we gave them fair warning, eh Lucy? You didn't hear any of 'em hollering did you?"

"No, sir." I sure had missed the way Uncle Red could make me smile.

"Well, then who am I to say there are no faeries in Missouri? Maybe I should hedge my bets. What do you think, Lucy?"

We might as well. Grandma said a little warning never hurt anybody. Standing next to Uncle Red in this quiet darkness made me feel warm inside, even more than Norrie's story had. He put his arm around my shoulder and hugged me in close to him. He was watching the clouds that feathered around the moon, saying that it looked like rain tomorrow.

"Uncle Red?"

"Hmm?"

"Do you think they are out there?"

"Who, Lucy?

"The faeries?"

"Well Lucy, let's just say that there may be faeries in your Grandma Fahey's yard, but not in mine."

On the drive home, Grandma Fahey hardly spoke a word, but Uncle Red chatted the entire time. He recounted stories about each of the precincts we drove through. He told us how he used to know the names of all the families in all of them. Pointing at the little frame houses we drove by, he ran through a list of names: "Tiny Mike" Hennessey, who could lift two fifty in his heyday, and "Tombo" Farrell, who never complained a day about the leg he left in France during the First World War. There were the Carmodys and Kelleghers, the Mulvihills and O'Kellys. We had many of the same names at Mary of Gaels.

"And there, ladies, is the boyhood home of one Martin 'Holy Water' O'Malley."

Uncle Red couldn't say the name without laughing. After Grandma said she'd just as soon not hear how his pal got his nickname down at Mr. Philsy Cannon's one night, he told us anyway. After Mr. O'Malley had sworn off all liquor for the third time and was struggling, he went back to his whiskey but cut it with holy water.

"He was a drowning man without a little Jameson's every now and then—and the holy water saved him, don't you see, from giving it up altogether. Jameson's and a spot of water from the Shrine at Lourdes, you gotta admit, is a powerful combination, Maeve."

Uncle Red had to slow the car a bit while he laughed about Mr. "Holy Water" O'Malley.

Grandma said, "This is the sort of talk that gives our entire race a bad reputation. And mark my words, Mr. Quinn, it's that reputation that'll keep a bootlegger's son like the Kennedy boy out of the White House."

What did the faeries think of Senator Kennedy not knowing his place? Did they have tricks in store for him?

"We are what we are, Maeve. Nothing more and nothing less. And Joe Kennedy never touched a drop. Poor old O'Malley's not long for this world anyway. He's laid up over at St. Joseph's. Been meaning to visit him myself."

I wished Grandma had just let Uncle Red tell his stories, because he turned a little sad now as he talked about how much had changed since our people began moving from the city to the suburbs, just like my folks had done. Things were not the same for the old parish after the last war and the GI bill.

When we pulled up in front of Grandma Fahey's large Tudor house on the boulevard, he perked up again, announcing the ward and precinct numbers, and the demographic profile as "low population density—leaving the faeries out of the counting for the present—and largely Republican."

"What's wrong with being a Republican, Mr. Quinn? It was good enough for husband, Will Fahey."

"Not a blooming thing. My own brother is a Republican. Conny believes in the Republic of Ireland, and that the English should give back to that Republic the six Ulster counties they stole."

Were there English faeries that could steal six whole Irish counties?

"You needn't see us in, Mr. Quinn," she said as Uncle Red opened her car door. "I've left the light on."

"Ah yes, I see it there. A beacon for the weary. Good night, Maeve. You've been a sport."

I didn't want to get out of the back seat not knowing when I'd get to see Uncle Red again. He had held the car door open for Grandma Fahey and helped her to the curb, and now he opened my door.

"C'mon, Lucy, pile out of there. And be careful helping your Granny through the dark and up the steps, will you now. And you be careful yourself, Lucy. No telling what's lurking about in this yard," he winked.

I didn't really have time to worry about meeting anybody or anything on our way up the sloping lawn to the front door. Grandma didn't see well at night, but refused to let me take her by the hand until we were halfway there. She asked if my great uncle was still watching us, and before I could answer she had reached out anyway and steadied herself on my shoulder. Uncle Red waited by the car until we were inside and the porch light went out.

Standing in her own front hallway, Grandma quickly took off her white gloves, folded them carefully, and then dropped them into her pocket book, saying just one word, "Preposterous!" The metal clasp on her purse echoed that judgment snapping shut on our evening.

Chapter 10: Communion

The kitchen was dark and empty when I went downstairs the next morning. I sat down at the breakfast table to wait for Grandma and watched a gray mist rising off the garden. I wondered why Uncle Red had teased Grandma so much, and what he had against the faeries particularly. He believed in all kinds of things that I had never heard anyone else talk about. I never doubted his stories. Once he told me that to escape being eaten alive by the hounds of King Leary, St. Patrick turned himself into a swift red deer and bounded off into the forest. I reported this fact to Sister Mary Columba at school the next day. She said that I had missed the point of St. Patrick entirely and that he was important for realizing that the shamrock proved the three-in-one Trinity.

I actually felt sorry for Sister Mary Columba if she thought that was a better story than a holy guy who could change into whatever he wanted, whenever he wanted to: a deer or a hare or a salmon, and once even a glint of the silver light that smiled upon the sea off Galway.

I jumped when the phone rang. Uncle Red's cheerful voice broke through the early morning gloom like sunlight. "Good morning, Lucy."

He asked for Grandma and when I told him that she wasn't out of bed yet, he chuckled, "Those half glasses add up. Does she think the Jesuits are going to wait to start 8:00 Mass until Maeve Fahey has risen from her slumber?"

His low laugh made me almost forget how mad Grandma was at him.

"Are you off to Mass by yourself then, Lucy?"

"No sir, I'm still in my PJs."

"Well, between you and me, I think it is best to not go every day. You can wear out your welcome if you do that, Lucy. I'd go to Mass more often myself, but I wouldn't want the Almighty taking me for granted. If I were in the same pew every morning, like your Granny Fahey, He wouldn't have to think about me. He wouldn't have to say to Himself, 'I wonder where the Hell old Red Quinn is?'"

I laughed mostly because I wondered lots of times myself what Uncle Red was doing when he wasn't around.

"I want to keep that other Old Man guessing as to my whereabouts. Get my drift, Lucy?"

"Is Grandma Keary still at the hospital Uncle Red?"

"She is, Lucy. Poor Maggie has worn out herself going back and forth. She'll probably be home today or very soon any way. I'm going over this morning to see them both."

"Uncle Red, why can't I go to see my mom?"

"For starters you have to be 12 to get in during visiting hours."

"Jackie gets to go and I don't?"

"Your mom needs as much rest as she can get right now and even very special visitors like yourself might wear her out, don't you see."

I didn't see that at all and didn't care to answer.

"She'll be home soon, too, Lucy. You wait and see. The time will go by pretty quick. She told me just yesterday that more than anything she wants you to have some fun this summer and not to worry about her. Speaking of fun, I nearly forgot why I was calling. We are having some music at your Grandma Keary's while the O'Fallons and McKees are still in town. I think we could all use it. You like to dance, don't you, Lucy?"

"I don't think so. I don't know how."

"Well you'll learn. There'll be some much younger cousins there on Saturday who'll show you the steps. I wanted to see if you and Maeve were free this Saturday night."

We were free all summer as far as I knew.

"Will Grandma Keary be home then?"

"Oh, she will, she will. Now tell your Granny Fahey we are having a bit of a *ceili*. If she's really from Mayo, she'll know what that means. Can you do that, Lucy?"

I didn't think that Uncle Red understood what Grandma thought of him.

"She won't let me come."

"I'll bet she will if you ask her very nicely."

"But Uncle Red, she, well, looks down on certain people."

"Do you mean me, Lucy?" I was relieved he knew I meant especially him and his laugh told me he wasn't bothered.

"Now how can she look down on me, Lucy, if I don't look up to her?"

Here was another of Uncle Red's riddles. I usually didn't know what he meant by them, but they could sure take your mind off your worries for a while.

"That doesn't mean you shouldn't pay attention when she is helping you with your school work for next fall."

Even Uncle Red knew I failed at school? I never felt funny and shy around him before. I hoped that Uncle Red didn't think I was lazy like practically everyone thought I was. He'd have to remember that I could memorize the words to any song he taught me, wouldn't he?

"Listen, Lucy, I've got to get out to the hospital now. Copy down my number for your Granny Fahey. Highland 4-0297. Tell her it is a *ceili*. She'll know what I mean. Bye now."

When Grandma Fahey appeared in the doorway, she was still in her bathrobe.

"Who was that on the phone, Lucy?"

I was amazed that she was not dressed and ready for 8:00 Mass.

"Was it your father? There should be some news today."

"No'am." I mumbled.

"Well, who then?"

I wished I had asked Uncle Red to promise never to tease Grandma again.

"It was Uncle Red." I watched her face closely to see how mad she still might be.

Her sleepiness left her completely as she sprang to her usual vigilance. "Is everything OK, Lucy? Was he at the hospital? Oh, where's the hospital number," she said, reaching for the phone.

"He wasn't at the hospital, Grandma."

She put the receiver down.

"He only wanted to say that he was very sorry he teased you last night."

"Oh, is that all."

"And he wants us to come over again, on Saturday night."

"What an exasperating man."

"Can we go, Grandma?"

She didn't even bother to answer. "Not on your life" was implied by her smirk.

"Oh, look at the time, will you. It is too late to get to Mass on time even if we took a taxi. Your mother's people wore me out last night. And if your great uncle had to interfere in our morning, he could have been thoughtful enough to wake us up in time for Mass."

Grandma cinched up her robe with one energetic pull. "Lucy, since there'll be no Mass and Holy Communion today, what would you say to a nice big breakfast?"

I didn't mind not having to fast until after Mass.

She struck a match to light a gas burner. The blue and white flames shot up so high that it looked like maybe the Holy Ghost was coming here since we couldn't make it to Mass. Water always boiled faster in her kitchen than anywhere else. Reaching for her oatmeal tin, she said, "Lucy, open the ice box and bring me that fine fat rasher of bacon. And the eggs too."

"Yessum. Right away, Grandma."

I was anxious to firm up plans for Saturday. There was a tightness in my body that reminded me of the tug of war at field day this spring. Our class had tried mightily to pull the other class across the line. When kids in front of me squealed and fell forward, I held on tighter although I could feel the grass sliding under my feet.

"Grandma, what's a gaily?"

"A what?" she asked, slicing the bacon thickly into the skillet.

"A gaily dance."

She squinted at me. I looked away. "Uncle Red said they were having a gaily dance, like in County Mayo."

"Oh he did, did he?" She cracked four eggs into a small skillet with some bacon fat. "The word is *ceili*, Lucy, it rhymes with gaily, but it's pronounced *kay lee*."

The bacon began to pop and sizzle and I could hear that word inside the sound.

"It is an Irish word, Lucy."

"Yessum. Uncle Red said you'd know that. He said you know all kinds of things that most folks have forgotten."

"He said that?" She raised her left eyebrow.

"Yessum." I lied again to Grandma.

"Well, I do try to take an interest in what's important."

"Uncle Red said I am to pay attention to what you teach about religion and catechism and stuff." I thought I might as well tell her anything to pull her in the right direction.

She jutted out her chin. "That is my specialty."

"Yessum, that's what he said. Uncle Red says no one since the Scribes and the Pharisees knows more catechism than you do."

I didn't know what slippery ground I was on.

"Oh, that'll do, young miss." She grabbed a knife and quickly sliced six oranges in half for our juice.

I wasn't sure what had set her off. Scribes and Pharisees sounded pretty official and important to me. I watched her turning and squeezing an orange half against the dome of her juice maker. I was eye level with the counter and close enough to be hit with the darts of juice.

"Do you even know who the Scribes and Pharisees were, Lucy?"

"No'am. Not exactly." I rubbed my stinging left eye and waited for her to finish with the first orange half. Grandma Keary always left some juiciness for me to finish off, but there wasn't much left but rind and flattened pulp when Grandma Fahey was through with an orange.

"I never understood it myself, the way Jesus takes the Scribes and the Pharisees to task in the gospels. He makes them sound like hypocrites. But who would keep track of things if it weren't for them. I ask you that? I say Jesus would have appreciated them more if he hadn't died young as he did. If he'd grown to old age, he would have appreciated the work that went into what they did, recording and teaching the important rules. All without so much as a thanks from anyone in the gospels."

She was gripping a handful of stacked orange rinds like she might throw them at someone across the room. When Dad would get really steamed at Uncle Natty for dying, he'd sometimes suddenly throw things. But Grandma never seemed mad about what happened to Uncle Natty, at least not the way she was now at Jesus for leaving before He could thank the people, like His mother, who taught Him everything He knew.

I was just as glad Grandma didn't throw anything. She lowered her voice as she poured the collected juice into a small white pitcher, "I wonder if the gospel writers got their facts right sometimes, Lucy. I think they might have been adding their own opinions. How could they know what Jesus really thought?"

The crisping bacon made my stomach growl and think more about breakfast than getting to go dancing at Grandma Keary's next Saturday. She seemed to be more irked with those old boys who wrote the gospels than with Uncle Red and Uncle Conny.

"Lucy, give the oatmeal a stir, will you."

I wished we could have breakfast like this every morning before Mass, but Grandma took the fasting rules very seriously, eating nothing from midnight until after Mass. Most days I would sneak some grape jelly rolled up in a piece of bread for energy to help me up the hill to St. Ignatius. At home, Mama always let me have orange juice before communion on Sundays so I wouldn't get cranky at church. By the time Grandma and I got home from daily Mass, it would already be too hot to eat a breakfast like the one she laid out before us.

As we sat down to eat, I wondered if God was really looking around to see where we were if not in Grandma's pew, like Uncle Red said. Polishing off the last of the bacon, fried eggs, toast and oatmeal, I said, "That was the best breakfast I ever had, Grandma."

She wiped some egg from my face with her napkin saying, "I'm sure that is not really the case, Lucy. Hunger is the best sauce. That wasn't much of a dinner at your great uncle's last night. A sandwich and some lemonade."

Grandma was holding her teacup with both hands and looking out the window at the garden. The damp fog was lifting off her pink and white peonies, making their broad leaves catch the sunlight like they were covered with little diamonds. She talked about the work that needed to be done today, the weeding, the edging around the garden, but she seemed too lost in thought or maybe just too tired from last night to spring to action. She took another sip of tea, and repeated the word, *ceili.*

"Did you know, Lucy, that in my Granny McNamee's kitchen we spoke only Irish?"

"How come, Grandma?" I thought it might be another rule, like only Latin in church.

"Well, that was her language, that's all she spoke, Lucy."

We were both looking out at the garden now.

"Just like the faeries, Grandma?"

"I think we've had enough talk of faeries for a time."

I didn't think so.

At least in the daytime, I wouldn't mind it if there were faeries around her peony bushes. Her back yard would be less lonely to play in. There had to be some nice faeries mixed in with the spiteful ones who steal things. The ones who danced at the crossroads near her Granny McNamee's cottage would be loads of fun to have around. They must have been friendly enough if they got that close to her cottage. They must be happy go lucky, if all they want to do is dance to their own music.

Maybe if I put some food out for them, they'd come and visit, like that little black and white dog that appeared quietly at our back step every day after Jackie and I fed him with milk and cereal saved from our breakfasts. I thought we had a pet forever, but before we could decide whether to call him Whitey Ford or Boston Blackie, the dog stopped coming. We waited and waited for that dog to come back, then Jackie kicked the screen door, said a swear word and went inside. I felt pretty much as lonely every day in Grandma's back yard as I did sitting by myself the day that black and white dog went his own way.

Having the faeries show themselves would make a big difference. Although I knew that Jackie would think I was being taken in for even thinking they were real, I thought it wouldn't hurt to leave some bread out for them. I wouldn't leave milk because that would bring the cats around and I'd seen Grandma go after strays with her broom like she was playing field hockey. Just a little bread ought to do it.

I'd like it if only the friendly ones showed up, but even if it were the spiteful ones, it might help my situation to show them I was thinking about them. Extra attention was what Grandma said they wanted the most, and I could understand that. I wanted the same thing as the faeries, just some attention and some help in getting back to where I came from. God, who wanted a bunch of attention—especially from Grandma Fahey—was still slow in getting around to hearing prayers as far as I could tell. I hadn't seen Mama in a month. Grandma's faeries seemed to fill the space between saying your prayers and God deciding if He was going to answer them.

When I'd asked Grandma did she think God played tricks like the faeries did, she had me write out 10 times this catechism answer instead of eating dessert, "God is a supreme being who can neither deceive nor be deceived." I guessed that meant "No."

Maybe if I left a little bread for the faeries, that would make them happier, less cranky. Taking communion bread every day sure calmed Grandma down. Maybe if I could just communicate with them, they'd see how much we had in common and that I could sure use their help.

"Grandma, how would your granny say bread in the faery language? Do you remember?"

"Oh, I remember quite a lot. I learned many important things from her. Why, when I was your age, I used to spend my days with my granny, and I was as happy as a clam at high tide."

I'd never seen a clam anywhere but trapped in her chowder on a Friday. They didn't seem happy to me. I needed an answer.

"Grandma, how do you say 'Here's some bread for you'? In Irish, I mean."

"Why you'd say *anseo ta aran*, Lucy," she answered without stopping her gaze out the window.

I chewed on that phrase with the crusts of toast I swiped from Grandma's plate. She was too distracted to even notice. Here were words the faeries spoke to each other. How could anyone, even Uncle Red, say they weren't real? The words were just as real as the coins that he brought me from Galway last summer. They were enough to prove that Ireland existed somewhere even though I'd never seen it. These words would be like coins in my pocket that I would spend someday.

"Hey Grandma, how do you say 'I'm Lucy Fahey' in Irish?" I'd need to introduce myself to them if they showed up for breakfast.

When she finally turned from the window to me, she looked like she thought I should be able to figure out how to say something as simple as that if I tried hard enough. "Well, now, Lucy Fahey, aren't you the one who promised to study twice as hard today if we went to your great uncle's last night? Let's get this day underway."

After breakfast dishes we set down to the Lists. These were words from my lessons that Grandma placed in alphabetical order for me to focus on. If Sister Mary Columba knew her stuff, she'd have thought of this herself. I had Lists for geography, history, spelling, and, of course, religion. We were up to the P's.

"Let's review, now Lucy, Pentecost and the other seasons of the church. We are in the season of Pentecost now, so what color should Father Hurst's vestments at Mass be?"

"Green." I knew that one easy. Father Hurst was short and kind of round and in his brightly colored vestments as he faced the altar with his back to the congregation, he reminded me of Charlie Parnell, Uncle Mickey's green parakeet.

"That is correct. Green is worn because it is the season of Pentecost. Please spell Pentecost, Lucy."

"P-e-n-n-y-c-o-s-t, Grandma?" I thought of buying penny candy at the sweet shop with Jackie when we got our allowances. She corrected my spelling and told me again that Pentecost was when the Holy Ghost turned into a bird and came to dinner with the apostles. I should have been able to remember something as silly as that.

"Is the Holy Ghost really a bird then, Grandma?" The idea delighted me because that meant any birds you saw could really be the Holy Ghost, including Uncle Mickey's budgie that I liked so well.

"Indeed not, Lucy. The Holy Ghost is the Holy Ghost. The Comforter. The Holy Paraclete.

"Parakeet, Grandma?" Charlie Parnell once flew from Uncle Mickey's finger to the top of my head. I drew my shoulders up towards my ears and giggled at the memory of how its little dancing claws tickled my scalp.

"Oh, Lucy, I said Paraclete not parakeet. The Holy Paraclete is a messenger from God the Father. Listen, P-a-r-a-c-l-e-t-e. Paraclete."

She was exasperated, but so was I. I thought I should get half credit because it all had to do with birds anyway, but she didn't agree.

"Lucy, we went over these just yesterday. What do I have to do to make you pay attention?" She said that yesterday, too.

"Grandma, can the faeries fly like birds when they want to?"

"Oh, again with the faeries, is it?"

"Do you think they are messengers from God the Father, too?"

"No, indeed I do not. I'm surprised by your interest in the Irish language. Do you really want to know this, Lucy?"

"Oh, yessum, I do."

"Well, I suppose it wouldn't hurt to put a few Irish words on a List. Mind you," she wagged a finger at me, "I won't have any of this coming up in general conversation with your mother's people."

It was an easy promise to make. I only wanted to talk to the faeries.

Grandma looked around the kitchen and began writing down Irish words for what she saw. My luck was already starting to turn. I'd have a List that was all in the secret faery language. It was like bread and wine at Mass changing into something more important when the priest whispered the secret Latin words. That morning bread became *aran*, water became *uisce*—which rhymed with whiskey—and butter turned to *im*.

I liked the sounds of these magic words right away. And I liked how one word could stand for another. It was as if the whole world magically split into two separate paths, and now I'd know the very path the faeries were on. I would work hard and learn what sounds they used. I didn't think I would even tell Jackie about the secret language. I was sharing these brand new words only with the faeries. If there were faeries out there, me knowing their secret words would change everything.

I listened as hard as I could with my good ear to the Irish sounds Grandma made, a wild tumble of whooshing sounds with sudden and surprising starts and stops, just like faeries themselves darting and dashing from place to place to avoid being seen or captured.

We started with a few words and then when Grandma went about her morning's work in the kitchen she left English behind completely. I passed the morning listening to a world of new sounds. It didn't matter that I didn't know exactly what she was saying. Once, I thought she must have been talking about rain on the roof, because that was the sound the words made. And when she spilled cool red apples on the counter to begin a salad for our lunch, they made a low rumbling and rolling sound that seemed like the apples were speaking this new language, too.

Mostly I looked out the window at the peony bushes while I listened to the stories her sounds were making.

"Grandma, can you see faeries in the daytime or only at night?"

I was surprised that she didn't stop to answer me in English. She was peeling more apples over the sink, but they could have been onions for the way she sniffled and patted away rare tears that rolled down her cheeks.

"Grandma?" I whispered, getting up from the table and going to her sink. I hoped she wouldn't cry too much, for what would I do then?

"Grandma?" I stood next to her, tugging gently on her apron. She shook her head a little and waved her hand in front of her face like there were cobwebs there.

"Oh, Lucy, it's you." She seemed startled to see me. "How the old language takes me back, child. I haven't spoken that much Irish in years and years," she sighed. She dabbed her eyes with her apron hem.

I wanted her to hug me, but she was not Grandma Keary.

She clapped her hands, saying "Back to your lessons. Take out your Big Chief tablet. Let's write down some of your new words."

I thought that was a very good idea, until she began to write out the strangest strings of letters that made me laugh when I tried to sound them out. Someone, Grandma or the faeries or both, was pulling my leg. I watched her face closely to see if she realized that these letters weren't adding up to any real words. When she said the word for her home, Mayo, there was a 'g' and an 'h' where a 'y' should have been, and no 'a' and no 'o' anywhere.

"Can't I just spell it like May with an 'o' in the end?"

"Certainly not in the Irish, Lucy."

She needed a little help, I thought, with the old words. "Grandma, how do you just say May in Irish then?"

She wrote down a jumble of letters and swore that it took all thirteen of them just for May. *M-i-N-a-B-e-a-l-t-a-i-n-e*. I figured it must have been the spelling alone that caused so many of my relatives to leave Ireland and come to America, where May was called by a simple bud of a word.

It was hard work being this Irish, unless the faeries let you in on the jokes they pulled in their language. I wanted in on it so I made her go on. She recited the sounds that stood for days of the week: *gee doe nee, gee loo in, gee marr ch, gee kay deen, jeer deen, gee hee neh, gee sah urn.*

This sounded as magical as the chanting at church.

"Once more. Listen carefully, child." I think she liked calling out the old words much more than just doing the Lists. That suited me, too. The lively sounds drew me closer in with each repetition. I studied her face as she recited these words. They seemed to be forming somewhere in those dark blue eyes, "Now you give it a try, Lucy *og*." She never smiled like this during catechism lessons, and neither did I.

I rubbed my hands together, anxious to show her what I knew. Her cadence had been imprinted, but only a few of the Gaelic syllables had. I looked at her furrowed face and tried to read it like a page. "*Gee loon ah, gee march, gee loon ah, gee loon ah,*" I sang. And then I added the day that sounded like garden, "*Jeer deen,*" and finished it all off with "*Amen.*"

I looked quickly out the window to the garden to see if anyone out there had noticed, or if anything was different.

Grandma said I got almost two days out of seven right. When I pointed out that was two more Irish days than I had yesterday, she laughed and called me Lucy *og* again. For the rest of my lessons that day, clear through to dinnertime, the faery language was used in her kitchen like a handful of invisible seasoning. As she sliced wedges of a cabbage into a pot where she was boiling potatoes, she said a word that had the same sound as the cabbage splashing into the bubbling water. *Cabawshtah*! I repeated as I threw a handful of celery seeds in after the cabbage. Irish words were in the air, like the steam that rose from her colander when she poured out the potatoes and cabbage, glazing her kitchen window and filling the room with a mineral, earthy smell.

Grandma seemed very pleased with herself as she buttered our potatoes for dinner that night.

"Is dinner about ready Grandma?" I asked looking up from my copying.

"*Ta, maise!*" she said as briskly as she salted our food.

I'd been waiting all day to head out to the garden, so I didn't mind at all when after dinner and before the dishes, she said, "Oh, Lucy. Let's not waste what light's left. My peonies need some tending." I bounded out the door towards the neat row of green bushes with wonderful sleepy looking pink and white flowers that grew along her gray stone terrace wall.

Grandma got busy staking the stems so the blooms wouldn't sway to the ground.

"Grandma, look at these ants." I began flicking them off the sticky green buds where just bits of pink were peeking out. I didn't think the faeries would like a bunch of bugs on their flowers.

"Oh, no, Lucy, don't do that. They'll never bloom if you do that. Let the ants do their work. It's their job to help the buds open. Nothing blooms without somebody's hard work."

I never knew that flowers were hard work for anybody. Lilies of the valley and wild violets just came up everywhere in Grandma Keary's yard.

"Life is work, Lucy. Hard work."

Grandma was down on her hands and knees digging up chickweed and dandelions with Great Grandpa Regan's rusty old trowel that she had lately taken to using in the garden. She was working away with a determination that reminded me of her lesson on how the medieval inquisitors dug up heresy by the roots.

I was bent over watching the ants do their work, when she called, "Don't dawdle, Lucy. Take that hoe to my row of peonies."

I began edging furiously, like she taught me, but stopped as soon as she went inside to do the dinner dishes. The shiny broad leaves swayed in the breeze and caught the last of pink and silver sunlight, and across one of the flat stones in the terrace wall a slug trail glimmered, pointing to one bush. I stayed in the yard even after it got dark. The mist and dew came back to the garden, a trio of locusts began to chant above me in the trees, and I heard a crickety sound that reminded me of summer at home.

I had worked hard at my lessons and now this day that had been so full of new and, I hoped, magical sounds was over. Even the ants on the buds had gone home to bed. Just one more thing to do in Grandma's garden. I pulled a crust of bread from my pocket and called out to any creature out there who might understand, "*Anseo ta aran*. Take this bread, if you want to."

I checked all around the garden to see where everything was in case there were changes by morning. I took two bites of the bread myself and left the rest where the trail ended and the green leaves began.

Chapter 11: A Stolen Child

A distant tinkling sound woke me very early the next morning. It might have been coming through the faery window, or lingering from my dream in which the faeries who appeared at Granny McNamee's crossroad in Mayo were dancing in glass shoes among Grandma Fahey's peonies. Were they coming today to take their communion on the stone fence? I sat up in bed as the click clink, click clink of their fragile shoes became clearer. I smiled. This will be the day everything changes.

"Good morning, Missus Fahey."

It must have been their leader who addressed Grandma Fahey by name. Even though the music of their glass shoes had stopped, I couldn't make out what he was saying to Grandma. Something about buttermilk. Should I have put out buttermilk with their bread? Why was he speaking in English and not Irish?

I ran to the faery window to hear what was being said.

"Two quarts buttermilk, Mr. Carmody. I've my granddaughter staying with me for the summer, trying to plump her up some."

Mr. Carmody was no faery, just the milkman with his case of bottles who came up the alley and over the terrace to Grandma's back door. I went back to my room and slammed the door. Just another faery trick. Just another day with Grandma and me.

We left for Mass at the usual time, but I never got around to combing my hair. Grandma fussed with it all the way up the hill. One side stuck up kind of funny from sleeping all night with my good ear towards the faery window, but she was only making it worse. We were both cranky by the time we got to St. Nat's.

I was glad to get inside the church because Grandma would quit fidgeting with my hair, but I made up my mind I wasn't going to kneel down and follow along the Latin in her missal. Neither the Irish or Latin did me any good. Nobody listened in either language.

"Lucy, if you have decided not to pray this morning, you may sit and read from today's church bulletin, St. Paul's epistle and the gospel, word for word. There will be a test on what you've learned before there'll be any breakfast when we get home. And don't slouch like that, Lucy."

It seemed some holy guys were miffed at St. Paul because he didn't make much sense to them, and they thought things should just be easier than they were, so he wrote them a letter to tell them they were all dopes and to pay better attention. I could see why Grandma liked this St. Paul. The gospel was more of the same. So, I just read the names of the parishioners who had died and had Masses being said for them this week. There sure were a lot more people dying off at St. Nat's than there were at Mary of Gaels. This might be an unlucky parish. In fact, the ad in the bulletin for Magilly & Sons Funeral Home was about three times the size it was in our parish bulletin. "Serving the Archdiocese since 1893." The biggest ad in our bulletin was for the Hoffman Garment Company, which made all our grade school uniforms. The Hoffmans were Lutherans, but they made enough selling navy blue jumpers and blazers to send all their sons to Notre Dame. My dad said it was good for business.

I looked back at the Magilly's ad and thought of Grandma Keary and Uncle Red and Uncle Conny. They seemed to talk about Magilly so often that I wondered if it were bad luck not to. Uncle Red would read the obituaries at Grandma's kitchen table and say, "Magilly got another one, Maggie." Magilly was always biding his time.

Uncle Red even kept what he called his Magilly shirt. When Grandma did his ironing, he'd put aside one white dress shirt every week, and say, "Maggie, this one's for Magilly. I want to be looking dapper when he finally gets a hold of me."

Sometimes nothing made them laugh any harder than talk of Magilly. I didn't think this was funny at all. Uncle Conny had his Ash Wednesday joke that they would all laugh at: "Did you hear the one about Paddy just off the boat showing up at St. Ignatius for Ash Wednesday? It seems a Jesuit was giving out with, 'Think this day upon your own demise, for not a one of you in this parish will escape the certain hand of death.' And your man,

Paddy, looks all around him and laughs. So, the priest tries to pin him to his pew with 'None, I repeat, none in this parish can hide from Magilly when his times comes.' Paddy laughs louder so the priest leans out of the pulpit and asks what the devil is so funny. Says Paddy, 'I'm not from this parish, Father.'"

I didn't like laughing at Magilly and I didn't particularly like the only Magilly I had ever met. The Magilly son that ran Uncle Natty's funeral was tall and scary and his hands were cold and white. I didn't like the way he tried to act like he was family, when I never saw him before in my life.

Under the Magilly ad were the Masses in Thanksgiving. One line caught my eye. A Mass to be said in thanksgiving for a miraculous recovery to health by the family of Martin J. P. O'Malley. It was "Holy Water" O'Malley. He wasn't dying after all like Uncle Red had said. It must have been the holy water that saved him.

I tugged on Grandma's sleeve to tell her that the bulletin says there had been a miracle, but she didn't want me interrupting her prayers. She gave me a look that said she wouldn't have cared if "Holy Water" lived or died. Sometimes I felt like nobody cared if I did either.

At the breakfast table, looking out on the garden where the faeries had played their latest trick—ignoring my kindness—I asked Grandma, "What's the strongest holy water there is?"

"Strongest, Lucy? That's an odd little question. Some would say the holy water from Lourdes in France because it has worked so many miracles."

Last spring two ladies, who were Mama's college roommates, came by to bring her some water from Lourdes. They all laughed and talked about the fun they had when they were away at St. Mary's College. Mama smiled and thanked them again for the holy water at the front door, but after they left, it made her cry because she knew she needed it.

"Or, from Fatima." Grandma went on. "Do you know of Our Lady of the Rosary appearing shortly before the First World War, Lucy?"

Well, sure, who hadn't seen *The Miracle of Fatima*? Sister Mary Columba packed us all on a bus to go downtown whenever it or *The Song of Bernadette*, about the kid at Lourdes, was playing. I liked the Fatima movie better because the ten-year-old who got to talk to the Holy Mother had my name, Lucia de Santos. Sister said it meant "holy Lucy." She got to tell the priest and the mayor that they'd better start praying the rosary for peace and for the conversion of Russia—or else. Even though she was really steamed about the Russians, the Blessed Mother was very kind and had all the time in the world for holy Lucy. She let Lucy de Santos be the one to warn the adults that they were in for it. You had to like that.

Grandma concluded, "But I'd say, Lucy, the holiest of all holy water is from a spring well in County Mayo, at a little place called Knock."

"How come it's the holiest?" I'd never heard of this one before.

"It is the holiest, Lucy, because it is from the stream near where the Blessed Mother, St. Joseph, St. John the Apostle, and a small white lamb appeared to some poor peasants."

That did sound like the best holy water. At Lourdes and Fatima, it was just the Blessed Mother all by herself. But in Ireland she had shown up with a bunch of extra saints, plus her pet lamb. I think she knew that if she went to Ireland by herself, she'd probably never get a word in edgewise. And Grandma said that instead of one or two people seeing the vision, in County Mayo there was a whole crowd of Irish kids and grownups there to meet her. With that many Irish people all in one place, Mary knew that chances were somebody would be starting a fight with her about something, so she needed her own pack of saints for support. If that crowd of Irish peasants was anything like the noisy pack of relatives at Uncle Red's the other night, she'd have been right.

As Grandma told it, Mary never got around to telling the Irish what to do either. At Knock she didn't give any orders to anybody, at least that anyone could remember, as she had in Fatima and Lourdes. She was just stopping by for a little visit to County Mayo, it seems.

"Our Lady appeared just when things couldn't have been much worse for those working the land. To let them know that they weren't forgotten, don't you know, despite the way things looked. And this all happened not long before I was born and not far from Granny McNamee's. What do you think of that, Lucy?"

I thought it would make a good movie, and Grandma said she thought so, too.

"With Barry Fitzgerald and Maureen O'Hara, do you think, Grandma?"

She objected to Barry Fitzgerald, who she said made the Irish look like they lacked all sense, but that Maureen O'Hara would be pretty good because she had a beautiful face, and red hair, just like Our Lady of Knock.

"Grandma, did they get to keep the lamb?"

"Who, Lucy?"

"The poor Irish kids?

"Well, no, it was a symbol, Lucy. A sign that they were favored by God, as only the poor can be."

"So, it wasn't a real lamb?"

"Indeed it was a real lamb. It was the Lamb of God. *Angus Dei, qui tollis peccata mundi*, don't you see. Lamb of God, who taketh away the sins of the world."

It would have been neater if the Blessed Mother had brought them a real pet to keep them company, instead of just giving those kids a vision. A vision must be as strong as about three daydreams, but even the very best daydreams can fade on you, so that you can't remember why they made you feel good. If you were lonely, it would be better to have a pet.

After we got home, Grandma forgot about the test on St. Paul in the bulletin and I didn't remind her. She went straight upstairs without even taking the pins from her hat, and then called for me to come up. Something was up. I hoped she hadn't found my locust collection again. She made me throw them all away once, and I had to start all over again. But she was in her room not mine and holding a small, dark blue bottle as delicately as if it were a flower.

"This has been with me since I left Mayo, some 66 years ago." Tapping the cork stopper she said, "And do you know, I've kept it sealed tight the whole while. It always meant more to me that way, having it just as it was given to me when I left my home. This, Lucy, is holy water from Knock."

"Wow."

"Wow indeed, Lucy."

"Who gave it to you, Grandma?"

"Well, Granny McNamee, of course."

She smiled as she placed it back in a little white box filled with cotton, alongside of a splintery old wooden crucifix and a small gray stone from a little road outside Granny McNamee's that she took with her the day she left Mayo. All of these things in the box seemed out of place in Grandma's room, except that the little box she kept them in, like the rest of her finery, was from Carson Pirie Scott department store in Chicago. She nestled the little blue bottle back deep into the cotton, and touched the crucifix like it might turn to ash if she was not very careful. I liked that Grandma had her own secret collection.

"What are the other things in the box?"

Sometimes the fun of a secret collection is to have people guess what the secret is. Grandma tilted her head and looked at me like she was trying to decide whether to play the guessing game.

"Did your granny give you that old cross, too?"

"Granny McNamee? No, it didn't belong to her."

"Well, did you bring it with you when you left your home?"

"Oh my, no. It belonged to someone else who left Ireland on a boat for America, long before I ever did."

"Who, Grandma?"

"It belonged to my father's own mother. This is the cross from her rosary." Grandma pulled it out of the cotton as tenderly as if she were pulling up a small plant from the earth, root and all. When she put it in my hand, I could see that someone had carved it.

"How come it doesn't have a Jesus on it if it is from her rosary?"

"Our Savior was lost, I suppose, somewhere on her voyage. Or maybe there never was one, I don't know."

I wondered what good a cross without a savior could be.

"Did she give it to you, Grandma?"

"I never met her."

"How come you never met her, if she left for America before you did? Wasn't she just in Chicago when you got there?"

"No, Lucy, she never made it to America, let alone Chicago."

I could tell by the looks of her rosary cross that she didn't shop at Carson Pirie Scott like Grandma.

"How come she never made it?"

"Never mind about that, Lucy," she said closing the lid. "I just wanted to show you what has been special to me since I was your age when I left Mayo."

I couldn't imagine thinking holy water and an old cross were the neatest things you could ever have as a kid. It's not exactly a box of locust shells or even a coonskin cap. I already knew I'd probably not grow up to be as good a Catholic as Grandma. There were so many rules.

All in all, the faeries were a bit easier to follow. They had only one rule I knew of to keep them happy, and that was never to throw anything out in the dark without warning them first. They must be sissies if they were afraid of a little water like that. Maybe it would make them melt like the water that Dorothy of Oz threw on the old witch. If Jackie were here, he'd advise a sneak attack on the faeries. Three water balloons out the back door would do the trick. And here was holy water from the faeries' and Grandma's own land to throw into the bargain.

"Would this holy water from Knock have more power than the faeries, Grandma?"

"Now Lucy, I will brook no more discussion of the faeries, do you hear me?"

I didn't think that was fair since she was the one who brought them up in the first place. I watched closely where she put the little box with her secret holy water. Top right dressing table drawer. I had taken to crossing myself with holy water from the little wall font at the top of the stairs right outside Grandma's bedroom every night since I first heard about the faery changelings. Grandma blessed herself now as we left her room, just as she did every morning and evening.

My dad called long distance during our dinner that night.

"What's the news today, Frank? Did Father Fitzgerald have trouble finding the hospital at that university? I still don't know why she didn't go to a Catholic hospital here in town after all, for something as serious as this. Well, that's all good news, then, Frank."

I looked up. She motioned for me to keep eating my dinner. There were three boiled potatoes left that I was sliding around my plate with my fork, avoiding the one Brussel sprout she forced me to take. Since she was busy, I cut it in half and put the halves under the rim of my plate. I could pitch it later without her seeing.

I was sure that Daddy would ask to speak to me when Grandma was through. Some good news she'd said. I put more butter and salt on my red russets waiting for my turn to talk to Daddy.

Grandma turned her back but I could still hear her say, "I see ... her heart ... I see. Lucy? She's fine, Frank. Lucy's just fine. Don't worry about her. Take care now. Get some rest and call again tomorrow, if you can. Good night, Frank."

It all happened so quickly and my mouth was so full of potatoes that I couldn't yell as I wanted to, "Wait. Stop. Don't hang up yet, Grandma!"

She put the receiver down, and turned back towards me.

"Whatever is wrong, Lucy? What face is that to make at your grandmother?"

"I wanted to talk to Daddy."

"Do not talk with your mouth full, Lucy. And besides it is quite an expense to talk long distance. Your father says everything is fine. He is worn slick, Lucy. He's been up for 24 hours, your poor dad has. Your mother's brother Mickey brought Jackie by the hospital, and they are all going home early tonight."

I thought the top of my head would come off. They were all there, and without me.

"How come Jackie got to go to the hospital, and I didn't?" I demanded, barely swallowing my mouthful of potatoes.

"That's not what is important now, Lucy. Your mother needs your prayers and you can't pray when you are so petulant."

I banged my fist and fork on the table, "I wanted to talk to Daddy at least, Grandma."

"Lucy, your father has got his hands full just this minute."

I glared out the window and then directly at Grandma as she told me again to calm myself down, and that I hadn't gotten enough rest this week, and what had she been thinking letting me stay out so late at my great uncle's.

"Maybe you had better spend some time in your room until you can act civilized, young lady."

That suited me. I unclenched my hand from my fork and stormed from the room. I didn't even care that she'd find my Brussels sprout under my plate. I would have walked right out the front door if I had anywhere to go. I might as well run away. I might as well be as invisible as the faeries. I wanted to make them all sorry for what they were doing to me. All of them. Daddy for not even wanting to talk to me, and Uncle Red and even Grandma Keary for leaving me stranded at Grandma Fahey's, and Jackie for being older and better at everything than me, and Mama, for being so sick. This was probably some really big sin to be so mad at her when everybody else was praying for her, but why wasn't she coming home when I needed her? Was she still my mom? If she was away for much longer, I was afraid that she wouldn't be.

I was so mad at everybody and everything that it made my jaw hurt, and sitting there on the edge of my bed, I wasn't sure these two fists would become just my hands ever again. What I hated the most since Mama got sick was that nobody ever gave me a straight answer. Not a yes. Not a no. Not even Uncle Red. And if I asked Grandma Fahey a question about my mom, her only answer was "Lucy, why would you ask such a thing!" Like it would all be my fault. I asked her if she thought that Mama might sort of forget to come pick me up at the end of the summer. "Lucy, why would you ask such a thing!" The more times she gave that as an answer, the more I began to worry that whatever I had asked about was probably what was going to happen.

Not one thing all summer long had gone the way I wanted, although I had pretty much done exactly what I was told. That was part of the joke on me, too, I suppose. One big dirty trick. I curled up on my bed in a tight little ball, making a smaller target of myself in case God came looking for the girl who was so angry at Him. I couldn't believe this anger beating as loud inside my head as a bass drum couldn't be heard by God, all the saints, and every last angel. The faeries never even paid attention to me so they probably wouldn't notice or care what was clanging around inside of me.

I'd pretty much stopped praying to God for anything, but maybe I had overlooked His answer— revealing the faeries. They must be the cause of all kinds of things. Jackie said God didn't make Mama sick, and Mama said it wasn't her first choice to send me to the wrong Grandma's. Sister Mary Columba flunking me in catechism sure wasn't my fault. This must all be the faeries. It was all their doing. Grandma Fahey said they love confusion more than anything, and nothing was as confusing to me now as the clash of my feelings. I didn't even feel like myself. Why did we have to give the faeries the warning if they never helped out in return?

I hated those faeries. I hated their faery guts.

But then creating those faeries may have been the best thing God ever did. I could hate them for what they had done to me and it wasn't even a sin. They weren't holy, and they weren't family, although Grandma Fahey seemed pretty close to them, so it was probably not even a venial sin to blame them and want to get even. God knew what He was doing when He made the faeries. I could feel myself unwinding, my spine straightening, lengthening, the more I thought about these tricksters. I'd show them I was on to them, and I'd do it tonight.

First, I'd need the strongest magic in the house. If I had learned anything from the church bulletin this morning—besides that St. Paul was a know-it-all—it was that you can count on holy water when the chips are down. It kept Mr. O'Malley safe from the power of Jameson's whiskey, and it would keep me safe from the power of the faeries.

Leaning over the banister to check on Grandma, I could see the light from her reading lamp in the living room and hear the rustle of the newspaper. I tiptoed down to Grandma's room, stopping once because I thought I heard her calling to me from down stairs, but it must have been the floorboards. I didn't remember them creaking so loudly like this. Her bedroom was dark except for two planks of moonlight that came in from the window and stretched across the room. My body kind of buzzed all over as I opened the drawer and the little box and then took the dark blue bottle from the holy well at Knock. I just needed a drop, I argued with some part of me that wanted to chicken out altogether. Just one drop, or maybe two at the most, then I'd put it back. Did I really have a choice? It was steal or be stolen. The faeries had their magic, well, I needed mine.

And who knows? Maybe Our Lady of Knock and the Lamb of God would appear to me, too, just as they had to the poor peasant kids who needed to know they weren't forgotten. Better than Jackie's dumb catechism medals if holy people appear to you.

The thought of all that made me bounce back down the hallway with Grandma's special holy water and the holy water font from the nail outside her door, entirely forgetting about the noisy floorboards.

"Lucy, what in Heaven's name are you up to?" she called. "You go on and take your bath and go on to bed. I'll be up to hear your prayers a little later."

Instead of answering, I went to the tub and ran a bath. It would cover any other noise I'd be making. I didn't have much time.

I climbed up on the little table under the faery window. The back door of the kitchen was right below me and I could see the peonies clearly in the moonlight. An easy target. I climbed back down. I took the thin crystal vase of flowers that was before the picture of Our Lady of Perpetual Help. The set of Great Grandpa Regan's jaw in his portrait reminded me that he wouldn't take any guff from anybody.

I took the cut flowers and put them on the floor. Then I poured all the holy water from the font into the vase, put my hand over the top of it, and shook it just like my dad making martinis. I'd need plenty of water so that those faeries would know they'd been hit, so I topped off the vase with some water from the running tub.

I wondered how much holy water Mr. O'Malley used in his whiskey. I couldn't take any risks of the faeries having more power than me. As I carefully twisted the dry cork off the holy water from Knock some of it crumbled in my hand. Thinking of how those wild faeries would be surprised, I kept twisting and pulling the cork until it popped out in my hand. I wondered what they'd sound like all yelling in Irish. I could feel my grin growing and looked up at Great Grandpa Regan's eyes that watched approvingly.

I tilted the blue bottle but the drop or two didn't appear. So I carefully tilted the bottle further, hoping it wouldn't spill out all at once. I needed holy water from the faeries' own land, so gave it a little shake. The bottle was dry as a relic. Did Grandma know the holy water from her childhood had evaporated?

I couldn't turn back now. I put the blue bottle in my pocket and climbed back up on the table. I raised the window screen, slowly, for it was the only thing that stood between the faeries and me, and leaned out of the window and swirled the holy and unholy water around in the vase three times to build up momentum, saying, "In the name of the Father, Son and Holy Ghost." I then threw my concoction upon the dark garden below. Oh, and one more thing, they'd need to know just who had pulled this fast one.

"Lucy Fahey is *ainm dom*," I called my name in Irish to the garden nestled in the stillness below. They wouldn't be forgetting me any time soon. I liked feeling in control like this.

I didn't hear anything right away, so I leaned farther out the window and turned my good ear towards the garden. Maybe I hadn't hit them squarely. I hopped down and filled the vase with more water from the tub. I threw two more rounds out the window at them. This was as good as three full water balloons. Jackie'd have approved.

Maybe silence is faery laughter. Maybe they weren't yelling because they thought it was all a pretty good joke on them. I couldn't keep my eyes from crinkling almost shut from laughing to myself. I got them but good.

But what if they didn't think this was as funny as I did. What if the faeries were going to wait to get back at me?

Realizing the last two rounds didn't have any protective holy water in them, I felt my scalp heat up and then chill suddenly, reminding me of the last time I meddled with invisible powers. I had tried to satisfy my curiosity about electricity by sticking my fork into a wall socket. I'd been knocked across the kitchen and there was a funny smell in the room, kind of like gun powder in the air on the Fourth of July. Jackie told me never to do that again because the current would probably kill me dead, or at least make my hair stand straight up like in the cartoons for the rest of my life. He said not to tell Mama because it would only worry her that I was such a chowder head.

What had I done exactly this time?

I could probably never go into the back yard again for starters. Grandma never said quite what the faeries did for revenge, but it was clearly their specialty. Even though it was still a warm night, I started to shiver all over like someone had just poured cold water on me. Slowly backing away from the window, I felt for my door behind me. I grabbed the doorknob, turned it as fast as I could and then slammed the door on the hallway.

"Lucy, you are not helping your case with me by all this door slamming today, young lady," Grandma called from the bottom of the stairs. "I'll be up to tuck you in and hear your prayers presently."

I didn't want to open my door and go back out there in the hallway, but I had to. She'd see right away that the holy water font was not on the wall as it should be, and the flowers to Our Lady were still on the floor. I moved as fast as I could dipping the holy water font into the bath water. It dripped all the way down the hall. I used my shirt tail to wipe it off before I put it back on its nail. I ran back to the table, jammed the flowers back in the empty vase, and shut the window, hard.

"Lucy! What in Heaven's name is going on up there? You start your prayers, and say an extra prayer tonight and ask Our Lady to help that temper of yours. I'm going to lock the kitchen door and then I'll be right up."

I was praying like crazy now that Our Lady of Perpetual Help had more power than a pack of riled-up faeries. What if they thought Grandma had done this without giving the warning they demanded? There she would be at the back door not knowing what I had done.

I climbed back up on the table and opened the window and screen and leaned out. I wanted to warn Grandma not to step out in the darkness for any reason whatsoever. But I had done enough yelling, even telling the faeries my name in their own language. If I hadn't told them, they'd never even figure out who did this to them. I don't live here. I'm not even *from this parish.*

She loved her peony garden best in the moonlight. She was standing at the back door, humming. I was scared she would step out into her garden, and then what? I jumped from the table and slammed the bathroom door, twice, as loudly as I could. The humming stopped. I heard her mumble, "That child." The kitchen door creaking shut meant we were both safe from whatever was out there. There wasn't time to put the holy water bottle from Knock back in her room, so I put it in my pocket, ran and jumped into bed with all my clothes on, and pulled the sheet over me. I rolled over with my back to the door, so I wouldn't have to face her.

Grandma called from the hallway.

"Lucy, leave this window open if you like, but please keep this screen down. There's no telling what could come flying in here at night. What are you thinking, child? Screen wide open. This place will be full of gilley whipples by morning."

As much as I disliked the green winged insects that she called gilley whipples, I wished that was all I had to worry about.

"Lucy, do you hear me?"

I didn't answer but lay completely still, except for my heart that felt like it was pounding to get out of my body.

"Lucy?" As she slowly pushed my door wide open, the pattern of light from the hallway grew on the wall in front of me like something trying to appear from out of the wallpaper. I closed my eyes as tight as I could.

"I know you can't be asleep yet. I heard you running around up here until a minute ago."

How could I tell her what I had done? Or what kind of danger I had put us both in?

"Well, you'll feel better after a good night's rest. Your father will call again in the morning if he can; you can talk with him then."

She stepped back out of the doorway and a second later called to me. "Lucy, you must remember to pull the plug on your bath tub when you're finished. You'll leave a terrible ring."

The sound of the water being sucked down the drain was not a sound I wanted to hear right then.

"Good night, child," she said turning out the hallway light. "And Lucy, don't neglect your prayers tonight."

I held on tightly to the empty blue bottle and prayed to the Lady of Knock that she would remember me as she had those poor Irish kids. Somehow I fell asleep, although there were bells, it seemed, somewhere, everywhere in my dreams through the night. Bells less like Mr. Carmody and his milk bottles coming down the terrace, and more like the head-turning, church-filling *Sanctus, Sanctus, Sanctus* bells at Mass telling you to stop your daydreaming and that Jesus wants your attention because something very mysterious is about to happen. The ringing ended suddenly and I found myself in a familiar place but by a river I never noticed before. I was in a small boat tied to a riverbank on which stood both Grandma Keary and Grandma Fahey. Grandma Fahey was swatting at gilley whipples with her *St. Andrew's Daily Missal* and telling me the Irish words for little boat. Grandma Keary loosened the boat's tether to the shore and gently launched me onto the stream, waving goodbye. The current started to move my boat but I had no oar. I had to remember the Irish word for boat or it would sink.

A real bell then. The phone downstairs. It was Daddy. Had to be.

When I heard Grandma on the stairs, I sat up in bed, and yelled out, "Can I talk to him now?" The faeries didn't seem so scary with Dad on the phone downstairs and the morning sunlight streaming into the hallway.

I was surprised that she didn't answer me. She just appeared in my doorway with not one but two rosaries in her hand.

"Child, I've got some news for you, some sad news."

I steeled myself for news about Mama.

"There's to be a *Requiem* Mass at St. Ignatius in two days, Lucy."

I couldn't feel my hands or feet.

"Mrs. Keary, your Grandmother Keary, has passed on."

I heard my heart pounding in both ears like hammering on an empty barrel. My lungs filled with air so cold I thought they would shatter like glass to breathe these words in.

"I am very sorry, Lucy. Mrs. Keary has gone to be with God."

I shook my head, and said my words very slowly so that Grandma Fahey would understand her mistake, "No. No, Grandma, no. She is coming home to go to the gaily dance on Saturday. NO."

"I'm sorry, child. She won't be," she said as she went to the hallway to cross herself with what would have been holy water—but for me—and knelt by my bedside to begin the rosary, with the First Sorrowful Mystery. I reached around under my pillow for the cold, empty bottle from Knock. How could I have known that there was no power left in it at all?

It felt like there was no air coming inside me, only going out, maybe for good, as I panted, "It's all my fault."

"That is nonsense. Mrs. Keary has just gone home to Heaven as we all will someday. Come, Lucy, and say the rosary with me for Mrs. Keary now, asking Our Blessed Mother in Heaven to kindly guide her on her journey home."

I couldn't move. I just stared at Grandma Fahey, waiting for her to take back all the words she had just said.

"Climb out of bed now, Lucy. We'll pray together. It will comfort you."

I did not pray. It would do no good now if the faeries had stolen Grandma Keary away from me. Grandma Fahey had started without me, but I only heard Grandma Keary's low laugh again, just as clearly as I had in the dream a few minutes ago. Maybe I was dreaming all this now? I looked past Grandma Fahey to the faery window in the hallway. Soft rounded clouds looked in at me through the very window where Grandma Fahey had seen the White Faery Woman when her mother passed over. I saw something quick and warm and bright as Grandma Keary's smile flash just outside that window, and then it was gone.

I knew then that I was the one stolen away. No faery changeling would have felt as alone as I did then. What else could explain how different my world suddenly was, how changed?

Chapter 12: Till Time is No More

It rained the morning of Grandma Keary's *Requiem* Mass and all through the night before. The air was so chilly that it seemed summer had disappeared, too. I sat alone in Grandma Fahey's kitchen in a scratchy bell-shaped slip and white anklets, still trying to make sense of Grandma Keary being gone forever. I was supposed to be getting dressed, but I only felt like staring at the drops of rain on the windowpane and watching how colors from the garden collected in the shapes they formed. Silver and black surrounded the green of the yard and the pink and white of the peony blooms. The smaller drops were only silver and black, too small to contain the background colors at all. These were the saddest to me.

I watched one big drop on the glass fill with colors and build into one heavier shape and then break into a path to another drop, another shape. Was there something in the color or the rain itself that made some shapes want to merge with others? Did the pink seek out the white and green to pull them all into the river of rain on the glass?

The entire pane of glass was alive with meaning if I could only understand it. The trails of rainwater might be forming words of a watery message, maybe in code from the faeries themselves. Since I first heard that Grandma Keary was gone, I tried to swim out of the notion that they had taken her from me for not respecting their power over me. That thought had hit me like waves off and on for the last two days. This rainy morning I thought I might drown in the possibility that we were going to her *Requiem* and not to a *ceili* because of me.

My body felt like it did on the opening day of the swimming pool last summer, when Jackie had dared me to go off the high dive. I had fallen through the air leaning back in can opener position. The water stung me hard on the back and knocked the wind out of me when I hit. I was stunned and lost and floating, gulping chlorine water when Jackie's arms reached me. I held on tight while he pulled us to the surface I thought had disappeared for good.

Now, I held tightly to the fact Uncle Red said there was no such thing as a faery. He had given me a dime and told me to call him at once if I ever saw one. I knew I had to face Uncle Red and Uncle Conny and all my relatives at church. I hoped they didn't know what I had done to stir up the faeries. I hoped that Uncle Red was still laughing at the idea of what the faeries were capable of.

When Grandma Fahey marched into the kitchen already dressed in a dark blue suit and matching hat and veil, she ordered, "Shake a leg, Lucy. I won't have us be late." She was carrying the shoes and dress she had bought me yesterday at Macy's.

"Come on now, child. Let me get you started." She bent down to slip the patent leather shoes on my feet. I let her, even though she made a pained noise when she did.

"Now stand up, Lucy."

My feet slid around in my new shoes and I thought of my first time on ice skates that were passed down from Jackie to me.

"They are too big for me, Grandma," I whined as if that alone was more than I could take.

Grandma said that I would grow in to them and that at my age dress shoes that fit were a bad investment. She had plucked them from the sales rack yesterday without even asking me to try them on, saying to the clerk, "We'll take these Mary Janes. Now kindly direct me to Better Dresses for Children."

I didn't want a new dress. I wanted the yellow dress Grandma Keary had made for me last Easter. It was hanging all by itself in my closet at home. Grandma Keary could make a dress so quickly you didn't even know what she was up to. I could still feel her hands holding the yellow satiny fabric against my back while I was bent over playing jacks on her porch. Next thing I knew, there was my new dress, and she was asking me to stand up while she whip stitched the zipper up the back. While she went to work on a yellow jacket with white piping to match, I picked out some buttons for decorations for the front of my dress from her assortment.

She didn't care that the buttons I wanted didn't match. I'd have the two white ones that looked like daisies, a shiny one that was as blue as the sky, and one big rhinestone just because it glittered and I knew no one would ever have such a dress as this. I told Grandma Fahey that it was the only dress I would wear to the funeral, but she hadn't listened.

"Nonsense, Lucy. You can't wear an Easter dress to a funeral. Shall I pick one for you then?"

I shrugged and she began going dress by dress in my size. When she pulled a navy blue one with a large lacy collar from the rack, I wanted to moan. It was the kind that the show off girls in the older grades wore. Not that kind.

"Well then, pick one, Lucy."

I didn't know why it should matter what I wore, until I came to a pink and gray dress that had a watch fob sewn over the heart. The watch made all the difference. The hands didn't move. It was always precisely twelve minutes after seven o'clock. I needed to have this watch and the dress that went with it and told Grandma so.

"Why Lucy, I thought you had forgotten how to talk. You haven't said two words all day." She checked the price tag and agreed to buy the dress because we had saved some on the shoes.

The time on my new dress would never ever change. Uncle Red carried his watch on the end of a gold chain that he clipped to a belt loop. At midmorning he'd pull his watch from his pocket and say, "Well, they are sitting down to tea about now in Galway City." I liked that his clock kept track of things that happened so far away. I would have liked to have a clock that kept track of time where Grandma Keary was. But I could at least imagine that the clock on my dress stopped short precisely when she left. In the taxi home, I consulted that frozen face over and over again. I had held on to it all the way home and afterwards, as I curled up on my bed, wishing everything could just stop.

Now Grandma Fahey lifted the veil on her hat to get a better look at the condition of my funeral dress.

"How did this dress get so wrinkled, Lucy? You didn't hang it up as I asked, did you. I'll have to press it."

She headed for her ironing board as if all could be made right by a little starch. "The taxi will be here soon," she called as she scurried from the room, "I don't want us to be late. You run upstairs and get your hat. Make sure your white gloves match. There's nothing that vexes me more than gloves that don't match."

"Can't I just wear my chapel veil?"

"You may not. This is a High Mass. You'll wear your Sunday hat. Get a move on now, Lucy. Time's not for wasting."

I thought about moving, but slumped back in my chair instead to watch the rain on the glass whose words were more mysterious than any in all of Grandma Fahey's languages. Yesterday she sat me down with her *St. Andrew's Daily Missal* to prepare me for the *Requiem* today. Inclining her prayer book towards my face, Grandma pointed to Latin words on the page. "Now, what does that say, Lucy? Read these words for yourself."

There was nothing there I could understand.

"Here, let me show you," she said as she traced some syllables with her index finger. "You see, Mrs. Keary will be led to paradise by the angels."

She said this as matter-of-factly as Sister Mary Columba told us that the earth was ninety-three million miles away from the nearest star. How far away are people when they are taken to Heaven? They must be farther away even than the distance to the sun. It was so far that they would never get back to earth. How could she go so far away without saying goodbye to me?

"See, here *in paradisum deducant te angeli*. Don't you see 'paradise' and the 'angels' in those words, Lucy?"

"I guess I do."

"Of course you do, Lucy," she had insisted. "You listen carefully for these words tomorrow. They will be a comfort to you."

She also said there was a perpetual light that would shine upon Grandma Keary and everyone who has ever died. She poured over these words in the missal much the same way she had the insurance contract the man from Hanrahan Life and Casualty had brought to her to sign a few weeks ago. But there was nothing on any page or in any of Grandma's languages that connected me to Grandma Keary or explained her leaving; only the secret language being spelled out on this pane of glass explained over and over that I would never see her again.

The rhythm of the rain was changing now as the drops fell more insistently. I turned my good ear towards the window to hear the sound of the neat, clear tap-ta-tap-tap. I wondered if my deaf ear would connect me to other things I had lost. Maybe I would hear more about what the rain was trying to tell me. I turned my head and cupped my hands around my bad ear and pressed it to the window. The glass was cold against my cheek. Grandma burst back into the room.

"Oh Lucy! Where are your hat and gloves?"

I quickly lifted my ear from the window.

"There now, child. Mrs. Keary wouldn't want to see those tears." The sharpness in her voice was softened by care. Holding my dress in front of me she said, "Now step into it, child, so that it doesn't get mussed again."

She began to button up the dress still warm from her iron and told me that I should be glad for the chance to go to Grandma Keary's *Requiem*.

"She would want you to be there. When my Granny McNamee died, I was in Chicago and she was home in County Mayo. I didn't get to go to her *Requiem* at all. Now dry your tears. Mrs. Keary has gone to be with God. That will make her happier than anything, don't you think?"

How could anything make Grandma Keary happier than playing Chinese checkers on her front porch with me while we waited for Casey and the music box sound of his ice cream truck? On summer afternoons, the little truck played "Casey Would Waltz with the Strawberry Blond," and Grandma Keary would sometimes sing that song as she went inside from her rocker to bring me a dime for two Popsicles. What would make anyone happier than waltzing around the porch, dime in hand, while Grandma sang, "He'd glide 'cross the floor with the girl he adored, and the band played on"? I'd waltz sometimes with Grandma, sometimes with her cane, and sometimes alone while waiting for the truck to make its way down to the middle of the block.

Once while we waltzed, I told Grandma Keary that I might marry Casey. She told me I could do worse than marry a man named Johnny Casey, who drove a truck for a living. I agreed wholeheartedly. I loved that musical ice cream truck. We'd talked then of what flavor Popsicle to choose.

"Do you want a grape or an orange today, Grandma?"

"Surprise me, Lucy!" she'd said, and I thought hard how to do that with such limited choices.

A pain caught in my chest now when I thought of what happened the day Casey caught us by surprise. He'd come by earlier than we expected him. Grandma was in the kitchen and I was in the yard.

"Grandma, Casey's already gone by. He's already passed us by. He won't wait," I yelled, hopping up and down on one foot.

"Oh, where's me purse?" Grandma had been frantic but laughing.

"Here, Lucy, take it all," she'd said pitching me her coin purse. I emptied it in my hand, dropped the purse and jumped from the porch steps. I'd wanted to yell out to Casey to stop for me, but instead put all my energy into beating the truck to the end of the block. He'd have to stop for the sign and then he'd see me. I began to breathe only when it was clear that I would beat the slow-moving truck to the end of the block.

As I stood alongside the truck, I noticed a new sign had been painted on the side, a giant ice cream in a dark sugar cone, dripping with chocolate and nuts. Under this vision was the suggestion "Try a Drumstick today! Only 25 cents."

"Made up your mind?" Casey had asked.

I'd cupped my hands and shook the change like dice. "I want that!" I'd said pointing to the drumstick sign. I opened my hands over his and emptied all the coins, mostly pennies, two nickels, one street car token, and some red and green plastic tax mils, that stuck to my sweaty palm and had to be flicked into the driver's hand.

"Is that all you got?"

I'd nodded and wiped my hands on the tail of my cotton shirt and waited for the drumstick. Casey shrugged and opened the case and handed me an ice cream cone that was much smaller than I thought it should be for 25 cents. But I eagerly tore the wrapper off anyway and bit into the chocolate covered ice cream that was so cold it made my teeth hurt. Walking slowly back, I lost myself on getting the most out of each bite, even the last one that tasted of copper pennies.

As I came up the steps Grandma Keary had called out cheerfully "Lucy, what flavor did you get me today? Is it grape or a nice orange one?"

The memory of coming home empty handed that day now made me cry in earnest.

"There, there, Lucy. Get a hold of yourself. You must calm yourself, child," Grandma Fahey said as she finished buttoning up my dress. "Oh, there's the taxi. Did you hear him honk, Lucy? Run down and tell him to wait for us." She checked the clock once more and dashed upstairs to find my hat and gloves.

Grandma Fahey and I did not sit in her usual pew, three rows back from the front on the Blessed Mother side of the church. Instead we sat on the Sacred Heart side, several pews behind the Quinns and Kearys, who were more still and somber than I had ever seen them. They seemed almost like statues of people I knew, all dressed in black. I couldn't imagine Mama in black like this. I wondered if Mama even knew that Grandma was gone.

In the rows in front of us I could see Uncle Red, Uncle Conny and his tiny wife, Auntie Cate, two of my mom's brothers and their wives. Because Uncle Mickey had no children of his own he sat several rows behind us and was in charge of the first, second and third cousins of my own generation.

I craned my neck all over the church looking for Jackie. Grandma Fahey said she wasn't sure whether he would be at the Mass, but she knew that my dad would be at the hospital all day.

I surveyed the boy cousins in the rows behind me. I never noticed how many dark-haired, fair and freckled cousins I had until I tried to find Jackie among them. Mixed in with dark headed Kearys, Quinns, and O'Fallons that all looked like versions of Jackie were the sandy-haired Herlihys and O'Deas and the redheaded McKee cousins from Chicago. Sitting in rows in their navy school uniform blazers and school ties, many of the boy cousins were hard to distinguish, one from another. I had never seen some of them all dressed up or so many all in one place.

Once or twice I thought I glimpsed Jackie in the jostling crowd of kids that tumbled into the pews with Uncle Mickey, only to check for his Kelly green and white Mary of Gaels school tie and find it was just another cousin. Jackie wasn't anywhere in the church.

Uncle Mickey didn't seem to mind or notice all the pushing and poking among these kids packed into the pews around him. It made me kind of mad that everybody back there seemed to be having so much fun and didn't care that my Grandma was gone. The look on Uncle Mickey's face, however, made the dark curly hair that fell forward on his forehead seem darker. His arms were crossed over his barrel chest and he looked down as if listening to sad music that only he could hear.

As I watched the pack of kids, one freckled second cousin caught my eye. It was the one they called "Limes" Quinn. He had already shed his uniform blazer and sat smirking in his shirtsleeves and crooked blue and green St. Ignatius clip-on tie. He saw me watching him and made a monkey face, then bobbed from sight like a duck on a pond diving for fish and reappeared as quickly with the shoe of one of the Chicago cousins who sat in front of him. The cousin must have slipped off his dress shoes to make himself more comfortable. I wiggled my toes in my own oversized shoes and suddenly felt like laughing aloud into the space all my tears had created. Anything funny in church seems about eight times as funny as it would be anywhere else. That's probably why God had that rule about going to church so often when you were sad or in trouble, just so you could feel how close you were to laughing.

Limes held the black shoe over his head like a trophy, then turned to the cousin next to him and bowed like an altar boy at benediction and handed him the shoe. The shoe was quickly making its way down the row when Uncle Mickey intercepted it.

"Whose shoe, boys?" he demanded in a low tone. The entire pew erupted into chuckling and shrugs. At the mention of shoes, the redheaded victim from the big city looked down to check on his. "Hey, it's mine. Mickey, it's mine!"

Uncle Mickey motioned to send the shoe back down the row to its owner. As soon as it was returned, the Chicago cousin turned completely around in the pew to take a swipe at his thieving cousin. "The lace is gone. Somebody took my shoe lace."

My uncle whispered, "The lace, boys. Who's got the lace?"

I was struggling with a laugh that wanted out more than I wanted to keep it in when Uncle Mickey returned a weak smile. I wished that I could have gone to sit with him.

"Lucy," Grandma murmured, "turn around now and pay attention. The Mass that is to send Mrs. Keary to the care of the angels is about to begin."

I checked my watch. Still 7:12. I blinked in a slow circle around the face of the clock. Mama told me that was the exact time of morning I was born. I never thought about it before, but the exact time I would die was also somewhere on the face of a clock, too. I hoped that it would be in the day and not the night and that I would not be alone. I hoped Grandma wasn't alone the last time she looked at her clock. I would have been there to say goodbye to her if she had told me she was going to leave. I would have been there even if it were in the middle of the night.

Grandma Fahey leafed through her black leather *Daily Missal* to the Masses for the Dead. The place was marked by a holy card that had my Uncle Natty's picture on it. He was smiling like he had just caught a pop fly with bases loaded, but the card was bordered with black and in heavy black letters it said, "A priest forever: Ignatius Loyola Patrick Fahey, S.J. *Requiescat in Pace.*" Grandma turned the card over. Her lips trembled as she read to herself the prayer on the back. I tried to read it, too. It began: "He hath set his tabernacle in the sun." Her hand was shaking so much that I couldn't read the rest of the card.

Suddenly the bells in the church tower began to chime and everyone rose in one whooshing sound. The *Requiem* was beginning; the perpetual light would begin shining soon. A very tall, silver-haired priest dressed in a long black cope that reached to the floor swept out on the semicircular altar followed by two altar boys. They all moved so mechanically that they reminded me of the figurines on Grandma Fahey's fancy clock from Switzerland, where a cuckoo pops out from the branch of a tree at the top of every hour, and underneath, forest people sweep by in the clearing ever quarter hour: a little girl with a lamb, at the quarter after chime; a smiling, red-faced man with an axe, at half past; at quarter to the hour, a trio singing, their mouths making little Os; and finally the old man stooping forward on a cane right before the clock strikes the hour and the cuckoo springs from the tree top, like it has all been a good joke.

The priest waited at the altar rail until the chiming stopped. A hush fell on the congregation as he began the mournful chant, *Requiem aeternam dona eis, Domine*. There was no turning back now. I looked back at Uncle Mickey. Even the cousins stopped their squirming and poking. I followed Uncle Mickey's gaze that was locked on the closed casket that stood before the altar.

The casket rested in the middle of the aisle with candles at its head and feet, but it couldn't really have anything to do with Grandma Keary, this beautiful shiny box. Her best furniture wasn't this nice. It had to be somebody else's grandma in that casket.

The priest began to circle it, shaking holy water that struck the dark wood like tears. My hands, already clenched for prayer, began to shake. A helpless sob tore loose from my throat. Grandma Fahey told me not to cry but to pay close attention to the rite she had tried to prepare me for. I listened as carefully as I could and heard the priest intone "... *et lux perpetua luceat eis.*" I thought I heard my name in the Latin words. *Luceat*.

I looked around to see if Grandma Fahey or anyone else had heard it too, before I buried my face in my hands and whispered my confession. "I'm sorry, Grandma. I didn't mean for this to happen to you."

I scooted closer to Grandma Fahey, hoping that I would hear nothing more that seemed to blame me publicly. The smell of incense started to mix with Grandma's perfume and make me woozy. When I lifted my face from my hands, the priest was swinging a silver censor on a silver chain over the casket. Incense smoke curled from it as he swung it like a pendulum. He might be trying to hypnotize me. I shook my head to keep from falling under its spell, but it did no good. All I could do was watch the silver ball swing this way and that, gathering light and color from all over the church. At the top of its arc it turned blue, reflecting the rows of dark blue glass votive lights which burned on Our Lady's altar. Arcing back in the opposite direction, it became red from the votive lights on the Sacred Heart altar. In between the two extremes it flashed green, blue, red, and purple from the light that streamed in through the stained glass. I was still staring at the silver censor when it stopped in front of the priest's vestments and turned again to black and white. Grandma Fahey whispered something to me about the certainty of death and angels, but I was too dizzy to care.

She nudged me gently. "The smoke is rising up to God now, child. Now is the time to add your prayers to all the prayers for Mrs. Keary."

I'd already told her I was sorry. What I wanted was a sign back from her that she knew it wasn't my fault. Then the *Kyrie* began. That was Grandma Keary's own prayer because it sounded like her name, "Keary, eh?" At church with her I'd waited for her joke at the *Kyrie*. She never concerned herself with the Latin goings-on at the altar except when they got to the *Kyrie*. Every time she'd act as if she were surprised and elbow me and say "Keary? Did they say Keary, eh? Are they talking about us up there, Lucy?" Today the prayer wasn't just recited, it was sung: *Kyrie eleison, Christe eleison, Kyrie eleison* in a long mournful chant that made Grandma's name seem to float in the air above me. Maybe it was still about us.

At one point the Latin gave way to English briefly. The priest asked for mercy on the soul of "God's humble servant that He called out of the world this day." God had called? I felt the muscles in my shoulder unclench. Maybe it was God after all and not the faeries that had taken her. I wanted this to be true, but how would I ever know for sure? If I could only talk to her once more, I'd know what happened. The priest was no longer walking around the casket but was facing the altar, praying that Grandma would not be "delivered into the hands of the enemy." He must mean the faeries.

When he prayed that God would "not forget her forever," I felt as lonely as Sputnik floating in space. I didn't know that God could forget you forever and needed to be asked not to. I wouldn't forget her forever.

I looked up at Grandma Fahey, who was intently following the words of the Collect prayer in her missal. Maybe she was right that I should listen to the priest, who was now praying for "we who are alive, we who are left." I was looking up into the high dome of the church, where the smoke from the incense still faintly lingered, as the priest promised that we shall be "taken up into the air together with all the dead to meet Christ in the clouds." Maybe Grandma was there in that haze now.

I heard no more English until the sermon, when the priest introduced himself as Dennis Ryan, a Jesuit at the College of St. Ignatius, and called Grandma Keary his second cousin, Maggie. He talked about Grandpa Hugh Keary being already in Heaven and about all Grandma's children, especially my mom in the hospital. He talked of Grandma's three homes, one in Loughrea, County Galway, one in Kansas City, Missouri, and now one in Heaven. When he said her smile was as welcome and expected as the flowers in the springtime, people all over the church made sounds between laughing and crying. I ached for her lilies of the valley, our own private spring.

He talked of how kind she was to all she met, and how each act of kindness was like a patch on the quilts she donated every year to the Little Sisters of the Poor raffle. He told us that she would be waiting joyfully in Heaven for all those who loved her, until time is no more.

But when he talked about her "mortal remains" here in the church, my chest froze and I couldn't listen. Mortal remains sounded like things left behind, unwanted things: old clothes, empty milk bottles, twice broken tea cups that could no longer be mended. It could not mean the gentle warmth of Grandma Keary's lap, her soft, low singing, her easy laugh. I didn't know or want to know that the phrase contained, just as the casket did, the cold body of Grandma Keary.

Grandma Fahey kept busy during the sermon, leafing forward in her *Daily Missal* to the *Credo* so that she would be ready with the next prayer when the sermon ended. The multicolored liturgical ribbons separating the parts of the book were frayed, and the gold was worn away from the edges of the pages she turned faithfully, day after day, year after year. As Grandma continued pulling liturgical ribbons from their places and moving them forward to bookmark the rest of the *Requiem* prayers, the green ribbon made my heart sore. Grandma Keary had always let me play with her Missal, which she carried to Mass on Sundays but never read from. She'd let me braid the red, white, green, blue and purple ribbons together, trying to decide which color I liked best. Once I interrupted the rosary that she always said during Mass to announce that I liked the green ribbon the best. Grandma Keary'd said simply, "That's for the Irish in you, darlin'."

That was all the liturgy I needed then, or ever would need.

When the rows of relatives and friends of Grandma began streaming past the casket towards the communion rail, I felt a chill go through me as I realized that I didn't really want to be any closer to anybody's mortal remains. If God had taken her, he should have taken everything. At least when the faeries take you, they take body and soul and no one sees hide nor hair of you again.

"Up for communion, Lucy," urged Grandma Fahey as she led the way. As we drew nearer the casket, I peeked around Grandma Fahey and saw people kissing or patting it as they went by. What was I supposed to do?

As scary as an open casket was, it was a much better idea than a mysterious closed box. I'd seen Uncle Natty in his coffin at his wake, but it didn't really seem like him with his eyes shut and without a smile on his face, so it was easy to think it was just somebody I didn't know. And with an open casket you could get out if you needed to, like Tim Finnegan in Uncle Red's song, who came back to life to dance at his own wake when someone spilled whiskey on him by accident. Jackie told me that people are sometimes buried alive by mistake and that when they finally open the casket it is too late, they find fingernail claw marks on the inside of the coffin.

I couldn't breathe thinking that Grandma was in there. I wanted more than anything to be with her, but if this box was how you got to Heaven, I wanted no part of it. I bolted from the communion line and hurried back to my seat.

I'd be in serious trouble for not going to communion. I hoped that Grandma Fahey would wait until after Mass to ask me what kind of child is it that doesn't take communion at her own grandmother's *Requiem*. I watched for Grandma Fahey to head back after communion. When I spotted her coming back down our aisle, I bowed my head pretending to pray harder than I even knew how. Grandma Keary wouldn't have minded, would she? But Grandma Fahey was another matter. When I raised my eyes, there she was steering my way and only a few feet from our pew.

Out of the corner of my eye I saw her walk right by me. Had I become invisible, really stolen by the faeries? I turned to watch her walk about halfway to the back of the church before she stopped and began looking around at the purses, Missals and other things that people leave in their pews, like bread crumbs, so that they can find their way back after communion.

How could Grandma Fahey be lost in her own church?

"Here I am, Grandma," I whispered, but she didn't hear me. Mr. Carmody, the milkman, had taken her by the arm and was trying to help her locate her pew. I jumped up and went to her, took her hand that seemed colder than I had even imagined Grandma Keary's might be in the casket, and repeated, "Here I am, Grandma."

"Oh Lucy, I lost my way." She squeezed my hand.

"Yessum. I know," I said, leading her back to our place.

The High Mass was winding down now. It had been much longer than the ordinary Mass, but I didn't want it to end. As our priest cousin was saying the final prayers over the casket, from all over the church came sounds like little birds cawing. Handkerchiefs came out of suit coats and pocket books. From my place in the pew behind them I saw Uncle Red's shoulders moving up and down almost like they did when he laughed really hard, and saw Uncle Conny's hands closing in two red fists at his side.

It was time for Grandma's sons, Mickey, Dick and Dan, and some McKee cousins to carry her casket down the aisle to the waiting hearse that would lead them all to the cemetery.

My dad was to have been one of the pallbearers, I heard my Grandma Fahey telling a group of parish women in the vestibule as the mourners emptied the church. "He and Jackie are at the hospital today with Mrs. Fahey. Rose should not be alone, today of all days."

So Jackie was there. They were all there together again. And I was here with both my Grandmas for the last time. I just stared at the little pearls on Grandma Fahey's gloved right hand. It was the only one for me to reach for now.

When Uncle Red came up to us, Grandma stopped her chattering and said almost in a whisper, "I am sorry for your loss, Mr. Quinn."

"Thank you, Maeve."

"It was a beautiful Mass and a fine sermon. I'm sure your sister would have been pleased."

"Oh, Maggie wasn't one for ceremonies of any kind, but she'd like seeing so much family and all the little ones all in one place. Lucy, would you like to ride with some of your cousins to the cemetery? With your Grandmother Fahey, of course."

"No sir, Uncle Red," I blurted out like my life depended on it. I didn't want to be anywhere near the cemetery. Both Grandma and Uncle Red looked at me. I could barely catch my breath thinking about the casket being covered over with earth. I remembered when they put Uncle Natty's casket in the ground how my dad and some Jesuits had thrown in handfuls of dirt, one by one, as they passed by. It sounded like a sudden rain shower on the wood casket. My mom and dad had held Grandma Fahey when her knees buckled under her. Jackie said she would have jumped into the grave if they hadn't.

"Lucy, are you sure?" Grandma asked.

"Yessum," I held her hand so tightly I could feel the seams on the fingers of her glove.

"Well, we are off then," said Uncle Red. "You'll both come by the house after, Maeve?"

His eyes, red rimmed, seemed bluer and clearer than usual.

Grandma raised her voice to be heard over the bells of St. Ignatius that had begun to chime the hour again. They were louder here in the vestibule than anywhere else inside or outside the church. "For the rosary, Mr. Quinn," she called between the clangs of the great bells. "We'll be there, for the rosary."

I watched as Uncle Red and a crowd of Kearys, Quinns and McKees disappeared into rows of black cars. Two policemen on motorcycles stopped the busy traffic on Troost Avenue for the procession to Calvary Cemetery, as Grandma Fahey and I started down the hill alone to her home.

Chapter 13: The First Sorrowful Mystery of the Rosary

Back at Grandma Fahey's kitchen, I stood eye level with her rolling board as her fist disappeared into the first of three mounds of yeasty dough that had been left to rise since early this morning.

"The past is the past, and a person can't be out of it too soon. Remember that, Lucy," she told me as she kneaded the sticky mass of dough. "You must work with what you have today and never look back."

"What are you making, Grandma?"

"Coffee cake. Everyone appreciates coffee cake at a time like this. We will bring three nice cakes for after the rosary."

"Can't we make green apple pie? Grandma Keary loves green apple pie."

Grandma looked at me for a moment before she answered in the voice she used to wake me in the middle of the night to give me my earache medicine, assuring me that something bitter tasting would make me better. Now the same direct voice was saying, "Lucy, you know Mrs. Keary is gone. You need to get used to that."

I could feel her watching me closely, waiting for me to swallow this bitter fact as I would the penicillin.

"It won't always hurt, Lucy."

I didn't really want the hurt to go away if it was what connected me to Grandma Keary.

"She has gone to be with God. You understand, don't you, Lucy?"

"Grandma, do you think that it could have been the faeries that took her instead of God?"

"Why would you say such a thing, Lucy?"

There was that answer of hers that didn't mean yes and didn't mean no. I knew she wouldn't tell me if she knew. It still made no sense to me that Grandma hadn't said goodbye.

"Things are not always as we want them to be, particularly when we are small. You know, Lucy, when we left Mayo, Granny McNamee didn't come with us. I had to leave her there rocking in her chair, stirring the ashes. She refused to come to America and refused to look up from the fire to see us off. She wouldn't talk to anyone, not even me. Not even me, her Maeve *og*."

She daubed at the tears that burned on my cheeks with a corner of her apron.

"Even after she died, it was hard for me to believe that she was in Heaven. No, I couldn't imagine her anywhere but by her own hearth, where I left her."

I knew exactly what she meant. There was a hollow place inside me that ached to be back at Grandma Keary's.

"But Ireland was so far away, Lucy. That little *boreen* that led to her door might have been in Heaven or another world once we were on to Chicago. I have one little grey stone from the path to her door."

I knew it was the stone she kept in her dresser with her Knock water and cross.

"You are fortunate to have gotten to go to your granny's funeral Mass, don't you see."

I only felt lucky that she was going to take me to the family rosary and gathering at Grandma's Keary's house. Something might make sense if I could be at her house again.

"Grandma, can't we just bring Fig Newtons or something. Why do we have to wait for coffee cakes? They'll take forever."

"Now you are a fine one to talk about hurrying off anywhere, when I couldn't light a fire under you this morning to save my life. The yeast won't be hurried, Lucy, and neither will I."

"But Grandma, how long will that take?" I whined, staring at the ceiling.

"We'll be there in time for the rosary. They have to get out to the cemetery and back before they'll be ready to greet visitors. And it is the proper thing to do to bring something fresh baked, Lucy. You can't show up empty handed."

She went back to her kneading and rolling. As she worked the flour sifter with her strong right arm, I noticed how the muscles in her forearm kept the familiar freckled skin tight unlike the skin of most old people. Grandma Fahey's hands, always red or scuffed from some work or another, were blanched white with flour. These were hod-carrying Regan hands that now reached for another lump of dough.

As she slapped the dough down on the board she put up a little cloud of flour. "No, I say the past is the past and it never did anyone any good at all to dwell on it."

Now I was really becoming frantic. I had come to recognize this particular warning about dwelling on the past as a signal that one of her longest stories about the past was about to follow. I didn't know what would take longer to rise completely, the yeast, or the memory of Chicago or County Mayo that was bubbling up inside of Grandma as she worked her dough. Usually I liked her stories, but not now.

"Grandma, what if we miss the rosary?" Missing a chance to pray should hurry her up I thought.

"If I know these people, and I believe I do, the rosary will be last on the agenda for the day. We are in no danger of missing the rosary. They'll carry on and on about dear old Mother Ireland and other nonsense before anyone reaches for the beads. Your mother's people live in the past, they nurse the old wounds. That's why I didn't want you at the wake last night, Lucy. They don't even try to act like Americans."

She wagged her flour sifter in my direction and then spread the powdery flour over a mound of dough and onto a rolling board as if there was more work to be done than anyone could ever imagine.

"There's nothing that hard work can't put right, Lucy. Your grandfather, Will Fahey, didn't need any help from any union or the Democratic Party." Grandma was now waving one doughy hand in the air as if to discourage imaginary helpers. The way she punched and rolled the dough as she talked of the past reminded me of the story she told of Jacob wrestling with the disappearing angel.

"Will Fahey was from quality, Lucy. He lived in one of the biggest and finest houses out by Lincoln Park, don't you know. I remember the first time I saw him. He was such a gentleman and he spoke so well. My brother, Packy, worked for the Fahey household just as I did. Packy shoveled the coal for that neighborhood." She laughed. "You should've seen the way he would look when he'd come around to Mrs. Fahey's back door. After working with that coal all day, I mean. He looked blacker than any Negro, except around his forehead where his cap kept his skin like snow. It always looked like a halo to me." She laughed and went on. "I'd feed him there at the back door. I wasn't supposed to. He worked for wages only and not room and board like me. I did it anyway. Didn't amount to much, some sandwiches, maybe some beer for his pail. Oh, there would've been the devil to pay if old Mrs. Fahey had found out. She was a skinflint if there ever was one ..."

I never knew Grandma worked for the Fahey family in Chicago and said so.

"Well, that's a very long time ago, Lucy. It was what they called scullery work at the time. I started out in the Fahey's kitchen and made my way from there. And I'll thank you to keep that to yourself."

She was silent for a while but her hands never stopped moving. What would Uncle Red make of this working in the scullery? Scullery was a scary word that reminded me of the skull and crossbones on pirate ships. She flipped over a flattened circle of dough onto a mountain of flour in the center of her rolling board. The flour flew up in jets around her face. She brushed some of it from her forehead with the back of her hand. "Poor Packy. He never did get on too well with Will. No, not at all. We ran away to get married, Will and I. I didn't tell a soul I was leaving Chicago, except for Packy of course. He told me, 'Don't marry him, Maeve!' He said the Faheys are Lace Curtain and that the Lace have no respect for us and they never will."

"Who are the Lace, Grandma?" I asked tracing the letters l-a-c-e in the flour on her board.

Grandma looked at me as if she'd already said too much. "Well that's a long time past now, Lucy. And sure aren't we all Americans after all?" As she flattened the dough with her rolling pin, a smile came over her face, "But Packy used to say that the Lace were the Irish who had flowers in the house and nobody dead."

Grandma Fahey asked me to bring her the cinnamon from the cupboard and the sugar canister. "Your mother's brothers just don't try hard enough.

Dick drives a truck for Anheuser Busch for a living, Mick drives a milk truck ..."

Uncle Mickey. He'd already be there. He'd probably be waiting for me to get there. I remembered how, like a miracle, Uncle Mickey had appeared last summer on Grandma Keary's porch with a wooden milk bottle crate full of shaved ice from the back of his dairy truck. I'd seen him through the window as he stood talking to Grandma Keary.

"Hot morning already, Ma," he'd said, taking off his McGrath's Dairy cap and wiping sweat from his forehead.

"It's the dog days for sure, Mickey. Come on in and have some tea over the ice," Grandma said.

"Can't stay, Ma. The snow's for Rosie's little girl."

As I burst onto the porch, Grandma Keary had smiled, "Here's our Lucy now."

"Hi, good looking," said Uncle Mickey as he pinched my cheek. "C'mon, let me show you what's in the yard for you. You'll be the only kid in Kansas City who can start a snow ball fight in July." As he turned over the crate on to the green grass he said, "Here Lucy. Have fun." Then he reached down and pitched some snow underhanded at me. I tried to dodge it but got hit with snow on the back of my neck. I squealed. He laughed.

He reached in again to the mound of melting snow with both hands this time and began looking around for a real target. I had run laughing up the hill to the porch and Uncle Mickey had turned and yelled, "Hey, O'Brien!" to a teenaged boy who was reading comic books on the porch across from Grandma's. The boy looked up just in time to get hit by the spray of ice as the snowball fell short of its target. I knew that Uncle Mickey could have hit him square on if he'd wanted to.

"What the heck?" the startled kid yelled.

Uncle Mickey had roared out a laugh and wiped his hands on his white trousers. As he walked back towards his truck, I charged down the hill for the snow and hurled a loosely packed handful in Uncle Mickey's direction. He'd bobbed and weaved, "What an arm! Jack Fahey's not the only pitcher in this family."

I liked that about Uncle Mickey, the way he was on my side and didn't always think Jackie was better than me at everything.

As he stood in the street with one leg up on his truck, I'd seen that he had on one blue sock and one green one.

"Hey, Uncle Mickey, your socks don't match."

Without looking down he'd said, "Sure they do, Lucy. I've got two pair exactly like this—the other one's at home." He'd winked and then disappeared inside the green and white McGrath's truck. Grandma had laughed that Uncle Mickey's jokes could have killed vaudeville if it weren't already dead, and waved goodbye from the porch.

The memory of that mound of snow on the grass last July melted into the present reality of this dry mound of floured dough on Grandma Fahey's counter. I hadn't been paying much attention to Grandma Fahey going on about her favorite relatives for thinking about my Uncle Mickey. When I listened in on Grandma to see where she was in her story, and how close to the end she might be, I heard her saying, "The Democratic Party is like a house of cards that will collapse someday and leave old Red Quinn out in the cold. Why, he wouldn't even have a job if not for the Democrats."

I didn't see anything wrong with that. Uncle Red worked as hard as anyone else. I'd shivered with him on a very cold night two Novembers ago when we walked up and down every street in Grandma's neighborhood, replacing Republican yard signs with signs for the Democratic candidate, his pal Judge O'Hara. Uncle Red said that those folks would thank him later when it would be an embarrassment to have backed the wrong man for county judge.

"... and what have any of your mother's people done of importance, lasting importance? I ask you that," said Grandma Fahey.

I didn't think she was being fair at all now. If I could listen to her stories about people I would never meet, like her brothers Petey and Packy Regan, she should be nicer to living people on the other side of the parish, who were waiting for us to show up. And besides, there were famous people on that side of my family. Uncle Red, for example, had done some pretty important things. I heard once that he had healed an entire ward. Although I was never sure just what it was he was healing it from, they always said that in his day, he could turn a ward around like nobody else.

But by the way Grandma was wielding her rolling pin, pointing one end in my direction to emphasize her notion that nothing good ever came from my mom's side of the family, I figured bringing up Uncle Red just might not be the right thing.

Well then, there was always Famous Aloysius. She'd never met him, so she couldn't have already taken a dislike to him. And she'd have to see the importance of what cousin Aloysius Reilly did that got them all laughing last spring and swearing more than Grandma Keary allowed in her kitchen.

They called him the Grand Inventor, and Grandma and my great uncles and Uncle Mickey and Uncle Dick couldn't stop laughing when Aloysius Reilly stomped out of Grandma's kitchen that day. Uncle Conny had said, "There goes Famous Aloysius," and Uncle Red had said that he was probably the only shot at real fame in our family.

"There's the Grand Inventor, Grandma. There's a famous cousin, Aloysius, who is an inventor." I really thought she should know.

"Do you know what an inventor is, Lucy?" she said irritably.

I thought I did but she thought I needed to be told.

"I'll tell you what an inventor is—it's a man who can't pay his own bills. An inventor, to be sure. What's he ever invented?"

"He invented a rosary you can say while you drive," I said.

"A what?" She dropped her sifter on the counter.

"A rosary that fits on your steering wheel so you can say your prayers while you drive. Uncle Mickey showed it to me. It's for truck drivers."

She looked at me suspiciously, for blasphemy was serious business whether it was mine or Uncle Mickey's, and asked very slowly, "Lucy, are you sure of your facts?"

"Yes ma'am. Uncle Dick and Uncle Mickey both have them. The beads go right around their steering wheels."

She was silent for a time, resumed her sifting and then declared, "Well, at least one of those boys is on the right track."

It made me smile to remember how they sat around Grandma Keary's kitchen table teasing the Inventor. Uncle Dick was reporting some difficulty in using cousin Aloysius Reilly's invention.

"The main problem with the thing, Ally, is when I get half way through the rosary, I'm at the beads at the top of the steering wheel. Well, I have to turn right whether I want to or not, just to finish my prayers. I'll have Busch distributors all over town waiting for me to show."

Then Uncle Red started in, "Oh Aloysius, you should have it so the lad here can finish the damn thing and not have to drive around the same block until he does."

Cousin Aloysius Reilly got very red in the face and said that the Patent Office of the United States of America would not have granted him a number if it wasn't a new idea, and besides that, Uncle Dick wasn't using the Steering Wheel Rosary correctly at all if he had that problem with it.

Uncle Mickey seemed pretty serious when he said, "You know, I've got the opposite problem from Dickie. Every time I turn a corner I lose my place in my beads. And I goddamn well don't want to say any more prayers than I have to."

Cousin Aloysius stood up and shouted to them all, "You have to actually be smarter than a bloody goddam rosary to say one." Grandma followed him down the hallway to the front door.

Great Uncle Red looked at his nephews, "Have either of you fine boyos ever used your Steering Wheel Rosaries?" Uncle Mickey and Uncle Dick both shook their heads from side to side and the laughter started up again. Grandma Keary returned to the kitchen and told them all to lay off teasing Ally for a while, but she was smiling when she said, "I mean it now, boys. He's hopping mad at the lot of you."

"He'll get over it, Maggie," Uncle Red said as he drained his beer bottle and rose from the table. "This Busch beer is nasty stuff, Dickie. Why don't you sell something worth drinking? But I guess it beats the buttermilk that you peddle for a living, Mick. Where did I get these nephews? What would you say to going for the genuine article?"

I knew that he was heading for Mr. Philsy Cannon's bar. I always wanted to go along whenever they'd all leave Grandma and me behind in the kitchen. Kissing Grandma on the cheek, Uncle Red said, "Maggie, I'm taking your boys off to Philsy's—to get them canonized."

This kind of canonization had nothing to do with becoming a saint though. I know because Sister Mary Columba kept me after school to explain exactly what was wrong with my homework assignment on how Mother Seton became the first American saint. Apparently there's another kind of canonization that had nothing at all to do with Mr. Philsy Cannon's bar.

But now I knew that they would never all meet again and laugh that hard in Grandma Keary's kitchen. I couldn't even think of that place without her. From the looks of my great uncles and uncles at the funeral, the laughs might have all been drained out of them, maybe forever.

I felt another sob coming from deep inside my chest. Grandma Fahey had just uncovered the last portion of the dough that had risen perfect and smooth in its bowl. She put her square scullery maid's fist in the middle of it. I looked at the dent she had made in the dough, and wished I could force back my pain that same way.

With my hand to my chest I stammered, "What makes it rise up like that?"

"The dough do you mean, Lucy? It is the yeast, salt, and soda. You have to keep punching it down if you are ever to make anything worthwhile of out of it."

So I pushed my sadness down deeper, while Grandma pummeled the dough and threw herself into kneading the last of the three cakes. The sweet and sharp smell of baking sugar and cinnamon filled her kitchen just as it would Grandma Keary's kitchen on pie baking days. I was surprised by how ferocious my hunger to be back at Grandma Keary's had become.

When our taxi dropped us in front of Grandma Keary's, I helped Grandma Fahey carry the coffee cakes up the steps. Paying the driver $2.50, she said this had been an expensive day.

There was a tall blue votive candle in the window, like the ones that cost a dollar at church. Grandma's house had always reminded me of a face with the brick of the chimney separating the two front windows like a nose does two eyes. The blue light in the one window made it look like a winking face tonight.

"Look, Grandma," I said, thinking she'd see the face, too.

"Oh, that's just the old way. A light is set in the window to guide the departed soul back to its own before it leaves this earth forever, or so the old ones say."

Walking the path to the familiar porch, I watched a few small sparrows that hopped and flew around in the yard. Birds were always more than just birds to both of my Gaelic grandmothers. They were messengers. They brought you news, and if one got in your house it was only bad news they were bringing you.

No matter what news came from my mom's doctor, Grandma Keary had always acted as if things were just as we wanted them to be, until the day this April when a bird had gotten trapped in her flue. She'd fretted like I had never seen her do when the panicked little bird batted itself around inside the chimney. She phoned Uncle Mickey to come over and see to it. He'd teased her about being so superstitious as he stuck his arm up the chimney to open the flue completely. The bird had fallen into the ash from last winter. Mickey said it must have broken its wing. We'd watched the bird exhaust itself spinning in tight circles and trying to fly from the ashes. It was so nearly covered with white ash except for its tiny black eyes that I thought it looked like a sea gull. Uncle Mickey had said it looked more like the Holy Ghost and laughed as he reached for the bird. Grandma said it was unlucky all the same and to take the little creature with him.

Holding the bird with two hands, he asked, "Lucy, do you want to pet it?"

Grandma Keary shook her head solemnly like she thought it would be a bad idea, but Uncle Mickey urged, "Go on, Lucy. It needs a friend."

Slowly leaning towards it, I'd seen that its chest puffed with each quick beat of its heart. As I'd reached for its ash-covered head, it lurched its beak towards my finger and made a high-pitched screech.

Uncle Mickey said calmly, "Try again. It's just scared. It has no idea where it is: one minute it's singing in the trees with its pals and the next, it's beak down in somebody's fireplace."

I'd lightly touched its head and felt its entire body tremble through my index finger. We had the same pulse, this wounded bird and me. Some ash came off onto my fingers. I hadn't felt right about dusting it off. It was somehow like ashes on Ash Wednesday that you weren't supposed to wash off until it was time for bed.

Following Uncle Mickey out on the porch, I'd asked, "Will it live?"

"It might. I kept Charlie Parnell's old parakeet cage when I got him a new one. I'll put this little guy in the old one and feed it for a day or two to see what happens. You never know about these things, Lucy."

"Does it have a soul, Uncle Mickey?"

"Oh, of course it does, Lucy."

Now that I was standing at the front door of Grandma Keary's where I had been longing to be, my heart was beating as wildly as that rescued bird. I felt helpless to quiet all the noise I heard coming from inside the house. I'd never seen so many people at Grandma Keary's before. I only wanted to see Grandma once more. Uncle Mickey answered our knock on the door.

"Sorry for your trouble, Michael," said Grandma Fahey.

He smiled slowly at me and said, "Thanks for coming, Mrs. Fahey."

Grandma handed him the coffee cakes like they were the price of admission.

"What time will the rosary start, Michael?"

"We were just waiting for you to get here, Mrs. Fahey."

I don't think she knew whether or not he was pulling her leg.

"Who will be leading it?"

"As you can see there are priests coming out of the woodwork," Uncle Mickey nodded towards the noisy crowd in the front parlor. "It'll probably be Prof over there, Prof Ryan. Teaches history down at the college."

"The Jesuit who said the Mass?" Grandma Fahey asked.

Uncle Mickey said, "Yup," and headed back towards Grandma Keary's sunny little kitchen. I took off after him. I wanted to ask him about that little bird and about the light in the window. I looked back at Grandma Fahey. She wouldn't miss me. She had already latched on to a young priest from the college, who sometimes stopped to talk with her after daily Mass. He had known my Uncle Natty at the seminary in St. Louis.

I followed Uncle Mickey to the kitchen and was amazed that it was the quietest place in the house today.

"Uncle Mickey?" I tugged at his suit coat.

"What's up, Lucy?"

"Will Grandma be here somewhere today?" We both looked at her empty chair at the kitchen table.

He only sighed, and said, "It's a tough old time, Lucy. And your Grandma wouldn't want you to worry about her."

"Uncle Mickey, did that little bird, the wild one from Grandma's fire place, did it live?"

His eyes were so sad that I wished I hadn't asked him. I'm not sure he could even remember the little bird.

"Here Lucy, put these cakes on the counter for Mrs. McElliott, will you. I've got to get the door."

I put the cakes down and looked up at Mrs. McElliott, Grandma Keary's good friend who always visited her on Thursdays. She was slicing bread and arranging food on trays that were handed to some women from the parish to serve to relatives and guests.

Mrs. McElliott was not a relative, but she knew exactly where everything was in Grandma Keary's kitchen. Mrs. McElliott was not a lady from our parish either. She explained to me last August, when the Feast of the Assumption came around and she stayed with me while Grandma Keary went off to Mass, that hers was an orange name, not a green one like mine. Holy Days of Obligation didn't matter much to Mrs. McElliott. She said then that it was sometimes lucky to have a few orange, Protestant friends.

People with orange names were still Irish like us, but they never went to our church. It's kind of like a Canadian penny or dime. They look so much like our coins that nobody cares that they aren't, except for

Uncle Conny who said he didn't particularly care to see the Queen of England's mug making an appearance in his change.

Mrs. McElliott spotted me and came over with a jar of tomato preserves. "Look what I found, Lucy. Your favorite. Do you remember last summer when the three of us made these?" Handing me the jar, she continued, "Look at the label, Lucy. There's your name, Lucy F."

I recognized my own handwriting but felt like it belonged to some other kid who hadn't ever been to a *Requiem*. Toward the end of last August, Grandma Keary asked me to go to our garden and gather up all the tomatoes left growing there. The red ripe ones for preserves and the green ones would be for pickling. I made three or four trips from the garden to the kitchen where the two old friends were boiling jars and chopping up vegetables. I sat on the counter and helped put rubber washers in the lids of Ball jars while Grandma and Mrs. McElliott chatted and laughed.

"I found all our tomatoes here in the cupboard," said Mrs. McElliott.

She began to open the jars to serve the mourners. The vinegary smell of the pickled green ones and the sweet, rich scent of the red tomato preserves flooded my senses. It smelled like the end of last summer, like the end of summer for all times.

I broke away from Mrs. McElliott and ran down the back hallway to Grandma's bedroom. Her bed was made up in an unusual way, not her way. I opened the closet. Her clothes were still there. Her shoes were under the bed and her cane was hung over the bed board. For an instant there was a light, feathery feeling in my chest, like something was trying to fly out of me, like a hope that she'd need these things and she'd have to come back for them and for me, too.

I began to examine her things more closely now. Someone—not Grandma Keary for this was not her way—had hung her apron on a nail on the back of her closet door. I ran my fingers over the pattern of wild violets on her apron. I put the hem of her apron that smelled faintly of baking apples to my cheek. Would the sound of her voice fade, too, like the scent of her kitchen? Where had the sound of her gone? It scared me that right now I couldn't remember her singing voice. What if her voice that I carried inside of me had left with her? I didn't want to know it if when someone leaves you forever, that something deep inside of you has to leave with them.

I staggered from the closet to her dresser. Her hand mirror, combs and brushes had been neatly arranged in a way Grandma never would have taken time to do. It worried me to think about other people touching Grandma's things. Strangers touching her things might confuse the mother bird of her soul. I knew that a mother bird can tell if a stranger has touched the eggs in a nest. She never comes back for them. She leaves them cold. I couldn't risk Grandma's soul never returning because the nest had been tampered with by strangers, so I ran my hands over everything on her dresser so that she'd know it was still me here waiting for her. When I looked in her hand mirror, instead of my own face, I saw Mrs. McElliott, who had walked quietly into Grandma's room. She had her hand on the unfinished quilt that was folded over the bedstead. As her hand went back and forth over the pattern, she said, "The dear, dear woman."

I threw myself on the bed and sobbed deeply into her pillow, "Where has she gone and why didn't she say she was going?"

Mrs. McElliott sat on the edge of the bed and stroked the back of my head saying, "I'm sure she didn't want to leave you, Lucy. She just got very tired. You'll understand someday."

I pounded my fist and the tears came in waves until they gradually slowed and I rolled over on my side and looked up into Mrs. McElliott's kind and questioning face. I looked over at an open window and the table where Grandma had placed the vase from the Vale of Avoca that she had mended after I broke it. A gentle breeze was lifting the lace curtain behind it, like a melody just out of memory's reach.

"I thought she could fix anything, Mrs. McElliott."

Mrs. McElliott kept brushing my bangs away from my eyes as I kept staring at the hand-painted scene of shade trees bending over the little stream in a valley, and all the cracks that ran through it in a pattern as familiar as the back of Grandma Keary's hand.

"Have you ever been there?" I asked her.

"Where, dear?"

"There, on the vase. That place in her song. It's in Ireland."

I don't even know why I asked. No one else knew that it was our place and our song. The song was just an empty shape inside of me now, although the words that I must have heard five hundred times rolled sadly by like the little stream, "Oh sweet Vale of Avoca, how calm could I rest in the valley of shade with the friends I loved best. Where the storms that we face in this cold world should cease, and our hearts like thy waters be mingled in peace."

But it was only me repeating the words. There was no magic in that without hearing her voice that used to be as close to me as the warmth of her skin against my sad, heavy self.

"Can you sing the song, Mrs. McElliott? Do you know it?"

Somebody had to sing it to me.

"How does it go, Lucy?" she asked.

I felt myself slipping away, like in the dream the morning she died. Hadn't she put me on the water without her? I sat up and reached for Mrs. McElliott who hugged me and said, "I'd sing it for you if I knew it, Lucy. Was it a nice song?"

Sobs washed over me. How could that place we loved exist, how could Ireland itself exist, if Grandma wasn't here to sing our song? Where would there be a place for me now? I hated Heaven. It was a place that it hurt to think about because it was so far away, maybe the way it always hurt her to be so far away from Galway. If her soul was supposed to come home for one last visit to the places she loved the best, I hoped it would come here first. I hoped that she loved her home here with me and Mama and Uncle Red and Uncle Mickey and everybody more than the one she left so long ago. I didn't want her soul to fly off to Ireland first and get to visiting with folks and not have time to stop here with me. When I die, I would want my soul to come right here, to Grandma Keary's house. Nowhere else. Not even to Heaven, that was just one more place like Ireland that I had to believe existed.

"Are there lilies of the valley in Grandma's yard, Mrs. McElliott? She said they would always come back on her birthday."

"I don't know, dear. Why don't you snuggle in for a little nap?"

I closed my eyes and Mrs. McElliott put Grandma's unfinished quilt over me. I could hear furniture being moved to make room for the mourners to kneel for the rosary. I heard cousin Prof Ryan announce "The First Sorrowful Mystery of the Rosary: The Agony in the Garden," and thought that nothing could be more mysterious and sorrowful than being here in Grandma Keary's room with the other things she left behind.

The priest quickly began the first of the repeating prayers like a train conductor calling out the stops from here to St Louis: "Hail Mary, full of grace, the Lord is with thee, blessed art thou among women and blessed is the fruit of thy womb, Jesus." Though I was curled in a tight little ball, I bowed my head at the mention of the Holy Name as we were taught to do and as I could imagine the relatives in the front room doing. They would bow their heads when the priest said the name as if that were the cue to begin their part of the Hail Mary: "Holy Mary, Mother of God, pray for us sinners now and at the hour of our death. Amen."

When Jesus' name came round on the second Hail Mary, I did not nod, even slightly. It hurt to move or even breathe. The responding women's voices rising above the men's voices comforted me almost like my mom's own voice. I could almost feel her soft cheek and cool slender hands in the soothing cadence of the women praying, "Pray for us now and at the hour of our death. Amen."

I didn't realize how much I had loved kneeling next to Mama at the monthly rosary circle in our parish. She'd dressed in her best dress and spectator pumps and spritzed us both with a little of her favorite perfume, White Shoulders, on those mornings. Women and their daughters gathered at a particular home once a month in the middle of the week to say the rosary and have treats. The entire cycle of prayers was long, but I knew that somewhere between the Sorrowful and Joyful Mysteries our hostess would slip off to the kitchen to put on the coffee. The percolating coffee in the background always seemed to speed up the Hail Marys in the concluding decades of the Glorious Mysteries. When the last mystery, "The Blessed Mother is crowned

Queen of Heaven" had been announced, I knew that I'd be served fresh butter pastries from McClain's Bakery with cold milk.

Now I tried to attach myself to Mama through the rhythm of the rosary, but I was becoming too sleepy to concentrate. I'd miss the start of one Hail Mary and wait for the next. Soon the murmur of the rosary sayers in the next room seemed to recede from me, and the prayers went by like rumbling boxcars. I worried that the last car would go by without me, but I was too drowsy to care. My arms and legs were heavy and warm. The Hail Marys had become a distant jump rope chant. "Blue Bells, cockle shells, at the hour of our death. Amen." I was on the playground trying to time my jump into the big jump rope twirled by the most popular girls in Jackie's grade. I lurched awake when my legs got tangled in the rope and I missed my turn.

I heard The Fourth Joyful Mystery, "The Finding of Jesus in the Temple," being announced from Grandma's parlor. I rolled over and burrowed deeper into the sleep that reached out to me. I never liked this mystery anyway, Jesus having to wander off to church by Himself when He was only twelve. Sister Mary Columba told us that the gospels said He was angry with His parents for interrupting His preaching in the temple, but I knew He was just mad that they hadn't noticed that He was gone any sooner than they had. I'd be mad, too.

"Blue bells, holy shells, easy ivy overs." I suppose I must have fallen asleep for it was no longer a strain to imagine my mother in the next room with the other women. I let go and felt myself drop off the edge of something into a deep blue space where I was suddenly no longer sad or scared but simply held by the comforting chant that I took for Grandma Keary rocking me one last time. The prayers that reached me had become like a song. The voices I heard came from Mama in the hospital, Grandma Keary in Heaven, Grandma Fahey on her old knees in the front parlor, and Mrs. McElliott who'd never said a Hail Mary.

I woke up some time later when normal conversation and laughter began again. I could hear pipes being tapped against ashtrays or heels of shoes and the muffled clinking of beads as rosaries were dropped into men's suit coat pockets or ladies' handbags that snapped open and shut. I sat up in bed to find lilies of the valley in the mended vase where Mrs. McElliott had left them.

CHAPTER 14: OLD TYRANTS APPROACHING

I realized with a jolt that I'd missed the rosary and that Grandma Fahey would be looking for me to find out why. She'd probably even want to leave now that the rosary had been said. I crawled out from under Grandma Keary's quilt and headed for her kitchen before I remembered with a pang that I wouldn't find Grandma Keary there. Uncle Red was sitting by himself at Grandma's kitchen table, her rosary in his right hand and a fresh glass of stout in front of him. Watching him from the dark hallway reminded me of seeing the actors off stage the time Uncle Red took Jackie and me to a play at the college. There was the King of Ulster, his crown in his hand, looking at his wristwatch between acts, and the great warrior, Cu Chulainn, tending a hangnail. Now here was Uncle Red in a black suit that I didn't know he owned, staring blankly. I never noticed how much he looked like Grandma Keary when he wasn't singing or ribbing somebody about something.

As I stepped into the light he perked up slightly, "Oh, Lucy, you been playing out in the yard with your cousins, have you?" he asked straightening my hair.

"No, sir. I fell asleep."

"It's been a rough day, eh Luce?"

We both looked at her rosary in his hand.

"Would you like to have this, Lucy?"

I took it without saying anything. I fingered the familiar brown wooden beads that I always imagined were apple seeds, like the ones that I snapped from their cores to play with when Grandma and I made pies in this kitchen.

My great uncle tilted his glass of dark brown stout saying, "Here you go, Lucy, take a swig of this. It will bring you around sure enough." I sipped in only foam that tasted as bitter as the smell of coffee grounds. As I lifted my face from his glass, I came away with foam on my lip and nose and his face lightened until Grandma Fahey appeared in the doorway.

"This is a fine how do you do, Mr. Quinn."

I wiped the traces of a smile and the stout from my face.

"And Lucy," she continued with genuine disappointment, "I looked for you when the rosary began. It was the reason I brought you here. Where were you, child?"

Before I could answer, Uncle Red said, "She was with me the entire time, Maeve. Never missed a bead, this one."

She looked at the rosary in my hand and said, "Well, as long as she said her rosary, my duty is done."

I tucked Grandma Keary's rosary in my pocket along with the double guilt I felt for lying about saying prayers. But it was really Uncle Red's lie, and he looked so sincere that it was hard to believe that he was really lying.

"We said our prayers and now we are having a pint, Lucy and me. Why don't you join us, Maeve?"

Grandma didn't budge from the doorway but watched Uncle Red slowly rise from the table, lifting his hefty body with his forearms. As he began to draw more stout into a clean glass, he said, "You must be exhausted from your prayers, Maeve. A half glass will do you fine." A weary smile came over his face as he brought the stout to Grandma.

"Please sit down," he gestured towards the empty chair.

Wait a minute. How could Uncle Red invite her to sit at this table? There was something not right about seeing Grandma Fahey at Grandma Keary's table. It might confuse Grandma Keary's soul trying to find a place to land to see someone else in her chair.

"Please sit with us, Maeve. You remember what the signs said when we were young pups, 'Guinness is Good For You.' Remember, Maeve?"

Grandma watched the tan foam rise towards the top of her half glass and said, "Well, I do have a bit of a thirst, Mr. Quinn."

"Of course you do, Maeve. Of course, you do. Praying is thirsty work," Uncle Red said placing the glass in front of her. "And the better you pray, the thirstier you get."

I sat between them with my hands on my cheeks, waiting. No matter how politely their conversations began, they always ended in loud talk or hurt feelings. Grandma sipped her stout as Uncle Red set a glass of lemonade in front of me.

Uncle Red looked around like nothing could please him more than to have time to chat with Grandma Fahey and said, "There now, we are all set for a little visit."

I wondered how many glasses he had already had. I drank my lemonade at the same pace Grandma drank her stout, trying to imitate exactly how thirsty I might be if I had really said the entire rosary, too. Just because she was thirsty didn't make her any less suspicious of Uncle Red and even me.

"Prof Ryan did a hell of a job on the rosary. He sure knows all his mysteries of the rosary, doesn't he, Maeve? I could never keep the damn things straight. That's the only thing that kept me from being a Jesuit myself."

There it was. I felt like I was shot suddenly into the air and suspended on the high side of a teeter-totter. The weight of Uncle Red's swearing in front of Grandma and showing disrespect for the Jesuits by suggesting that he could have ever been one was more than enough to keep me dangling in mid-air indefinitely. I worried about falling into a hard landing.

"I didn't realize until today that there was a Jesuit in your family, Mr. Quinn."

Uncle Red laughed as if she had just congratulated him that not all his people died in jail. He explained between gulps of stout, "Dennis Ryan. We just call him Prof. He's smart as a whip, but don't tell anybody I said so."

"He teaches here in St. Ignatius, I understand?" asked Grandma.

"Yup. He had both of your boys in class, Maeve. He always had good things to say about Frank Fahey and Nat, too."

"He knew Nat?"

"Yes, and Frank as well."

"Would you like to meet him, Maeve? Lucy, could you go and fetch cousin Prof for your Grandma? Tell him Mrs. Will Fahey would like a word."

I didn't like being banished from Grandma Keary's table even by Uncle Red, but my assignment brought my side of the teeter-totter back to the ground. I was glad of that and jumped up to find cousin Prof Ryan.

I had met Prof Ryan only once, but I knew he would be easy to spot even in this crowd of look-a-like relatives. Last summer when Uncle Red introduced me to him at Cleary's Drug Store between Grandma Keary's house and the college, I thought he was the tallest man I had ever seen. Uncle Red had promised me a cherry phosphate for helping stuff envelopes for the Hibernians, so I was not interested in slowing down to meet any more of his pals or old relatives, but this one stopped me in my tracks.

"Lucy," Uncle Red had said, "this distinguished chappie is your mother's second cousin."

I squinted up towards the ceiling. His freckled face seemed to come out of the light fixture at Cleary's. The slow way he bent over to shake my hand reminded me of the graceful giraffe at the zoo, bending over for the leaves on the lower branches. His blue eyes seemed enormous behind his thick rimless glasses as his face met mine. He seemed so much like a gentle animal in a picture book that I was almost surprised when he spoke.

"We are praying daily for your mother, Lucy."

I didn't know if I was supposed to call him Father. He was wearing a Roman collar but he was a cousin after all, so I said nothing and looked at the soft freckled hand that enveloped mine.

"You have a brother at the top of his class don't you, Lucy?" The charm of this imposing presence was quickly broken. I couldn't escape the shadow of Jackie's reputation even here. I looked towards the soda fountain and tugged at Uncle Red's arm.

"You are barking up the wrong tree if you think you can put your Jesuit curse on Jackie Fahey, that is, if Frank Fahey has anything to say about it," laughed Uncle Red.

Uncle Red knew as I did that my dad didn't share Grandma Fahey's enthusiasm for the Jesuits. In fact, even if Jackie wanted to become a priest, I don't think my dad would have let him. Dad didn't even like Jackie being an altar boy. On the Sundays that Jackie served Mass, he'd yell about him wearing "that damn dress, just like Nat."

"Lucy," he continued, "Prof here would have Jack ruining his eyes over Aquinas or spending his youth translating *Goren on Bridge* into Latin, or some such thing."

As the two old men bantered, Prof Ryan opened his purchase, a deck of cards, which he began to shuffle with one hand. The phosphate could wait. I was mesmerized by the way the cards moved in his hand. It was exactly the way my dad began all of his card tricks. Once I asked Daddy to teach me one, thinking it must be magic.

"There's no magic to anything, Lucy," he'd said like he was mad that there wasn't. "A little sleight of hand and how to hold my whiskey were about all I learned from the Jesuits. I am not like my brother, you know."

Tonight as I wandered out into the smoky parlor I immediately spotted Prof Ryan. The kindly giraffe was leaning over a card game, giving advice to Uncle Conny. Grandma's card table, on which we had played endless hours of Old Maid and Crazy Eights, was opened and a group of silver-haired cousins and the young priest from the College were playing poker. I didn't like them using Grandma's card table and I didn't think they should be smoking either. Grandma never let anyone, even Uncle Red, smoke in the parlor.

Uncle Conny shouted "Bloody hell!" and threw down his hand as the young priest opposite him quickly swept up all the match sticks from the center of the table.

"Sorry Conny, I seem to have miscalculated," Prof Ryan smiled.

"Like hell!" Uncle Conny replied. "There are too damn many Jesuits at my sister's funeral is all I have to say."

"Where can I cash these in, Mr. Quinn?" deadpanned the other priest.

"Just put them in the collection plate for me next Sunday, Father Logan."

"Why don't you come to Mass and do that yourself, Conny?" laughed Prof Ryan. He was standing up straight now and I didn't think he would be able to hear me so close to the ceiling, so I told Uncle Conny that Uncle Red wanted to see cousin Prof in the kitchen.

"One more hand, Lucy, then I'll turn loose of this bad luck priest," Uncle Conny said as he anted up two wooden matches. I could see he was holding two jacks and then he drew one more. He looked at the priest across the table from him and continued his heckling. "You know what they say about Jesuits at a funeral, boys? They come out like worms on the sidewalk after a rain."

Prof Ryan seemed to laugh the loudest of all of them. The giraffe could see the three jacks, too. When Uncle Conny raised the bet, the other priest looked quickly up at Prof Ryan who slowly pulled three times on his ear, quickly crossed his arms and then looked down to smile at me. I thought of Jackie's third base coach giving the bunt signal. The young priest folded immediately, but the betting went on.

"If we come out like worms it is only to remind us of our mortality I am sure, cousin," said Prof Ryan after the betting had concluded.

"That, and where to deposit any unneeded cash on our way to Heaven," sputtered Uncle Conny. "Well, my sister had no money. All she had was this house."

"What are you going to do with it, Conny?"

"I hate the thought of it, Prof, this is where everyone meets, always has been, but we'll have to sell it. What else could we do with it?"

"You might consider St. Ignatius. The college could always use a property this close."

I blinked slowly to keep the room from spinning. How could they even talk of giving up Grandma's house? A light was just put in the window for her soul to find its way back. What would happen when Grandma's soul found strangers here? This was serious. I needed to know just how long it takes for a soul to find its way home.

The Jesuit priests at the card table would know about such things. Dad said the Jebbies were especially good at calculating such things as how many angels could dance on the head of a pin, but these priests were too busy with poker to answer my questions.

Uncle Conny slammed down his three jacks, smirking at the young priest across the table. The old cousins laughed as Uncle Conny grandly rolled all the matchsticks into his Ohio Blue Tips matchbox.

"Well played, Conny," said Prof Ryan.

"Your pal, young Father Logan there, folded a little early. Uncanny, don't you think, Prof? That's twice he's folded early when I had some cards to play."

"It's the wisdom of the innocent that St. Thomas spoke of at the end of his life I am sure."

"That must be it," he answered, shuffling the cards. "Well, this innocent little cousin says Red wants to see you in the kitchen. Run along now Prof, maybe he's back there drawing up the deed to Maggie's house for you right now. Probably needs help with the Latin word for swindler."

"I'll let you know how it turns out, Conny," laughed Prof Ryan.

My giant cousin bent down and looked me in the face and asked, "Maggie was your grandmother, wasn't she?"

I didn't want to make small talk. They were making plans to sell this house. I blurted out, "How long does it take for a soul to find its way back home, Father?"

"Back home? You mean Heaven, the true home of all kind souls like your grandmother? I don't know exactly how long it would take to get there. Heaven has its own time that is not like ours. That is an interesting question for such a little girl to have. Let me think."

I bit my lip and wished that my question had a ready answer like the number of dancing angels. Nothing was going to keep me from being here when Grandma's soul came home.

"Not Heaven, Father. I was thinking about her soul coming here. When will she pass through here, do you think? Do you think she's gone to Galway first and will come by here later? I know that she'll be able to see the light in the window, but how will I be able to see her?"

"Ah, the light in the window. Who told you that story, Lucy? Was it Red?"

"No, Father. My Grandma Fahey."

"Well, there's another very interesting question." As he continued, the answer I needed was lost in the

~ 166 ~

general buzz of conversation and sudden bursts of laughter of the relatives in the crowded room. I supposed that, being so tall, he was closer to God. I found myself walking next to him on tiptoes and imitating his loping strides, straining to hear his answer as we headed back to the kitchen. As he ducked down under its arched doorway, Grandma Fahey jumped up from her chair although Uncle Red stayed seated. This was the reverse of what my mom always taught Jackie, that gentlemen stand when ladies enter a room.

Uncle Red made the introductions, "Mrs. Will Fahey, wealthy widow, meet Dennis Anthony Ryan, S.J. A match made in Heaven to be sure."

They both ignored Uncle Red.

"Mrs. Fahey, I am delighted to meet you at last," Prof Ryan said squeezing Grandma's hand. Even her powerful Regan hand seemed dwarfed in his. "I was so sorry not to have been at your son Nat's funeral. I was out of the province on sabbatical in '57. He was a fine young man; we all had high hopes for him. Such a loss to your family, and to our order as well."

Grandma looked dizzy the way she did sometimes in her kitchen when she would say suddenly, "Lucy, I must sit down."

"Thank you, Father Ryan," Grandma whispered as if she were struggling to catch her breath.

Prof Ryan held her chair although he didn't sit himself but leaned his lanky frame against the doorway. "It is certainly a blessing to have your younger son," he said softly.

"Frank do you mean?"

Who else could he have meant but my dad?

"Yes, Frank. I was sorry that the Frank Fahey dropped out of school when he did. Then I thought he might come back to college after the war. A lot of our boys did on the GI bill, you know. Frank Fahey was a wonderful tenor soloist and had the quickest glove at second base that St. Ignatius ever had."

I never knew that Daddy had played second. He was always pushing Jackie not to settle for any position less than pitcher.

"They came from far and wide for the funeral," Grandma said.

I wasn't sure whose funeral she was talking about. I thought we were talking about baseball until Grandma continued with a quiver in her voice, "From Rome, Father Ryan. There were two Jesuits who came all the way from Rome. They had studied there with Nat."

"From far and wide," echoed Prof Ryan. "They say that was the fullest St. Ignatius Church has ever been. Nat was well loved, Mrs. Fahey."

As always happened when people talked about Uncle Natty, the conversation just trailed off into silence. Grandma Fahey, who had by now finished two half glasses of stout supplied by Uncle Red, said after a pause, "I wonder how many will come to my funeral?"

Uncle Red leaned forward slowly and patted her gently on the hand, then said, "Don't worry, Maeve, I'll come. And if it'll make you feel better knowing it, I'll promise to bring a few of my pals, from the AOH."

"Oh really, Mr. Quinn," Grandma bristled.

Prof Ryan turned his head to smile down the empty hallway and Uncle Red continued, "Oh, you've plenty of life in you yet, Maeve old girl. You won't be going anywhere any time soon."

I was glad that this was Uncle Red's opinion. Talk of another funeral had made me clutch Grandma's rosary in my pocket so tightly that my hand hurt.

"Tell me, Mr. Quinn," Grandma glanced from Prof Ryan to Uncle Red, her voice gathering indignation, "do you take nothing at all seriously?"

"Not much, Maeve."

"You have no respect for the dead then, Mr. Quinn?"

"It's death I have no respect for. Why should I give it its due? What did it ever do for me? The way I see it, death is an enemy we can never defeat. It's rather like the English when you think about, eh Professor? So we laugh at it, or we spit in its face because it obliges us to steal from it until we are caught. And it catches up to all of us for all we can do. How's it go," he said, trying to come up with the words to a song about digging a great hole in the meadow to bury some old fiddler named Rosin the Bow. He was pounding out a steady beat on the table with one fist and raising his glass with the other: "I fear that old tyrant approaching, that cruel and remorseless old foe. And I lift up me glass in his honor. Take a drink with old Rosin the Bow."

Grandma crossed her arms and shook her head as he sang. "Can everything in life, even our own mortal end, be reduced then to a few comic words? Tell me, Mr. Quinn, do you have a song for everything?"

"What choice do we have, Mrs. Fahey? What choice?"

Uncle Red was suddenly so serious that it worried me. I wanted him to keep singing. He was happier when he sang.

"Prayer and devotion to the Blessed Mother is the only proper way to honor the dead. You must pray for their souls through the intercession of Mary, not sing them a little ditty as if you expect to see their faces before the night ends." Grandma squinted a look that only Uncle Red could bring out in her.

"You'll forgive me, Mrs. Fahey, but I am all prayed out. A little music would make Maggie seem a bit closer. I hate the thought of her off somewhere with no music to cheer her," he said wiping his nose with his handkerchief. I did, too. I hated it something fierce.

"Prof, did you know that Ned and the McKees were planning to have a bit of a *ceili* here? We'd planned it all before Maggie ..." Uncle Red's voice broke and he shook his head. "I still can't believe it. It was so sudden."

Prof Ryan had his enormous hand on Uncle Red's heaving shoulder and said calmly, "We should have it anyway don't you think, Red? It will be one last family gathering at Maggie's."

"Uncle Red," I whispered, "are you going to give Grandma's house to the Jebbies?"

He slumped further down in his chair. "I hadn't thought anything about the house yet, Lucy. It is too soon. Too soon."

I hadn't meant to make him any sadder, but I needed to know. I was relieved when after a few seconds he lifted his head from his hands and announced, "Not until we've given a proper farewell. If there is anything still standing after our *ceili* on Saturday, we'll let the Jebbies take it for a song, Lucy." He hammered the table and said, "That seems fair to me." He laughed and coughed and cried all in one sound.

"Uncle Red, will Grandma's soul find the light in the window by then?"

"Oh Lucy, Maggie wouldn't miss this night, a *ceili* with the family all here. Oh, she'll be here with us on Saturday. We'll make such a commotion that there will be no sleeping on Saturday night in the city of the dead. Maggie'll be here, trust me, they'll all be here, all of our own that have passed on," he said tapping me on the nose.

This was more ghosts that I was interested in having around, but I knew I would risk everything, even my place with Grandma Fahey if I had to, to be here this Saturday.

"Prof, we didn't have much of a wake for Maggie. Not really. What with Rosie being ... away. Now we have one last chance to do it up right." His old face crinkled into a smile. He was happiest when there was organizing to do, whether for the Holy Name or the AOH or the Democrats. "We can do it the way they used to when we were all young. Remember, Professor, the way the old ones used to carry on for days when we were lads?"

"We are none of us young anymore, Mr. Quinn. That boat has sailed," Grandma said sternly.

He ignored her and instructed his cousin, "Make sure the McKees are still planning on staying until Saturday. Old Ned'll know all the steps and no one plays a fiddle like Old Ned. It'll be like it was when we were all pups."

"I'll do that, Red. Now, no more stout for you, old cousin. And you turn in early tonight." Prof Ryan slowly lifted the glass from Uncle Red's hand.

"Quitting time for me is it?" He sounded like a sleepy little boy.

"Something like that, you sacrilegious old Mick," he chuckled.

Uncle Red sat empty-handed at Grandma's table, smiling at something that must have happened long ago.

Grandma Fahey broke the silence with, "My house and land are bequeathed to the College upon my death, Father Ryan."

She looked at Prof Ryan as if she expected personal thanks. Uncle Red had turned to watch the last of his stout being poured down the sink, but now he swung slowly around in his chair and focused on her like he had just remembered she was in the room.

"I was wondering, Professor, what is the church's official position on *ceili* dances?"

"Oh, we are for them, under one condition implied in canon law: that there will be card playing, too."

"Been cheating at cards again, Reverend?"

"All for a good cause, Red. And it wouldn't hurt if your brother Conny came with a little extra cash on Saturday."

"He was born a chump, that brother of mine. He should have been a priest."

The grouchy little sounds that Grandma made at that remark brought her back into Uncle Red's focus.

"Ah there, Maeve. No sin in a *ceili* dance. You've heard the opinion, ah, how's it you boyos say it, Professor? *Ex cathedra*. You see there's no reason not to come back on Saturday night for some music and dancing."

"Lucy and I have plans for Saturday, we cannot make it, Mr. Quinn, and besides, it would certainly be disgraceful to fill this house with wild racket so soon after Mrs. Keary's passing. I suppose you'll be singing those Fenian songs of yours?"

"That may happen. We might have a rebel song or two. We just might want to thumb our noses at all the old insulting tyrants. Death. The English. They are all about the same to us when you get right down to it."

Although Uncle Red was beyond arguing with her, Grandma summoned her child-scolding voice, and said, "Just why do you think raising a shindy is the proper thing to do?"

Looking for support for her position, she turned to Prof Ryan but he only said, "Mrs. Fahey, may I ask you a question?"

"Why certainly, Father Ryan." She folded her gloved hands in her lap. I thought that, being a Jesuit, he was probably about to ask her a really hard catechism question. Maybe the nine orders of angels. I could never come up with more than six, well, actually five since Uncle Red told me that Orioles was a baseball team and not an order of angels. But nothing could stump Grandma Fahey.

"May I ask, Mrs. Fahey, what county are you from? Originally, I mean."

"Oh, that'd be Cook County, Chicago, Illinois. I know what you are thinking Prof, but Maeve is from Chicago!" Uncle Red's laugh ended in a coughing fit.

Grandma smirked the smirk she seemed to save up just for Uncle Red, and then looked at the priest's pale blue eyes like she'd seen them somewhere before.

"Oh, my mistake, Mrs. Fahey. It's just that you remind me of my own mother. She was from Mayo. I haven't heard anyone use that word, shindy, since I was a boy."

We took a taxi home that night. Uncle Red didn't offer to take us. Grandma Fahey gave the driver three dollars and told him to keep the change, mostly because she was too tired to care. Three dollars was a lot more money than I could come up with to get back to Grandma Keary's this Saturday night, but even if I had to set out on foot, I'd be back.

When we got to her home Grandma Fahey sat down in a living room chair across from her grandfather clock that was chiming the hour. "Oh my, I had no idea how much time had gone by. Lucy, I think I'll rest here for just a little while. I'm too tired to go upstairs yet. Will you bring me my comforter and put something on the record player, anything at all. Whatever's on the turntable will be fine."

I put the needle down on one of her old RCA Red Seal recordings of John McCormack. His tenor voice reminded me of my dad's. I found Grandma Fahey's blue and green plaid comforter in the reading chair by her bed. I never knew how scratchy the wool was; it was not the type of thing that I would have wanted tucked in around my face. Grandma Keary's quilts were made of scraps of soft cotton and linen that she gathered from anywhere. Once a shirt of Jackie's showed up as a flower in a quilt for the St. Ignatius raffle. Good thing it wasn't for our parish.

Coming down from upstairs I could hear John McCormack's lyrical tenor singing to Grandma Fahey: "The eyes that shone, now dimmed and gone, the cheerful hearts now broken."

Grandma Fahey was asleep. I left the light on by her chair, covered her with the comforter and then sat down by her feet. The grandfather clock standing in the dark corner suddenly seemed like a tall intruder, maybe even death itself. The scene of Grandma asleep in her chair was reflected in the round pendulum that seemed to rock her as she slept.

Chapter 15: Leaving Limbo

"We will not be going to any *ceili* dance tonight, Lucy. And that's my last word on the subject."

It was Saturday. All that remained was for me to decide exactly when I would leave for Grandma Keary's on my own. I didn't think Grandma Fahey would take me back if I ran away, but I didn't have any choice. I had to be there by dark. They'd be putting one last candle in the window for her tonight.

I'd wait until after dinner. Grandma Fahey had been napping in her reading chair lately after the dishes were done. I sure knew how get to St. Ignatius on foot, but the way from there to Grandma Keary's on the other side of the parish was still fuzzy. Jackie had said I'd need a map to find my way to Grandma Keary's, but how hard could it be? I had all afternoon to figure it out.

"Did you hear me, Lucy? Not tonight."

"Oh, yessum."

"I am glad you agree with me, Lucy. You are showing some signs of maturity," she said browsing through the albums neatly filed in her record player console. "Trust me, Lucy, it is precisely that wild music that kept the Irish in service and sculleries and in low paying jobs. Your grandfather, Will Fahey, would not have that music in the house. People look down on it."

Blowing a little dust from a portfolio of 78s she said, "Here, I found it. *Lucia di Lammermoor*. It is time for a lesson in serious music. Irish music is not serious music and it never will be. It is only the *ceol tire*, the folk music. Opera is real music. There is a very fine tenor on this album, Lucy."

"Is it John McCormack, Grandma? I like him. Prof Ryan said Daddy was the best tenor in his school. Is he better than John McCormack do you think?"

"Lucy, you are to call your cousin 'Father Ryan.' It is unseemly to call him by his nickname. And by the way, you are always to refer to the order as the Jesuits."

"But Daddy always calls them ..."

"Not in my house," she interrupted, "will either of you show any disrespect for the Society of Jesus. Have you got that, Lucy?" She wagged a finger.

"Yessum." *Jebbies, Jebbies, Jebbies*, I yelled in my head.

It was not John McCormack on this record, but an Italian tenor. According to Grandma, John McCormack was a tenor that could melt your heart, but he is important only because he sang songs in Italian like Caruso. But I'd heard him sing "Mother Macree" and "Kathleen Mavourneen" in her living room more often than the music she had planned for this Saturday afternoon, probably my last one with her.

"Here Lucy, listen to this," she insisted as the first record dropped on the turntable. "This was one of Will Fahey's favorite operas."

My dad liked this, too. He'd whistle or sing some of the tunes around the house. His high voice always made me think of bells ringing. Lucia's boyfriend had a nice tenor voice, too. I wondered what my dad was doing right now. I tried to forget how angry I was that he didn't call to talk to me after Grandma died. I closed my eyes and pretended I was in my own living room with everyone home the way it used to be. Mama would be playing her piano while Daddy sang some old song that made them both smile.

"Lucy, let me tell you the story so you can pay better attention. Lucia is a very fine person, but she falls in love with a young man without money or a title or any land at all."

Grandma clearly disapproved of this Lucia until she marries a nobleman and ends up living pretty high on the hog.

"Did she have her own castle?" I asked looking for something interesting about her.

"She did, Lucy. She lived in a fine old castle. That is all she had except for her family name."

Just like Grandma Fahey and her big house, I thought.

"It is a sad story as you can tell, Lucy."

The really sad thing about this opera was that it was going to trap me here for hours. The stack of LPs she set on the spindle weighed me down and made me itch, like the time I was caught miles from home on my bike in jeans and a heavy shirt on a day turned suddenly hot. It would be a long, uphill ride home. I'd wanted to throw off my flannel shirt and tie it around my waist like the boys do. I knew it was against the rules, but I wasn't sure why. So, I'd just suffered all the way home and offered it up for the poor souls in Purgatory. Sister Mary Columba said that stuff we suffer here in the name of the poor souls is like giving them a drink of cool water when they are parched and burning up, Purgatory being not that far from Hell.

I liked having extra penance already in my pocket to spend any time I liked. Jackie said that the prayer on the back of the holy cards we got this year at Easter would be worth one thousand days off Purgatory when the time came. I wasn't sure if a thousand day indulgence was enough to cover all my sins since coming to Grandma's, especially the one I was about to commit. So, maybe a little suffering through Grandma's opera wouldn't hurt.

I tried to avoid getting behind with balancing my indulgence prayers with my sins because there was nothing I hated more than going into a dark confessional and turning myself in. I hid in the bathroom stall this spring when they rounded up my class to make sure we were all free from mortal sin before Easter Sunday. If God didn't already know what I had done, there didn't seem to be any reason to point it out to Him. Uncle Red agreed that this was clear thinking. And besides, before this summer with Grandma Fahey, I never had much to confess except for being jealous of Jackie and stealing stuff from his room. I always got exactly two Our Fathers and two Hail Marys for that. Sometimes I had to make up sins just to have something to say, and that was a lie that I had to confess then next time. This would have gone on forever, so I put a stop to it by not going to confession anymore. Therefore penance in advance was my only way out of Purgatory.

Listening to opera was some pretty powerful penance in my book. I rocked myself back and forth trying to make the music go by faster.

"Oh, for the love of Mike. Stop that fidgeting, Lucy," Grandma chided. "How can I enjoy this if you are going to squirm so? What is on your mind to make you so restless?"

"Purgatory mostly, Grandma."

"What about Purgatory?"

I stalled, trying to think of a catechism question important enough that might make her shut off the record player. "Well, I was wondering, is it above Limbo or below?"

"You know this already, Lucy. Limbo is neither above nor below Purgatory. It is the place set aside unto itself for the unbaptized. Good people who through no fault of their own are not baptized."

"Like pagan babies who die?"

Jackie and I saved up every year for the pagan baby drive at school to buy them food and rosaries. Jackie paid for so many pagan babies that Uncle Red told him someday they would all show up at the door to shake his hand, and ask to borrow more money. So this year Jackie gave half his money to plant trees in Israel instead.

"Yes, I suppose, like pagan babies," she said leafing through the libretto.

Watching the needle move slowly through the grooves on the face of the long-playing record, I wondered if pagan babies in Limbo ever work their way up to Purgatory.

Since neither of us could remember being baptized and since anyone can baptize, Jackie had looked up the words in the catechism and baptized me and then I had baptized him just to be on the safe side. Jackie had said he wasn't going to spend eternity in Limbo with a bunch of pagans on a technicality.

In the pause between the first and second record I asked, "Do you know the song, 'Mick Maguire'?"

Thinking she must know Uncle Red's song, I began to sing: "Johnny, get from the fire get up and give the man your seat. Can't you see it's Mick Maguire and he's courtin' your sister Kate. You know very well he owns a farm a wee bit out of town. So get up me darlin', Johnny get up, let Mr. Maguire sit down."

"Shush that nonsense, Lucy."

For my money there was no song about marrying somebody for a fortune like "Mick Maguire," and it didn't take all afternoon like *Lucia di Lammermoor*. It always made Grandma Keary laugh. I'd ask Uncle Red to sing it tonight.

My daydreams about being rescued from my lonely family castle carried me along until the music on the record intruded and I opened my eyes to Grandma's high ceiling. The whole opera had overheated and was bubbling over like something left too long on the stove. Everyone was singing at once: Lucia, her brother and her boyfriend, their priest, her maid. Each voice rose and fell, but Lucia's was still the loudest of them all. As it rose and fell, it reminded me of something.

"Tornado siren! Did you hear it, Grandma?" I was on my feet, shouting.

"Hush, Lucy, this is one of the most famous sextets in all of opera."

"Don't you think we should go to the basement?"

"Please be still. It is not a tornado siren. We have no need of them in the city. This is not Kansas after all."

I stretched out on the floor close to the speaker, and stared at the little RCA dog with its head cocked, perpetually listening to the whirled ear horn of an old fashioned Victrola. I wondered if he wouldn't rather be playing in the yard like other dogs.

How much more could they all sing about? I began to wonder if people in Hell ever think they are only in Purgatory, and maybe after a few hundred years of looking for the back door, they give up and realize there is no escape. They'd been tricked all along.

The exact route from St. Ignatius to Grandma Keary's was still hazy, and the rain that had just started was going to complicate things. Grandma Keary and I usually rode to Mass with Uncle Red because it was too far to walk. I sat in between Uncle Red and Grandma in the front seat of his Ford and could barely see out the windows or pay attention to the route. Mostly I stared straight ahead at my shoes that stuck out in front of me, while Uncle Red made a fuss over whatever homemade dress I had on. Then he would kid Grandma about her dress or her hat, telling her she was trying to impress the Quality. Sometimes he'd sing the one about the Irish washerwoman who put on her best for church.

"'Hallelujah! Hallelujah!' sang the choir above her head. 'Hardly knew ye! Hardly knew ye!' is what she thought they said."

If it was still raining when I left, there was the yellow slicker Grandma Fahey had bought me just for walking to Mass on wet mornings. I thought of the anxious look in her eyes when she would fasten it up to the top and pull the hood down so far that I could barely see out.

"To keep out the elements!" she'd announced.

Keeping elements out sounded a whole lot more serious than just keeping dry. As she talked about opera this afternoon, I had the feeling that she was trying to wrap me up in another kind of coat. She had the same slicker-fastening look on her face when she stressed, "Will Fahey used to say that only the Italians really understood opera. We've got all we need with Donizetti and Puccini and Verdi. We don't need any *ceili* music. No, we do not."

Grandma reached for her basket of darning and began to attack the worn heels of the thick walking socks she had bought me when I first came.

"There, good as new." She smiled at her handiwork and reached into her basket for my other pair of my socks, then suddenly dropped her needle and said, "Lucy, you won't always be staying with me you know."

"Ma'am?" I didn't move. Had she seen the escape route I'd been drawing with my index finger on the carpet?

"We won't always be together like this, you and I, so we should make the most of it."

She was still smiling. Was she on to me?

"Here, Lucy, take these socks to your room on your next trip up the stairs, please."

I looked carefully at Grandma's face as she handed the walking socks to me and realized she didn't have a clue what I was up to. I couldn't believe it. I lowered my head because I was embarrassed for her. But the socks would come in handy tonight, although I knew that if I ever got back to my own neighborhood, I wouldn't be caught dead in them. Kids would make fun of them in the suburbs, and besides, I could ride my bike everywhere anyway and wouldn't need walking socks. My bike. I could sure use it now for the journey ahead. If I took a wrong street, it wouldn't take me as long to double back on my bike. All the tree-lined streets and small houses on Grandma Keary's side of the parish looked alike. I could get lost and never find my way back to this living room.

I watched Grandma cheerfully working the darning needle. She was always happiest with work that showed instant results. "I thought we'd have corned beef hash for dinner. You like that well enough don't you, Lucy?"

It was one of my favorites. She was in a rare mood. I suddenly felt sorry that I would have to leave her all alone in this big house. Would she miss me when I was gone? I hadn't broken anything in several weeks and lately she told me that I reminded her of things, sometimes very important things from the past and her time with her own Granny McNamee. Maybe I could get to Grandma Keary's and back without her knowing I was gone. Sometimes I could play in the yard for what was probably hours, or just stare out my window when she thought I was studying my lessons upstairs before she came to check on me.

She was looking out the window when a record came to an end. She put down her darning needle and said, "Thank God, that's over for a while now."

"The opera, Grandma?" I asked, happy as a pagan baby unexpectedly sprung from Limbo.

"No, child, the rain. We are only in Act II of the opera."

Lucia and her brother and her boyfriend and their friends raged on until it was time for dinner. The opera had clogged my head so completely that I couldn't have remembered the tune of "Mick Maguire" if my life depended on it.

"Why Lucy, you certainly are helpful this evening," Grandma Fahey smiled, as I brought the plates from the table to the sink, whisked the crumbs from her tablecloth and swept the floor without being asked. "I appreciate the help. I am anxious to get to my *Saturday Evening Post*. I've been saving it all day."

I hadn't counted on *The Saturday Evening Post*. Time stood still for that magazine. She'd read every word, wetting her index finger to turn the slick pages instead of taking her nap. I followed close behind her as she picked up the magazine and headed into the living room to nestle into her reading chair.

"Aren't you sleepy like last night, Grandma?"

"Not in the slightest."

"Are you sure, Grandma, because you look kind of sleepy?"

"Not one bit, Lucy, but aren't you the sweet girl for asking."

I couldn't remember her ever calling me a sweet girl before. My sweaty hands turned itchy as she lingered over this week's cover. When she finally lowered the magazine it was only to announce, yet again, that Mr. Norman Rockwell is a very clever man, for a Protestant. She looked up at me standing next to her chair. "Do you need something, Lucy?

"No'am."

She patted my hand that gripped the arm of her chair. "While you're up then, please turn on my reading lamp. I need to get a better look at these details. It is getting darker earlier now, have you noticed?"

It must be later than I thought. I had to make my move. I turned on the light and quickly kissed her on the cheek.

"Well, what's that all about, child?" She touched her hand to her cheek.

"Nothing, Grandma. I'm just going outside to play jacks is all," I said showing her the pouch I kept them in. For my journey I had crammed a few things I thought I might need into my shorts' pocket: Grandma Keary's rosary, one pair of newly darned socks, and my jacks.

"Stay close to the house then, so you can hear me call." She picked up the magazine again.

From the front steps I could see her reading by the lamp. I sat down to put on my socks and looked up the street towards St. Ignatius. I started up the hill faster than I ever had, turning at every sound behind me, wondering if I was being followed, sometimes hoping someone would stop me. The sounds inside me and outside me seemed louder going up that hill alone for the first time. My heart beat loudly in my good ear and I never before noticed all the commotion that roosting birds make at the end of the day.

I didn't stop to catch my breath until I reached the edge of the campus. I could see St. Ignatius Church from there. I must be about halfway. I could imagine Grandma Fahey behind me nodding in her chair, *The Saturday Evening Post* open in her lap—and Uncle Red lighting the votive light in Grandma Keary's window ahead somewhere in the distance.

CHAPTER 16: THE LIGHT IN THE WINDOW

I heard the rain start again before I saw it. A tapping sound came on the broad maples leaves high above. The sidewalk in front of me began to fill with dark blotches. The rain was cold on the back of my neck as I reached the stoplight at the intersection that divided the campus and the church. I began to cry for the warm dry place I had left. Even the opera didn't seem that bad now.

There were so many streets that might lead from the church to Grandma Keary's. I looked up and down Troost Avenue. This summer rain put up a veil of silver-gray in both directions and steam rose from the cooling pavement in front of me. The water on my face started to taste salty. I was glad for the rain so at least kids, safe and dry in the passing cars, wouldn't know that I was lost and crying about it.

I stepped back from the curb to keep from getting splashed by the traffic that rumbled by. When the light turned green in a puddle of water, I ran for shelter under the covered portico over the side entrance to the church.

This is where Uncle Red would let Grandma Keary and me off. But had we come up or down the street to get here? I hoped to remember that much by the time I reached the covered drive. As I ran, I counted backwards from ten, like Jackie told me to do when I needed to remember something. "Three, two, one," I puffed, but only the memory of Grandma's hearse waiting here to take her to Calvary Cemetery hit me when I finally reached the side door.

Now she would be leaving earth for good, they would be signaling her again with the light in the window and I wouldn't be there. The blood pulsed in my legs. I started to count down from ten again as if it were the holiest prayer I knew. I couldn't stop my tears any more than I could have stopped the rain.

I thought about going inside the church. Sister Mary Columba told us that God was always there and always ready to listen. I didn't think He had done such a good job lately. Uncle Red would be more reliable if only I could reach him. If I had a dime I could call him to tell him to wait for me, and not to light the candle until I got there. He'd listen. He'd come get me.

There was a pay phone off the vestibule by the rack of Legion of Mary pamphlets. The clinking of the jacks in my pocket gave me hope that there might be a dime lodged in with them. My mom had always placed a dime and a Kleenex in my pocket and told me never to stray far from home without both. I emptied my pockets and turned them inside out. No dime. Now I knew what Grandma Fahey meant when she warned me that there was nothing emptier than a pocket when I suggested that we spend her extra change at the checkout counter at the grocery on a Baby Ruth or two.

There would be dimes in the church. I sniffled. I could use a Kleenex, too. By each saint statue there would be a tray to pay for the candles. The small votive lights were exactly ten cents.

Stealing from the saints wouldn't really be a sin because I was only going to borrow their money for a while. Uncle Red could pay it back when he got here. He always had plenty of change in his pockets. He practically jingled when he walked and if I ever asked if he had any extra, he'd gladly flip me one of the new dimes and say, "Render unto Roosevelt that which is Roosevelt's, Lucy." What he meant didn't much matter to me. The new Roosevelt dimes spent just as well as Mercury head dimes.

All I needed now was any dime, but I didn't think anything would make me brave enough to go into a church twice the size of Mary of Gaels and lift one from under the nose of a saint. It was Saturday and the church was probably dark and empty. Not even Grandma Fahey went to church on Saturday. There was nothing more frightening than being alone in an empty church, as I had learned last spring with Jackie. Even he was spooked by being alone in God's place, with all the eyes of the saints watching you. I had left my uniform sweater at Mary of Gaels church after Tuesday night novena, so we turned back to go inside the darkened church. We'd walked slowly down the long aisle to the pew where we sat for the novena.

I'd been amazed that the candles were still burning.

"Look, Jackie. I thought they blew them out when everybody went home," I whispered.

"Nope. They are always burning. God is here even when we aren't."

"Like the light in the refrigerator?"

"No, you chowder head. That light just comes on when you open the refrigerator door."

The fact that the refrigerator light knew you were there seemed more mysterious and God-like than its being on all the time, but I didn't say so.

"Where is God exactly, Jackie?"

"Everywhere, but mostly in the tabernacle," he'd answered pointing to the altar where one large candle flickered in the eerie darkness.

"Saints' eyes are always open on the statues, too, Luce."

"Saints' eyes, Jackie?" I had suddenly become less interested in finding my sweater than in getting out of there.

"Yep, it's true. They use real eyes for the statues. From rich people who have died or something." Jackie, who was devoted to Vincent Price movies added, "And their eyes follow you wherever you go."

"Cut it out, Jackie," I'd begged, but I suspected that he was right. I felt the eyes of St. Joseph and St. Patrick from the statues behind us on the back of my head. I was afraid to turn around and meet their gaze.

"Here it is, Luce," he'd said, grabbing my sweater that had slid underneath the pew. When we'd turned to go, we both noticed a floodlight that shone across the larger-than-life crucifix hanging over the back door we planned to leave from. Jackie stared at it. I knew he hated crucifixes, even the one on our wall when we were smaller and shared a room. He always got up after Mom had heard our prayers and turned out the light to hang whatever was handy, usually socks or underwear, over the face of the suffering martyr so we could sleep.

"Let's scram, Luce. This place gives me the creeps," he'd said and we'd bolted for the door with me inches behind him clutching the back of his jacket with both hands.

When holy stuff turned on you, it was scarier than anything else.

Now I stood alone in front of St. Ignatius Church, trying to dry my face and arms with my wet shirttail. I couldn't turn back, but I sure didn't want to go into an empty church. I couldn't think how much I wanted Mama now or I'd never stop crying. I'd settle now for the soft and certain comfort of a novena to Our Lady of Perpetual Help like we had every Tuesday at Mary of Gaels.

Uncle Red said novenas were the court of last resort. If you begged politely for nine weeks in a row, Our Lady could plead with God to change whatever had happened to you. It was like my own mom persuading my dad after his mind had been made up about something.

People prayed differently at a novena than they did at Mass on Sunday. Nobody could afford to pretend at a novena. They were there to admit that they were lost and didn't know where else to turn but to Our Lady of Perpetual Help. Every week I'd watch the faces of adults around me when they sang: "Mother dear, oh pray for me whilst far from Heaven and thee. I wander in a fragile bark o'er life's tempestuous sea."

Now I was in the same boat.

At least I knew that novenas worked if you did them right. Week after week Father Fitzgerald proved that when he read from the list of answered prayers: "For a job found, for a return to health, for a deathbed conversion."

I'd only tried to make a novena once, for a pony to put in my backyard. Every Tuesday night for eight weeks after my dad said there were absolutely no ponies in my future, I imagined that Father Fitzgerald would soon be adding to the list of miracles: "For a pony, with saddle." I missed one week because of an ear infection and never started over. But this was different. I was desperate. There was nowhere else to turn but to the Holy Mother who was as invisible as my own mom was now.

I knew how those adults at the novena felt, with their desperate singing faces. It was how I felt now about getting to Grandma Keary's. I shook the rain from my head like Uncle Mickey's spaniel and sat down on the curb to pray. The cement seemed colder against the back of my legs as I realized that no one in the world knew where I was at this moment, not Mom or Dad or Uncle Red or even Grandma Fahey, maybe not even Our Lady of Perpetual Help herself.

I'd get my dime. I was going in.

Saturday night confession was underway. Families were coming and going. At least the lights would be on and I wouldn't be completely alone. I wiped my nose on my shirttail. My legs felt almost too heavy to move and I teetered when I stood up. I followed a family of strangers inside but didn't go to the pew where they lined up for confession. If I went to confession, I was afraid with what was on my mind, the priest might jump up and open the door on my side of the confessional just so he could see what kind of kid had such a sin. He might haul me right out of there.

My sin was too big to fit inside the confessional. I was angry with someone who was sick and in the hospital. The fury I felt deep inside for being taken from my mom in the first place was like a wild animal, growing in the darkness. I knew it was there because of the clawing in my stomach at night. I had to keep it to myself. I'd been angry for so long and she'd been sick for so long that I couldn't really remember which came first. Maybe my hidden anger was what caused her illness.

I wished there was someone who would just give me a dime, but this was not my parish and I didn't know anyone. I had no choice about stealing and I looked around for the least scary statue. I wanted one far from the tabernacle candle, too, to be on the safe side.

A bent old woman in a black mantilla rose from the communion rail where she had been saying her penance and slipped some coins that clinked one after the other into the Peter's Pence box. I was surprised how the sounds echoed through the quiet church, like a warning to the saints of what I had planned.

St. Ignatius had most of the same statues as we had at Mary of Gaels and then some. I started walking down the right aisle. There was St. Ann, Jesus' own grandma, off one alcove. I didn't think it would be right to steal from a grandma. I passed up St. Jude of Hopeless Causes, too. There were already two people on the kneelers in front of him. I kept moving to avoid suspicion, passing by St. Martin de Porres and even St. Vincent de Paul, who had a friendly enough smile.

I stopped in front of St. Anthony, patron saint of lost objects. I knew he was a powerful saint. The only time I ever saw Uncle Red pray was to St. Anthony when he lost the bank deposit bag for the Holy Name Society. St. Anthony found it for him in Mr. Philsy Cannon's backroom.

I didn't think I was allowed to pray to him since I was what was lost. Grandma Fahey could pray to him to find me, but that was different. Besides this statue, like all the others at St. Ignatius, was much larger and seemed more important than ours at Mary of Gaels. Looking up at St. Anthony, I didn't think he could even hear someone as small as me. I suspected that my novena hadn't worked very well for the same reason. No one up there could see me well enough to hear my nine prayers.

The Infant of Prague was the littlest statue in the church so I slowly headed for it, even though Jackie said this statue of Jesus as a little kid made Him look like a sissy, wearing that nightgown and that crown with jewels on it.

I would go for the plate and pretend to be making change for the candles as I'd seen other people do. Maybe I should take two dimes and call Grandma Fahey. But what if she didn't know I was gone yet. Or what if she did know I was gone and had called the police? Would there be sirens when they came looking for me? Maybe that wouldn't be so bad, a little attention. All the cops in the parish knew Uncle Red after all. They could drop me off at the *ceili*. But what if Grandma told the cops that she suspected that the faeries had stolen me away. I imagined her shaking an index finger and saying, "What else would explain Lucy going up into thin air like that. It must be the faeries." The cops would have the same opinion about the faeries as Uncle Red. I didn't want her to be laughed at. I'd be just as happy without the cops.

I hoped that she only told my dad. I liked to think of him all red-faced and yelling. He'd be scratching that little patch of freckles on the side of his right hand that turns bright red when he is upset.

As I got closer to the statue, I slowly lifted my eyes just in case Jackie was right about the eyes watching, but the Infant of Prague seemed to be smiling at something over my left shoulder. He seemed not to notice that I was here to plunder.

This was easier than I thought. No one was really around, just a few people lined up for confession, and statues aren't as spooky when the lights are on. The closer I got to the change plate, the more I started to think maybe I'd steal three dimes and light a candle myself, but then I thought of Billy Sheehan. He'd gotten kicked out of Mary of Gaels and had to go to public school for lighting whole rows of votives without paying. Jackie said he had to go to juvenile detention later for burning down a barn in the field in our neighborhood. Three dimes might be pushing it.

I was in front of the statue reaching for my dime when I heard a voice from behind me call my name.

I stopped cold.

It seemed to have come from my right. It could be any one of the saints that I had passed on my way to the Infant of Prague. I didn't turn around to see which one. *I'm going to pay it back*, I said as loudly as I could inside my head.

I waited and heard nothing. Maybe it had only been my soggy shoes squeaking on the marble floor, nothing more. I looked down at my shoes as I took another step and then froze again when I heard the voice clearly ask, "Lucy Fahey, is that you?"

The voice seemed closer this time but didn't sound annoyed like any saint that might know what I was up to.

"Did Mrs. Fahey bring you, Lucy?"

I knew this voice. I turned around slowly and didn't see anyone at first because I wasn't looking up high enough. But there was Prof Ryan nearly as tall as the statue of St. Ignatius himself. He had a purple stole around his neck to hear confessions. The biretta on his head made him seem even taller.

"Are you coming to confession, Lucy? You must be with Mrs. Fahey. I'm sure Red Quinn didn't bring you," he laughed.

"No, Father Ryan." I answered as politely as I could, remembering that Grandma Fahey told me not to call him by his cousin name.

"Surely you aren't by yourself?"

I lowered my voice "Yes, Father."

"All alone?" He seemed a little angry and like he was about to give somebody a couple of Our Fathers and Hail Marys right there on the spot. I was ashamed about being alone. My face felt hot and my woolen socks seemed even more heavy and scratchy when two girls in summer dresses and white cotton anklets breezed by with their mom.

"Did you come to confession for a reason, Lucy?" He was bending over to talk to me.

"No, Father."

"I see. I see. You know, Lucy, God knows what's in our hearts and forgives us long before we even ask."

This was like being handed a Roosevelt dime by Uncle Red. I didn't understand what Prof Ryan meant, but I put it in my pocket for later just the same.

"I was just on my way to Grandma Keary's house."

"Oh, and you thought you'd stop in to make a visit and say a prayer. Your Grandma would be proud of you, Lucy. Were you going to light a votive for her, too, Lucy?" He nodded toward the row of lights in front of the Infant of Prague.

I didn't answer and tried to fill my head with noise. Everyone knows that priests could read your mind in the confessional. I didn't know if they could do that in other places too.

"I am heading over there now that I'm finished up here. Can I take you, Lucy? Surely you weren't going to walk all that way by yourself."

"Father Ryan," I blurted, "I need to be there before dark when they light the light in the window. I don't want to miss her."

"Ah yes, the light in the window, as Mrs. Fahey told you. Well, you won't get there by dark on foot. If you can wait for me to change, I'll give you a ride. You must be quite a dancer then Lucy if you are willing to walk all this way by yourself for a *ceili*. Is this something else Mrs. Fahey taught you, to dance a Mayo step?"

"No, Father. I can't dance at all. Can we please hurry?"

"I won't be a minute, Lucy. While you wait, why don't you light a candle here for your Grandmother Keary?"

I hesitated, hoping he wouldn't expect me to produce a dime.

"Go on, Lucy. This one's on the house," Prof Ryan smiled.

I knew it wouldn't be the same as lighting the candle in Grandma Keary's own window. I didn't know how she felt about the Infant of Prague. I chose one blue candle that seemed kind of lonely at the end of a row and whispered as I touched the flame to the wick, "It's me, Grandma."

I turned to watch Prof Ryan lope down the center aisle. He stopped in front of the altar while he took off the purple stole that he kissed before putting it in the pocket of his cassock. He stood for another moment with his hands crossed and then genuflected and disappeared into a door off the altar.

I stared with satisfaction at the blue flame I had lit. The wood taper I used to light it was still in my hand. Who would know if I lighted another one? It was on the house after all. Too bad Billy Sheehan didn't have a Jesuit cousin. He wouldn't have had to go to both jail and public school. Maybe I'd light the dollar size votive, like the one that would be in Grandma's window. I was about to light a tall red votive when I turned to see the dark accusing eyes of the old lady in the mantilla. These eyes were scarier than any saint statue, she was so stooped that she was no taller than I was. She was making the Stations of the Cross and had waddled nearly alongside of where I stood.

She crossed herself in front of the ninth station but kept her eyes on me the whole time. I felt like a wild rabbit being watched by a dog as I waited for her to move on. She looked disapprovingly at my shorts and then quickly at the top of my head. I hadn't thought that I was in church without even a chapel veil. Venial sin probably, but Prof Ryan hadn't said anything, so maybe not even that. Who runs away from home wearing a school beanie anyway?

I didn't move until I heard three quick whistles behind me. Prof Ryan had emerged from the sacristy and was motioning me to come to the altar. Extinguishing the votive taper in the sand, I walked right past the old lady like I had been called to the front of the line at the movies because I knew the head usher. She sniffed twice as I walked by and then went back to her prayers. I wanted to shout, "I'm with cousin Prof Ryan."

Prof Ryan led me through a door off the sacristy, down a hall and out a door by a garden behind the rectory. The rain had stopped.

"All this rain's been good for my flowers, but I'm just as glad these storms are moving on," he said scanning the sky.

As he opened his car door and I climbed in he said, "You'll see her again, you know, Lucy." When he slid in on the driver side, he added, "That's hard for you to believe now, isn't it?"

The only thing I believed in now was my relief to be inside a car heading for Grandma's as the darkness was gathering. As I stared at the green backlit dials on the dashboard of Prof Ryan's car, he continued, "You see, Maggie's a little like the stars in the daytime, Lucy. You can't see them in the daytime, but you know they are there because you've seen them many times before. Souls in Heaven are like stars in the sky."

I leaned my head out of the window to check for stars. The clouds were breaking up and blowing fast across the sky like ghosts. Patches of deepening blue shown briefly as if through windows on Heaven. At the first star I spotted, I said a prayer to myself, *Hardly knew ye. Hardly knew ye, Grandma.*

Chapter 17: The Jiggin' Jesus

When we pulled up in front of Grandma Keary's, there was already a red votive light in the window. I dashed from Prof Ryan's car, ran up the steps and around the side of the house and knocked on the kitchen door.

"Well, Lucy," Uncle Red said looking over the top of my head. "I didn't think you'd be coming. Where's Maeve?"

Prof Ryan poked his head in the door behind me and said, "I found Lucy at church tonight. I think she's run away, Red."

Uncle Red looked at me like the one time I beat him at checkers, then laughed, "Well now, that's what I call moxie, real moxie."

Prof Ryan wasn't smiling at all. "I think you'd better call Mrs. Fahey."

"Don't Uncle Red! Please. She'll never forgive me for leaving her. Please don't. She might not even know I'm gone."

"Let me handle Maeve, Lucy."

Uncle Red took a towel to my head as I sat at the kitchen table. Then he took off his sweater and put it around my shoulders.

"Warm you up a bit, Lucy. You're drenched."

I liked being enveloped in his maroon cardigan. It smelled like pipe tobacco and Luden's cherry cough drops. There was a Kennedy button pinned on the front and two smaller buttons for Estes Kefauver and Hubert H. Humphrey in one pocket. He always told me it was smart to hedge a bet no matter how sure you were about a thing.

"Grandma will really be mad at me when she gets here, won't she?"

Uncle Red laughed as he tried to comb my hair, "Madder than a wet hen, Lucy. You've defied her, and Faheys, more than most folks, find that highly insulting. But don't worry, we'll keep her occupied when she gets here. Prof, here, will be giving her a personal lecture on the history of the Jesuit order, won't you Prof? Show some photographs of St. Francis Xavier as a lad, that kind of thing?"

"Whatever it takes," smiled Prof Ryan.

"I've got five dollars says I'll get her over to our end of the parish to attend our little hooley. You game, Prof?"

Prof Ryan raised his eyebrows. "Sounds like easy money to me."

"And who knows more about easy money than a Jesuit."

"Make it ten, Red, and I'll see if Conny wants in."

They both laughed. I'd seen Uncle Red and Uncle Conny bet on baseball, dogs, horses, primaries, and the weather, but it gave me a funny feeling to think they were betting on Grandma Fahey.

Uncle Red was still tugging his comb through my hair. "Lucy, I can't make your hair hold a part, but at least you won't catch cold now."

When Uncle Red reached for the phone book, I could hardly stand to be in the room. I pulled Uncle Red's sweater up over my head and held my hand to my good ear, but I could still hear his part of the conversation.

"She's fine, Maeve ... I am sure that she's just not playing jacks in the yard. Fell asleep over *The Saturday Evening Post*, understandable. No, she walked." Uncle Red boomed his laugh and then listened for quite a while before he began. "Oh, I'm sure you did Maeve. No one's faulting you. I'll bring her home, but let her stay for the music, won't you Maeve, now that she is here?"

I peeked out from the sweater.

"Well, if you think it is best, Maeve. I'll bring her home right away."

Uncle Red winked at me.

"It is just that, well, it might raise questions, Maeve, if Lucy left suddenly now that everyone's seen her. People might wonder how she got here in the first place."

Uncle Red's face had that same surprised look he would get just before he double kinged me at checkers, like he didn't know how that had happened.

"Oh, excuse me Maeve, a friend of yours just came through the door. What's that, Prof? To be sure. I'll tell her. Maeve, Father Ryan wanted me to tell you that he is looking forward to seeing your Mayo steps tonight."

He listened a while, then said in a confidential tone, "I'll just say that you sent Lucy on ahead and that you'll be here shortly. That would explain it don't you think?"

Now he was about ready to clear the board completely. "Ah yes, I am quite sure I can be that discrete. I'll be by in an hour ... No trouble at all, Maeve. Until later then."

"You're in like Flynn, Lucy," Uncle Red beamed as he hung up the phone. "Make yourself at home. The place will be filling up with your little cousins and the music should be starting soon."

Prof Ryan was shaking his head, "Trading on the Society of Jesus just to get a date to your own *ceili*. That's a new one even for you."

"Twenty quid says I'll have the old girl dancing before it's over, Professor," laughed Uncle Red.

Prof Ryan made a quick little sign of the cross in Uncle Red's direction, "*Absolvo te, Johannes Quinnorum.*" I was glad that I hadn't crossed myself at the Latin words like I thought I was supposed to when they began to laugh.

The wheeze of an accordion in the living room was followed by a penny whistle running up and down a scale.

"There's the McKees warming up," said Uncle Red.

It was a clarion call that emptied other rooms and brought people in from the porch to the living room.

"Go on and listen to them, Lucy. They play for money in Chicago, you know. Run along now," he said, transferring his pipe and tobacco from the pocket of his sweater to his shirt pocket. "I've got some things to do here before I go to pick up Maeve."

I hoped he had a thousand things to do before he went to Grandma Fahey's. He pulled his comb through his straight silver hair and bent over to look at his reflection in Grandma's coffee percolator on the counter.

I stood up. Uncle Red's cardigan came down to my knees and covered my shorts.

"Uh, Lucy, do you want me to pick up a party dress for you at your Grandma Fahey's?"

I didn't even understand his question.

"What am I thinking? You look grand as is, just grand. Go on in and join your cousins."

When I wandered into the living room and saw that the girl cousins from Chicago had on navy skirts and white bobby socks, my own walking socks seemed soggier than they had before. But I hadn't come to dance.

The Chicago cousins all looked like they knew what they were doing at a *ceili*. At the far end of the living room Old Ned McKee said to his grandsons, "Let's try 'Drowsy Maggie', lads." As he threw himself into the reel tune he nodded to his fiddle player, a serious, dark-haired teenage boy intent on keeping up. But I couldn't take my eyes off the red haired penny whistle player who was about my age. His fingers seemed to be detached from his hands as they flew up and down the whistle. His blue eyes went around the room as he played. Other Kansas City cousins were making faces at him trying to make him laugh while Limes Quinn crawled up to where he stood and began tying the laces of his high-top basketball shoes together. When the red haired boy stopped his playing to giggle, Old Ned McKee looked up from his accordion to see what happened to the harmony from his whistle player. Every Kansas City kid in the room including me laughed when he stomped his foot and shot a stern look in the direction of Limes, who shrugged his plea of innocence, just as he had when he'd stolen the shoe at the funeral.

Old Ned called over the music to the penny whistle player, "You're up, Jim Pat. Step forward now."

The red haired cousin didn't miss a beat even though the corners of his mouth turned up into a smile as he kept his eyes on the gang of boys. Everyone clapped at the end of his solo and the tops of his ears turned red. The other boys teased him so that he couldn't play.

Older cousins were busy rolling up rugs in Grandma Keary's living room. Smaller children dove to retrieve the treasures found there: hair pins, pennies, plastic tax mils, and one black checker that I recognized as the one missing from Grandma Keary's game. We would use an Oreo cookie in its place and the winner got to eat it at the end. Over the hardwood floor a dusting of powder was spread to make the stepping and shuffling easier for the dancers. The lost checker reminded me of my mission.

I headed by myself for the small parlor at the front of the house where the only light in the room was the tall red votive light in the window. If it hadn't been for all the people and the bright music in the next room I wouldn't have been able to think about going in alone.

I stood in the doorway of a room I'd run in and out of a thousand times before. I didn't know what I would see or even exactly what I was looking for. I'd never looked for someone's soul before, but I was pretty sure that it could only be seen in the candlelight. Why else would they put the light in the window as a signal to it? I was glad for the rosary in my pocket when I considered that the faeries might lurk in the darkness, too. You could never have enough protection. I pulled the rosary over my head to wear it for good luck, even though Mama didn't believe in such things. Once she wouldn't let me leave the house although we were running late for the All Suburbs Swim Meet until I took off the miraculous medal that I had donned for good luck in my event.

"It is not our way," she had said lifting it from my neck.

But at the meet I wished I had it on. I was so scared I would forget how to do the backstroke in my event that I crossed myself before I curled up against the starting block waiting for the starter pistol. Mama scolded me afterwards and said this was not something we did in public.

"Other kids do," I objected.

"I don't think we want to bother God with the eight-year-old and under twenty-five meter backstroke event."

"But I won, didn't I?"

"Lucy, we don't wear our religion on our sleeves."

"What sleeves?" I asked as she wrapped a towel around me.

Later I asked Jackie about it. He said it would make our God look bad if I crossed myself and lost to public school kids. But I was good at the backstroke. And what was the use of even having a God if He didn't help you out in a jam?

No one seemed to understand how lonely it was to start down the swimming lane by yourself. Now I was here in this room tonight all by myself. I decided that since this was the city, I could cross myself whenever and wherever I pleased. They crossed themselves in public a lot more in the city than they did in the suburbs. Once when Grandma Fahey and I were going downtown to shop, the *Angelus* bell was ringing as we got off the bus. Grandma crossed herself right there on the sidewalk. She was mumbling the *Angelus* prayer so seriously as we walked through the revolving department store door that I thought it must be a prayer to deliver us from inferior linens and dry goods at Macy's.

I took one step into the dark room and then ran straight for the love seat against one wall. Grandma Fahey might be here to take me away before I could have a chance to find Grandma Keary's soul. I wasn't sure which grandma would appear first.

From my position I could see both the tall votive light and the large portrait of Jesus with His chest all aglow that they called The Sacred Heart. That picture was so familiar that it seemed less like a holy picture of Jesus than it did a very old member of the family. Nearly everyone I knew kept an identical picture of the Sacred Heart in their houses. Grandma Fahey had a large version prominently displayed in her living room. The further you got from the city and St. Ignatius parish, however, the smaller the pictures became. Mama had one in a back hallway of our house where she kept the palms from Palm Sunday year round. Grandma Keary's Sacred Heart loomed out in the candlelight as the only other face in the room but mine.

The Sacred Heart's face always looked rather peaked to me, but then He had probably just risen from the dead and He would be pretty worn out. He only faintly smiled while He reached out with his left hand and pointed with his right hand to his heart. It was that flaming heart with its crown of thorns that always drew me in. I thought of that glowing heart, shining through His white tunic under His red robe, whenever Mama would rub Vick's Vapor Rub on my chest for a cold. However congested I might be, I knew that the Vick's and the Sacred Heart of Jesus would see me through the night. There is something holy about being down with a cold and breathing in camphor. I hoped that they were giving Mama a vaporizer full of Vick's every day at the hospital.

The candle flickered faint red light over everything in the room. Maybe seeing Grandma Keary's soul would be like the time Uncle Mickey showed me how photographs developed in the red light in his dark room. There was only blank paper to stare at, but the more you stared and the more Uncle Mickey washed it in some solution, the clearer the picture became. I knew I had to pay attention.

Almost immediately there seemed to be a fluttering at the corner of my vision. I gulped hard and turned my head in the direction of the candle. I couldn't make out what it was. If I blinked slowly and then opened my eyes it was gone. I wasn't even sure I had seen anything at all until I heard a little pinging sound against the votive glass. I held my breath as I stared at the edge of the darkness above the candle where something definitely was going on. I was starting to feel a little dizzy and was glad to exhale when a flitting moth came plainly into view. Just a moth. It must have gotten in through the tear in the screen that Uncle Mickey was always going to fix for Grandma.

I watched the moth wheeling openly now above the candle and noticed it was going lower and lower with each circle. I knew it would die if I did nothing. Catching a moth was easy, but making a move in this room where anything might happen was hard. I wanted to be safe. It started to dive bomb the center of light. "Wait!" I heard myself whisper as I lunged across the room and cupped my hands around it. Its batting wings tickled the inside of my hands. When I opened them I saw the streaks of silver-white dust on my palms. Their power is in their dust; if too much of it comes off, they can no longer fly. The moth must have noticed that I opened my hand for it to escape. It stopped fluttering and spread its shimmering wings long enough for me to see the patterns of little circles on them. They were like rows of eyes. Jackie said that they have them for camouflage. It makes birds looking down on them fly right by, thinking there are several tiny creatures looking back at them, not just one tasty moth.

This must be the cleverest of moths because it had large eyes and small eyes all over its wings. I admired it as it crawled to the tip of my finger and lifted itself into the air. It flew right towards the flame and before I could stop it was inside the glass. Its opened wings looked even more beautiful behind the red glass, but its legs were mired in the liquid wax and in an instant its wings went up like two sheets of paper in the fireplace. I turned away when its body began to singe and curl and my eyes met those of the Sacred Heart who calmly presided over the scene. He could do something if He wanted to. When I turned back again the moth was completely gone.

Jesus played for keeps, and it was hard to know what was on His mind.

You'd think if Jesus really wanted to make friends with everyone, He might come across more often in a pinch. And He'd make more of an attempt to smile in his pictures. I was tired of His pitiful face and that crown of thorns and all. I had my own problems. It burned me up that the Sacred Heart had been as much help to me as to that moth. It was probably a really big sin just to think that, but it was true. I gulped hard and stared back at His pale, changeless face.

Sister Mary Columba told us there were three ways to sin—in thought, word, and deed. Sinning in my head was easiest for me. She'd told me to busy my mind to keep from sinning. She suggested rehearsing spelling words in my head, which is what I tried to do now as I waited for Grandma Keary's soul. "Sacred" was itself a troublesome word to spell. Even though it came up in my homework with some frequency, I seemed to miss it about every other time. Just one letter needs to jump out of place to make it "scared." Tonight, there should be just the one word for how I felt being alone with my anger in the presence of the Sacred Heart of Jesus. I hoped He wouldn't know it was me sitting there in the dark.

Now that the moth was gone, His sacred eyes were the only others in the room. I reckoned I could see Him better than He could see me, but just to be sure I slowly moved to my left on the sofa to see if His eyes would follow. I squinted as hard as I could, but I still couldn't tell for sure. What if He was watching me? I pulled my knees up under Uncle Red's cardigan against the sudden chill. I held my knees and started to see if He would follow to the right. I moved a little too quickly, lost my balance and fell over on the sofa just as a breeze picked up outside and blew a gust through the screen. The candle flickered and caused light to dance across the holy face that seemed to wink at me. And who was there to say He hadn't?

Something must be underway.

When Uncle Conny appeared suddenly in the doorway, I figured he must know what was up because he walked directly to the candle and picked it up, but he only lit his cigarette from it. When he put it back on the ledge he sighed heavily and then leaned forward and stared out the window at the sky. He began to hum the tune that had been skirling around the living room a minute earlier. I figured what he had seen out the window made him happy, although I couldn't decide whether some of this *ceili* music was really happy or sad music. I suppose it didn't matter much because it was the beat that made them all dance just the same.

I didn't move but whispered very quietly, "Is it her, Uncle Conny?", hope clashing with fear that he had seen Grandma's soul.

He jumped and said, "Who's there?" as he bent over to pick up the lighted cigarette that had fallen from his mouth.

I didn't know if he was talking to me or to whomever he had seen out the window. I could see him and I figured he could see me.

"Is it Grandma, Uncle Conny?"

"Oh Lucy, is that you there?" he laughed, working the bit of ash into the singed carpet. "So much for the new owners, eh."

"What do you see, Uncle Conny?"

"Nothing Lucy. Just the old moon as she ducks in and out of the clouds. She's nearly full," he said pointing out the window.

His white shirt almost glowed in the sudden shaft of moonlight that he stood in. The room was bright enough to see the red pack of Winston's in the pocket over his heart. I thought he made a better Sacred Heart than the one on the wall.

"What are you doing here in the dark, Lucy?"

"Waiting."

"For your Grandma Fahey, do you mean, Lucy? She'll be a while yet. Red hasn't even left to get her."

"No sir, I am waiting for Grandma's Keary's soul to come home."

"Oh, I see. Mind if I wait with you then?" he smiled as he came to sit next to me on the sofa.

"No sir."

"Boy, oh boy, I am older than I realized and these knees are stiffer than I thought. I was trying out my old steps while McKee was warming up his boys. Can you keep a secret, Lucy?"

"Sure I can, Uncle Conny."

"I dance worse than I sing, and that's not a good thing to say about a Mick."

He fell onto the sofa without bending his knees. He reminded me of a tree being felled in a movie I saw about a very old forest in California where trees had been growing since the days of the crucifixion. I was glad I was not alone in my vigil, but I had to stop him when he reached for the table lamp.

"No, Uncle Conny. We won't be able to see her."

"Oh true enough, true enough." Then turning to me, he chuckled, "Lucy, you look like a little old lady at a wake, all huddled there, holding that crucifix. A little old Mayo woman, at that. You really should be out there dancing and playing with your cousins, not in here by yourself."

"She's coming, isn't she, Uncle Conny? Why else would Uncle Red have put the candle here?"

I didn't think he even heard my question.

"Lucy you're not wearing that rosary, are you?" He laughed, "They are not for wearing, you know."

"I need it for protection."

"Exactly whom do you need protection from, Lucy?"

"The faeries. I think they took Grandma away," I confessed.

I found myself telling Uncle Conny things I couldn't tell Grandma Fahey or even Uncle Red. I had tried to tell Uncle Red about the faeries before, but he didn't seem to understand.

If anyone were to ever understand my situation it would be here and now in this room. Uncle Conny seemed different in this light from his usual boisterous self. He was bigger than Uncle Red and since he smoked only cigarettes he didn't have the sweet rich pipe tobacco smell to him that Uncle Red did. I sat close enough to him to notice that a licorice smell was coming from the Sens Sens he kept in his shirt pocket with his Winstons. I hadn't spent as much time with him as I had with Uncle Red, but sometimes strangers are best to talk to.

Once I asked the man who was filling the dairy case at the A&P if milking hurt the cows. This was something I had felt bad about for some time. When the stranger smiled and said, "Not at all," I felt much better about the way the world works. Uncle Conny wasn't a stranger, but I don't remember ever talking to him as I was now unable to stop myself from doing.

He didn't take his eyes off me while I talked, and the look on his face passed from alarm to a smile and back again, as quickly as the moon outside passed through the clouds. I felt better just telling Uncle Conny everything.

"I didn't mean for it to happen, but they took her away to get back at me for trying to play a trick on them," I concluded.

"Is that what you think happened, Lucy?"

"I need to see Grandma once more to tell her I am sorry."

His face lighted up from the glow of his cigarette, "Lucy, there are very few things in life that I am as certain of as the fact that the faeries didn't take your grandmother. Do you hear me, Lucy?"

"How do you know that, Uncle Conny?"

"Simple logic, Lucy. Your grandma is a Quinn, is she not?"

I nodded.

"Well there is no Quinn that has been bothered by the faeries since they left Ireland."

"How come?"

"Faeries don't travel well, Lucy. It is universally known that faeries get terribly seasick. And when they got a look at some of the leaky old boats our people left on, they decided not to follow them to America but to seek employment on dry land, closer to home. Many of them went to Ulster. They pester folks there to this very day."

"But Grandma Fahey says the faeries steal stuff just to get your attention. And that they knew that

Uncle Natty had died and brought her a rose to say they were sorry for it, even though they might have caused it."

"Ah, but Lucy, those would be the Mayo faeries. We are from Galway. Big difference there. Let me look at your face a bit closer. Oh sure, sure, you are safe from them, too. You've enough of Galway about you. You don't need any special protection from the faeries."

Uncle Conny left his cigarette dangling from his mouth as he lifted the rosary from around my neck. "So you see, Lucy, you are off the hook. Maggie's passing was not your doing."

If it wasn't the faeries, I needed to know what other trickster was in charge of things.

"Who took her away then?"

"No one took her, Lucy." The smile drained from his face. "It was just her time to go. Everyone has one. This was Maggie's."

His eyes filled.

"Uncle Conny, does my mom know that Grandma is gone?"

"Yes, she knows, Lucy."

"What if, what if she wants to go on to Heaven with her own mom more than she wants to stay here with me?" I spurted this out with warm tears that surprised me. I didn't even know that this was what I thought.

Uncle Conny looked surprised, too, as he told me not to cry anymore because crying children made him nervous.

"Look, Lucy, your mom misses you like the devil. Just give her some more time. It won't be that much longer. What she has been through takes some getting used to before she comes home to you. She's much better Lucy. It is a big adjustment."

What about me? What about what I had been through?

"Does she even know where I am?"

"Red called your dad at the hospital after he called Mrs. Fahey. You worried them both, Lucy, fleeing the ancestral House of Fahey as you did." Uncle Conny laughed, "I think you got their attention. Come to think of it, you running away may be the thing Rosie needs to put her mind off her troubles."

He looked at my eyes like he was checking to make sure I wasn't going to start crying again. "And you'll see your Grandma Keary in Heaven someday too, Lucy, unless you aren't planning on going there yourself. Somebody out in those suburbs might slip you a cheeseburger on a Friday. Then who knows?" He laughed his fierce Uncle Conny laugh that shook the love seat.

"I'm pulling your leg, Lucy. Don't look so worried. You've got it made. What do they call your parish out there again, Mary of the Social Climbers?"

"No sir, it's Mary of Gaels."

"Oh, of Gaels, is it? I keep forgetting," he said as he took another long drag on his Winston. "Lucy, do you know what a Gael is?"

I thought that it had something to do with a storm. Once during a tornado warning, I heard Grandma Keary say that the wind was blowing with the force of a gale and that we would have to go to the basement. I thought therefore that a gale was the force that caused storms, but wasn't sure so I didn't say so.

"No, sir."

"Well," said Uncle Conny as if he expected that answer, "I'll give you a clue, Lucy. I'm a Gael. So's your Uncle Red and your Grandma Keary. And even your Grandma Fahey."

I considered Uncle Conny's riddle half because I wanted to figure it out and half because I knew Uncle Conny didn't want me to cry anymore. It seemed to make sense that he came from some sort of stormy gale. While I didn't think that Grandma Fahey had much in common with Uncle Conny, except that they could both become blustery storms when giving their opinions, I couldn't relate Grandma Keary's quiet and gentle ways and Uncle Red's mild humor to what I assumed was a Gael.

Uncle Conny snuffed out his cigarette in an ashtray on a table next to him and laughed, "Give up, Lucy? Well, I'll tell you. The Gaels are your tribe, so to speak. Your race. Your people are from the same bit of ground in east Galway since rocks could talk."

Laughter and clapping exploded in the next room as one furious fiddle tune ended.

"Am I one, too, Uncle Conny?"

"You are indeed, Lucy, that's exactly my point. You are what you are." He patted me on the knee. "You are indeed a Gael. And you have some good Norman blood in you too, being related to the Burkes and the Mansfields as you are. But all good Irishmen. And did you know that we have special saints that watch out for our kind, Lucy? St. Brigid, for one. She's your Mary of the Gael."

I looked away from him. I didn't want to hear any more about saints who were supposed to help out but never got around to it. It made me feel worse if they helped out other kids, but not me. Besides, I knew by the way he talked about St. Brigid that he didn't really believe in her as much as he believed in being a Quinn. I could only take so much cheering up.

"Uncle Conny, you don't think she's coming tonight, do you?"

He only sighed.

"I just want to know. I won't cry. I promise."

He drummed his fingers on the arm of his chair. "Have you not been paying attention at all, Lucy Fahey?"

I'd never tried harder to understand anything since Grandma died.

"Dead or alive, the clan is still the clan. You belong to her and she to you. She's here because you are, because we all are."

"Prof Ryan says she is like the stars, do you think that is true?"

"Hmm," he said.

I wished he could tell me that she was some place a little closer to home.

"I don't know what all happens when you die, we'll leave that to Prof and his cronies to speculate, but what I know is that there are things that never change, Lucy. Your grandma will be looking out for you and you may not ever even know it."

"But why did she have to go?"

"I don't know that anyone knows that Lucy," he said softly. "But did you never hear the story that's passed down of your great grandmother Keary?"

He started twining Grandma's rosary around his tobacco stained index finger as he began the story. "She lost her way as a child far from her home and was out the entire night trying to find her way. She climbed over stone fence after stone fence, cutting across the farm lands with the moonlight her only guide. She was so cold and of course she was very hungry, this being in famine times, and then the snow began to fall. She gave in to her weariness and fell asleep not knowing if she would ever wake. It was the warmth of the blanket and the steam off of an oatmeal porridge over a fire that woke her in the middle of the night. An old man, and him with a missing leg, sat beside her stirring the fire. She asked his name and was told it was Declan. He told her she has only a mile to go to the road back to her town of Drumkeary. She ate and fell back to sleep knowing she'd make it home. Next morning the old man was gone, and no sign the fire had ever been."

"Where did he go, Uncle Conny?" I sat up to ask my question. He didn't answer but kept weaving the rosary between his fingers to make a cat's cradle. "Did he know her?" I was on my feet standing in front of him demanding to hear the rest.

"Oh, he knew her all right, Lucy, but she didn't know him."

"Who was he?"

"Her people told her, when she made it home again, about Declan Keary who had died years before from his leg wounds in the uprising of 1798. Shot through by the Brits. He tried to make it home but died along the roadside, a mile or so from Drumkeary."

"Maybe she just dreamed she saw him. I always have dreams that seem real to me."

"You'd think that, Lucy, except for one thing. He left her the blanket. She had it wrapped around her when she made it to her home." He reached over and buttoned the two top buttons on Uncle Red's cardigan that hung from my shoulders. "In the daylight she saw what looked like powder burns and blood stains."

I looked at Uncle Conny's forearms to see if his hair was standing up like mine. "Where is it now, the blanket?"

"Well Lucy, that was a very long time ago, and it was an old thing when the little girl was given it. They may have left it in Galway when they left. Or, maybe it just went to dust."

"I wish I could've seen that blanket." I could hardly wait to tell Jackie this story.

"Here's your rosary back, Lucy." He wound it around my right hand and gave it one tug to tighten it. "So remember, Lucy, kin are kin even after they leave this earth. Well, I see you are on your feet now. You feel like dancing, do you?"

I could feel the rhythm of the dancers' feet on the floorboards like the beat of a heart.

"No sir, I don't know how to dance."

"Yes sir. No sir," he echoed. "You are the politest little kid I've ever seen. Is it your old man that makes you come up with the 'yes sir, no sir' routine?"

"Yes sir."

"It is just like the Faheys to be always looking for ways to put on the dog. Well, you don't have to call me sir, in fact I order you not to. I demand that you address me as Cornelius Arthur Quinn."

"Cornelius?" I laughed.

"An outrageous moniker, don't you think?"

"I guess so. What's a moniker?"

"My name. You have my permission anytime to say to me, 'Cornelius Quinn you old gray con artist, how the hell have you been?'"

I knew I would never say that, but I liked the idea of it.

The crowd in the next room was growing in size and rowdiness. I could hear more people walking up the front steps and shouting hello to one another. It was the familiar squeak of Grandma's screen door that made me finally ask, "She's not going to come back tonight, is she, Uncle Conny?"

"How do you know she isn't already here, Lucy?"

I didn't.

"Come on now, Lucy, help me up from this couch."

I took both of his hands and pulled as hard as I could. He lifted himself, laughing, from the love seat, but couldn't resist making a show of falling backward again when I let go of his hands. The jolt of him falling back against the couch and the wall made the little parlor shake. It was enough to knock the Sacred Heart picture crooked on its hook.

"Will you look at that, Lucy," he said, pointing to the picture that seemed to sway in time to "The Red

Haired Boy," a jig tune coming from the living room. "It's the jiggin' Jesus, Himself."

Uncle Conny gave the picture another swing when it started to slow down, saying, "We'll make Him dance to our tune for once, eh Lucy?"

I thought it was scary to make fun of Jesus, but because Uncle Conny enjoyed his own joke so much, Jesus seemed more of a pal that Uncle Conny might slap on the back.

"C'mon, now Lucy. Let's go and enjoy the evening while we can. Mrs. Fahey will be here soon and that will put a damper on everyone's fun. You know now, Lucy, your Grandma Keary wouldn't want you brooding over her. Not on a summer night like this with all your little cousins about."

"Yes sir, Uncle Conny."

He raised his hand to correct me, but before he could I added, "you old gray con man." That seemed close to what he had told me to call him.

"It's artist, Lucy. Your great uncle is an old gray con artist."

Then he winked.

Chapter 18: The Cyclops

When a pack of local boy cousins ran by the parlor laughing and heading for the front door, followed in hot pursuit by a Chicago cousin, Uncle Conny laughed and said, "Go on Lucy, run outside with your cousins while you can."

I stood in the hallway and looked back to the dark room where Uncle Conny was straightening up the Sacred Heart picture. I didn't really want to leave the room at all. I was surprised how far down the votive light had burned. I worried that it wouldn't last all night.

Just short of the front door Limes Quinn, who had been caught by a bigger Chicago cousin determined to give him an Indian burn, was calling out for reinforcements.

Uncle Conny had lighted another Winston from the votive candle and turned to me as if he were surprised I was still there. "Go on now, Lucy. You go play before you forget how."

But what if something happened here while I was gone? I was torn—until Jim Pat, the red haired penny whistle player, ran by. I quickly took off Uncle Red's cardigan, tossed it to Uncle Conny, and bolted towards the front door.

"Good girl, Lucy. I'll hold down the fort here," called Uncle Conny.

As I pushed open the screen door of Grandma's porch, I thought I heard her voice so clearly in the familiar squeaking of the door, telling me, "Don't stray too far, darlin.'" When I turned back to peer in through the screen, the porch was empty.

Out on the curb there were seven boy cousins. Limes was leading them in howling at the full moon. I recognized some of these far-flung cousins from other family gatherings. Most of them had sat behind me at Grandma's funeral Mass. There was Jodie, who was from Arkansas and could catch lizards with his bare hands and outrun even Jackie. Mike was friendly with Jackie; his brother, Leo, was my age but the smallest one in the group. Little Pat on the other hand was taller than even Limes. He was called Little Pat because his dad was already Young Pat Herlihy. This was almost like having Jackie around to play with, except I never felt shy around him.

As I walked towards the group, Limes called, "Hey, I saw you at the funeral. You are not from Chicago or anything weird like that, are you? Larry here thinks Chicago guys are better than us."

He jabbed his thumb at the biggest cousin in the gang. Larry leaned against the street light pole with his arms crossed and coolly answered, "I don't think it, I know it."

"I'm from Chicago," said the penny whistle player proudly.

"You're too little to even count, Jim Pat," said Larry.

Jim Pat looked about my age.

"I'm from here," I said, admiring the way Jim Pat carried his whistle in the back pocket of his jeans.

"You don't go to our school, do you?" asked Limes.

"I go to Mary of Gaels," I answered, although that sounded like another country even to me.

"I heard of them," Limes said. "They stink at football. Kids from the fancy schools over on the Kansas side fall down before they even get tackled."

"The Gaels are good at baseball," I said. "My brother Jackie is the pitcher."

"Hey, she must be Jackie Fahey's sister, Limes," Mike said sizing me up.

I guess I didn't mind Jackie's name opening one more door for me.

"I'm Lucy."

"I'm Limes Quinn."

"I know who you are, Limes." Just saying his name made my mouth pucker and water. "How come you have a name like that?"

"I had a nun in second grade who couldn't pronounce my real name, Liam. She was from Georgia or some place. Sometimes she called me 'Lamb.'" Larry hooted at this. "And sometimes it sounded like *Liiime*." He drawled out the short word into a long one that made everyone laugh. "My dad said I reminded him more of a lime than a lamb, so he just called me Limes. I like limes. It's like my trademark."

"Yeah that's how they figured out who pulled the stunt last Holy Saturday night at church," laughed Little Pat.

"I put lime fizzies in the holy water font during *Tenebrae*," he proudly explained. "You know, when they put out the candles and shut off the lights and everybody has to wait in the dark for them to light the candles again. I got three days suspension with no school."

Even tough Larry from the big city smiled at this form of bravery.

"How come you did that?" I asked.

"I had to. It was a dare." He answered so solemnly that the dare seemed more sacred than the *Tenebrae* ritual itself. He laughed and rubbed the back of his legs where a belt might have struck when he got home.

"Anybody want to play Truth or Dare now?" he challenged the group, eyeing Larry.

"Can I play?" I asked looking down at my shoes.

"She can't play, can she Limes?" asked Leo.

Everyone looked to Limes. I'd seen similar looks on boys' faces the night of the campfire in the field behind our house. Jackie's friends had looked at him that same way before he told me to turn my back when they all took leaks into the fire at the end of the night.

"You really want to play, Lucy?" asked Limes.

"Hey wait, she's not part of the club. She's a girl," said Little Pat.

"What club?" I asked.

"Just the club, we don't have a name or anything," said Limes.

I'd heard about this club from Jackie. It was a loose affiliation of cousins that met to play Truth or Dare at family reunions. Jackie told me about his initiation when the family was gathered at some cousin's house near the cathedral in St. Louis. He'd taken a dare that nobody else had. Since this was their neighborhood it was up to the older St. Louis cousins to set the dare. That night they gave him a map that led up the hill, across a busy boulevard to a place called the Hall of the Reptile King. When he found it, Jackie had to pound on the door three times, shout his name loud enough so that the Reptile King could hear him, and then turn his back and count backwards from 100 to see if it would snatch him.

I'd shivered when he told me the dare, and shivered again when my dad drove us up the hill the next morning on our way back home. We passed a huge domed building whose greenish tiles looked like scales, a likely reptile headquarters.

"Look, Jackie, the Hall of the Reptile King?

"Yup, that's it, Luce," he'd said looking out the window. "But in the daytime it's called the St. Louis Cathedral."

"She can't be in the club unless she does a dare, like everybody else," Little Pat insisted now.

"Can't I just tell the truth about something?"

Truth didn't matter much to these cousins, in fact, I don't know why they even called it Truth or Dare.

"Nah, we need a good dare," Limes said. "You'll have to put a spell on somebody."

"I don't know any spells, Limes."

"Don't you even know the black cat hex, Lucy?"

I shook my head.

"It's a secret spell that only we know. We'll tell you, but only because you are a cousin. You can't help being a girl," Limes said.

"If she does her dare, does that mean she can be part of the club?" Little Pat asked indignantly.

Leo said, "Don't worry. She's not going to take the dare. We'll make it a really good one."

Limes said seriously, "Now here's what you do to cast the black cat spell. You have to say three times, 'Scat! Scat! Now you're an old black cat!' But it will only work when there's a full moon like there is tonight."

We all looked up to the moon and Mike and Jodie started in on the howling noises again.

This hex didn't seem so hard. I looked around the ring of round faces to make my choice of which cousin I'd most like to see as a black cat. Probably Little Pat.

"Wait a minute, Lucy, you can't put the hex on any of us. You have to go down the street and around the corner, and go down the alley to find your victim." Limes pointed to the darkness beyond our little circle gathered under the streetlight.

This changed everything. I avoided the alleys even in the daytime. When I rode my bike around Grandma

Keary's neighborhood, I always built up speed to whisk myself by the opening to that alley. We didn't have alleys in Mary of Gaels parish, but Jackie told me to stay out of them in the city because they have rats. I'd never seen a rat but I liked the little field mice that came into our garage when the weather got cold. Jackie told me that rats are absolutely nothing like that. They were much larger with long tails, pointy teeth and they travel in big packs like public school kids. If they bit you, you'd get sick and die.

"Do I have to go there by myself?" I asked, trying not to sound too scared.

"Nope," said Limes looking around the group. He suddenly turned and pointed to Little Pat and said, "He'll go with you."

"No way, Limes," sniffed Little Pat.

"You have to go with her. How will we know if she does the dare?" said Limes.

"How come I have to go?" Little Pat protested.

Mike and Leo made chicken noises.

"Because I said so," said Limes.

"I'm not going down the alley. I got nothing to prove. I'm already in the club."

The chicken clucking had gotten louder by the time Jim Pat announced, "I'm not scared. I'll go with her."

I looked gratefully at him as he sat on the curb to undo the knot that Limes had tied in his shoe earlier. Jim Pat's round smiling face under his copper hair reminded me of a new penny.

"Step forward, Lucy Fahey," commanded Limes. As I stood in the center of the circle, Limes put both hands on my shoulders and asked, "Do you know which alley I mean, Lucy? It's the one behind the brick apartments."

I knew the one he meant. It is the worst alley there was. The rows of brownstones that made up the two sides were much taller than any houses in Grandma's neighborhood so at night it seemed to swallow up any streetlight or moonlight. It was narrow and deep and so dark that you just assumed there was no end to it. They say stray cats would go down the alley and never return. Any noises that woke me up at night at Grandma Keary's I figured came from that alley.

"But Limes, what if there's nobody in the alley?" I hoped that would be the case.

"You'll just have to find somebody to put the hex on. You can't come back until you do. Those are the rules. I can't change them just because it is a dangerous mission and you are a girl. But take my rabbit's foot ... well, just in case." He untied the furry white object that was fastened to the belt loop of his jeans. "Here, take it, Lucy. No one goes down that alley at night. No one knows what might be in it."

"You scared, Lucy?" grinned Little Pat.

"No," I lied my biggest lie all summer.

"Remember, Lucy, three times, or else we are all dead by tomorrow night."

"But why, Limes, why would we be dead by tomorrow night?" I would have preferred to stand around in the familiarity of Grandma Keary's yard discussing the finer points of casting spells than to head towards the unknown.

"That's just the way it is," he pronounced. "Go on, you two. Unless you're too scared."

"I'm not scared one bit," countered Jim Pat so confidently that I believed him.

We stepped out of the ring of light and started our long walk to the alley. Jodie called out, "We'll never see them two again," and Mike started droning, "Pray for the dead and the dead will pray for you."

The bright music and laughter that came from Grandma's house became fainter and fainter as we proceeded down what was a friendly street by day. The night, however, was full of eyes. The full moon itself seemed a great watchful eye—sometimes alert, sometimes sleepy, sometimes smiling, sometimes worried—depending on the angle of the clouds that arched over it like an eyebrow. As we walked along I watched the moon's reflected eye change in the puddles along our way. I splashed my shoe in the middle of one puddle where an angry reflected eye stared up at me and thought of Grandma Fahey on her way to Grandma Keary's house.

"My feet are cold," I complained to Jim Pat, who had on black high-top Converse basketball shoes.

"That's because you have on girl shoes," he said as if I had any choice in the matter.

My socks hadn't been dry since I ran through the rain to St. Ignatius. I wished I had Uncle Red's cardigan.

We walked on in silence until Jim Pat asked, "So, who is Rose Fahey anyway? My mom has us praying for her second cousin, Rose Fahey in Kansas City. Who is she?"

There wasn't any easy answer. Sometimes my mom didn't seem real to me anymore. Her absence had become like an empty space that enveloped me, sometimes like a comforting memory, but sometimes frightening like the darkness that surrounded me now. If I reached to try to touch the empty space, there was nothing there.

"Everyone's been praying for her all summer so that she won't die."

"She's my mom. OK?" His words were as hard to hear as it was to see through the deepest part of this dark night. And I was embarrassed that we needed anybody's prayers. "That's stupid. She's not going to die. My Uncle Red says so."

"You mean 'cause everyone in the whole family has been praying?"

"No. How can she? She's our mom. That's stupid."

"Hey, don't get so mad. I was praying for her and I didn't even know who she was. I was just asking is all. I'm sorry, Lucy."

I wanted to talk about anything else, but all I could think of was to pick on Jim Pat for being from Chicago. "Yeah, well, people from Chicago talk funny."

"No way. People from Kansas City talk funny. You talk too slow down here."

"Do not."

"Do so."

"I'm from Kansas, not Missouri, anyway."

Jim Pat laughed and said after a pause, "If you want to hear somebody that really talks funny it's my Grandpa McKee, especially when we wake him up from his naps. My mom says he talking in Irish, but its sounds the same to me as when he talks without his dentures. He's all *a musha musha a hammish*."

I giggled as Jim Pat gummed out more sounds.

"So what. My Grandma Fahey talks in Irish whenever she wants to. She's teaching me so I can talk to the faeries."

"Faeries? Nobody believes in them except old ladies. My Grandma Gargan thinks they drowned her cat in Lake Michigan. It really got hit by a bus, but my dad didn't want to tell her that since the driver lives in our building. So he pinned it on the faeries."

"How do you know they don't exist, Jim Pat? My Grandma's granny says that they can steal you away if you listen to their music, and guess what, you have to wander the earth as a faery changeling."

He just shrugged like nothing could be more mysterious and scary than the alley we were now in front of. The moonlight made jagged shadows of the brownstone apartments on our path. I wished I were back at Grandma's Keary's noisy living room, even if Grandma Fahey was on her way there. I'd rather have faced her anger than the alley that loomed before us.

"Wait a sec. Did you hear that, Lucy?"

I hadn't heard anything except my heart pounding in my ear. Now I heard what sounded like some creature splashing through a puddle. It could be a rat coming out to bite us on the ankles.

"My Grandma Fahey will be really mad if I'm not back at Grandma Keary's house when she gets there. I've got to explain why I ran away, and ..."

"Pipe down, Lucy. It's coming this way. Listen," Jim Pat said.

Another sloshy, rummaging sound and then an opossum padded its way to the streetlight. It was the biggest one I had ever seen and the only one I had seen up close. It was a spooky creature with its chalky, mask-like face that looked like death itself. It stood between the alley and us. There was more to living in the city than I realized, like knowing rats from opossums. I liked that about Jim Pat, that he knew the difference. Jackie would have too.

It sniffed the air like it was us that brought that dank smell.

It was the weirdest animal I had ever seen except in a dream. I reckoned it was already trapped in some awful jinx that made it as ugly as it was and forced it to live in that alley full time. It probably wouldn't even notice another little spell more or less.

"Hey, I'll just cast the spell on it. Then I can get back before my Grandma Fahey gets here."

"I don't think so, Lucy. It's gotta be a real person."

Jim Pat shouted at it, but it did not move. He ran up to it yelling as if he were going to kick it, but the opossum still did not budge. Something about the way it stood its ground reminded me of Grandma Fahey. Jim Pat was looking around for something to throw.

"Here, take this," he said handing me some gravel. "We'll pelt him when I count three."

"I don't think we ought to make it mad," I argued.

"If I tell them you were scared of a broken down opossum, you'll never get into the club," he taunted.

When Jim Pat threw his handful of gravel, I threw mine, too, but turned away hoping that it wouldn't hit the target. The rain of stones hitting the critter was followed by a hissing sound but the opossum did not give an inch. When I turned back around the fur on its back seemed to stand up and made it seem like it was getting bigger, or trying to.

"I got an idea." Jim Pat took his penny whistle from the back pocket and blew a loud high scale of notes. The animal scurried one way and then the other and finally gave up the entrance to the alley.

"I thought that music spell would get him." Jim Pat crossed his arms and smiled like I'd seen Jackie do after holding the door for a girl at the CYO mixer. But this was no school dance.

I squinted into the dark alleyway. I wanted to turn back. Grandma Fahey really would be double mad at me if I wasn't there when Uncle Red brought her to Grandma Keary's. I was the only one in the whole place she liked, and she might not even like me much anymore. The light in the window was burning still, but how much longer? And what if Jackie found out I didn't live up to my dare?

"Do you want me to stand guard here or go in with you?" Jim Pat asked. When I didn't answer, he said, "C'mon, Lucy."

My eyes were beginning to adjust to the alley darkness. We were no more than ten slow steps into the alley, when the back door of a first-floor apartment only yards in front of us suddenly swung open and a man came out. He quickly lifted the metal lid of a trash barrel and dropped something into it, all the while talking to his wife who sat in the well-lighted kitchen.

We froze in the shadows and looked at each other. He was too quick to cast a spell on, so we moved on. From other apartments we could hear sounds that grew as we approached and then faded as we passed by. It was like turning a radio dial very slowly to bring in one station and then another. Women were doing the dishes and rising steam made the kitchen windows glow. I thought I might cry to look in at these warm cozy homes feeling like such an outsider. TV sets flickered fuzzy gray light on our otherwise dark path. Jimmy Durante was disappearing in and out of his trademark spotlights saying good night to Mrs. Calabash from most sets.

We had nearly come to the end of the alley when we heard the voice of a radio announcer coming from a screened porch on the second floor, where a man sat in the dark listening to the baseball game.

"A swing and a miss," the announcer proclaimed.

We stopped and watched the man in silence. I flinched when he stood up suddenly. Did he know why I was there? The man began to pace the floor of the little porch. His rimless glasses flatly reflected the light in the sky. I imagined a monster with two vacant white eyes.

When the next pitch was announced, he stopped his pacing, crouched in a batter's stance with an imaginary bat.

"Two and two the count at the bottom of the eighth. Runners on first and second. Here's the pitch. Low and inside. ..."

"Good eye." The man quietly congratulated himself for not swinging.

Jim Pat looked at me and said, "He's your only chance, Lucy."

We continued to watch my victim as he took a few warm-up swings between pitches.

"Here's the 3-2 pitch ..." The announcer's voice rose, and then sank. "A swing and a miss on a pitch that was high and away. That's the inning folks."

The man collapsed in his chair and with his head in his hands and cried, "What a bonehead! It was 3 and 2. Those bums will never get out of the cellar."

Jim Pat pointed at the fire escape that ran up the side of the building next to the porch. That would put me in spell casting range. I put my foot on the first rung and grabbed the cold metal railing. I felt some paint flake off in my hand.

"Go on, Lucy. It's the perfect setup," Jim Pat said.

In the cheering from the radio as the A's pitcher caught fire against the bottom of the White Sox order, I clambered up the ladder imagining myself as smugly, happily part of the boy cousins' club. The fans were cheering me on.

By the time I reached the landing next to the porch our pitcher had retired the side. I watched my victim sitting in silence. The light from his cigarette as it moved from his mouth to his side was red and menacing. The orange glow of the radio dial was reflected on his belt buckle. His undershirt was as white as the moon. The quick double pop and fizz of his beer can being opened punctuated the radio announcer's patter. If Limes' hex really worked he wouldn't know what hit him.

I opened my mouth and tried to utter my spell, but I had forgotten how to talk altogether.

"Go on, Lucy," Jim Pat whispered from the alley below me.

The sound was just enough to rouse a sleepy old dog that sat on the floor next to the man. The dog barked. The man called, "Who's out there?"

I froze to the metal landing until I realized that he was talking to his cocker spaniel, "Is somebody out in your alley, Polly? Some big cat after you? You're worthless," he said affectionately to the dog that had circled its spot on the floor and curled up again.

There was no more noise from Jim Pat in the alley below. I clung in silence to the fire escape. The voice from the radio hung in the air like the full moon. "Well, we're at the top of the order here in the bottom of the 9th. It's do or die for Kansas City. Two away. The Sox lead by one."

Suddenly Jim Pat whispered again from the darkness. He was just a few steps away from me on the stairs. "Lucy, you don't have to. I'll tell Limes you did. That guy might call the cops or something. Let's scram." We both stood silently watching the eye of the cigarette as it moved through the darkness.

"There's the first pitch, what a beauty. O and one."

I couldn't move.

"Here's the wind up," sang the sports announcer.

"C'mon. Let's get the hell out of here," said Jim Pat.

Never thinking I wouldn't take the reprieve, Jim Pat turned so quickly on the metal landing that his Converse squeaked. The sound alerted the dog that was barking wildly by the time Jim Pat's shoes slapped the alley.

The man jumped up and demanded, "What's going on out there?"

I felt as exposed as a slow change up pitch coming over the plate suspended above the alleyway as I was.

He tilted his head to get a better look at me, "You better not be one of the Morrissey kids again. I'll call your parents this time. Leave me alone and get off my fire escape."

"Man, oh man, he connected on that breaking fastball." The announcer was yelling above the noise of the crowd.

I did not move or answer. The dog was now on its hind legs leaning against the screen, still barking.

"The center fielder will have to hustle to get under this one, folks. That ball was hit a mile high!"

"Quiet down Polly," the man hollered pulling her by the collar. He waved me off with his free arm. "You get down from there right now or I'll call your mother."

Let him try.

"He's going back, back, back. He's back to the warning track," sang the voice from Comiskey Park.

The man let go of the dog to turn up the radio for the final play. It was now or never for my spell. "Sca-sca-scat," I stuttered.

The dog charged the flimsy screen that separated us, barking louder. The man bellowed, "Don't tear that screen again, you mutt!"

The announcer's voice was high and thin over the swelling sounds of the fans and the husky woofing of the dog underneath. All of this racket was just like the opera at Grandma's earlier today. It gave me an idea. From some unfrozen part of me came a voice like that of my namesake soprano, Lucia di Lammermoor, that sang, "Scat, scat, you old black cat."

The shrill pitch of my spell-casting voice caused the pace of the dog's woofing to quicken, nearly drowning out the announcer so that only intermittent phrases could be heard: "It's off the wall ... he bobbled it!"

The man yanked the dog away from the screen again.

"Cut off throw kicked up dust at second. ..."

I wound up and pitched my spell loud and clear at him a second time. "Scat, scat, you old black cat!"

The dog's barking was now frantic, almost hoarse, as the man dragged her over so that he could turn the radio up even louder. In exasperation he roared, "Shut up, Polly. And I told you to go home!"

"They're waving him home, folks. The fans are on their feet."

I turned and scrambled down the fire escape. I wanted nothing more than to join up with Jim Pat who was now nearly halfway down the alley. "Scat, scat," I yelled as loud as I could, not looking back. I held my breath and dropped from the bottom of the ladder, just as Jim Pat had, and exhaled "you old black cat." My feet hit the alley with a sting. The dog was yelping over the crescendo of the fans and the rising and falling voice of the announcer whose words were indistinguishable, except for the final one, "... thrilling."

"I missed the last play," the man whined. He reminded me a bit of the clown, Pagliacci, in Grandma's other opera record.

"That's the ballgame, folks. I wish the fans at home could have seen this finish at Comiskey Park," said the announcer.

"I wish this fan could have just heard this one," the man moaned. He turned the radio down as it went to a commercial for Gillette razor blades. "Ethyl," he called to someone inside the apartment, "call your brother and find out what happened."

I was now running up the alley as fast as I could. Lights were going on up and down the alley, and off in the distance I heard the caterwauling of what I imagined was a real black cat doing battle somewhere with that opossum. I ran faster when I thought that maybe my spell had worked and the eerie sound was the man turning into a black cat. I didn't stop running until I cleared the alley and made my way to Jim Pat, who was bending over with his hands on his knees, still breathing hard.

We looked at each other and took off running again. We ran wordlessly back to Grandma Keary's where Jim Pat announced to the other cousins as he caught his breath, "Lucy put the spell on a guy at the end of the alley."

"What guy?" Limes asked.

"Last apartment on the right. Two floors up," Jim Pat panted.

Mike and Leo looked at each other and laughed nervously and Leo said, "Uh oh, that's Mr. Daugherty, he's the meanest man in the building."

"He calls the principal at St. Nat's anytime a lousy pumpkin gets smashed in front of his building and somebody happens to slip and fall, or a snowball accidently breaks something," Mike complained. "Serves him right to be turned into a cat who can't dial a telephone anymore."

Leo laughed, "He'll be an ugly cat. Will he still have to wear those thick glasses when he's a cat?"

Little Pat said, "Leo, you dope," but then chortled, "How about it, Limes, will he still walk to church on Sunday wearing his big hat on his little cat head?" Little Pat and Leo fell into the silliness of this possibility.

But Limes took this seriously and said to me as he looked from Jim Pat's face to mine, "Lucy, did you say it three times?"

"Yeah, she did. Right to his face," said Jim Pat as I nodded my head to confirm.

"Did the spell take?" asked Limes.

"Probably not right away," explained Jim Pat. "He chased us down the alley and so did his dog. It was a wild dog. A hunting dog. It was fierce. You should have seen it. It tried to get at Lucy." He made a claw of his right hand and swiped at the air. "Right, Lucy?"

"Yeah, it tore a hole in the screen and jumped on the fire escape. It had fangs, too." I improvised a few details that seemed mostly true.

"Yeah, long, white fangs, like a saber tooth tiger," Jim Pat rejoined.

"The man was yelling at me the whole time," I added.

"Hmm," said Limes judicially. "He probably knew the counter hex. What was he saying?"

"We couldn't make it out, Limes, it might have been the counter hex," Jim Pat said.

"He threw a baseball bat at us," I said, looking at Jim Pat.

"A baseball bat?" asked Mike and Limes together.

"Well, we ducked. We had to get out of there quick. That wild animal was starting to catch up to us, so we ran like hell," said Jim Pat careful not to let the drama fall off its pace.

"Yeah," I said, "and the guy took off his belt to swat us if he caught us."

Limes rubbed the back of his leg, looking worried for the first time, and asked, "Did Mr. Daugherty really chase you? He might figure out who we are."

"He doesn't know Lucy, and Jim Pat's from Chicago," assured Little Pat.

"Don't worry Limes, he wasn't fast enough to catch us. We wore the old man out. But not that wild dog," said Jim Pat.

"If this is true," said Mike, "where's the dog now? How come the dog didn't chase you all the way here?"

Jim Pat and I paused in our story telling frenzy, looked at each other, and then he raised the stakes. "Now that's just the weirdest thing. The dog chased us to the end of the alley and then it stopped because it was starting to change into something else ..."

"Just like in that werewolf movie we saw, Limes." Leo was caught up in the spell of the moment.

"Yeah, it was just like a werewolf, Leo," Jim Pat said, a bit relieved.

"But why would it change into something else. It was already a dog and that's close to a wolf. Werewolves are guys who become like wolves," Little Pat questioned.

"Shut up, Little Pat. What did it change into?" demanded Leo.

Jim Pat looked at me. I searched for something fearsome to say. He gave me a worried sidelong glance, knowing that he'd most likely have to agree with whatever I said next. Then it hit me. I turned to the assembled members of this select club and said, "The wild dog turned into a huge 'possum that hissed steam at us."

Jim Pat looked crestfallen, but that small opossum was scary enough to me.

"Oh, that's not so scary, Lucy, 'possums aren't scary," said Mike. "Even Leo's not afraid of them. We have them in our alley."

But Jim Pat said slowly, "Lucy's right. It was a 'possum. A giant, white 'possum, six feet tall, with long pointy teeth," and as he looked around at Limes, Mike, Little Pat, Larry, Jodie and Leo, added, "with blood on them."

Mike "oohed" appreciatively at the turn the story took, but Leo looked anxiously down the street and mumbled something that might have been the opening lines of the Act of Contrition. Limes, however, proceeded with the wisdom and authority of being the oldest, saying, "He was white you say?" He raised an eyebrow "Did he have one eye or two?"

I was thinking three, but Jim Pat spoke first, anxious to redeem himself in the eyes of his male cousins. "Just one, but it was bright red and in the middle of its face."

After surveying his cousins' faces, Jim Pat continued, "Yeah, it spit blood and came right for us, but I still had the bat that Daugherty threw at us so I poked him right in his eye. It howled a frightful howl, Limes. Couldn't you hear it from here?"

"I heard it howl, Limes. I'm sure I did," said a wide-eyed Leo.

"And that's how we got back alive, me and Lucy. But it was a close call."

Limes looked at me and I nodded my head quickly for it seemed only a slight exaggeration at that moment. The circumstances seemed true enough if few of the facts were. Limes rubbed his chin where a few red whiskers grew and said solemnly, "You've seen a cyclops. And a fierce one by the sounds of it. Maybe even Polyphemus, King of the Cylcopses. I read all about him in Classic Comics."

Everyone nodded at the mention of that authority. Jackie read them all the time. Limes announced his conclusion again to the assembled cousins. "They have seen a cyclops. I thought we would have to go across Troost to hunt for them, but they came looking for us it seems."

"What's a cyclops?" blurted Leo, who had been saying a Hail Mary as fast as he could under his breath.

"A monster with one eye that guards caves," said Mike, who'd read more Classic Comics than Leo.

"Yeah," continued Limes, "and they can disguise themselves. They can appear anywhere and anytime. That's what makes them really scary. You never know when they will appear—or who or what can turn into one!"

A story told outside on a summer night is always scarier than any other and there was no stopping Limes. He embellished the story that Jim Pat and I had started beyond recognition, teaching us that cyclopses live in alleys but can't be seen by day because they come out only at night when the moon is full. He told us matter-of-factly that cyclopses were probably to account for all kids who were murdered in their sleep.

Leo asked what kids were murdered as he edged toward the center of the circle of cousins under the streetlight.

"But how come you can't see them in the daytime?" I asked.

"Well, they take the shape of other animals," said Limes.

"Like the 'possum?"

"Yeah, Lucy. Like the 'possum. Or even cats and dogs and squirrels."

Although I was fully aware that the giant, one-eyed opossum was pure fabrication, the hair on the back of my own neck stood up as the story grew and I imagined the terrifying ability of normal daytime creatures to turn into alley-dwelling cyclopses.

"This is a dopey story," said Larry, his face stuck in a smirk. "How could it change from one thing to another? That can't happen."

"Lots of things are other things at the same time, Larry," said Limes.

"Yeah, like what?"

I couldn't believe that I would have to point out what was so obvious to these older cousins. "Like the Holy Trinity, of course!"

"Yeah," said Leo. "Do they have that in Chicago?"

"Lucy's right," smiled Limes.

I continued, "God can be an old man with a white beard and then His own son, the Sacred Heart, and then a Holy Ghost that nobody's ever seen. All three things are really just one thing."

I looked at Jim Pat and decided not to mention that the faeries, too, can change into whatever shapes they wanted. Just as God can be an old man, a young man and a white bird that appears at the apostles' dinner table, I'd been taught that a faery can appear as an old banshee lady, then a beautiful swan, and later as a gust of wind. Boys, including even Uncle Red and Uncle Mickey, just don't seem to understand the faeries—or their catechism—like me and Grandma Fahey.

"Yeah, well, I still don't think this is scary, somebody's dog turning into a 'possum," said Larry, "and you don't scare me neither, Limes. I never heard of no cyclopses before. We don't have them in Chicago. Limes is always lying about Kansas City because Limes is just a big liar."

Limes let Larry have his say. When it was clear that Limes wouldn't be drawn in that easily, Larry looked for an ally in another out of town cousin. "Jodie, do you have cyclopses where you live?"

Being apparently more closely related to Limes, Jodie said immediately, "Sure we do. And we've got some lizards in Little Rock as big as dogs. They are called gila monsters and when they bite you, they don't let go until the sun goes down. But by then you are dead, so it doesn't matter."

Limes' blue eyes squinted in delight at this new horror and its effect on his audience, particularly Leo and Little Pat. I tried to show no fear but decided not to stray far from my cousins' front porch next time we were in Little Rock. But Larry was unmoved.

"You are all dopes. Liars and dopes," Larry said. "We have much scarier stuff in Chicago. Real stuff that's scary. Not made up stuff. My dad showed me where these gangsters gunned down these others guys," he said, making a machine gun noise and shaking as if by the force of the gun. "In Chicago, in this place called Cicero. We have real gangsters in Chicago. We don't have to make up scary stuff."

Limes said, "We have gangsters, too, you know."

"Big deal. Everybody knows that Chicago has the best gangsters," smirked Larry.

"Says who?" Mike demanded.

"Says me. Eliot Ness and the Untouchables didn't work in Kansas City," said Larry with big city superiority.

"Yeah, but I bet you can't go anywhere to see real bullet holes in the wall," Limes said.

"Yeah," said Mike who knew where Limes was going, "my dad took us to Union Station once to see the bullet holes in the walls from the machine gun massacre there. Those were Kansas City bootleggers and gangsters."

Limes added, "And people on the trains that come into town after midnight can see their ghosts. Bloody gangster ghosts."

We Kansas City cousins all looked approvingly from Limes to Larry, glad to have one upped the Chicago cousin on such a grand scale.

"Well, if cyclopses are so terrifying, how come they didn't hurt Jim Pat and Lucy?" demanded Larry.

Limes thought hard, then asked confidently, as a lawyer might of his own witness, "Jim Pat, are you wearing a medal or your scapular or anything blessed?"

"Sure," said Pat, as he pulled the green cloth St. Patrick's scapular from his shirt.

"Lucy?" directed Limes.

I pulled out Grandma Keary's rosary from my jacks pouch and handed Limes back his rabbit foot.

"There's your answer, Larry," concluded Limes.

"You're a dope, Limes. Like a scapular and a rosary could save you from cyclopses?" mocked Larry.

"Guess so, how else do you explain them getting back alive?" smiled Limes triumphantly.

"Limes, do they work against gila monsters, too?" inquired Leo, who was being sent to summer camp in the Ozarks.

Before we could speculate and Limes could issue an off the cuff opinion on this important issue, we heard a familiar but wholly unexpected sound that made us all—even Larry—jump. Uncle Mickey's laugh boomed from behind us as he came down the steps of the porch, "What if you were being chased by an agnostic cyclops, or worse—a Protestant gila monster? Where would you be then, Limes? And, of course, even a miraculous medal didn't save Capone or Machine Gun Kelly," chuckled Uncle Mickey.

Everyone laughed while Larry and Mike fired imaginary but noisy machine guns at each other, and

Leo and Little Pat fell, clutching fatal wounds, humming the theme song of *The Untouchables* television show.

"Liam Quinn, they ought to get you off the streets and get you into the seminary with your imagination. I'll talk to your old man," Uncle Mickey said as he swatted Limes lightly on the back of the head. Everyone laughed again.

"Come on in now, Lucy," said Uncle Mickey

I knew the jig was up when I saw what he had in his hand.

"Your Grandmother Fahey brought these for you, Lucy." He presented me with a carefully folded pink and white cotton dress, anklets and my oversized Mary Janes. As I took the dress, the smell of starch and a hot iron replaced the smell of wet city streets, opossum fur, metal fire escapes, and the dank, slightly sweet smell in the alley, and even moon flowers that must have been blooming somewhere on that night.

Jim Pat chided as Uncle Mickey held out my dress, "Yeah, Lucy's just a girl."

"Am not!"

"Are too!"

"I can run faster than you, Jim Pat McKee. I could beat you down the alley."

"Well, howse come you didn't?"

"'Cause you started running before me, you were scareder than me."

The others hooted at this.

"Was not!"

"Was so!"

The cousins picked on Jim Pat for a while as a scaredy cat, saying that he was scared of an old blind opossum. Mike added that he was even scared of a cat that wears glasses, while Leo speculated that Mr. Daugherty couldn't have run that fast because Mr. Daugherty's pants probably fell down when he took off his belt.

I was sorry that the other cousins were turning on Jim Pat, but I wished they had noticed my bravery. I was the one who actually put the spell on the man after all. From the depths of his misery he said, "Sure Lucy, you had to tell them it was a 'possum, like that's a good story, like that's really scary."

"It was scary enough, Jim Pat," I answered quietly.

"I wasn't scared one bit."

"Pipe down, the lot of you," Uncle Mickey laughed.

"Mickey, are there gangster bullet holes at the train station?" said Mike looking at Larry.

"Yep."

"We told you so," gloated Leo.

"Can you take us there tonight to see them, Mickey?" implored Limes.

"Nope," laughed Uncle Mickey.

"Uncle Mickey, are there real cyclopses? I mean really real ones?" I asked, concerned that, as had happened with the faeries, talking about them might make them take some action.

"No Lucy. There are not," said Uncle Mickey as he took me by the hand. "Come on in now, Lucy. Hurry inside. There's somebody that wants to talk to you."

"I know. Is Grandma Fahey really mad, Uncle Mickey?"

He smiled. "Well, isn't she always peeved at something? But that's not who I meant."

Uncle Red and Prof Ryan were standing in the living room with their ears to the phone listening, the extension cord pulled taut. I hoped it wasn't that Mr. Daugherty from the alley already. How did he find me so quick?

Prof Ryan bent over me and said, "Here Lucy, long distance call for you."

When I heard a voice, a familiar voice, say "That you, Lucy?" For a wrenching, dizzying moment I thought that it was Grandma Keary's soul.

"Yes, ma'am, It is me. Lucy." After all the weeks of thinking I heard my mom's voice in the wind or other people's conversation, here she was.

"I've missed you, Lucy."

I didn't know how painfully I had missed her voice until it was there again.

"Mama?"

"Yes, Luce. It's me."

"Mama," I repeated simply because I could, my chest aching, "Grandma's gone but it is not my fault."

"Of course not, Luce. How've you been?"

I didn't know what the question meant. So much had happened since I had last seen my mom that I didn't know where to begin, so I began with tonight.

"Mama, do you know who Limes is? He dared me to go down the alleyway to put a spell on this man and I did and I was the bravest one."

"You were, Lucy?" I could almost hear her smile. "My good girl."

"Yessum. I took the dare. I shooed away a 'possum and went all the way to the end of the alley all by myself, except for Jim Pat McKee, and then we got chased by a dog, except not really, and then we told them it was a fierce wild dog that changed into a giant 'possum ..."

"Don't wear your mother out now, child," Grandma Fahey was saying. She and Uncle Red were bending over me trying to listen in.

But I had plenty of stories for Mama to catch up on, so I continued, "Then Limes said that wasn't scary enough, so Limes says it was really a cyclops. They're a whole lot scarier. Do you know what they are, Mama?"

"Enough, Lucy!" The sternness in Grandma Fahey's voice startled me. I hadn't heard this voice since I broke one of her delicate teacups from Beleek. I stopped so suddenly it felt like the words were jammed in my throat. Tears began to burn in my eyes.

Something was wrong but I didn't know exactly what. I lowered my head and looked from side to side.

"Mama, when are you coming back?"

I couldn't have been more confused if she were really a ghost. Was she back or wasn't she? Did she still want to be my mom? I felt a pang in my chest and a pressure building in my lungs.

"That was a long walk, Lucy. Next time you'll just tell Grandma Fahey before you think about setting out like that, won't you?

I didn't answer her and threw my dress and shoes into the empty chair near the phone.

"You'll promise, won't you, Lucy, that you won't run off again?"

She wouldn't promise me that she wouldn't run off from me.

"C'mon, now, Lucy," she sighed weakly.

Before I could explode with my demand that she come home right now, tonight, she gently said, "I want to be completely better before I come home so that I won't have to leave ever again, Lucy."

But I wanted her to be here tonight.

"It's all of us here now, Rosie." Uncle Red shouted above the music. Mama shouted back to Uncle Red that the McKees sounded good and the *ceili* was a good idea.

Some of Mama's cousins crowded around and Prof Ryan raised his huge hand like he was parting the Red Sea, saying gently, "Give Lucy some room."

Everything was going slowly around me and voices around me seemed so distant that I wondered if I wasn't somehow under water and just didn't know it. Faces floated above me—Uncle Red, Uncle Conny, Uncle Mickey, Prof Ryan. I heard Grandma Fahey ask for the blessing. I saw them all cross themselves well before I heard Prof Ryan's voice, *"In nomine Patris, et Filii, et Spiritus Sancti."*

I looked up at him as he bent over to put his hands on my head to say "Christ above me, Christ below me, Christ before me, Christ behind me."

I felt the vibration of Mama's voice buzz in my good ear as she said with the others, "Christ in the hearts of all who love me." I heard Grandma Fahey say "Amen" before anyone else.

"Well now, Lucy," Mama's voice was breaking up and the static on the line sounded like spiteful faeries. "It won't be long now before we are all home together. I'll be back very soon."

"Mama?" I knew she was slipping away again, as easily as the leaves on the willow branches over the creek in our yard. No matter how hard I held on to the branches to swing over the water to the other side, the leaves could slip off and drop me right into the creek water.

"It'll be a short trip this time, Luce."

The leaves in my hand were like little yellow and green fish that always surprised me by the numbers of them.

"Be a big girl now for me, OK, Luce?" Mama was saying through the static.

"Goodbye, Mama. Goodbye." I hadn't gotten to say goodbye to Grandma Keary.

"Big ... girl ... now ... Luce."

Someone, I think it was Uncle Mickey, stood behind me trying to help me unclench the receiver from my sweaty hand, but he didn't understand about willows. Mama and I were two separate people again, on opposite banks of the creek.

Jim Pat McKee was crawling on his hands and knees through the group of adults. I didn't care that he saw me crying. He waved his penny whistle and then looked away.

"Now, now, child." It was Grandma Fahey's voice.

There was a hush, and then an empty dial tone. It was as if the room breathed out pity in a single word, "Rose."

CHAPTER 19: FOLLOW ME UP TO CARLOW

I ran out the front door and into the night, with Grandma Fahey calling after me, but I wanted the darkness. This was where Mama seemed most real, among the stars, one of them maybe Grandma Keary already, maybe Mama was becoming one, too. I felt a hand on my shoulder and didn't have to turn to know it was Uncle Red.

He wasn't in any rush to go inside either judging by the way he was looking up into the old elm tree like he'd never seen one before. He didn't want anyone to know that he had been crying.

"Uncle Red?"

"Hmm?"

"Can I go home with you?"

"You have a fine comfortable place with your Grandma Fahey, haven't you Lucy?"

"But what if she doesn't want to take me back?"

"Oh, Lucy," he chuckled. "Your Granny Fahey's not going to hold what happened tonight against you. She knows you had your reasons. She's kin to you and kin have to forgive you anything. Those are the rules."

"But Uncle Red ..."

"You know, Lucy, you might get pretty tired of my cooking. I do myself. And the meatloaf down at Philsy's would take years off your life."

Having to leave too early tonight because Grandma wanted to go home would kill me off sooner than the food at Mr. Cannon's.

"Are you ready to rejoin the family now, Lucy?"

What did he mean by *family*? My *family* was all at some hospital. I never thought about anybody but Mama and Daddy and Jackie as my family. Even Uncle Red and Grandma Keary were "the relatives." I looked in at the house full of relatives and realized this was my family for tonight and maybe until Mama came back for me. There was light inside and laughter that came in swells and a thin line of fiddle music stitching it all up together. Looking in the windows at the relatives gathered in the warm light of Grandma Keary's house, I thought the word *family* must be like an ark—always able to hold one or two more than it had before. Mama would be coming back for me, even if it took forty rainy days and nights.

"Lucy? Mr. Quinn? Are you still out there?"

Grandma was calling in earnest for us now.

"Do I have to go back, Uncle Red? I want to stay here with you, at Grandma Keary's with everybody. She'll make me go home right now."

Neither of us answered her. With the light from the porch behind her, she was a dark silhouette. I checked to see if she was carrying her purse, a sign that she was ready to leave. I couldn't tell for sure. I couldn't see her face either to gauge her mood. We continued to watch her from our place in the dark. Uncle Red took out his hanky, rubbed his eyes, and then blew his nose so loud that he ended up laughing. It sounded like an elephant.

"Mr. Quinn, that must be you?"

"The jig's up, Lucy," he shrugged, then called out cheerfully, "Here we are, Maeve. Here were are. Just on our way inside." He put his arm around me and led me toward the steps.

"Ah, there you both are." As we stepped into the pool of amber light at the bottom of the porch steps, Grandma announced, "Lucy, I could only find a polyester sweater, but that'll have to do." She marched down the steps and put some other kid's white spring uniform sweater around my shoulders.

"But I'm not cold, Grandma."

"Yes you are, Lucy," she insisted taking my hand. "Come along, child. We need to get you home."

"Grandma, I don't want to go home yet. Can we please stay a while?"

"Oh, sure you can, Lucy," Uncle Red boomed from the bottom of the porch steps. "Sure you can."

Prof Ryan was at the screen door now holding it open for Grandma and me. Uncle Conny had stepped onto the porch behind him.

"It is late. Lucy and I must be on our way. This child'll catch a chill."

"Here now, Maeve, a little music and dance and being with her own family will be enough to warm her up. You both must stay." Uncle Red sounded like he was in charge of everything at Grandma Keary's house now. "We're here as a clan to bid farewell to Maggie. Isn't that what we are about? Everyone is eternally welcomed here."

There. That sounded good. I looked up at Grandma.

Cousin Prof said gently, "Mrs. Fahey, it may be good for Lucy to be around her own people tonight, don't you think?"

Grandma answered first with her chin. It jutted out so sharply that it seemed like the edge of a flint. In this crowd it'd be easy for just about anything to spark her fuse, and once it was lit there was nothing to stop it. I was glad she let go of my hand before she answered. She might have crushed a few of my fingers if she squeezed any tighter.

"I am Lucy's grandmother," she said slowly. "Certainly she is with her own people when she is alone with me at my home."

Uncle Red slowly made his way up the steps, his eyes even in their sorrow weren't far from some game. "This is a farewell *ceili* and there's dancing to be done yet. Am I not right, Father Ryan?"

Prof Ryan continued, "What I meant to say, Mrs. Fahey, is that your steady guidance in the faith is a wonderful lesson for Lucy, but the music and dance may be good for her as well. More distraction for the child here tonight, don't you think?"

Grandma unclenched her jaw and listened to Prof Ryan like he was the only person on the porch. "These Quinn boys, your cousins, think they have invented *ceili* music," she said.

Uncle Red and Uncle Conny laughed as if she'd meant for them to.

Prof Ryan's understanding smile seemed to calm her like receiving Holy Communion and she didn't object when he said, "Why don't we all listen to the music? Ned and his boys will be playing again here shortly."

When Prof Ryan stooped forward to link arms with her and proceed to the living room, she looked like a little girl walking arm in arm with my tall cousin.

"Look at that old duffer. He'd have been quite the lady's man if he were in the business," Uncle Conny whispered after them.

"You think I can be outwitted by a Jesuit, do you Conny? I've got twenty bucks says I'll get Maeve out on the dance floor before the night is over."

"You? You're daft. She hates the very thought of you. Twenty-five says you can't and I'm sure Prof'll want some of this action."

"Funny, that's what he said of you."

"Yeah? Well, I think he just likes to keep the betting going to raise the stakes. He never seems to remember having placed a losing bet, in the grand tradition of the Jesuits."

"True enough," Uncle Red rumbled out a low laugh, wheeled around taking my now-free hand in his and asked, "Did anyone ever teach you to dance, Lucy? Maeve maybe?" He had the same smile on his face as he did the time he paid me fifty cents to put up a campaign poster for his pal, Judge O'Hara—in the De Molay Mason's Hall.

"No, Uncle Red, I don't know how to dance and I'm sure Grandma doesn't either." I couldn't imagine her dancing at all, especially as I'd seen Mama's Chicago relatives do.

"Oh, you must learn to dance, Lucy. What is it the Poet said? 'Oh body swayed to music, oh brightening glance. How can we know the dancer from the dance?'"

"I give, Uncle Red. How can we?"

"Who knows, Lucy," he shrugged with a laugh. "All I know is when the world gives you questions too hard to answer, you just give it back an even bigger riddle. That way you stay on top."

Was this in the catechism?

"And this much I do know," he continued, "by the end of the evening your Uncle Conn will be paying me twenty five bucks."

"How come?" My smile matched the one on his face.

"Mostly because he's always on the wrong side of a bet and he's a chump," he chuckled as we hurried down the hallway to catch up with Grandma Fahey and Prof Ryan.

Plunking himself down next to them in the living room, Uncle Red said cheerfully, "Sounds like West of

Ireland here tonight, wouldn't you say, Maeve? With Ned sawing away on that fiddle. Hard to keep from dancing just like you did in Connaught."

When Grandma didn't answer him, he rubbed his chin and asked, "What do you call that step they are dancing, Maeve?"

"It is the 'Siege of Ennis'," she said, squinting a judgment on the skill of cousins of all ages who had taken to the floor. White haired men from Chicago were shambling around the floor holding hands with teenaged girls or ladies Mama's age. I was surprised to see Little Pat paired up with his tiny Grandma Herlihy. As I watched I wondered how they all knew just how to keep weaving in and out as they did and when to drop hands with one partner and join up with another cousin. And then there was the spinning. It made me dizzy just to watch.

"Do they still teach them to dance young in Mayo, Maeve?" Uncle Red leaned back to light his pipe.

"I suppose they do, Mr. Quinn, but this is America, isn't it."

"What's the name of the tune they are dancing to, Maeve? Do you know?" he asked between puffs.

Grandma looked at Uncle Red like he'd just asked did she remember her own maiden name.

"It's 'Follow Me Up to Carlow' of course. My father used to sing this. It was a particular favorite of his."

I was nearly hypnotized watching the opposing lines of cousins dancing in and out. When I heard Old Ned McKee call "Advance and retreat—advance and retreat," I imagined that one line might be our tribe, the Gaels, and the other, the Saxons. The pace of the music sounded merry, but the music was in a minor key, like one of Uncle Red's riddles. And maybe when the sadness got too much to even sing about, a furious dance was all that you could do to cheer up again. Maybe this was all anyone could do before they closed up Grandma's house and gave it to the Jesuits.

Uncle Red and Prof Ryan were clapping their hands in time to the dancers' motion. But Grandma seemed agitated, as if she had misplaced her coin purse. Her right foot shuffled from toe to heel to the beat that contained the last phrase, and her heel hammered the syllables of the word "Car—low" to the wooden floor.

She did something I'd never seen her do in Uncle Red's presence, she clapped her hands and laughed aloud, "My lord, I hadn't thought of that in years." She looked apologetically from me to Prof Ryan.

"Well," said Uncle Red springing to his feet, "who'll follow me out to the dance floor? Lucy? Maeve?"

I almost giggled at the thought.

Crossing her ankles, Grandma said, "My dancing days are dead and gone, Mr. Quinn."

Prof Ryan objected, "You can't just jump into the middle of a set, Red."

But Uncle Red ignored him. "Will I be all alone out there then?" He tugged at his suspenders and then charged onto the dance floor like he knew exactly what he was doing. I'd never seen Uncle Red dance at all, but there he was in the middle of a line of Chicago relatives who were holding hands and shuffling towards another line of relatives.

"Look at that old fool," sniffed Grandma, "For all his talk about the dear auld sod and he can't even dance a proper reel."

I was keeping an eye on him because I didn't want to be invited to dance again and not know how. He made it seem easy enough until the lines split into smaller groups and someone grabbed Uncle Red and spun him around and handed him off to another cousin who pulled him in another direction entirely with no partner in sight. Old Ned McKee finally put down his fiddle and bow and ordered him from the floor. When he came back to where I sat with Grandma and Prof Ryan, he puffed, "It's in my blood wouldn't you say?"

"You call that dancing, Mr. Quinn?"

"Do you know, I think the Chicago cousins made a particular point of showing me up? What do you think, Prof?"

"That wouldn't take much, Red."

Grandma scoffed, "You've made a shambles of the old dance, Mr. Quinn." Uncle Red laughed and collapsed on the couch cushion next to Grandma with such force that she tilted against him until she could right herself. The collision made me laugh.

"I need a good teacher it seems." He was still puffing out his cheeks. "Do you know, Maeve, that Lucy doesn't know how to dance either? That little mug and she can't dance a step. Appalling."

"Why should she, Mr. Quinn? She is an American child."

But when Uncle Red and Prof Ryan excused themselves to the kitchen for more stout, Grandma turned to me like maybe I had forgotten one of the Holy Days of Obligation, "Lucy, surely you know at least the threes and the sevens? It is basic."

"Threes and sevens, Grandma?" Jackie had taught me to jitter bug so that he could practice before CYO mixers, but that's all I knew of any dance. He always complained to Mama that I stepped on his feet and could never keep up.

"It's three simple steps up, and three back."

Grandma seemed unaware that her feet were counting out steps as she talked until she saw me watching them. "Remember it this way, Lucy: three for the trinity, seven for the sacraments. Threes and sevens. You advance three, and then retreat for three."

It was pretty much what I had seen opposing lines of the cousins doing.

"Have you got that much, Lucy?" Grandma asked.

I nodded that I did although I had about as much idea about how to dance as how to knit. Watching the dancers' feet, I thought of the clicking and clacking of Grandma Keary's knitting needles and her telling me not to think of the stitches as much as what it would look like when finished. There's a pattern to commotion if you can see it.

"Now, for the sevens," Grandma Fahey said getting up from the couch. "You go to the right for seven and then back to the left seven." She looked around to make sure no one noticed before stepping off the seven to the right. With her right foot pointing in front of her and her leg raised from the knee, she stitched her way through a series of seven crossover steps. I was concentrating as hard as I could, trying to memorize what she had done, but gave up when she said, "Then you simply undo it all by moving seven to the left. Like this."

Clearly, the same people who made up the Irish language thought up this dance, too.

She looked down the hall to make sure that Uncle Red was nowhere to be seen. Then she told me, "Always begin the sevens to the right, like this, Lucy," in the same tone she might have said "always genuflect on both knees, not just one, after benediction." She made a little hop step that made it seem she was briefly suspended above the floor, her front foot striking the floor a second after her back one.

My whole heart went out to this step. But as I jumped up to try, Grandma was reaching down to straighten the seams in her silk stockings that looked like vines climbing two trellises instead of straight lines up the backs of her legs. As quickly as she had been up dancing, she sat down again as if this magic had never happened.

"Show me again, Grandma."

Her face was bright, the perspiration on her brow and determined chin collecting and reflecting the light in the room. She was dabbing her forehead and throat with a navy and white embroidered hanky from her pocket when Uncle Red reappeared.

"This will fix you up, Maeve, one half glass, just as you ordered."

"I never ordered such a thing and you know it, Mr. Quinn," she protested before taking two long sips.

"Conny is the best dancer in our family, Maeve," Uncle Red said pointing to his brother in the midst of the dancing Chicago cousins.

Grandma looked shocked. "He's not much better than you."

When the reel was over, Uncle Conny made a beeline over to us to say how awfully hot it was on the dance floor.

Uncle Red announced to him cheerfully, "Did you know Conn, that 'Follow Me Up to Carlow' was a favorite of Maeve's father. A rebel tune at that. He used to sing it to her. May be hard for Maeve to sit still with McKee and the boys going after it on the old man's favorite song. What do you think of them apples?"

Uncle Conny eyed Grandma and then leaned forward like he was giving her very confidential information, "Mrs. Fahey, I'd pass on the opportunity to dance were I you. I thought I'd pass out myself. Miserably hot out there tonight."

"I have no intention of dancing." Grandma folded her arms across her chest.

"That is wise. You've the best seat in the house, Mrs. Fahey. Pleasant little breeze through this window here," Uncle Conny said fanning himself.

"My mother used to dance the Haymakers' Reel, Mrs. Fahey. Did you ever dance that as a girl?" Prof Ryan asked sincerely.

"Where exactly was she from, Father Ryan?"

"From Kilkelly, in County Mayo like yourself, Mrs. Fahey. When I was little, they never said Mayo without saying 'God help us.' I swear to Christ I thought the name of the county was 'Mayo God Help Us.' Poorest and most unlucky place on the face of the earth."

Grandma smoothed her dress and fussed with the hem of it that broke a few inches below her knee like Prof Ryan had just announced from a pulpit on Easter Sunday that Mrs. Will Fahey's slip was showing.

"What use would Mrs. Fahey have of a step dance?" Uncle Conny said. "She is from Chicago, Prof. She's as American as Mamie Eisenhower."

"I'll bet Maeve could dance a hornpipe in her sleep," said Uncle Red.

"No doubt, no doubt," huffed Uncle Conny, "but I wouldn't advise it. No, not tonight. Whew! For a minute I thought I saw Magilly himself circling like a vulture."

The mention of Magilly, the undertaker, made my great uncles and even Prof Ryan wheeze with laughter. I didn't understand how they could still make jokes about Magilly, but if Grandma Keary were here she'd probably be laughing right along with them. Uncle Conny's face was bright red and shiny and his shirt was so damp that the pocket that contained his pack of Winston's stuck to his round chest. I didn't think old people could really dance themselves to death, but I'd learned that they could go without a warning.

"Maeve," said Uncle Red, "what do you think of Conny's dancing? Do I want him dancing at my wake?"

Grandma said seriously, "Are either of you gentlemen aware that there is a pattern to these dances?"

"I was better as a younger man, Mrs. Fahey." Uncle Conny acted like his feelings were hurt. "Dancing is not for the old."

Uncle Red said as quickly as he could jump three of your checkers in a row, "Here's a thought now. Why don't you show us, Maeve? You name the next dance and show us."

"Oh, no, Red. Mrs. Fahey doesn't want to dance here. A woman of her refinement doesn't want to get out there and sweat." Uncle Conny was pulling on his shirt that still clung damply to his chest. "It wouldn't be proper for a woman her age to kick up the dust."

Grandma turned slowly in Uncle Conny's direction and then folded her hands in her lap like she was ordering from the menu at a fancy restaurant on the Plaza. "'The Walls of Limerick,' Mr. Quinn. I'd like to see them dance 'The Walls of Limerick.'"

Uncle Red stood up and shouted to Ned. "We need a Waltz of Limerick."

"No, no," laughed Grandma, like she could barely stand it. "It is 'The Walls of Limerick.' There's nothing grand enough in Limerick to call it a waltz. The dance commemorates my father's namesake, Patrick Sarsfield, at the walls of the city in the battle for Limerick."

"Oh, Sarsfield again is it?" asked Uncle Conny.

I was hoping there wouldn't be a row like there was the last time she mentioned her one and only approved Irish hero, but Uncle Red said, "He's as great as your man Danny Crocker at the Walls of the Alamo, Lucy."

Now I was giggling at him too. "It's Davy Crocket, Uncle Red."

Uncle Red set about organizing the next dance by trying to cajole sweaty old men and women to get back out on the floor. They waved him off like he was crazy. Only the younger people jumped up when Old Ned McKee called, "All up for 'The Walls of Limerick.'"

As the lines formed, Uncle Red came to Grandma and said, triumphantly, "There Maeve, they are ready for you to join them."

"Oh, I am not going to dance it myself, Mr. Quinn. I only wanted to see it danced once more before I die. And Lucy, you might want to see how to put the threes and the sevens to use." She eyed her empty stout glass and said, "It is rather warm in here, your brother's right about that at least."

I wished Uncle Red had pulled her to her feet. I thought I'd die myself if I didn't get to see her hop step again, but he was off making plans with Ned McKee, and Uncle Conny was off to the kitchen for more stout.

Returning he said, "Here's some refreshment, Mrs. Fahey. You can just settle in for a comfortable sit, we'll leave the dancing to the younger folks. You don't see Norrie O'Fallon out there do you? No indeed. You are wise to stay put."

I couldn't tell if it was just that Uncle Conny always irked her or if it was his suggestion that she couldn't do something that riled her most. We walked to Mass every day precisely because her doctor told her that she should take the taxi or not go as often.

When Uncle Red came back Old Ned was in tow. "Here's Ned, here to play whatever tune you want, and you can show us a Mayo step or two."

"Ned, you know some Mayo tunes, surely. How about it, Mrs. Fahey?" entreated Prof Ryan.

"Oh my, no. My day has passed and gone," she insisted again.

"Is that three times she's denied us, Prof," Uncle Red said with his hand over his heart. "Very Biblical don't you think? You know I almost expect to hear a cock crow."

But Prof ignored him and said enthusiastically, "Give us a real Mayo set, Mrs. Fahey."

"Would 'The Blackbird' do, Missus? Or 'The Stack of Barley'?" asked Old Ned McKee. He seemed suddenly shy in front of Grandma Fahey, like one of the tradesmen that would call at her back door.

The lines of cousins that were assembling to dance 'The Walls of Limerick' had followed Uncle Red over to Grandma's side of the room.

"What tune would you like to dance to, Maeve old girl?" chuckled Uncle Red.

Grandma looked up like they had all gone mad. But when Prof Ryan put out his huge hand to pull her up from the sofa, a cheer came from the room. I heard Uncle Red tell Uncle Conny that the betting was closed and he wouldn't take another of his rubber checks. Cash only.

"Maybe just a step or two," she said almost girlishly looking only at Prof Ryan. "Do you know 'The Men of the West,' Mr. McKee?"

Old Ned started bowing the melody as his answer.

"That's the ticket, Maeve." Uncle Red was practically crowing. "We all know that one, Maeve. Words and all."

"If you can slow it up a bit, Mr. McKee. It is just a trifle," she blushed "but, if I must dance ..."

"Yes, Missus, I can," Old Ned said slowing the pace just a touch.

Grandma was standing so stiffly that I wondered if she were even breathing. As Old Ned played on, she pointed her right foot, brought her hands firmly to her side and raised her head with her usual pride. She counted out a measure without moving at all, one, two three, one, two three, ooone two. Then suddenly she clicked her right heel against her left, stepped forward, then back, but stopped suddenly, saying, "Oh, I'm dizzy with this."

"Careful now," cautioned Uncle Conny. He stopped whatever he was writing on a paper napkin, "Don't strain yourself, Mrs. Fahey. It's not too late to just sit back down and let the young people take the floor."

Uncle Red said, "C'mon Maeve, you're among family. Would it help for us to sing along?" He fixed his eyes on Grandma and sang the chorus with the fiddle: "Then over the hill went the slogan to waken in every breast, the fire that's never been quenched, boys, among the true hearts of the West."

"You're off to a good start," shouted Prof Ryan, "Don't stop now. Take us home to Mayo. Mrs. Fahey."

She looked from Prof Ryan to Uncle Red and then at me. "Pay attention now, Lucy. I'll only be doing this once, so you'll see how it's properly done."

"Yessum." I sat on the floor to get the best view of her feet. It was like she was on stage.

"Lucy, the sound of the shoe on the wood is as important as the music," she instructed. "Granny McNamee kept an old door that she put over her stone floor—just for dancing."

When she smiled at the pitch her solid heel made as she tested Grandma Keary's old floorboards, she might have been knocking with her dancer's foot on a door that led back to her own Granny McNamee's hearth, at last.

"Now then, Mr. McKee." She nodded and began again with her hands properly at her side and her head held high. She was tapping her pointed right foot in time. At the end of a measure she began with a smart click of her heels, a waggle of her ankles, a syncopated stomp of her heavy black shoes, and then a straight-legged pointing of both feet that suddenly shot out in front of her, one after the other. This one quick mesmerizing movement ended in another stomp that raised a bit of dust from the floorboards and coincided with the loudest beat in each measure. It reminded me of a sudden rain shower on the roof.

I waited eagerly for each stomp and each time noticed the little plumes that shot up where her foot struck the ridges of dust that had been concealed by the old rug. The plumes rose into the light behind her like birds, only to dissolve midair and fall formless again. Each rhythmic stomp caused these birds of dust and light to rise again, like the phoenix bird that Jackie told me could rise again and again from its own ashes. It seemed for a moment that she was a queen, maybe like the Queen of Heaven borne aloft by a cloud of white birds on my Assumption Day holy card.

I could hardly wait to try myself. I stood up with my hands at my side and hopped around on one foot, but there was no matching her. The room cheered whenever her legs shot out one after the other or she hammered the floor with her heel in quick succession. Old Ned himself hollered, "Yeeeooow," at one point. She was breathing heavily but showed no sign of wanting to quit. Uncle Red and Uncle Conny only looked at each other like they couldn't believe it, but then they had never tried to catch up with her bounding up the hill to St. Nat's every morning for Mass.

"Look at her raising Old Ned. She could dance rings around the best of us, boys," Prof Ryan said with his gangly arms draped around Uncle Red and Uncle Conny. "You might think about donating your earnings to the church, Red. Or will we have to split your windfall with Philsy Cannon like always?"

Uncle Red didn't seem to hear him, he was watching Grandma that closely. When at last she nodded to Ned McKee and he drew his bow slowly over the last note, the room erupted in shouts and laughter. Grandma sank into the couch, and pulled out her embroidered hanky again, saying, "I am parched, Mr. Quinn."

But Uncle Red stood speechless, and didn't even notice Uncle Conny putting the paper napkin IOU in his pocket.

"Half glass coming up, Mrs. Fahey," Uncle Conny laughed.

Prof Ryan loomed over her. "You are a grand dancer, Mrs. Fahey. Just grand."

Uncle Red only nodded.

Grandma put the hanky to her forehead and looked around the giant Jesuit at me, "Did you get that down, Lucy," she panted. "I went through it twice for you, did you see?"

I bit my lip. I would have traded my soul and all the catechism she ever taught me to dance like Grandma Fahey just had.

CHAPTER 20: THE WEST'S AWAKE

I never thought Grandma Fahey would be the center of attention in the Quinn gathering place, at least not for something they appreciated. But here she was, breathing hard, one gloved hand over her heart, her whole face a rosy color that I had only seen flash in her cheeks when she would get caught up in telling me stories about the mighty Regans of Mayo. It was not her sunburned, working-in-the-yard face that would holler to me to "Yank the dandelions by their roots" before she went after them herself with her father's rusty old cement trowel; she hated dandelions the way my Uncle Conny hated the English. The color in her face now, after her dance, had a deep and even tone that made her eyes seem clearer and her hair more silvery. She smiled like there was nothing she could do about it.

"Grandma?" I touched her arm that was warm with perspiration. "Grandma, can you teach me to dance just like you?"

"Lucy," she puffed, "I taught you ... everything I know. It's just ... the threes ... and the sevens."

Uncle Red's burst of laughter brought him back to speech. "Oh, it was a bit more than that, Maeve. You should dance more often. The world needs this kind of grace, Maeve."

Grandma was trying not to look Uncle Red in the face. "Oh, go on with you ... Mr. Quinn. I wasn't ... a bad dancer ... in my day."

"Grandma, please, will you dance some more?" I was tugging on her hand.

"Lucy ... I'm talking ... to Mr. Quinn ... as you can plainly see."

"Yessum," I slumped onto the couch next to her. The relatives who had gathered around her had started to drift back to their places across the room. It was no use. Grandma didn't even seem to care that we—well, mostly her—were being admired so.

Then Old Ned McKee announced as he put his fiddle down, "No one in North America can top stepping like that. And if anyone wants more music, they'll have to play it themselves."

There'd be no more dancing tonight.

Uncle Conny took Old Ned's announcement as his cue to organize some singing. "How about 'The West's Awake.' C'mon Red. Will you join us, Mrs. Fahey? You've more than proven you are still from the West."

That was it. She could sing for everyone. Why would she squander an audience, as Uncle Red would say? She'd danced them all speechless and she'd sung on stage before in Chicago. How many times had I heard of the green silk dress she wore to sing? I tugged again on her hand but she snapped, "Oh Lucy, not now."

She didn't even bother to answer Uncle Conny and neither did Uncle Red, who was usually the ringleader of any singing, so Uncle Conny marched off to find someone to play the piano.

"Maeve, you should have been dancing all these years." I'd never heard Uncle Red speaking so quietly and gently to her. You'd almost think he was talking to Grandma Keary.

But Grandma Fahey answered him, still catching her breath, like he lacked all sense, "I had work to do, Mr. Quinn. Children to rear. Where would dancing have gotten me?

Uncle Red only smiled at her like her answer had not much to do with his question.

"Oh, I did dance ... as a girl in Ireland. And afterwards in Chicago ... some."

"Well, what was it made you stop?"

"Will Fahey ... my husband ... thought it best to get on with the business of being American. He didn't approve of the ... immigrant ways." She sighed deeply, finally catching her breath and asked, "Did you know Will Fahey, Mr. Quinn?"

Grandma always said my Grandfather's name with the same reverence she said the word, America, or something with stone pillars, like the Commercial Bank of Kansas City where he had worked. Grandma always pointed out the tall building downtown as the very place where Will Fahey had been the highest-ranking and only Catholic bank officer.

"Surely he didn't make you stop dancing, Maeve."

"Did you know him very well, Mr. Quinn?"

"Not well, but he certainly kept the Hibernians in the black when I was president."

Grandma looked a little confused. She never mentioned this when she went through all Grandpa Fahey's important contributions to the parish, not the least of which was providing a Jesuit son.

"Will Fahey was the main financial supporter for years. I assumed you knew, Maeve."

Grandma didn't answer but began to smooth and straighten her hair although it didn't seem to me that even a strand was out of place in her permanent wave.

"Well, he didn't want it getting out, to anyone I guess. He made that very clear every year when he wrote the checks," Uncle Red explained. Then he quickly pulled the top of his shirt collar tightly as if he had buttoned the very top button and mugged, "I don't want this getting around. Do you hear me, Quinn? I don't want every loafer in town thinking I have money to burn, because I haven't."

Yikes. I'd never heard anyone say a word against Grandpa Fahey. Ever. Grandma crossed her arms. This was becoming more interesting than the dance. She might land on Uncle Red with two feet any second and with more than her hop step. She didn't say a word, but began to watch him very closely.

"I'll cut you off without a penny if word gets out, Quinn." Uncle Red continued his mugging. "And I don't want to hear of any of my money finding its way into the back pockets of any Democrats. Have you got that, Quinn?"

I wondered if my Grandpa Fahey really blustered like that as I watched my great uncle's face turning red from the tightness of his collar. I didn't dare laugh, and neither did Uncle Red, until Grandma's face tightened as she fought off the smile that since her dance was closer to the surface than usual. She said, as quietly as if Grandpa Fahey were in the next room, "You did know him, then."

Uncle Red let loose of his collar finally and grinned. "I did, Maeve."

Grandma Fahey was staring at the loose threads from which the top button on Uncle Red's shirt had slipped off long ago. Uncle Red never sewed buttons back on shirts and sweaters because he told me it made a bachelor look more eligible. I knew it wouldn't impress Grandma Fahey. She couldn't stand the sight of a missing button. I knew by the way she squinted at it that she was itching to take a needle and thread to Uncle Red's shirt. Or maybe it was his neck that she was making a plan for.

"You know Mr. Quinn, that Will Fahey was ..."

"An important man in the parish." Uncle Red interrupted Grandma to finish her thought. I'd never seen anyone do that to Grandma Fahey when she was making a pronouncement of some sort. She looked more startled than offended. But it was Uncle Red's face that interested me the most. He had that intense look he had when he'd shown me just how to reel a fish into his boat at the Lagoon. "Set your hook in 'em first, then reel slowly, ever so slowly now, Lucy. So it doesn't turn and run on you."

Uncle Red called out to Prof Ryan, who was walking towards us with a tray on which were three glasses, a full pitcher of stout, and one small glass filled with ice cubes and dark green Kool-Aid. "Will Fahey was a big man in St. Ignatius, wasn't he, Prof?"

"Indeed he was."

I think Uncle Red might have had two fishes on the same hook, by the way Prof and Grandma smiled at each other.

Prof Ryan poured the stout and handed full glasses around with the same large freckled hands he wielded the chalice at St. Ignatius, and for a long moment the three drank in silence. I took a sip of the Kool-Aid. I wasn't nearly as thirsty as Grandma, who drank her stout like it was water.

Uncle Red smacked his lips and said, "Wasn't Maeve's stepping marvelous, Prof?"

"A revelation to us all," he smiled.

"Will Fahey wouldn't let her dance. What do you think of that?"

Grandma lowered her glass and frowned at Uncle Red like she would at me, to remind me not to tell our business to anyone outside the family. Beads of moisture ran down the side of the glass into the linen hanky she wrapped about it. Was she getting ready to turn and run? She had downed about half the stout in the glass and was settling in to quench her thirst with what remained, although she told me that a lady always nurses her drink in polite company.

"But, Mrs. Fahey," Prof Ryan said more surprised than anyone, "surely your talent for stepping is a gift from God."

That color in her high cheeks deepened. Being praised by a Jesuit seemed to make Grandma relax nearly as much as the stout.

"Well," she said as confidentially as if to her confessor, "I used to sing some, too, in Chicago, Father Ryan."

Singing at church was for the honor and glory of God, but what Grandma told me this summer about where she used to perform topped all church singing in my book. I thought Uncle Red would be impressed too.

"My Grandma Fahey sings so good that they used to pay her." I slurped more Kool-Aid and smacked my lips just as Uncle Red had over his stout, and waited for Grandma to begin one of her stories that came after dinner as certainly as dessert and catechism. I couldn't believe it when all Grandma said was, "Lucy, it is 'well' that you mean to say. You would say a person sang well, not 'good.' Surely you haven't forgotten so soon what I told you about adverbs and adjectives?"

Prof Ryan lifted the pitcher to top off Grandma's glass. She let him. The slow purposeful way he poured the dark stout seemed almost part of a sacrament.

"You sang professionally then, Mrs. Fahey?" he asked slowly as the tan foam rose to the top of her glass.

She looked from Uncle Red to Prof Ryan and back again, took another long sip of the fresh stout and said, "When I was a single girl, I sang for extra money, but only for the household, mind you."

"Was it in your choir then? You must have been a paid soloist." Prof Ryan nodded his head to encourage Grandma to continue.

"Better than that," I said. "My Grandma Fahey sang on a stage with a feather in her hat." Wasn't she going to tell them about the bright blue and green feather she bought for her hat with the tips she saved?

Uncle Red put the back of his hand to his mouth but I could still see his smile as he asked, "What kind of stage would that be exactly, Lucy?"

"Just the one at the biggest music store in Chicago on Wabash Avenue. And everyone clapped and bought the sheet music to whatever you sang, didn't they, Grandma?"

"Enough now, Lucy," she said as she looked up at Prof Ryan. "It was a respectable establishment, Father Ryan. Our choirmaster at Immaculate Conception got me the job."

She gave two quick tugs on her best white gloves and then began to examine the seed pearl beading on the backs of them.

"I know your home parish, Maeve," Prof Ryan said enthusiastically.

Grandma put down her glass and looked as flustered as she did the Sunday at St. Nat's when she noticed that I had both a rip in my lace collar and mud on my white anklets as we came back from communion. I'd gotten a lecture on the importance of appearances.

"My family lived in that parish," she added quickly, "but Will Fahey was from St. Vincent's. Will Fahey went to St. Vincent's Academy, don't you know, and then on to the College there. They call it De Paul now. He sang tenor in the choir. He had such a sweet voice, like my boy, Frank. My boy, Nat, sang more, him being in the Seminary and all, but it was Frank that had Will's voice and graceful way with singing and ..."

Prof Ryan stopped Grandma's nervous chatter. "A lot of our people were from Immaculate Conception. Hard-working immigrants in that parish years ago, both Irish and German."

Grandma seemed to be re-absorbed in the pearl pattern on her gloves.

Uncle Red glanced at Prof Ryan and then said "Aw c'mon, Maeve, look around you. There's none of us here came over on the Mayflower. You are among your own here."

Grandma looked up from her pearled gloves when Prof Ryan said, "Your parish must have been an interesting sort of place in those days, Maeve. We had Ryan folks long ago out in the West Loop, St. Patrick's parish. Oh God, the stories they told. Tough end of the world then, eh?"

"Some of them still vote, don't they Prof?" Uncle Red slapped his knee.

Grandma had a strained, alarmed look on her face just as she did when we were far from home and she was trying to remember if she had left something burning on the stove. She reached for her drink. When she finished off the last drops, she curled her lips like she had tasted something more bitter than the dregs of her stout.

"Hinchy Street. We lived on Hinchy Street in Immaculate Conception and my old Da worked the week round." Her shoulders lifted like she'd just set down something very heavy.

"I can only imagine the hardship, Mrs. Fahey."

"What was the name, Maeve?" Uncle Red rubbed his ear like he needed to hear every detail. He could pretty much tell what part of the West of Ireland a person was from by the name.

"Patrick Sarsfield O'Regan. But he dropped the O' with his baggage when we got here, he used to say." She looked up briefly at Uncle Red's brimming face.

"Oh, that used to always fool the yanks," he roared. "They'd never have taken Paddy Regan for a Mick, I am sure."

Grandma gave Uncle Red a full-blown smirk this time. "He wanted his children to be Americans, Mr. Quinn. It took more than half of his life to get here after all."

"I'm only teasing you, Maeve."

"And I'll thank you not to use that epithet in front of my granddaughter."

"What? You know by now you're a Mick, don't you, Lucy?"

Grandma aimed a glare at Uncle Red and I decided that no one really was interested in my answer. Uncle Red might have gotten away with a laugh or two about Grandpa Fahey, but not Great Grandpa Regan. Grandma wasn't letting him up for air, but I was the one having trouble breathing.

"My father was Patrick Sarsfield Regan, Mr. Quinn, and proud of it."

Grandma said her dad's name the way Uncle Red said Franklin Delano Roosevelt, like you were expected to put your hand over your heart and say the pledge of allegiance.

If Uncle Red had ever been to Grandma Fahey's and seen the picture of her father that she kept in the hallway, I think he'd have shown more respect. Even in the picture of him laid out in his coffin he looked stronger than Uncle Red and Uncle Conny combined. She had only one formal portrait of Grandpa Fahey, in a starched white shirt, red tie and navy blue suit. But she had three pictures about the house of the man she had just lately begun to call, "my old Da," in her kitchen table stories.

I exhaled when Uncle Red, still smiling at Grandma and drumming his fingers on the arms of his chair said, "Patrick Sarsfield O'Regan is a grand name, isn't it Prof?"

"Oh, a grand name, Mrs. Fahey. A name full of history."

She eyed her empty glass, and didn't object when Prof Ryan poured her another half glass. I hadn't realized what a powerful thirst she had worked up, but quenching it so single mindedly seemed to make her a little sad. I thought bragging about her Da might cheer her up.

"Great Grandpa Regan carried the hod."

"A brick layer then? That is back-breaking work to do all week, Mrs. Fahey." Prof Ryan sat back in his chair as if he himself had been at it all day.

Brick layer? Boy, did Prof Ryan have it wrong. I waited for Grandma to start in on some story about Great Grandpa Regan. I wanted her to boast to them, like she had to me, that the day he landed he went to work building the great White City in the Chicago World's Fair.

"My father worked in the masonry trades, Father Ryan, and for a time in the coal yards."

This was barely a shadow of what she told me of the mighty Regans. How could she not want to tell Uncle Red and Prof Ryan her stories? I sat up on the edge of the couch, trying to think of something that would set Prof Ryan straight about the importance of Grandma's family in Chicago as I had learned it. I knew that Uncle Red would have liked the Regans much better than the Faheys, if he could only get to know them through her stories.

"Great Uncle Petey Regan was a professional pugilist," I announced.

"You mean he was a fighter, Lucy?" Uncle Red chuckled.

"A famous fighter. C'mon, Grandma, you tell it." She would never let anyone say he was just a fighter. She insisted that I refer to him as a professional pugilist and scolded me once because I might have been thinking that he was only a common street fighter.

I decided to warm her up by starting the story without her. "In those days they fought with bare fists, not with gloves as they do today." Grandma always began her best stories of the past with "Now in Chicago at the time" very much like the priest would begin a gospel story at Mass with, "At that time in Judea."

"Well now, a prize fighter in the family. Let's hear all about it, Maeve. Did he give John L. a run for his money?"

"He was a bull of a man, wasn't he, Grandma?" She never talked of him except to tell me that he was.

Both Uncle Red and Prof Ryan leaned forward, eager for details, just as they might to hear about a new relief pitcher the A's had just hired. I couldn't believe she wouldn't jump at the chance to fill them in.

Great Uncle Petey never lost a fight until one night when Grandma was about my age, the other brothers carried him home from the ring when he couldn't get up. In the morning when her mother found him dead in the kitchen she shrieked his full name, *"Peadar Padraig O'Riagan,"* so loudly that Grandma thought her mother was trying to call him back in Irish from the other world. This part of the story gave me the shivers and made Grandma tear up, so I was glad to skip over it.

"Tell them about the big wake, Grandma, and how the man with the green sash from the mayor's office brought all the flowers, and the Knights of Columbus with their swords and feathered hats marched at the Mass." This would surely impress both Uncle Red and Prof Ryan as it involved their specialties, politics and religion.

"That'll do, Lucy, the adults are trying to have a conversation here."

I looked at Uncle Red and Prof Ryan, who clearly wanted more of the story. I braved the stern look she sent my way and added very quickly, "Petey Regan could deck anyone in a fair fight, but the fix was in." I'd heard that many times before and I thought they should know.

"Lucy." There was her don't-tell-everything-you-know frown again, and I felt the full weight of it.

"Yessum."

"I'm sorry, Maeve. It is hard to lose a sibling at any age, but when you're both still kids. ... Well, that's almost too tough to deal with," said Uncle Red.

"Maggie was my sister for seventy-three years, and I was lucky for that, but I don't know how I'll go on without her."

He reached for her hand but Grandma began waving it in front of her like she was clearing away the remnants of a dream. "It was a long time ago and I remember very little of it."

"An ebb in memory is oftentimes a blessing, Mrs. Fahey," consoled Prof Ryan.

"In that case, my brother Conny must be the most holiest old fool around," Uncle Red said, jabbing his thumb at Uncle Conny and his son who were standing at the piano struggling with the last verse of "The West's Awake." "That old man can sing only two songs unassisted, one is 'Wearin' of the Green,' and so's the other one, come to think of it."

Uncle Red began calling out the words just ahead of Uncle Conny singing them, creating an echo in the room: "If, when all a vigil keep, the West should sleep. Alas, and well, may Erin weep, if Connaught lies in slumber deep. But hark a voice like thunder spake, the West's awake! The West's awake ..."

I imagined the land of Connaught as a great sleeping giant with a voice as loud as thunder, finally shaking itself awake and scaring the bejasus out of the English. It was probably this same Irish giant who'd "shake down the thunder from the sky" in the "Notre Dame Victory March."

Uncle Conny was teetering now like he was ready to fall forward and motioning to Uncle Red to hurry up and catch him with the last lines of the song, "C'mon Red, I can't remember how the bloody thing ends. What the hell rhymes with spake and awake? Other than, 'My brother's lower than a common snake.'" All the old cousins laughed, but no one helped Uncle Conny finish the song. Uncle Red laughed the loudest, but he turned his complete attention back to Grandma, who was leaning forward very slowly. But she sang out as clearly as a tolling bell the last lines like a responsorial at Mass, "Sing, oh hurrah, let England quake. We'll watch till death for Erin's sake."

It took one or two beats after the song for some old cousin to loudly chide, "Aren't you Quinn brothers fine old Galway men being done in by a Mayo woman— twice in one night."

"My old Da knew all the old songs," Grandma said sadly to Uncle Red.

Uncle Red patted the back of her hand the way I had seen him pat Grandma Keary's hand from time to time, and said, "Of course, he did, Maeve. I'm sure he packed them up with his boots and shirts when he left." He squeezed her hand and asked gently, "Or had he only the one shirt?"

Grandma tilted towards Uncle Red to whisper, "Well, we hadn't much more than that when we came," and ended up leaning into him like he was seated next to her on a bus that had just taken a sudden wide turn. She looked a little queasy. Except for tonight and the last time she was with the Quinns, I'd never seen Grandma drink anything more than a little spot of Mogen David on Sunday nights. Uncle Red kept hold of her hand to right her, then placed a sofa pillow between them at her hip to shore her up.

"There you are, old girl," he smiled as he would at a member of the family. "I'd say the West's still awake in ye."

Grandma was sitting contentedly next to Uncle Red in Grandma Keary's living room, and there was no way for her to turn and run now, even if she wanted to. She'd been hauled into the boat.

Chapter 21: The Same Boat Twice

Grandma spoke slowly, like she was having trouble focusing on Uncle Red's face. "My Father, Mr. Quinn, was a proud man, oh, very proud—and not the type of man to miss the same boat twice."

"Oh, there must be a story there, Maevsie."

I didn't much like him calling her that, if anyone was asking. He sometimes called Grandma Keary Magsie.

"What boat would that be, Mrs. Fahey?" asked Cousin Prof.

"The boat to North America, of course, Father Ryan." Then turning to Uncle Red she almost whispered, "Oh, my legs suddenly feel quite like lead, Mr. Quinn."

"But your thirst is gone, I'd wager," he laughed.

"Are you feeling OK, Mrs. Fahey?"

"I am right as rain, Father ah …"

"It's Ryan, Mrs. Fahey. Father Ryan," Cousin Prof said patiently.

"To be sure," Grandma said, shaking her head a little, "I think it was the dancing that went to me legs. I'm feeling rather lightheaded. I think I'll just sit here quietly a spell."

"I am sure it was the dancing, Mrs. Fahey, but we'll switch you to tea just the same."

I wasn't sure why they called it being in their cups when what made people tipsy came from tall glasses.

"Dancing legs should be hollow ones, Maeve." Uncle Red knocked on his own leg but Grandma didn't pay any attention to their laughter.

"My poor old Da was only a lad of eight or nine when he left Mayo for North America, the first time. It was 1847."

The smiles on Prof Ryan, Uncle Red and Uncle Conny's faces drained away.

"Black '47," said Prof Ryan. "The worst of the Great Famine then. My own mother's people were among the lucky ones who gave up soon enough and left."

"The Regans did not leave as much as they were forced out," she rallied to object. "It was leave your home or die where you stood. He was half ghost himself, he used to say, closer to the next younger siblings that had been carried off by the cholera, than to the older children. He was not much older than Lucy when ... Oh, where is Lucy, has anyone seen the child?"

"I'm right here Grandma." I hadn't moved from my place on the sofa next to her. I was sitting as still as I could. I'd never heard this part of the story of the mighty Regans. I couldn't imagine the old man in the hallway picture as a little kid.

Prof Ryan turned his head away from her like he was hearing her confession, "Was it on a coffin ship they set to sea, Mrs. Fahey? Oh, terrible business that. Imagine having your only escape a rat-infested, disease-ridden boat."

A coffin ship? Would they put little kids in them, too? Jackie'd want details when I told him this one.

"Grandma, did your Da sail all the way over here in his own coffin?"

Her wide eyes met mine. I was used to the look that would come over her when she'd forget I was there, especially when she would walk us deeply into a story as if it were a dark forest and then seem suddenly surprised to see me sitting at her own kitchen table.

It was Prof Ryan who answered me.

"They were not really coffins, Lucy. That is what they called the immigrant ships that many of our people left their homes on, many to die of disease on over-crowded ships or ships that foundered along the way and were never heard of again."

Grandma waved her hands and made the sort of throaty sound she used to scare the blackbirds out of her garden. Then looking into my eyes she said slowly and sorrowfully, "I don't think, Father, ah, Ryan ... I do not think that this is a suitable topic for young ears. Maybe for your history students over at the College."

"Oh, perhaps you are right, Mrs. Fahey," he demurred. "It was long ago, Lucy. You should say a prayer every day for the repose of the poor souls from the West of Ireland on those ships."

Grandma slowly put her hand to my face, and said, "Lucy, look at you, you've got that awful green

Kool-Aid all over your face. Please excuse yourself now and go and wash up."

Uncle Conny said, "Lucy looks a bit like what they said of the starved ones by the side of the road. The ones they say who were found with grass stains around their mouths. Their Last Supper in Connaught, while England stole our grain and cattle."

"Really Mr. Quinn. This is not suitable talk at all," Grandma huffed. "Lucy, you may excuse yourself now."

I hated being sent from the room by myself to do something that didn't need doing. It happened a lot when they talked about Mama. I stood in the dark hall wiping Kool-Aid from my mouth with the tail of my shirt and listening to the adults. They weren't talking about Mama at all. Grandma, who was doing most of the talking, was still telling them again and again that the famine was nothing anyone should speak of, ever. Uncle Conny said it was like the Great Depression. Uncle Red said it was much worse because it was like the Depression without Roosevelt, if you could imagine that. Prof Ryan said it was the British Empire taking deadly aim at our people just to clear the land. Grandma, of course, told them they didn't even know the half of it as she had heard from her old Da.

She lowered her voice, so I sat down on the floor and scooted as close as I could to the doorway. I wanted to hear how it took two whole ships to bring Great Grandpa Regan to America, not just one, like most people. I didn't think that any old famine would be a match for the Regans of Mayo.

"He went overland with his family to the harbor in Cork. They'd given up everything they had. Traded their lives to the landlord for just enough for six passages, when seven was what they needed. Since he was the littlest, they thought they'd just stow him away once they all got on board."

That didn't sound so bad, at least they all got to go together.

"They rolled him up in a bit of canvas—there wasn't much of him to hide—and made him look like a little parcel of something, and tucked him behind a davit on the deck."

I hoped it wouldn't take them long to sail across the Atlantic. I was sitting in the dark hallway glad to be able to wiggle my feet when Jim Pat McKee ran by and nearly tripped over me.

"Hey Lucy, we're playing Sardines. Limes is it. Where's a good place to hide at your grandma's house?"

I didn't even have to think. I used to hide behind the sofa that Uncle Red and Grandma Fahey sat on. There was just enough space between the wall and the angled back of the green velvet couch.

"Follow me, Jim Pat."

He dropped to his knees and then we crawled on all fours from the dark hallway back into the parlor— Uncle Red's eyes darted for a second from Grandma to us as we went by heading for the little cave. I didn't think he'd turn me in. If Grandma had noticed she would have stopped telling her story.

"Nobody would think to look here, it's too small a space," Jim Pat grinned after we slipped in behind the couch. I was feeling pretty important having saved him from Limes. It was a favorite hideout of mine while Mama and Grandma Keary were busy talking. I sniffed at a Double Bubble gum wrapper I had left from the last time.

Grandma's voice was muffled now, like it was coming from far away. "If you can imagine it, they told him not to move a muscle until they were well away from the harbor."

"Hey, Lucy move over some, will you," he whispered.

"I can't. There's no more room," I whispered back.

Jackie and I used to both fit in here, but that was a long time ago.

"Hey, Jim Pat, this is really just a Hide and Seek hideout. There's not enough room for any other Sardines in here."

"You're going to kick me out while Limes is on the prowl?"

"Pipe down. I don't want them to know we are back here."

"You're right, I guess, Lucy. This place is not so good for Sardines. There's no way we could pack anybody in here to hide from Limes if they came along. I've got to try for home base."

I didn't really want Jim Pat to leave but he scooted backwards out of the cave, started to stand up, and then quickly dove back in, headfirst. Limes was coming through the room, looking high and low for Sardines. I was afraid he'd spot us and we'd both get pulled out of there, and I'd get scolded again for eavesdropping. I'd caught heck the day after the funeral for trying to listen in on Grandma's phone call with my dad at the hospital.

Jim Pat and I were nose to nose. It was very hard not to laugh.

"Tell me when Limes goes by," Jim Pat whispered.

Jim Pat couldn't see as I could Limes's freckled legs as he went back and forth across the entrance to our cave. He went by the sofa three times before he stopped. He was so close I could see wisps of curly hair on the back of his legs. When he reached down to scratch a red blotch of a mosquito bite right in the middle of his left calf, I closed my eyes. I thought for sure we'd be found out. Then, I heard Uncle Red ask Limes what he was doing.

"Playing Sardines. I've caught every fish but Jim Pat McKee."

My throat felt itchy with a giggle. Jim Pat put his hand over my mouth to keep me from making any noise and tried to turn to see what he could of Limes.

"Jim Pat? Little red-headed penny whistle player? I saw him go by a while ago."

Jim Pat cringed.

"I believe he said he was planning on hiding in the pantry closet, off the kitchen. Make sure he hasn't eaten us out of house and home when you catch him, Limes."

Limes's downy legs were gone as suddenly as they had appeared. We gave into our giggles imagining the triumphant look on Limes's face thinking he'd find Jim Pat's hiding place. A second later, Jim Pat pushed himself out from behind the sofa, his sneakers squeaking all the way on the wood floor.

"Later, Lucy gator. I'm heading for home base."

"In a while, Jim Pat crocodile."

I thought about following him to play the next round of Sardines, when I heard a spring in the sofa twang underneath Grandma as she turned and said, "What is that racket I keep hearing? And just then, it felt like the couch was moving underneath me."

I froze so I wouldn't be discovered, but then found myself trapped by the rest of the story of what happened to her Da.

"A little more tea, Maeve? May keep the sofa steady underneath you," chuckled Uncle Red.

"Mrs. Fahey, how is it that you came to be born in Mayo, if your father stowed away when he was a lad?"

"Oh, they thought he was safe on board, but the men from the shipping line came poking and prodding every little place they could. They routed him out at the very last minute, with his mother begging that she would stay behind, not him. Well, they pitched him off the ship onto the pier like unwanted cargo, threw the ropes and were off without him."

"Holy Lord, Mrs. Fahey!"

Prof Ryan had a way of swearing that sounded like prayer, so I crossed myself. Now, I really wished I'd gone off with Jim Pat. I closed my eyes again and tried hard to make up a better story ending than that, one where God the Father or St. Patrick or the Lady of Knock, or maybe all three of them, come at the last minute and put him back onto the boat with his family.

"Well, what could they have done but leave him there and send for him later?" Grandma was asking. "The older children were stronger and could carry the family forward. He was a sickly slip of a boy."

I knew Uncle Red's silence meant that he would have thought of something besides leaving a little kid on a dock like that. I tucked my arms and legs in tighter and tighter in my hiding place. I would be a better stowaway than Great Grandpa Regan.

"The boat set sail without him, with his people shouting to him that he should get home to Mayo, by hook or by crook, and wait for word."

I went hot and then very cold feeling that I might as well be wrapped in canvas. I needed to move my legs but I couldn't yet. I needed to know how he did it. I needed to know how he survived to grow into those huge boots that Grandma showed me. My life depended on Great Grandpa Regan's story as much as his did.

"How did he live, Mrs. Fahey?"

"My father was spared actually by an English soldier named Sutton, as it happened. Put him on another boat, bound for Liverpool, if you can imagine that. Why, he wasn't much bigger than little Lucy."

I held my breath, afraid she'd ask for me again.

"English soldiers, Maeve?" pressed Uncle Red. "What were they doing in Ireland during the famine?"

"Why to guard the grain ships that were being loaded for transport to England. But there were not enough soldiers in Hell to stop the hunger of the people. A sort of mob stormed the granary. My Da was trampled and nearly killed in the melee. It was the soldier Sutton who pulled him out of the way just in time."

"Oh, there's a double Hell, Maeve, being saved by the English," said Uncle Conny.

"He used to tell the lads in Chicago that his nose was broken by the butt of an English rifle, but it wasn't so. Do you know when he heard my prayers at night, he always had me add one for Corporal Sutton."

I thought of Great Grandpa Regan's square, half-smiling face with its crooked nose that pointed in a direction other than the one his eyes were looking. His chin had the little Regan cleft just like Grandma's and Dad's and mine. I rubbed that place on my own chin now, for good luck.

"Christ, Maeve, what a tale."

"What of his family, Mrs. Fahey. They made it?"

I heard the ring of Grandma's teaspoon against a cup.

"Oh, he was wild to get back home and just as wild to get the news from America, his remittance letter with money so that he could join his family. It took him years, though, to work his way back home. He learned his trade in Liverpool. When he finally made it home to Mayo there was a small package that Moran, the schoolmaster, had kept for him. There was a letter in a language that no one, not even the schoolmaster, could make out. There was also a smaller package wrapped in a bit of oilskin that contained the wooden cross from his mother's rosary. That was all, just his mother's cross. He knew at once she hadn't made the voyage. Moran helped him with the Irish written on the inside of the package. It said only, "Stay in Mayo. Don't follow. God and Mary bless your efforts there."

"What of the letter, Maeve? It wasn't in Irish? Some of the others made it safely no doubt?"

"Moran thought it might have been in French. Well, no one could make heads or tails of it. No one could even tell who had written it. It took a while until they located a priest all the way up in Leitrim, who could help translate, but Moran told him not to get his hopes up because of the one word he could make out: 'quarantine.' My old Da carried it with him for months, just the same, trying to imagine the life of his family in America.

"'Imagine me, Maeve,' he'd say to me, 'Me with me hat in me hands while the priest tells me those cruel words, said they were all gone, all six of them gone. All perished. After me dreaming all the years of them living high on the hog, and me being off to America to join them.'"

"Did the boat founder, Mrs. Fahey?"

"No. The boat made it to New York but wasn't allowed to land for the disease was rife. Typhus and cholera, I suppose. They were turned away to Canada, to an island in the St. Lawrence. And there they died. A French priest from Quebec gave them final absolution, and wrote the letter and sent it to anyone in Westport, County Mayo who might know the family."

I heard Prof Ryan mumble, "Eternal rest grant unto them, O Lord," and Grandma answer, "And let perpetual light shine upon them."

There was that perpetual light again. I heard a clinking of a teacup and glasses being quickly placed on the table that meant they were crossing themselves. I didn't want to let go of the grip I had on my knees even though it would be bad luck not to make a sign of the cross at the mention of the dead.

"That was a lucky boat to have missed, I'd say," said Uncle Red, though his voice sounded funny and distant. "That's the Irish luck, something that seems like no luck at all until you see the story through to the end."

"I still have the cross, Mr. Quinn. The figure of Our Lord was lost somewhere along the way, but I thought I'd give it to little Lucy someday. She'll have a tough old trip herself if, well, you know ..."

"Oh, no, no, Maeve. Lucy'll never have need of such a cross. Not ever."

I didn't know why Uncle Red was suddenly talking so loud. I already knew about that splintery old cross in Grandma's dresser. Why would she think I should have something like that and not her best rosary with the blue glass *Pater Noster* beads and a sterling silver cross? What was the use of that beat up old cross without a Jesus to make it a crucifix? It would always be Good Friday and never Easter Sunday? What kind of luck could that bring me? I put my hand to my Regan chin again. I was glad the boy that got left behind made it to become my Great Grandpa, but I still didn't like their weathered old Regan cross. I didn't want to have anything to do with it or with being homesick forever. Why were they talking about me all of a sudden?

I needed to bust out of here. I felt sweaty and like my cave walls were moving closer to me. I wanted them to see me. I didn't want to hide anymore. I wanted them to see we were all on the same boat, Uncle Red and Grandma and Uncle Conny and even Prof Ryan. I didn't know the sounds I heard next were coming from my throat. My legs starting to kick against the back of the sofa.

"Now, don't tell me I am the only one that hears that racket?" Grandma asked. "I'm afraid there are mice around the baseboards. I know the sound of rodents when I hear them."

The mere thought of mice shot me out from behind the couch, and I scrambled into the center of their circle. Grandma looked more stricken than if I had been an actual sea rat scurrying into their midst.

"Lucy, how long have you been back there?"

"It seems she comes from a long line of stowaways," Uncle Red said pulling me to my feet and into a hug. My legs tingled with hot and cold needles as the blood rushed back into them. "Let me hold you, Lucy. Until you get your sea legs."

I wanted him to hold me forever, but I didn't need sea legs because I wasn't going on any voyage by myself like that boy left on the dock.

Grandma looked like she was going to collapse from the weight of her disappointment. "See what comes of dwelling on the past. Oh, what kind of story is this for a child to hear of her family?"

"A true one, Maeve. A true one."

I looked from face to face. I didn't know why everyone was still staring at me. It was Grandma that had told them the story of the boy left on the pier, not me. They all seemed stymied for something to say, almost like they were turning back into the statues some of them had briefly become at Grandma's funeral. I had never seen Grandma Fahey and Uncle Red sit together without some kind of ruckus between them. Even Prof Ryan only sighed a long, tall sigh, and he usually had plenty to say that sounded like he was reading from something at church.

I wished they didn't all look so worried and tired. I wished I could tell them how glad I was to be among them now, how even their silence calmed me and held me just as closely as Uncle Red's arms, just knowing we were all together like this. I didn't care what else had happened to anybody a long time ago. I didn't care that they looked at me like a storm was coming our way. I was with them now, what else mattered? It was almost as good as being huddled in the southwest corner of the basement with Mama, Daddy, and Jackie, waiting for a tornado to pass over. Gathering around the radio, the static somehow warming us like a crackling fireplace, listening to shutters slapping against the house and the trees in the yard turning shrill, and feeling you are not alone even in such a storm, to know you are safe because you are with family. For what could happen to the family? Weren't we all of us in the very same boat?

CHAPTER 22: OUR NATIVE HOME

When Grandma decided it was time to leave, she did so slowly at first. She looked around at the living room full of Quinns and McKees like she was trying to shake off the fuzziness of an afternoon nap. Then she got that urgent look that she would get when we were downtown in a crowd and would suddenly take my hand and say, "Lucy, we must take the next bus home," explaining that she needed to have her own things about her for comfort. Prof Ryan asked if she wanted more tea, but that only made her rub her head and look at the stout pitcher and glasses on the table.

When she finally stood up, all the men stood, too.

"Come along, now, Lucy. We must go home."

Something lurched inside of me and I heard myself say, "No!"

"What was that, Lucy?"

She didn't seem mad, only like she hadn't heard me correctly. Maybe a little politeness wouldn't hurt. It was one thing to run away from home when her back was turned and another thing to defy her to her face.

"No thank you, Ma'am. I'd like to stay a bit longer if we could."

I might not have said anything at all by the look on her face. "Tell your great uncles and Father Ryan goodnight now, Lucy."

Not yet. Not now. I hadn't made this entire day's journey up the hill from her house, down the cave of the Cyclops and nearly out to sea on a coffin ship only to leave without getting what I came for. Uncle Conny had told me Grandma's soul was here tonight because we all were gathered. Did that mean when I left that Grandma's soul would be less than it was when I was here? Would she feel part of her missing when I left tonight? I knew that part of me would be missing when I left. Not like an arm or a leg or anything you can see. More like the outline you feel of your own body. Or like the familiar shape I'd leave behind after getting up from lying back in her lilies of the valley and waving my arms and legs through the little white flowers to make an angel. How is it possible to leave any of that behind?

"What about the song, Uncle Red? You said that you'd let the Jebbies take Grandma's house for a song."

"Well, we'll insist on getting a little more out of Prof and his order, but we do need a song before the evening breaks up. You're right Lucy."

Most Quinn gatherings ended with singing something. Usually it was Uncle Conny trying to lead everyone in "A Nation Once Again" or "Wearin' of the Green." They couldn't just close up Grandma's house forever without the right kind of song, to sum it all up. I hoped it wasn't going to be "Danny Boy," although Uncle Red said that it sometimes helps when you are sad to sing the saddest song you know as loud and well as you can. I didn't think Grandma Fahey could take "Danny Boy" either. When somebody started to sing it when they buried Uncle Natty, my Dad had to ask them not to go on to the second verse.

"Grandma, we can't leave before the song, can we? Wouldn't it be like leaving Mass right after communion, before it was over?" She looked straight down her nose at people who rushed off after communion and didn't see the Mass through to a proper end.

"What shall we sing then?" Uncle Red looked to Prof Ryan.

All the chants and singing at Grandma's funeral were too sad and not like Grandma Keary at all. They all just stood there. Grandma Fahey seemed worn out by her story. Uncle Red fiddled absently with his pipe until he remembered that he had already put fresh tobacco in. He didn't seem to have the energy to light it. Uncle Conny was trying to light the wrong end of his Winston. Prof Ryan was looking at all of them as if he had just dealt them a hand of poker cards and was waiting for them to pick them up to see what they drew. Mostly I was feeling like some big old black bird was just watching us all.

Before Grandma's story I thought the famine happened only in songs that Uncle Red and Uncle Conny sang like "Revenge for Skibbereen," about a town in County Cork where nearly everyone died and mothers fell in the snow and "passed from life to mortal dream." I never knew that the famine had anything to do with us, that without a few turns of luck I wouldn't be me and Grandma Fahey wouldn't be here and there might not be anyone to tell the story of the mighty Regans of Mayo. I didn't like knowing this story as much as other Regan stories but it made sense that it was Grandma Fahey's story because she was the kind of person to find her way no matter what. I rubbed my Regan chin again and hoped that the Regan luck hadn't been used up just getting to America.

Grandma Fahey steadied her stance and leaned towards me and spoke as if I were the only one in the room. "Lucy, the Regans of Mayo were a great and proud people and you are never to forget that. Famine or not."

"Yessum," I said and nodded hard so that she would know there was no doubt that I still believed in them, particularly if it meant I got to stay longer.

"Those were very hard times and people did what they had to just to survive. It was a shameful time that is better forgotten," she said.

"Now, now, Mrs. Fahey," Prof Ryan soothed, "You'll make Lucy think there is something shameful in just being Irish."

"Being Irish was certainly deadly enough for a time, that's for sure," said Uncle Conny.

Whenever Uncle Red sang of Skibbereen, I thought about what it would be like to have to leave home before you wanted to, "They say it is a lovely land in which a prince might dwell ... then why did you abandon it, the reason to me tell?" I understood now that it was the abandoning that would cause a great hunger for some other place. Great Grandpa Regan took half his life just to catch up and find America. My own home in the suburbs with Mama, Dad, and Jackie seemed farther than an ocean away.

"It has been a long evening, Lucy. I am sure our hosts are tired. We should just ask for Father Ryan's blessing and say good night."

"We need a song, one final song," Uncle Conny said rubbing his eyes with his knuckles.

"Father Ryan," Grandma was saying, "shouldn't we sing something religious, if we are to sing at all, remembering our purpose here tonight."

"Perhaps you are right, Mrs. Fahey."

I had to act fast before church music broke out. It could even be one of those awful ones about the crucifixion. I hated being blamed somehow for Jesus being crucified. Although "Skibbereen" was almost like a church song—as sad as any we sang at Grandma Keary's *Requiem*—it didn't leave you feeling like you were as much to blame as the Roman soldiers who nailed Jesus to his cross. Crucifixion songs could make you wince with the nails and the crown of thorns and all, but at least Jesus got to rise from the dead three days later and go home. Not like the people who fell by the wayside in the snow around Skibbereen and were gone forever.

"What about 'Revenge for Skibbereen?' C'mon, Uncle Red." He only smiled a little at my effort to pull him from his chair. "Sing 'Skibbereen.'"

"Lucy, mind your manners, please. And I'll countenance no singing of that song, Mr. Quinn."

Grandma's cold words went up like a wall, but I knew Uncle Red could get around it any time he wanted. I was confused when he leaned forward not to stand and sing but to pat Grandma on her knee.

"Prof, can you start us off on a verse or two of 'Hail, St. Pat'?"

"Thank you, Red." Grandma almost whispered.

Red? I'd heard her call him a bounder and a boaster before, but never just Red.

Prof put hands on his knees and leaned his tall frame forward and announced as he might from the pulpit, "For God and St. Patrick," and then led us off signing the first verse. "Hail, Glorious St. Patrick, dear saint of our isle. On us, thy poor children, bestow your sweet smile."

We sang this hymn every March 17th at Mary of Gaels. I felt a pain in my chest that had edges as sharp as broken glass. I felt a pressure building in me that forced the air inside me out in puffs. By the time the second verse came around, I felt like there wasn't enough air in the room to breathe. "Thy people now exiles on many a shore, shall love and revere thee, till time is no more. And the fire thou hast kindled shall ever burn bright, its warmth undiminished, undying its light."

The light in the window. How had I forgotten about it? I tore off running down the hall to the darkened parlor. Grandma called out for me to finish singing the hymn, but Uncle Red said, "Let her be, Maeve. She needs to say goodbye."

There in the window was the light I hoped would never die. The red glow faintly flickered from the bottom of the tall votive glass. It seemed like one drowsy eye still opened on the room. I took the candle from the sill and tipped it to one side to drain the remaining wax away from the little well the wick burned in. The candle brightened like a momentary smile.

I wanted to wake Grandma Keary. I wanted to bring her back so she could see me and hear me before she drifted off to sleep forever. All I could think of to say or do was to tell her that I was learning to dance. So much had gone on tonight. Frantic, I stood in the middle of the empty room, hands straight at my side like Grandma Fahey had held them, and improvised a dance to the hymn coming from the next room.

I whispered to the light, for if she was anywhere, it was in the warmth of the light, "See, Grandma, see what I know."

I was shuffling toe to heel more than stepping and clicking my heels as Grandma Fahey had, but it wouldn't have mattered to Grandma Keary that I didn't really know the exact steps, or even that I had learned it from Grandma Fahey. She'd have said "Very nice, darlin'," no matter what. I was sure of that.

The hymn was slow enough to count off some threes and sevens to the words. I moved through the repeated refrain, "For God, and St. Patrick, For God, and St. Patrick," with One, TWO, three, one TWO three. I found seven easy steps as they completed the chorus, "For God, and St. Patrick, and our native home." I drew my foot across the worn carpet on the words "native home," and as I did, I understood that a native home is a place you came from and could never go back to again. Grandma Keary's house was becoming my native home.

I breathed in slowly and tried to memorize everything in Grandma's front parlor: the smell of the church candle; my great uncles' cigarette ashes and pipe tobacco in the tray; the red glow on the old wood furniture; and, the hymn of exile rising from the living room. I wanted to take all of it with me.

The flame in the votive light was sinking even lower. I swallowed hard at the thought that Grandma couldn't see me anymore. Reaching for the warm red glass, I held it in both hands and sang as loudly as I could along with the echoing hymn. I could hear Uncle Red singing loudly too, although his voice cracked in places. Prof Ryan's voice was low and steady like it had made the long journey from the bottom of his shoes to his mouth. Grandma Fahey's voice was, as always, clear as a songbird. Uncle Conny and others seemed to have fallen along the wayside, until they got to the chorus: "And our hearts shall yet yearn wheresoever we roam, For God, and St. Patrick, and our native home."

I didn't understand why anyone would leave their native home if they didn't have to and if it made them sad forever. Grandma Keary left me, so I didn't have a choice. Uncle Red told me that there were so many songs about Ireland because so many folks had to leave. If they'd stayed home, they wouldn't need to sing about it to keep it alive. It would be right outside their doors.

I didn't want to be left with just a song after tonight.

The votive flame made a little flicker, like a leaping hope, hope that none of this was happening. I held the candle to myself. With my eyes shut I couldn't tell where my heat and that of the candle began and ended. I wanted to believe that my love for Grandma Keary was fuel enough to keep the little fire from ever going out, but I didn't need to open my eyes to know that the fire had gone out for good. I could feel the heat draining away from the glass. I clung to the fading warmth like it was my own life. I promised her I would never forget our place on her porch or Galway, her native home.

The glass chilled quickly and it felt like coldness was spreading into my limbs. I was afraid that if I didn't do something that I would merge into that darkness forever. My hand trembled as I reached for the Magilly's matchbook on the ledge. I struck one match after the other and dropped them into the empty votive glass. Each match fell through the tall glass like a brief, red meteor but burned long enough to give shadows back to things. I desperately needed to see my own shadow again and prayed to St. Patrick that one of the matches would land just right on the little well of cooling wax and rekindle the spent wick. As I watched the last match go out, I slowly put the candle back on the edge of the sill. I didn't say goodbye for I was certain now that she had gone.

I tried hard not to think of whom the faeries might call to next. It is very hard not to think of a thing when you don't want to.

I went back in to Grandma Fahey, who looked at me once or twice like she had just remembered she had a pet of some kind, and stayed close to her. I didn't even object when she stood up to leave, but I was glad that Uncle Red was going to see us home.

"I don't want you navigating by yourself, Maeve. That stout stays with you a while longer than you think."

"Pfft, Red."

"Let me just see if I can borrow my nephew Dick's beer truck. ..."

She wasn't sure as everyone in the room that he was kidding. He reached into his pocket for the keys to his Ford and found a folded napkin, Uncle Conny's IOU for $25. He tore it up and smiled at me and said, "Are you ready to go now, Lucy?"

I stopped in the yard to look back at the front of Grandma's house with its two windows looking out like eyes now shut on either side of the stone chimney. I had been here when the candle winked out.

"Come on now Lucy, it's time to leave. Maggie's gone on to her new home."

I took Uncle Red's hand and walked across the yard for the last time.

Chapter 23: Heading West

By the time the summer evenings seemed to come sooner, I was used to having Uncle Red stop by to sit with Grandma Fahey and me. He almost always brought us something nice, a pint of ice cream from the dairy where Uncle Mickey worked or a couple of flowers that he had picked somewhere along the way. Once he brought me two goldfish in a little bowl that were left over after a Holy Name fundraiser.

"Are they really mine, Uncle Red?" I tapped on the side of their bowl to get their attention.

Grandma said she objected to goldfish because no matter how much care you give them, they don't last.

I glubbed back at the vacant fish faces that looked around at nothing in particular. I liked them immediately.

"You'll only disappoint the girl, Red," Grandma went on. "She'll become attached and they'll be gone before the fall."

"Well, if you're absolutely sure they'll be gone by this fall, maybe Lucy should name them Dwight and Mamie."

Grandma said, "Save that kind of disrespect for one of your clubs."

"You'll have to make sure that Dwight and Mamie don't spawn, Lucy." Uncle Red seemed serious.

I was willing to do anything to keep the fish. "Yes sir, I will, Uncle Red. How do I do that?"

"Red, you'll please mind your tongue."

Bending over to get a better look at them, Grandma announced that my gold fish were dead ringers for Bess and Margaret Truman and didn't look a thing like either of the Eisenhowers.

"Oh, right you are, Maeve."

Uncle Red laughed so hard the water in the fish bowl began to sway from side to side. I tried to steady the bowl so my fish wouldn't slosh around and end up on the floor. Pressing the bowl against Uncle Red's belly I felt it shake with his laughter. It was hard to remember a time before he'd started calling on us.

At first, he came by regularly every Tuesday to drive Grandma to her Legion of Mary meeting at St. Ignatius. They never discussed it or made plans for it, but she would put on her hat and gloves and wait at the door and say, "Where is that vexatious man? It's nearly half seven."

He was never late for *Death Valley Days* on our nights to watch TV. In fact, he got there early so that he would have time to warm up the television. He moved the rabbit ears on Grandma's TV as carefully as if he were making a house of cards. Then he'd raise his hands over the set like a magician, causing the images of the Old West to come into focus. Backing up slowly from the set and feeling behind him for his chair, he'd say, "Quiet, now, everyone."

But when the announcer for 20 Mule Team Borax came on the air, Grandma would loudly say, "Och, I've no use for that Ronald Reagan or any Reagan for that matter, putting on airs with adding an unnecessary 'a' in a fine name. They were tinkering with their immortal souls just as surely as they were tinkering with a good Catholic name. Ronald Reagan will regret that fancy spelling someday, at the gates of Heaven."

Uncle Red laughed sometimes whether Grandma meant for him to or not, and said, "The announcer has a nice face." He studied it the way he did everything on Grandma's TV. He didn't own a set himself.

"Mark my words, no good can come from any of the Reagans." She picked up her little green leather volume of Thomas a Kempis and pretended not to watch the show.

When the first wagon train flickered into Grandma's living room, I knew where Jackie was—in front of a set somewhere. We never missed *Death Valley Days* when we were at home. He'd strap on his Colt .45 gun and holster and holler, "Luce, it's on."

TV was kind of like what Grandma told me about the Mass being exactly the same the whole world over, from the *Introibo ad altare Dei* clear through to the *Ite, misa est*, so it didn't really matter what parish you were in. But Jackie and I would always cheer whenever a pioneer mentioned that he had just come from the Santa Fe Trail. We thought of the Santa Fe as our trail since it passed through Mary of Gaels Parish not far from our own backyard.

"Santa Fe means Holy Faith, you know, Luce."

I thought it might just be called holy faith when it passed through our parish.

"Nope. It's the Santa Fe Trail all the way west from Independence, Luce."

I figured that the other one, the Oregon Trail that veered off from the Santa Fe, must be for Protestants since they never named their churches after saints or holy things but called them 75th Street Baptist church, Prairie Presbyterian, or Shawnee Mission Methodist.

Although we could run down a stretch of it where the grass grew over the ruts made by the wagon wheels any time we wanted, somehow hearing about the Santa Fe Trail on television made it seem bigger, more important. Jackie said that when you were in a place where something actually happened long ago you could see it if you concentrated. Squinting at the wide open clover field that buzzed with honey bees and shimmered in the blazing midday, it wasn't hard to imagine the wagon trains clacking and rumbling by.

But *Death Valley Days* at Grandma's seemed to get dustier and dustier every week, always the same. Usually someone died dreaming of a destination in the far off green hills of California. Although they never actually showed anyone dying, you knew a man was a goner if they showed a brittle old steer's skull or the rut of a wagon wheel while he mooned over how green and lush everything was suddenly becoming.

Whenever this happened at home Jackie would thump his head with the heel of his hand, "It's only another mirage."

"How do you know Jackie? Maybe they're seeing into the future, maybe there are some real things in mirages, maybe they're seeing all the way to California."

"Nope, it's what they call an oasis, Luce. It's like a dream you can live in for a while, usually just before you croak. They happen when you want something so bad that you think it is really there. They see them all the time when they are in the desert and running low on water."

But sipping the ice-cold ginger ale, sitting happily on the floor between Grandma Fahey's and Uncle Red's chairs, I wondered for the first time why these pioneers didn't just stay at home instead of wandering around in rickety old wagons week after week. If I ever made it back to my own home, I didn't think anything would make me leave it.

I closed my eyes in the breeze from the floor fan until Uncle Red said to the screen, "Oh, look out there, boyo. I wouldn't be drinking from that pool if I were you."

I opened my eyes in time to see a thirsty pioneer wiping his sleeve after taking a long drink. He hadn't seen the three piled stones that all westerners knew meant poison water, especially if there was a steer skull close by.

"Did they have a lot more poison pools in those days, Uncle Red?"

"They did, Lucy. But that was before the 20 Mule Team company drained the borax and alkali from them to sell back to us as laundry soap today."

Grandma smirked like she wouldn't put it past any black-hearted Reagan with the extra letter in his name.

As the crawling man reached the back wheel of his wagon, his wife shouted "Oh, Hiram, no." Uncle Red shook his head, "Poor devil," and drained the beer from his bottle. "Just think," he continued, "a little Pabst Blue Ribbon would have saved that lad."

At the last commercial Grandma complained about how hot the day had been and how dry the air.

"Well now, Maeve, a little cold beer's what you need, too. And I think I'll have another. Let me get one for you."

He jumped up and ran to her kitchen like the house was on fire. She followed behind protesting with a rare chuckle that sounded like she'd already been into the beer. Grandma had given up her objection weeks ago to Uncle Red leaving some beer in her refrigerator between visits, although at first she'd complained to me about how much extra electricity it took to keep so many bottles cold.

No doubt about it, watching pioneers was thirsty work, but I waited until Ronald Reagan finished telling about the scenes from next week's episode before I went for more ginger ale. I didn't know exactly what was going on in the kitchen when I got there. Uncle Red was standing on his tiptoes on a chair in front of a cupboard, saying, "Are you sure they are here, Maeve?" His voice sounded muffled as he had his head deep inside the cupboard.

"Of course I'm sure. They were a wedding present. Top shelf, all the way to the back."

"I'm going to have to unpack some of these other things if I am to find them. Here Maeve, take these." He began passing down small floral plates with gold rims.

"Oh, look at these. I haven't had these dessert plates out in years. They are up there for safekeeping. I got them at a shop on Michigan Avenue when I was still single. Be careful now, Red, I can't replace them. I never use them because the gold wears off too easily."

Uncle Red's laugh from inside the cupboard caused a ripple of tinkling sounds among the glass wear, like a toast was being raised. "Why, would you care then about protecting something too precious to use?"

"Just be careful. They are fragile and you're an old bull in a china shop."

"I'll have to move these, too," he said as he handed down the pieces of a silver tea service, one by one.

Soon the kitchen counters were strewn with so many fancy old things that it looked like they were getting ready for a party, or clearing up after one that might have happened long ago.

"There. Got 'em." Uncle Red handed down one tall crystal glass and then another. He stepped slowly off the chair and they both laughed when he blew into the glasses and dust flew into his face. I never knew dust to be a laughing matter to Grandma. It was evidence of at least a venial sin, and sometimes a mortal one if it was at someone else's house. When she'd squeaked them clean, she slowly began pouring beer from a brown bottle. He never took his eyes off her as she poured. Mostly I watched the bubbles. The glass was so tall that they had enough room to grow large into a full celebration of being a bubble. Now that was elegance in my book.

"Can I have some more ginger ale in one of those glasses?"

"No, Lucy, these are my crystal Pilsners. They are just for adults."

When the foam began to settle as she finished the first glass, the etching on the side of the glass became clearer. A large scrolled F unfurled and then a smaller W and a J appeared. F for Fahey, of course.

"Hey, it says W.J.F. like William J. Fahey for Grandpa." I'd never seen such fancy monograms on glasses before. When I looked up at Grandma, I saw Uncle Red's hand on hers to steady and guide it as she poured the second glass. Grandma Fahey never needed any help doing anything around her kitchen. What was Uncle Red thinking?

"We'd want to use our finest crystal for our guest, would we not?"

She was blushing as she had a few days ago when Uncle Red pronounced that the roast she served was the finest in Christendom, when we all knew she'd done better.

"Here, Lucy, a little more ginger ale?" Uncle Red tilted a soda bottle over my empty jelly glass. Good thing it was ginger ale because my stomach felt like it was going to turn over completely at any second. I liked that they got along well enough for Uncle Red to come visit, but I didn't know what it would mean for me that they were getting along this well. Uncle Red was my pal long before he was Grandma's and I didn't like being excluded.

Most nights after Uncle Red had left, Grandma said it was to his credit that he never stayed too long. I guess she didn't notice that he'd reach for his straw fedora whenever she reached for her rosary, excusing himself with, "My sacred iliac is acting up, Maeve. It wouldn't do for me to kneel on your floor tonight. Lucy'll pray extra hard for me, won't you?"

I didn't want to have to pray any more than I had to or to have him leave, either one, but I liked it that he winked only at me when he left for Mr. Philsy Cannon's backroom.

But recently there was less praying the rosary and less time being spent at Philsy's, the AOH, and the Holy Name. And a lot less time watching the cowboy shows I wanted to watch with Uncle Red.

One day last week, Grandma said, "So soon, Red?" when he got up to leave. Grandma put her beads aside and Uncle Red seemed happy to sit back down. When he asked if there was any more strawberry shortcake, she served him the last sliver on one of her gold-rimmed, floral dessert plates. It looked silly in Uncle Red's big hands, like they were playing house with a tiny tea set. I expected him to make some crack about Grandma putting on the dog, but he didn't. And I had been hoping to have the last of the short-cake myself.

"I was wondering, Red, if you could see to the TV reception. Bishop Sheen will be on soon."

All the strawberry shortcake in the world wouldn't make my Uncle Red sit still for Bishop Sheen. Even Grandma Keary couldn't keep him in the same room when Bishop Sheen was on. He always told Grandma Keary that Bishop Sheen was wound a little too tight for an Irishman and he didn't need anyone on TV wearing a purple beanie to tell him that God loved him.

So, I couldn't figure it when he stayed for Bishop Sheen's sermon, particularly when he wouldn't stay to watch *Bonanza* when I asked him last Sunday night. I never heard him say that Pa Cartwright was wound too tight. He liked all the Cartwrights and I thought he liked watching them with me even though he called them the Ponderosas and said he never heard of Italian cowboys. If anyone was asking, I didn't always like having to share Uncle Red with Grandma.

Although I was used to having him around Grandma's in the evening, when I heard Uncle Red's laughter echoing in the kitchen one Sunday afternoon, I came running.

"Uncle Red, what are you doing here?"

"Why, I came to see my best gal, Lucy."

I hoped he still meant I was his best gal. He didn't think Grandma was his best gal, did he? I hadn't seen any more hand holding in the kitchen, but Grandma had scolded me last week for startling them in the hallway before her Legion of Mary meeting. Uncle Red was standing behind her at the mirror and adjusting her hat and veil with both hands.

"And how's old Dwight doing?"

"A little green around the gills, I think." It wasn't true, I couldn't tell Dwight and Mamie apart, but I liked to see Uncle Red's face shine the way it did when we talked about my fish.

"That's a good sign, maybe he's thinking about moving from the castle."

"I think he is."

He roared.

Neither of my fish could still fit through the little plastic castle in the bottom of the bowl as they had when I first got them, but they seemed happy enough.

"Tell me, Lucy, you haven't let them spawn have you? Two of their kind is enough."

I still didn't know what this meant or how to prevent it so I couldn't be sure, but I said I hadn't anyway.

"Good work, Lucy."

He stopped Grandma from whatever she was winding up to say by snapping his suspenders and telling her he would die if he didn't have a ginger ale. "Hottest day yet this summer, Maeve," he said wiping his forehead with a handkerchief.

What he said next took me by surprise more than a bowl full of goldfish.

"Lucy, how would you like to accompany me ..."

"Yes sir, I would, Uncle Red."

"Wait, Lucy," he laughed, "wait until I tell you the details."

He told Grandma that Senator Jack Kennedy was making his way through town and that he had heard him with the boys from the Al Smith Club that morning at a breakfast sponsored by the Jackson County Democrats.

"Kennedy in Kansas City. Pfft." Grandma said.

"He's over at the College right now talking to the Jesuits, as if you could get a word in edgewise with a room full of those chappies."

"Oh, that boy. He should know his place. He'll bring us all to shame when he loses."

I didn't understand Grandma's alarm.

"But Grandma, how could Senator Kennedy bring us shame if he's a Democrat?"

She didn't answer. Uncle Red laughed, but he didn't explain either.

"Lucy, do you mean to tell me you are a Republican, too?"

This put me in a jam. I wanted to go to see Senator Kennedy with Uncle Red so I could have him all to myself for a change. Grandma was the only Republican I really ever knew.

"Well, Lucy, what party will it be?"

The only party I was interested in was the one Uncle Red was going to take me to. I guess Uncle Red knew I was a Democrat because I was about the only one in the family who still asked him to tell about chasing live turkeys in a snow storm one Christmas when he was my age. He'd been hired by Alderman Pendergast to deliver turkeys to all the Democrats down in the west river bottoms. The turkeys had run wild when Uncle Red accidentally left the cage open. Each time he told the story more and more turkeys got away. I was glad for the ones that got away and so was Uncle Red, I think.

Grandma was looking me square in the eye, "Democrats have no sense of propriety and they never will, Lucy."

I knew that word, propriety. People without it didn't wear white gloves to church, or worse, they wore white patent after Labor Day.

"And Red, I must tell you, I don't like that Kennedy boy thinking he can be President. What would others think of us? That we all expected to have one of ours in the White House? Preposterous."

"Oh Maeve, he's far from a shoo-in. I just want him to give them a run for their money, like Al Smith in '28. Better than Al Smith even, Jack's Irish on both sides, Maeve. Cork and Wexford."

"His grandfather was only a saloon keeper in Boston, did you know that?" she lowered her voice like there was someone else in her kitchen to overhear.

"Well, a saloon keeper, now that's high praise, Maeve. You remember what Big Jim Pendergast told them years ago when they tried to keep him out of politics just because he ran a saloon."

I'd heard this before. I liked knowing a joke that Grandma didn't, even one she wouldn't think was funny anyway.

"Oh, I know, Uncle Red." My right arm raised itself like I was back in Sister Mary Columba's class. I hoped I could get it right, I didn't want Uncle Red to lose interest in taking me with him. Grandma had a way of wearing you down.

"Lucy, what did the Alderman say about barring saloon keepers from holding public office in Kansas City?"

He waited for my answer just as Grandma would for answer to a catechism question.

"He said that keeping saloon keepers out of public office would only improve the reputation of ... the saloon keepers?"

He tapped his index finger on his nose to let me know I'd gotten it right, and laughed like I had told him Dwight was floating belly up in his bowl.

"See now, Red, there's a good example for you, that Pendergast machine. When they threw that Tom Pendergast boy in prison it was a disgrace to the entire faith. People didn't say just that he was a crook, they said he was an Irish Catholic crook, and that's what comes of letting an Irishman have too much sway in government."

"Jack Kennedy is no crook, Maeve."

"Democrats don't have much concern for how the rest of the world sees things."

"I hope to hell not, Maeve."

The room seemed even hotter. I didn't know if it was the weather or the politics that made Grandma so cranky, but it was pretty much okay with me that things were back to how they had been before they started holding hands in the kitchen.

"What time will we be leaving, Uncle Red?" I ventured in the silence between them.

"Soon, Lucy. Soon."

I wasn't so sure. This was Grandma Fahey's house where she made the rules, but Uncle Red smiled and lowered his voice a bit. "Look Maeve, Rosie asked me to see to this. She'd take Lucy herself if she could. He's going right through their own parish, right past Mary of Gaels. She may never get another chance to see a Catholic running for President. It's been thirty-two years since Al Smith. It's practically like Halley's comet coming around again."

Grandma unclenched her fist that she held tightly at her waist.

"C'mon, Maeve. Rosie wants her kids to at least see the man while they have a chance."

Kids? "Is Jackie going to be there?"

"You bet, Lucy. Mick is picking him up after his game today. We'll meet up with them."

"Oh, Grandma." I bit my lip to keep from begging because I didn't want her to think I didn't have a sense of propriety.

She was tapping her fingers together as she tried to find fault with the plan. "You propose to drive all the way to Mary of Gaels in this heat?"

"I thought of that, Maeve. We are taking Mick's dairy delivery truck. It is nice and refrigerated. Conny is going, too."

Uncle Mickey's truck. What a day this was turning into. Jackie and I never got to actually ride in it no matter how we begged. I loved that green and white truck from McGrath's Dairy with a shamrock for an apostrophe. It was like Christmas Eve even on the hottest days inside Uncle Mickey's truck.

"You like fudgecicles don't you, Lucy?" Uncle Red asked, looking at Grandma.

They were my absolute favorite. I hadn't had one since I left home.

Uncle Red continued, "Well, Mick said something about fudgecicles and things left over from the week, and he needed some help eating them all, Lucy."

"Oh, Grandma, please can I go?" I was begging now and I didn't care how it looked. I must be more of a Democrat than I knew.

Grandma was tapping her index finger on the table like it was Morse code for no, no. no, no, no.

"Sure you don't want to ride out into the fancy Kansas suburbs in the back of a milk delivery truck with us, Maeve?"

"I do not. You and your brother Conny over in Mary of Gaels. Now there's a sight for you. There's two more Democrats in Kansas than there is room for. You do know that your boy Kennedy doesn't stand a chance on the Kansas side of the line?"

"He has precisely a snowball's chance in Hell, or Kansas in the summer, if you can tell the difference between those two locations."

I couldn't wait another second for her to make up her mind, but Uncle Red was slowly making circles on the white napkin with the bottom of the ginger ale glass and he smiled at Grandma like he held three aces.

"I am not in favor of having my granddaughter out on such a hot day just to hear a lot of palaver from the Democrats. But I'll just touch up the dress you wore to church this morning, Lucy. I won't have you out on a Sunday afternoon in shorts. You run and get some fresh anklets from the clothesline now."

When Grandma left the room, Uncle Red pushed his ginger ale over in front of me. "You want this, Lucy? I never touch the stuff myself."

I was only allowed soda once a week, during *Death Valley Days*. The anklets could wait. Savoring the way the bubbles rose and popped at the surface, I asked Uncle Red, "Do you think the faeries would be for or against Senator Kennedy?"

Tilting my good ear to the bubbles popping at the surface, I smiled back at Uncle Red who laughed, "What's Maeve been putting in your ginger ale, Lucy?"

"No, really Uncle Red. What do you think?"

"The faeries must be for Jack. What else would explain Missouri going for him at the Democratic Convention last month over Missouri Senator Symington, the favorite son."

I thought of Jackie.

"Uncle Red, how does my mom know that Senator Kennedy is here?"

"I told her, Lucy."

"Do you ever tell her about me?"

"Oh, I do, I do, Lucy. And she is glad that you are having such a good summer, and learning so much. Don't worry Lucy, it won't be much longer before she's home."

"How come Mama wants us to see Senator Kennedy so much?"

"Well, she has a special interest in long shots like Jack Kennedy. Also because this race is unique. If he makes it all the way, he'll be the first Catholic, Irish or otherwise, elected to the presidency."

"No, really, how come, Uncle Red?" The bubbles in the cold ginger ale bristled inside my mouth making me smile as I watched his face for signs of a punch line.

"That's the reason, Lucy. There's never been a Catholic President."

I couldn't believe Uncle Red didn't know that President Eisenhower was a Catholic. Why else would they have his picture on the wall in my classroom at Mary of Gaels, right under the American flag and right next to Pope Pius' picture and his yellow and white flag. They both looked old and tired to me, but they had nice flags.

On TV President Eisenhower sounded like any of the parents at Mary of Gaels who prayed every week for the conversion of Russia when he talked about not trusting the Soviet Union. And wasn't he always saying "God Bless the United States of America" like he had more of a right to say it than anybody else? What more would a President have to do to be a Catholic one?

"Are you sure President Eisenhower's not one?"

"One what, Lucy?"

"A Catholic."

"Let's just say, the Eisenhowers in Kansas City are not in your parish or in mine," he smiled.

"But Uncle Red, there are plenty of Irish guys on TV already, why wouldn't they just let Senator Kennedy take over for President Eisenhower on the TV?"

When I started to name the ones I could think of—Jackie Gleason, Art Carney—Uncle Red started to laugh like it hurt him somewhere.

"Stop. Stop, Lucy."

"Ed Sullivan. What about him?"

"You're serious then? Well, the President has a bigger job than Ed Sullivan. The President does more than just appear on television to introduce a pack of Hungarian plate twirlers or a family of trained seals every Sunday night."

"But that's the only time you get to see President Eisenhower is when he's on TV."

"Sure, the President comes on every so often but even if he came on every week as regular as Fulton Sheen, God help us, it would still be just a little bit of what he gets to do. If young Jack got to be President, don't you see he'd get to tell the bankers and the unions and the farmers and the railroads what to do. The bankers and the farmers, especially the kind you have over there in Kansas, don't want a Catholic telling them anything."

"But President Truman is a Catholic, Uncle Red. You said you were at Mass with Harry Truman and his secret service men over at Visitation church when one of the Pendergasts died. Remember?" I was confident that he would correct his mistake.

Grandma rounded the corner back into the kitchen with my pink and gray dress all tidied up.

"Judge Truman a Catholic? That's rare," she laughed. "Maybe that's why they cancelled his membership in the Ku Klux Klan out in Independence."

Uncle Red wasn't laughing. "That was just a rumor, Maeve. He denied that charge over and over to the Party."

"That doesn't mean he wasn't actually in the Klan."

I liked smiley old Harry Truman. I sort of assumed he was part of a clan, maybe even our clan. Uncle Red even had lunch with him at the Muehlebach Hotel once. My mom always let me send him a birthday card every May 8th when the TV news and *The Kansas City Star* made a big fuss about him strutting around downtown with his cane.

"But if he is a member of the clan, doesn't that mean he's got to be a Catholic?"

"Not that clan, Lucy. Or any other. You'd better get changed, we don't want to be late."

"Yes sir, Uncle Red."

"Lucy, make a trip past the clothesline for your anklets. And please put a ribbon in your hair," Grandma said as she daubed the perspiration at her brow with a hanky. "I won't have you running around on a Sunday afternoon looking like a hooligan even if you're only going to the suburbs."

"Yessum."

I was halfway up the stairs to change when I remembered that no one would be caught dead in a dress in the summertime in Mary of Gaels and decided to change into my pedal pushers. Nobody wore socks with their Keds back home in Mary of Gaels either, so I saved my clean anklets for another time by throwing them in my closet. I wasn't going to wear a ribbon either. Only showoffs wore ribbons. Uncle Red was wearing his straw fedora, so I'd wear the felt cowboy hat he brought me earlier in the summer. I'd have to wait in my room until the last minute so that there wouldn't be time for Grandma to make me change.

I could hear them bickering about the Pendergast Machine. I never understood what the Pendergasts needed a machine for, but any time Grandma mentioned it, I saw a long row of Christmas turkeys being delivered on a conveyor belt.

I heard Uncle Red say that he wanted to drive me through the old wards down by the river just to round out my view of Irish politicians.

"You'll go straight to Mary of Gaels and right back home, Red Quinn. I won't have her driven through those broken down old places down in the river bottoms. They're unsafe."

I was glad when I heard Uncle Red call from the bottom of the steps. "They'll be waiting for us, Lucy. Let's go."

Before I hit the bottom step, Grandma began to fuss, "Oh, Lucy, this is the last straw. It's Sunday. You can't wear that. Just look at you."

"She looks fine, Maeve. I'm not taking her to dinner on the Plaza. She's heading west to her home in the Kansas suburbs. This is how we dress on the prairie, am I not right, Lucy?"

"You have her home early, Red. I'll have some supper waiting."

I couldn't have been happier. Going out by myself with Uncle Red, picking up Jackie and heading back to Mary of Gaels in Uncle Mickey's dairy truck. And I could add seeing Senator Kennedy in person to the list of things I wanted to tell Mama about when we both got to go home.

I wanted to make sure Uncle Red noticed my hat, so before we headed out the door, I asked, "Uncle Red, is my hat on right?"

He stopped in the hallway at the mirror. "Hmm. Let me see, Lucy. Let me see," he said as he tightened the strap under my chin just a bit. "There. You look grand. I'd say you look better than Dale Evans."

"Uncle Red, do you think we can watch *Bonanza* together tonight?"

"You bet. I'll have you back home before Little Joe and Hoss have time to ride into Carson City for supplies, Lucy."

I knew it. Bishop Fulton Sheen had nothing on an entire family of Cartwrights. And I was still his best gal.

CHAPTER 24: WEARIN' OF THE GREEN IN KANSAS

When Uncle Red and I pulled into the dairy parking lot Uncle Mickey and Uncle Conny were waiting for us. I ran across to the truck and Uncle Mickey sprang open the door. There in the storage behind the front seat was my brother Jackie sitting on an overturned wooden milk bottle crate.

"Hiya, Luce," he said without taking the fudge-cicle from his mouth.

"Hiya, Jackie."

"Hop in, Lucy. The cold air's getting out," Uncle Mickey called from the driver's seat.

Jackie turned over another crate for me to sit on and said, "Hurry up Luce, my fudgecicle is melting."

I jumped up on the high step on the side of the dairy truck and scrunched past Uncle Conny who was sliding over in the front seat to make room for Uncle Red, and saying, "How the Hell are we all going to fit in here? We should have taken a car."

"Want one?" Jackie asked, reaching behind him into a little metal fridge door. When he opened it, a cold fog rolled in waves and settled around me like a long sigh on this hot August day. I was as happy as I had been since I left home.

I unwrapped my fudgecicle. The pioneers could have used a refrigerated truck like Uncle Mickey's heading west on the Santa Fe Trail. This was no mirage like on *Death Valley Days*. Sinking my front teeth into the fudgecicle made me shiver with delight.

My mouth had already frozen into a smile when Jackie said, "You should see all the stuff that's in here, Luce." He patted the side of the metal fridge like he'd found a treasure.

"All in?" asked Uncle Mickey.

"All in," answered Uncle Red. "Head 'em up, move 'em out, Mick, lad. We're heading west into the Shawnee Territory."

"No, Uncle Red," I tried to say. "Nobody calls it that anymore, it's just Kansas," but my mouth was so full of icy chocolate slush that no one seemed to know what I said.

"That Indian language you're speaking there, Lucy?"

Even Jackie laughed.

"Just the same, I'll ride shotgun for you, Mickey. In case we are attacked by any wild injuns wanting our scalps. Shawnees, Pawnees, and maybe Cherokees. Who knows?"

"More likely Methodists, Baptists, and Planned Parenthood," Uncle Conny said.

Jackie grinned like he was all grown up or something, laughing at a joke I didn't get.

"Hey Red, what did it cost you to get the back window on your Ford replaced? Uncle Conny asked.

"Not too much. The damn thing shattered and it was easy to replace."

"Must have been a shotgun then," grumbled Uncle Mickey. "Big rubes."

"At least if anybody shoots out the windows today, your boss McGrath will have to pay the tab, Mick," smiled Uncle Red.

"Well, Red, we are not going to be so daft as to drive a car with 'Back Jack' bumper stickers all over it."

The stick from the fudgecicle Jackie was finishing off fell from his mouth. "Somebody tried to shoot Uncle Red?"

"No, no, Jackie. I wasn't in the car."

Jackie was leaning over into the front seat demanding details.

"Nothing for you to worry about, kids. Just an election prank, you might say."

"Hell, Red, swiping yard signs is an election prank. I've never heard of the likes of this."

Uncle Red was trying to turn around in the crowded front seat saying, "Jackie, why don't you have another fudgecicle and see if Lucy wants one, too."

Jackie didn't budge.

"What happened, Uncle Red?" he asked, feeling for the Black Cats firecrackers he carried in the back pocket of his jeans. Wherever Jackie was, explosions followed. He'd spent all his grass cutting money to buy fireworks wholesale. Black Cats were his favorite, although whenever Dad found any he'd ground Jackie and put them in a bucket of water.

"Well, a few days ago, I was out here on the Kansas side, you see, running some papers at the end of the day from Judge O'Hara's office out to the Johnson County court in Olathe. I know a lot of those boys, nice boys, in the court so I chatted them up. By the time I came out, let's just say somebody had expressed a political opinion on Jack through my rear window."

"Wow."

I was glad that Uncle Mickey's truck had no back windows.

"And Lucy," Uncle Red added, "no need to tell your Grandmother Fahey any of this. We don't want to worry her."

"Yessir."

Jackie sat back down. "Double wow."

I moved over closer to Jackie on our milk crate bench.

"Did you miss me, Jackie?"

"Not much."

I used to be able to tell if he was kidding or not, but his A's hat was pulled down so far over his head that I couldn't see much of his face. I missed him, how could he not have missed me, too?

I wanted to tell him that I missed him every day, but the dairy truck seemed too cold a place to say it, and besides, he was busy rummaging through the fridge. He opened a dreamcicle, took one bite and then put it back and dug deeper, until he found a Bomb Pop.

"Does Mama miss us do you think?"

"Don't be a dope, Luce, of course she does. She misses us a lot. And don't eat that fudgecicle so fast or you'll get that headache right between your eyes again if you do."

I didn't have to slow down if I didn't want to, but when it felt like my brain was starting to freeze, I decided to take a break from my fudgecicle, but not because he told me to.

"Jackie, how come if you put a Snicker Bar in the freezer it would freeze solid and fudgecicles never do?"

"Just does. It's science. Molecules and stuff."

"Do I get to take science next year?"

"Nope. You have to wait until you are older unless you win the science fair like me and get special permission. And you have to pass catechism first, Luce, before you can take science."

I didn't like him bringing that up. "How come?"

"Because catechism is good training for science. You have to be able to understand invisible things in catechism before you can understand invisible stuff in science."

I could tell him I'd already learned plenty from Grandma Fahey about how invisible things work but I liked having my own secrets, so I didn't mention the faeries.

"Luce, you're going to take off that cowboy hat when we get to Mary of Gaels, aren't you?"

"Why? Uncle Red got it for me. We watch television together all the time. Just me and Uncle Red."

"Oh right, Luce. Like I'm sure Uncle Red goes all the way to Grandma's just to watch TV with you."

"Well, sometimes Grandma watches too, but mostly it is just me and Uncle Red."

Uncle Conny ribbed, "Going to the Widow Fahey's to watch TV, eh Red? The set at Philsy's broken, is it?"

Uncle Red wasn't talking. And Jackie kept after me about my hat, "How come it's green?"

"Why not? I like it."

"Cowboys didn't wear green hats, Luce. They were all black or white, like on TV."

"Everything's black or white on TV, Jackie. Anyway, how do you know?"

"Well, I know that they weren't that color."

I was glad when Uncle Red came to my defense, "Not so, Jackie. Two Shillelagh O'Sullivan wore a green hat. And he was the slickest Mick in the West."

That reminded me of Senator Kennedy. "Oh, Jackie, did you know that they only let a Catholic run for President every 32 years?"

"Yeah? How come?"

"Just cause. It's like Bill Haley and the Comets." I already knew a little science myself.

"No, it's not, Luce. For one thing, Bill Haley is the guy on American Bandstand. And for another thing, Halley's Comet comes every 75 years, not 32. It came last time in 1910, so we can see it again in 1985."

"1985," I repeated slowly. I hoped I'd be driving my own McGrath's Dairy truck by then.

Uncle Conny said to Uncle Red, "Hey, we'll have to go to Calvary Cemetery to call on you in 1985."

"You think so, do you, Conny? I think we both should have paid more attention back in 1910 if we wanted to see Halley's Comet."

"What do you mean?" Uncle Mickey said, "You'll both still be drinking that embalming fluid down at Cannon's."

"At least we'll know where we are headed, Mick. Do you know where the hell you are going now?" asked Uncle Conny.

I couldn't believe they didn't know how to find Shawnee Mission High. It was only the biggest public school around anywhere. Although it was just a few blocks down from Mary of Gaels, Jackie and I wouldn't be going there for high school.

"How the Hell did a parochial school get all the way out there, anyway?" Uncle Conny said.

Uncle Red said that a farmer had willed his land directly to the church since the big developer on the Kansas side wouldn't sell land for a Catholic Church or a Jewish Synagogue.

"Go all the way to Stateline and turn right, Uncle Mick." Jackie said, as proudly as if he'd just saved a wagon train, and announced, "Entering Shawnee Territory."

I was now riding through my home parish for the first time since I left. I pulled myself up to stand behind Uncle Red and look out of his window to see if I saw anyone I knew. I thought I saw some kids from my class but I couldn't be sure, so I waved anyway.

"Cripes. Sit down, Luce," Jackie said.

The red light was about to change at the busy corner of 75th and Mission Road. Uncle Mickey said, "Red, why don't you and the kids get out here. Conny and I'll park the truck."

"I'll stay with you, Uncle Mick," Jackie said.

"OK. OK," Uncle Red took a deep breath before he made the jump off the high step from Uncle Mickey's truck to the street.

"Hurry up, Lucy," Uncle Conny said.

The car behind us was honking as I squeaked out of the back.

"We'll look for you in the crowd in front of the church," Uncle Red called to them. When he took me by the hand, I thought he was shaking a bit, but it might have been just from sitting in the cold of Uncle Mickey's truck. He stooped to pin a "Back Jack" button on my cotton shirt, looked around at faces in the crowd, and then stiffly put his arm around my shoulders and said, "Let's walk a little quicker, Lucy. We'll want to be in front of the church, so young Jack knows where we stand, eh?"

The crowd was starting to thicken on both sides of the blocks of Shawnee Mission Road between Mary of Gaels and the public high school. Policemen on motorcycles zipped up and down to keep people from standing in the street. There were more people in front of Mary of Gaels than I had ever seen at the school, more even than during May procession when all the parents would gather around as every kid in the school swayed in a long line out and around to the grotto that faced our church. We sang "*Ave! Ave! Maria*" as one 8th grade girl crowned the statue of the Holy Mother in the grotto with flowers.

I didn't recognize all of the faces from Mary of Gaels as I would at May procession. The police were putting up wooden barricades all along the curb in front of the church, but there was our neighbor Mrs. Sweeney's cheerful face. "Hello Lucy. How have you been? We've been remembering you all in our prayers."

Uncle Red tipped his straw fedora. "Thank you, Missus."

I liked Mrs. Sweeney, but all the praying that everyone was doing hadn't brought Mama home yet.

"Lucy, here's a good place to stand." Uncle Red was pointing to the back of the stone grotto. "Climb up there so you can see our boy when he drives by. Too bad the Blessed Mother is facing the other direction, she would have gotten a kick out of this, too."

Mrs. Sweeney chuckled and said, "So would your Mom, Lucy. Do you thinking climbing on the grotto is a good idea?"

As I was trying to get some traction on the back of the Blessed Mother's statue with the slippery soles of my Keds, Deirdre Mannion, a girl from Jackie's class came up to us. She was the only seventh grader to be one of the Living Rosary beads at the May procession, an honor usually reserved for eighth graders. She got to wear a white dress and stand in the circle of 50 other girls who took a turn leading the Hail Mary. She acted now like the Mother of God was a special friend of hers. Jackie was the only seventh grade boy to be one of the five living Our Father beads last year because he got the highest score in the school on the Iowa Basics math test.

Dierdre, a red ribbon in her blond hair, looked at me and said, "Sister doesn't like it when anyone climbs on Mary's grotto."

Uncle Red nodded his head like she had said something extremely interesting and said, "I'll take that up with Sister after the election." Then he proceeded to help me find a niche and anchor myself in the stonework. I knew right then and there that I would never be asked to be a Hail Mary bead.

"Is he your Grandpa or something?" she asked, like Uncle Red didn't matter at all to her, a famous rosary bead.

"I don't have a Grandpa," I said. "He's my Uncle Red."

"His hair is white not red."

"So what." I never felt like I had to defend Uncle Red just for being old out in the new parish, but you only saw white hair in Mary of Gaels when people's grandparents came out for Sunday dinner or something.

"Anyway, is your brother here?"

"He's out there somewhere."

"Tell him I said 'hi.' And tell him that we are all meeting at the Velvet Freeze after Kennedy's car goes by."

I knew that I wasn't invited but I didn't care much. I was with Uncle Red and, besides, the inside of my mouth still felt numb from fudgecicles. I was glad when she wandered off and Uncle Red assured me the Blessed Mother wouldn't mind a bit me using her statue.

Someone shouted, "Here he comes!"

"Go ahead and lean on me, Lucy."

I looked down the street as far as I could see. Uncle Red was right about this being a good place to watch. I was leaning out so far that my green cowboy hat slid off my head and down my back. Dale Evans sometimes wore hers that way, too.

"Can you see him yet, Lucy?"

I saw a suntanned man waving from a white convertible as it came around a bend. People were spilling onto the street and the car nearly slowed to a stop. When Senator Kennedy waved at one side of the crowd and then the other, it was like watching the sun and wind sway grain growing in a field. Arms were waving back like stems of wheat and people were shouting "Mr. Kennedy!" or "Senator!" as the car slowly made its way. For all the police could do, people were running up to the car to shake his hand or touch his arm, and the crowd brought the car to a complete stop.

Suddenly there was a loud popping noise from the crowd in front of the Senator's car. Then, three more noises just as loud. Pop. Pop. Pop.

"Lucy, where's Jackie?"

I couldn't see Jackie anywhere in the crowd around the car. Now, a policeman on a motorcycle broke away from where the Senator's car was swamped by shouting people. He was clearing the way like a cop at a funeral. When he stopped in front of our Mary of Gaels grotto, his motorcycle made two louder pops. I felt Uncle Red's shoulders drop as he laughed, "It's only a backfire. Just a backfire. Sure, I didn't think Jackie would have a reason to set off those firecrackers with Jack coming by. He should save them in case Richard Nixon ever comes to town."

The cop was off his motorcycle and making people move back behind the barricade so that the car could get through.

"I see them now, Uncle Red. I see Uncle Conny and Uncle Mickey. They are right across the street from us. Look." I waved but they didn't see me because Uncle Conny was talking to a man with a sign of a cartoon-like drawing of a dead fish.

I waved again at Uncle Conny, but he didn't see or hear me shout his name. I knew from the set of his chin what was going on between him and the stinky fish sign man. I didn't see Jackie, but I knew he couldn't be far away. When the Publics called us "fish eaters" it made Jackie steaming mad. That's why he started his club, the Moggers, after our MoG school emblem in the first place, he said, to give the Publics a taste of Hell, where we knew they all were heading when they died. I never minded us being called "fish eaters" and "mackerel snappers" that much because I enjoyed my fish sticks and tater tots in the cafeteria on Fridays. Uncle Red thought Jackie's club was called the Mongers, and when he would ask him, "How are your fish monger friends? Staying out of the way of the law, are you?" Jackie would grin proudly.

I wondered how Senator Kennedy felt about being a "fish eater" like us. When more signs started springing up from the crowd like dandelions in Grandma Fahey's back yard, I asked Uncle Red, "How can he go back to Rome? I thought he was from Boston."

"Boston is closer to Rome than to Shawnee Mission, Kansas."

The police had finally cleared the way for Senator Kennedy's car to start moving freely on the street again and some girls and even some moms started to scream. I thought of how the older girls screamed in the theatre when Jackie took me to see Elvis in *Love Me Tender*. I didn't even think I knew how to make some of those noises. Jackie said then girls shouldn't be allowed to go to Civil War movies at all if they had to do that.

The closer the car got to us, the louder the crowd around us got. The dead fish sign began to bob up and down directly across from us. Uncle Conny had his hand on the sign man's chest. The police whistle turned suddenly shrill when the car was a few seconds away from us. The crowd seemed pulled towards the street by a magnet. I was glad for my place on the grotto and hung more tightly on to Uncle Red's shoulders.

"Can you see him, Lucy? Can you see the man yet?" Uncle Red was yelling.

"He's waving like he knows us all, Uncle Red," I shouted down to him.

"Well, your little mug ought to be familiar enough to him Lucy," he laughed.

Out of the corner of my eye I saw Uncle Mickey. He was behind the sign man, bending down to tie his shoe or something. He'd better stand up soon or he'll miss Senator Kennedy. Uncle Conny, who still had his large hand on the sign man's chest, started backing him up into the boulder Uncle Mickey had become. With one shove the man tumbled backward over Uncle Mickey's broad back and the sign went down like a hatchet just before the Senator's car, now picking up speed, reached us. From out of the crowd behind Uncle Mickey came one black high-topped sneaker, and then another. My brother's feet landed squarely on the dead fish sign just as Jack Kennedy's smiling face whisked by between us. Jackie was doing what any Mogger would do.

Uncle Conny had his arms crossed like nothing had happened. Uncle Mickey was bending over with a smile and a hand to help the sign man up, but the man reached for the front of Uncle Mickey's shirt instead of his hand and tore his pocket off. I never knew that grown ups played Moggers versus Publics, too.

"Did you see the chief, Lucy? Did you see him?" Uncle Red was laughing like he was going to cry, the way my dad did when Notre Dame won an important game. Uncle Red hadn't shouted or waved as people around us had, but only gave a two-fingered salute off the brim of his hat as the Senator passed.

I didn't want to tell Uncle Red that I really hadn't seen that much of him as I stared at the back of Senator Kennedy's head. I was surprised that his hair was reddish brown like Dad's, and not at all the way it looked on TV. He had a cowlick worse than Jackie's, but that may have been from riding in a convertible.

Uncle Red turned to help me down from the grotto. "Tell the Blessed Mother thanks for her hospitality and hop down from there now, Lucy. We've got to move quick if you are to hear him speak." His face was stuck in a smile but his eyes were rimmed with red.

I wasn't sure if Uncle Red had seen what Uncle Conny and Uncle Mickey had done, but he took me by the hand and we headed towards them. The man with the dead fish sign still had Uncle Mickey by the shirt and was still shouting at him. The commotion had attracted the attention of a motorcycle cop who was streaking towards them. With his white helmet he looked eight feet tall. I knew this one. He was the meanest cop in our suburb. Jackie and the Moggers called him "Cochise" after the Apache sheriff on TV. He'd been after Jackie since the Moggers dropped exploding Black Cats off the roof of the public junior high just to rub it in that we had the day off for eating fish on Friday and they didn't.

Uncle Red knew all the cops by first name in his parish but not in Mary of Gaels. He sized up "Cochise" and put his thumb and index finger to his mouth and whistled so fiercely that the sound could be heard above the noise of the crowd. Jackie squirted out of the crowd and ran over to us. Uncle Red put his arm around Jackie, gave him a little shove in the direction of the high school, tipped his hat at the giant helmeted cop and we were off to hear Senator Kennedy.

"Just as well you stay with us, Jackie." Uncle Red led the way. "We need to pick up the pace if we are going to get to the school to hear the chief speak."

Jackie seemed very glad to see Uncle Red and I was glad that Jackie was safe. We fell in behind Uncle Red, and Jackie seemed like his old self for a while.

"What? Why are you staring at me, Luce?"

"You lost your hat, Jackie. Your favorite hat."

"It got knocked off of me when that guy, ah, fell over. Quit staring, Luce. You're giving me the creeps. What are you looking at?"

"Nothing."

"Look, Luce, the guy was a jerk, OK? He was asking for it."

"He was outnumbered. You ganged up on him."

I had seen Jackie join fights on the side of the underdog even when he didn't know what anyone was fighting about.

"I'd knock down all these dumb signs if I could get to them. Big rubes."

"Did you know Deirdre Mannion is here, Jackie?"

"Oh yeah? Did you talk to her? What did she say?"

"She told me not to climb on the grotto."

"I guess so. Why the H were you doing that?"

"Uncle Red told me to, so I could see the parade."

Jackie lowered his voice, "Cripes, she didn't talk to Uncle Red did she? Did she say anything about me?"

"She told me to tell you she was going to the Velvet Freeze, or something stupid like that." I didn't figure he'd go. We had a whole freezer of stuff to eat on the way home.

"Who else? Did she say who else was going to be there?"

"I don't remember." Seventh grade girls all got too much attention in my opinion. "Probably some other stupid rosary beads."

"Think, Luce. It's important. What did she say?"

"She told me to tell you that you were getting stuck up and not fun anymore."

"Am not." Jackie slowed to nearly a stop. I could tell he was wondering if Deirdre Mannion had really said that.

"C'mon you two, pick up the pace," Uncle Red called. "I promised your mom you'd hear Jack Kennedy speak, and so you shall."

By the time we got to the gymnasium it was packed. There were bright lights and cameras everywhere around the entrance where he was expected.

"It's full, Uncle Red, I heard the guy at the door say so. We'll never get in. Let's just watch him on TV," Jackie whined.

Uncle Red led us to a less busy side door that was just being shut and said "Three more?" to a man with a walkie-talkie.

"No way."

I felt Uncle Red's hands on my shoulder blades inching me towards the door.

Then he reached into his pocket for some change and said, "What'll it take to get in?"

The man who was bending over to unlatch the stays on the big metal door stood up, suddenly more interested in Uncle Red.

"What have you got?"

"I've a little collection of silver here, some rare stuff." Uncle Red was pawing through his change.

Jackie looked around like he wished he had his Kansas City A's hat to hide under.

"No bills?" the doorman asked.

"Oh, cripes," Jackie said as he disappeared, probably heading for the Velvet Freeze.

"Nope, but this ought to do it." Uncle Red flipped a big coin in a high arc towards the Kansan who reached for it with both hands. Uncle Red's pitch was off center enough to draw the man away from the door. Uncle Red chuckled when he put his foot in the metal door to stop it from slamming. His hands on my back felt like two springs as he pushed me forward and through the door.

"Hey, what kind of coin is this?" the man said getting a better look at it.

"It's an Irish one. It'll spend better come November."

"Baloney!" said the Kansan, walking away.

I was inside. But I didn't know what to do next. Uncle Red wouldn't fit in when I barely did. Uncle Red peeked in from the doorway and smiled, "Go on now, Lucy. I'll wait here."

I never knew it was possible to freeze in a crowded gym in August. I couldn't believe that he wasn't coming with me. I was surrounded by strangers. I didn't know which were the type that Uncle Conny might like to knock down so I covered my Kennedy button with my hand.

Uncle Red was scanning the room, looking over the heads of people seated and ready for the speech. "Go on now, Lucy, move to the front and sit on the floor." He pointed to a spot I couldn't see but had to believe was there.

I didn't want to go anywhere all by myself. Everybody had someone else to be with but me. I was all alone. Jackie was off looking for Deirdre Mannion, Mom and Dad were together at the hospital, Grandma Fahey was waiting for Uncle Red to come home and adjust the set for Bishop Sheen, and even Dwight had Mamie. Where did that leave me?

"But Uncle Red ..."

"Go on, now, that lad'll be important someday. I'll wait here for you, don't worry. It's the future."

Uncle Red took off his straw hat and wiped his forehead with the back of his hand. His shock of straight white hair that he always kept neatly combed hung down on his forehead. He looked tired like he did at Grandma Keary's kitchen table the day of her funeral. He had told me to look to the future that day, too.

How sad the word "future" seemed to me then. Something to believe was there when other things were falling away from you. The future was a big sad gap in something comfortable.

"Lucy, make your move. Find your place," he shouted.

I darted as fast as I could towards the front of the room, making my way by crawling under several rows of cafeteria tables that held TV camera equipment. I emerged from out of a jungle of cables and wires into a blaze of hot lights to the left of the podium where Senator Kennedy stood with his hands jammed in the pockets of his suit coat, waiting to be introduced to the crowd.

He looked dazzling under those lights. I was surprised that he was taller and skinnier than he looked on Grandma's black and white TV. The blue suit that hung on his thin frame was the color of his eyes. His smile looked familiar. It was part Uncle Red and part my dead Jesuit uncle.

I thought Grandma Fahey might be right that he was too young to run the whole country even though he was two years older than my dad. With his tan he didn't look much older than one of the lifeguards at our pool. I could see him wearing red trunks and swinging a whistle on a shoelace the way the guards did.

He took some note cards from his suit coat pocket and held them by his side. When he glanced down to read them, his blue eyes met my staring ones for just a second. I was afraid I was going to make noises like the girls at the Elvis movie.

As he stepped up to the podium, he was introduced as "the next President of the United States." He nodded to accept what cheers there were, and ignored the boos that were much louder. I was just as glad that I was safe under the table where no one could see me, or the "Back Jack" button on my shirt.

Senator Kennedy didn't seem to mind the boos as much as I did. He began to make cracks about who would win the annual Kansas Jayhawks versus Missouri Tigers football game in November, and soon the boos were all at the Missouri Tigers. A smile grew on his face as he said, "I hope to be occupied with other equally important matters this year in *Novembah*." Everyone laughed and some people clapped, and someone in the back shouted "Go Jack!" For the first time all night, I was glad that Jackie, Uncle Mickey, and Uncle Conny had knocked the dead fish sign man down. I wished I'd shown him my button when he looked at me, but maybe he recognized my face anyway, like I recognized his.

As I looked around at the other faces, I wasn't exactly sure just who had been doing all the booing earlier. When I realized it could have been anyone, I decided to find a short cut out of the gym. I crawled back under the tables and headed for a door behind the makeshift stage. I was surprised to find myself in a hallway that was as empty and quiet as the gym had been crowded and noisy. I hoped I could find my way through these hallways and among the trophy cases and pictures of championship teams. There was what looked like light from the outside shining on the school mascot, a knight in its suit of armor. It stood at an intersection with a wider hall, so I headed quickly in that direction.

I'd never been in a public school before. The Shawnee Mission High School knight loomed even larger the closer I got to it. It was taller than the statue of the Holy Mother that I had climbed on to see Senator Kennedy go by. I noticed that they had the same picture of President Eisenhower that we had on our wall at Mary of Gaels, but there was a blue and gold Kansas flag where we had a yellow and white papal one.

I barreled down that hallway towards the knight and the crossroad that led hopefully to an outside door, and I didn't see the man rushing around a corner until it was too late. I looked up to see a rumpled grey suit just as I felt the bony knee that knocked me down. The collision sent me sliding along the polished linoleum on my bum, as Uncle Red would have said. The man had been reading from a little spiral notebook that he quickly rolled up and shoved into his suit pocket when he bent over to help me up.

"Excuse me, *theah*, little girl. I didn't see you."

I hoped I wasn't going to get in trouble for being somewhere I wasn't supposed to be.

As he helped me to my feet, I noticed he had the same reddish-brown hair as the Senator did, but he looked like he had been sleeping in his suit, and Dad would never let Jackie get away with going without a haircut for so long. It was easy to see family in a face. Anyone could tell Uncle Red and Uncle Conny were brothers, and Grandma Keary always said that Jackie and I were peas in a pod.

When he smiled, I knew for sure I wasn't in trouble.

"My big brother stomped on a dead fish sign in front of our church before Senator Kennedy went by," I bragged and proudly pointed in the direction I thought our church would be.

"Thank him for us, won't you?"

I nodded.

"What parish are we in?"

"Mary of Gaels, sir." I looked up at the empty suit of armor of their mascot. I guessed the inside of the public high school could be considered part of the parish.

"Would you like to meet my big brother?"

The man continued his quick pace down the hall and opened a door, and there was Senator Kennedy sprawled on a chair, scribbling on note cards. A heating pad at his back was plugged into the wall. He took off his reading glasses and looked up when his brother said, "Jack, this little girl's brother has just taken on the local John Birch Society singlehandedly."

"Oh, it wasn't just Jackie, it was my great Uncle Conny and my Uncle Mickey." It seemed important to have all the facts right. When I explained just how they had taken down the sign man, Senator Kennedy laughed loudly and said, "With a name like Uncle Mickey, what else could a fellow do?"

The other brother said, "But, for the record, we are for free speech, even in Kansas."

Before he went back to his note cards, Senator Kennedy asked, "What is your name?"

"I'm Lucy Fahey."

"Well, I'm Jack Kennedy."

As he shook my hand, I wanted to ask if he could really sing "Wearin' of the Green" like Uncle Red said. And tell him that Uncle Red says he'll be the next chieftain, but a man came in and unplugged the heating pad and said, "Break's over, boys. We've got a plane to catch back to St. Louis where they actually have electoral votes."

His brother took off the button on his lapel and asked, "Would you like another button?"

"Yes, sir, I would." He must have seen me eyeing it. It was bigger and much fancier than my "Back Jack" button. It had a picture of Senator Kennedy that I knew from the red and gold cover of Uncle Red's paperback copy of *Profiles in Courage*. It was almost a profile of him looking off towards something in the distance, maybe something only he could see. Maybe it was the future. I was very glad that someone could see a future out there that brought them a smile.

He placed the button in my hand and then they were gone.

I found Uncle Red waiting near the back door of the gym.

"Well, Lucy, did you get to hear our boy?"

"I met him, Uncle Red. I met him!"

"You mean you wedged your way in and got a good place to watch him from. Good girl. Rosie'll get a kick out of hearing this."

"No, Uncle Red. I met him, and his little brother, too."

Uncle Red stopped walking and looked at me like I had just told him that Brian Boru and a couple of other old chieftains had stepped out of one of his songs to have a little chat with me down at the public high school.

"When you say met, Lucy, you must mean ..."

"Look, they gave me this." I told him all about it.

Uncle Red took the button like it was a rare coin from an ancient land.

"What did you say to him?"

"I told him I hoped we win."

"Oh Lucy," he boomed, "You're a pip, a real pip."

Uncle Red whistled and sang all the way back to Uncle Mickey's truck, pausing twice to laugh and punch at the air like a boxer. I felt like singing, too.

CHAPTER 25: AUGUST

Although I'd waited for it all summer, I almost missed the moment that Grandma Fahey said I'd be going home. It came as unexpectedly as the news that I was being sent away at the end of the school year.

On what turned out to be my last night at Grandma's I went to sleep with my window open to let whatever breeze there was into my room. A cool mist during the night had blown in the first rain of the fall and I was dreaming that my own arms and legs had become shapes I didn't recognize, driftwood floating on the ocean maybe, so far from the forest or any other trees. The sad little tangle of wood was drifting gently towards a shore where something creaked out my name again and again, louder and louder until *bang*—the window next to my bed that Grandma had been trying to pull shut finally slammed soundly and I was awake. I stretched my arms and legs, glad they were not made of soggy wood, though my eyes still stung from what must have been the salt water of the ocean.

My legs ached as they did mostly at night when Grandma fed me sugared water with aspirin in a spoon for the growing pains, with the advice that an ache in the legs is a good thing. It would make me tall and a good runner.

"The Regans, Lucy, were all tall, practically giants."

Now Grandma's voice was trying to keep me awake, but the ocean in my dream kept tugging me back out upon it.

"Lucy … Lucy, come on now child. Lucy."

I yawned. It was another day, but I wasn't ready to open my eyes. The smell of orange oatmeal muffins had followed Grandma up from the kitchen. She was sitting on the edge of my bed, as she had when Grandma Keary died. She was patting away the rain that had blown in on my arms and legs that were twisted around a sheet. The driftwood. I stretched my legs again and wondered if they had grown during the night. I felt a tea towel soft on my face and heard her whisper, "Lucy *og*." I opened my eyes to her.

I knew this smile as the one that came over her when she watered her annual flowers outside her kitchen door, especially when she thought that no one saw her. She moved her pots of bright blue lobelia and red geraniums around the yard to keep them in the sun, and then out of the sun so that they wouldn't freckle like the two of us.

"We won't be going to Mass this morning."

These words were as welcome as the sound of the rain on the roof last night. She helped me untangle myself from the sheet, so I could slip deeper under the cool cotton.

"But there's nothing, mind you, that daily Mass won't improve the complexion of." She'd have wagged her finger if her hands were free. "Besides our Blessed Lord expects it."

Jesus wouldn't be expecting daily Mass in the summer if He hadn't grown up in a desert and had known the pleasure of sleeping in on a rainy morning.

"Now, Lucy." This was her morning announcement voice. Two weeks ago she startled me awake with it like the world was coming to an end just to tell me we would be leaving for Mass 20 minutes earlier than usual. It was August 15, Feast of the Assumption of the Blessed Mother into Heaven, and we'd better get our show on the road if we were not going to miss the Holy Day of Obligation rush at the eight o'clock. But this morning there was nothing I had to do but wonder exactly what was baking in her kitchen.

It was easiest not to listen to Grandma in the morning. She'd repeat whatever was important and, besides, she wasn't really asking my opinion on anything. So now I listened lazily to her voice, following it like it was a kite flying free. My great uncle would be coming by earlier than usual today, probably before lunch. That was to my liking. There was something about taking a test at Mary of Gaels, but even that wasn't enough to snag the kite in the treetops.

"You'll be ready for it now that you've been taught well. We've worked hard, you and I, and I'm confident that you'll pass. I've talked with Sister Mary Columba myself. Let me tell you it doesn't hurt your class standing that your Uncle Nat was a Jesuit. She didn't even know that about you, Lucy. I can't imagine Frank not mentioning your pedigree."

The thought of my dad talking at all to Sister Mary Columba made me laugh; he stayed as far away from the school and the church as he could.

"Now that you know your catechism, and she's feeling up to it, your mother is coming home so that she can prepare you for the start of school ..."

Mama is coming home.

I sat up, but slowly, not sure I'd heard this right.

"My mom is coming home?"

"Yes, Lucy, that's what I have been telling you."

Something heavy gave way in my chest.

"Yes, and you and I have a big morning. There's the washing and the packing to do, and ..."

I rolled out of bed and my feet hit the floor before she could finish her thought.

"What time, what time, Grandma? Is she coming here to get me?"

"Frank is taking Rose home from the hospital today and your great uncle will be over before lunch and ..."

"Is Jackie coming home, too?"

"Of course, Lucy."

I knew she was annoyed to be interrupted but I didn't care, I was pulling on my shorts over my seersucker PJ bottoms.

"You have plenty of time to dress properly. There's no need for that kind of drama, Lucy."

She'd held up the pink and white shirt with the Peter Pan collar she had bought me a few weeks ago, three quarter sleeves so I wasn't likely to grow out of it as I had the others.

"My iron's all heated up. What'll you wear home with your new blouse?"

"My shorts."

"A skirt or culottes would be nicer, Lucy."

Why would anyone care what I wore? Mama wouldn't care.

"Do you think Mama will notice how much I have grown?"

"Oh Lucy, you must have grown a foot."

She never laughed when I looked at my feet and said, as Uncle Red had taught me, "Nope, still just the two of 'em," so I didn't bother saying it. Besides, she was looking at my fish on the table next to my bed like she was hoping she didn't have to pack them. Her prediction hadn't come true; they were still here. I knew that Uncle Red was wrong when he said that it was what he named them, and not the fish themselves, that Grandma didn't like. It was just as well the three of us were leaving the city.

She stood up slowly, or maybe it just seemed slowly since I was moving so quickly, but soon she was all business, going through one of my dresser drawers.

"Lucy, I want you to gather up anything that doesn't fit you anymore and get it ready for St. Vincent."

She always talked like she knew St. Vincent de Paul personally. She was looking at things I'd grown out of this summer like I'd done it on purpose.

"Some other little child could use these cotton shirts."

I was thinking we could just cut the sleeves completely off of the one I liked best, so that it would fit.

"The darts would all be wrong then."

I didn't argue this morning because I didn't know what a dart was, and because I wanted to get this day on the road as Grandma had told me at 7:00 every morning all summer that we should do.

"Be sure to go through that closet closely. You really must learn to be more neat, Lucy. And sweep under that bed. God knows what all's under there."

I'd almost forgotten about my shoebox full of locust shells.

"And, Lucy," she turned in the doorway.

I stopped my scurrying because her voice sounded funny, kind of tight and thin, like a rubber band pulled too far that was ready to end up stinging somebody. My dad had the same voice sometimes.

"Lucy?"

"Yessum?" I waited.

"Be sure and take a dry towel to that window sill and bedstead. You'll ruin all my wood if you continue to sleep with that window open in all kinds of weather."

"But Grandma ..." I didn't finish what I was going to say because it just hit me I wouldn't be sleeping there tonight but in my own bed. Jackie'd be in the room next door and my mom and dad down the hallway.

"I'll call you for breakfast, Lucy."

When Grandma left the doorway I saw the little gray suitcase that I had brought with me. I'd never forget the heavy feeling in my stomach that went with the definite thud of it being placed in her attic last May. At Grandma's, things not worn to a nubbin or given to St. Vincent were placed in her attic, where even the spiders were bored with them. At home, we only put things in the attic at the end of Christmas: ornaments and lights, all that fragile brightness nesting in shredded paper, putting away the hope and the warmth of Christmas with nothing but getting through the winter to look forward to.

Now my suitcase was down from the attic and standing in the hallway like my best friend.

It wouldn't take me all morning to pack. I didn't know what Grandma was talking about. Most of my favorite things were on the floor of my closet or the back of the doorknob. I threw these things into the suitcase whether they still fit me or not. Anything that didn't fit in after that I'd give to St. Vincent's. They had kids of all sizes.

Next, I reached under the bed for my locust shell collection. If Jackie wasn't still mooning over Deirdre Mannion, he'd flip when he saw how many I had. An entire shoe box full.

Here they all were, as dry as the husks of the summer days now past. I'd gathered them like days on the calendar when I was the loneliest, each one different if you studied them. Some faces seemed blank, and some like they were laughing, some like they were trying to scare away their own fear, some like they'd been holding on so tight that they never saw it coming when the new greeny locusts inside burst out to fly away.

Grandma called up to say that the muffins would be out of the oven in three minutes. "I don't have time to butter yours warm, so don't dawdle, Lucy."

"Yessum," I hollered back.

Most of them at the bottom of the box had gone to dust already. I wasn't sure what to do with them. I couldn't just leave them here for Grandma to find again. A box of bug shells under my bed was something she'd probably never get over.

I guess it was up to me to decide what they meant and what to do with them.

"Lucy, come down now unless you want a cold breakfast."

I closed the lid, put the box under my arm, and ran down to breakfast. At the bottom of the stairs I found that Grandma had already tied up all my school books with brown twine: my navy blue *Baltimore Catechism*, my red Big Chief tablet, spelling notebooks, and the American history book with a priest in a canoe that I better know by now was the famous Jesuit explorer, Father Marquette. There were also loose-leaf pages with her writing, neater even than Sister Mary Columba's, followed by my practice writing.

My math workbook was off to one side. She'd said in May that I wouldn't need much of this, except to know cups and quarts and pecks in the kitchen.

She had baked orange oatmeal muffins. Those and a little hot tea were my favorite. Grandma acted surprised when I told her that. But then, she acted surprised when Uncle Red said he especially liked an iced cold Papst Blue Ribbon when that was the only beer she ever served him.

She stood over me for a second and then sat down. Something was in her hand. When I saw the little blue vial of holy water from Knock, my scalp began to itch.

"Did you know, Lucy, that the holy water in here had evaporated years ago, before you were born, even before your Uncle Nat and your Dad were born? So, imagine what I thought when I found it full of water after these years."

I tried to explain what had happened, but it seemed silly even to me, so I just stopped talking and looked up at her face.

"Was it holy water you put in here?"

I didn't answer.

"I thought not," she sighed. "You might get this water blessed someday, Lucy."

"Yessum."

"Granny McNamee left this for me before we left for America, as you know. Not that she spoke to me to

~ 312 ~

say goodbye, mind you, she was not like that. She gave it to my Da and said 'Give it to the littlest, she'll have the most need of luck'."

She moved the bottle in front of me.

"Oh, no, she was not one for goodbyes, especially to her children, she'd lost so many. I know what it is to lose a child."

I knew she was starting on the long walk back though her memories of Uncle Nat. Usually she would fall silent for a spell and then come back and ask, "Did I ever tell you of *Tir Na N'Og*, Lucy, the Land of the Young, beyond all time, the land where nothing changes? It's off the western seas of Ireland as the story goes."

I would usually say "No, Grandma," because it made her happy to tell about it after she thought too long about Uncle Nat.

This morning, however, she told me that it was not an easy thing to give up a child, even for God.

"Within seven months both my boys were gone from my house, with so much still to learn, especially your father, Frank. And they weren't going around the corner either." Her nod towards me let me know she was still aware I was there.

"Frank was off to fight in France, and Nat was off to study in Rome. How I worried about Frank dying unconfessed on some beach in France, and all the while it was Nat in mortal danger, not of his soul, of course, but it was Nat that came home dying. Tuberculosis."

So, it had a name, it was not the faeries that took him.

What my mom had had a name, too, but I only overheard it twice. The first time, I thought I heard Grandma Keary say it was an answer that made Mama sick. I wondered what Mama's question had been. I was afraid of asking the same one until Jackie told me it was cancer and a secret.

"There I was worried sick about Frank fighting in France when all the while it was Nat breaking his health, studying till all hours in a damp little basement room in Rome. He couldn't get out of Italy for the war, and then he barely said goodbye before he left for Santa Fe to dry out his lungs. I wonder if Rose still thinks of Nat."

Why would my mom think of Uncle Nat any more than anyone else? Especially since it was my dad who was still the maddest about everything.

"They got along so well. So sad, yet so understanding when he left for the seminary. It killed Will when Nat died. But we women have to be stronger than that. We have to carry on. And teach the faith as we know it."

She patted my hand. Her walk through memories always brought her full circle back to the present if I waited long enough. I wasn't used to her telling me so many of the details. I felt more important knowing them.

I picked up her granny's holy water bottle.

"Thank you for this, Grandma."

"Oh, sure enough, Lucy. Sure enough." She patted my hand again. "Now, you'll be needing another suitcase. You are leaving with more than you came with."

It was true that I now owned more white gloves than I ever thought I'd need in a lifetime. But I'd be leaving with stories I never knew, too, especially about the boy who had survived the famine times.

"You can borrow my suitcase. I'll just go to the attic and get it. You finish your breakfast. It'll need to be aired out, so I'll leave it by the back door for you."

My box of locust shells was on my lap. After Grandma left, I opened it again. These were as important to me as other things I'd collected this summer: two types of Kennedy buttons, Grandma Keary's rosary, and now Grandma Fahey's holy water bottle from Knock. I knew the Regan cross from the famine time would be mine someday. But somehow it didn't seem right to take these shells away from where they had appeared just for me this summer. They belonged where I found them. I knew what I had to do.

At the base of the tallest elm in Grandma's yard, I opened the box, took one last look, and then threw them all up in the air. Some twirled and tumbled briefly on a puff, most clung to each other as they fell to the ground, a light brown, almost golden dust settling over them a few seconds later. I felt something that I hadn't felt since leaving Grandma Keary's house. All I could think to do was to bless them with the water in the holy water bottle from Knock.

Grandma had left her suitcase at the back door to air out. It was a leather one with a strap that fastened around a worn leather button; no metal on it anywhere. It still smelled musty and made me think of movies where people were trapped in the pyramids. The scent of mummies still came through the lavender sachet and new lining paper Grandma had put in it.

I took the suitcase upstairs and put into it whatever was left of my stuff. Grandma looked around the room with me and helped me haul the two suitcases to the front step, where I waited for Uncle Red. Grandma busied herself inside, coming to the door every few minutes.

When Uncle Red pulled up in front, Uncle Mickey was with him. They honked, then Uncle Red started up Grandma's walkway from the boulevard.

"They're here, Grandma."

Grandma appeared at the door, but without her hat and gloves. It never occurred to me that Grandma wouldn't be coming with us out to my house.

"Are we all ready?" Uncle Red seemed as confused, too. "Maeve?"

Her voice was tight like a rubber band again.

"This is Rose's moment with her children. There's no place for two women of the house. She'll want her own little family around her."

Uncle Red whistled to Uncle Mickey and pointed to the suitcases and the gold fish bowl. Then Uncle Red opened the door and I followed him in.

"I won't be going out to the house with you, Red. My work is done. You two go on now."

Uncle Red took off his hat and threw it on top of a table by the door, "C'mon, Maeve old girl, you've been through worse, much worse. Buck up now."

Then he pointed to my cowboy hat that I'd left on top of the TV console, "Here's your hat, what's your hurry?" he chuckled.

He wasn't going either? I never counted on that. If I was just home from the hospital, I'd like to see Uncle Red. Everyone liked seeing Uncle Red, even my dad, although he would grouse about it.

Uncle Mickey was at the door.

"Time to go now, Lucy," Uncle Red said gently. "Your Grandma needs a little help around the house today. And I'll see you up to St. Nat's tonight. You've got Legion of Mary tonight. You're not forgetting that, are you Maeve?"

She shook her head to say she hadn't forgotten, her back still to me.

"Grandma?"

"Go on now, Lucy *og*." She launched each word with great effort.

I thought of her lesson that in Irish there are two separate ways to say goodbye, one is just for the person leaving—and the other just for the person staying behind. I never knew until now exactly why you needed both.

"Grandma, *slan agat*."

"*Agus slan leat*. Safe home, Lucy."

We had secrets only she and I knew, things not even Uncle Red knew. Wasn't I standing on the very step where the faeries, or someone, had left her a white rose the day she learned that Uncle Nat had died?

"I'll remember all of it, Grandma."

"That's a good girl, Lucy," but she made no motion towards me.

I turned to Uncle Mickey. He was flicking his finger against the saran wrap Grandma had pulled taut over my fish bowl.

"And who are these chaps, Lucy?"

I was too old now to be cheered up so easily.

"We have to put them in steerage on this trip, with the rest of the Finn family, eh Red."

"As you say, Mick." He had his arm around Grandma again. "We'll see you soon, Lucy," he smiled.

Uncle Mickey's arms were so large that my luggage looked like toys. His hands were large too, but tender enough to have taken the wild bird out of Grandma Keary's fireplace and cradle it for me to touch its beating little body.

"Did its wing ever mend, Uncle Mickey, the bird at Grandma Keary's house that day?"

"Oh, Lucy that was a while back. Let me think. Yes, yes, I believe it did. It flew quite handily."

I didn't think he was telling the truth, but it didn't matter to me as much now. I was heading home for good.

Chapter 26: Coming Home

My dad was at the kitchen door off the driveway when I hopped from the car. Uncle Mickey followed with the suitcases.

"Well, well," was all Daddy said.

I put my fish bowl on the counter.

"Hi, Daddy. Where's Mama?" I wanted to shout but I didn't. I had been so used to whispering around the house before she left for the hospital.

When I pecked him on his smooth, freshly-shaved cheek there was the sweet and smoky smell of his Jameson's. He gave me a quick hug.

"Is Mama upstairs?" I asked as I headed for the stairs.

"Just a minute, Lucy. There's something I need to say first, just give me a minute."

Mama was probably resting anyway.

"Thanks for bringing Lucy, Mickey. Where's Red? I thought he was coming."

"Oh, he stayed behind. Your mom sort of asked him to."

"What the hell for?"

I'd never heard my dad swear because Uncle Red wasn't coming to our house.

"Go figure, Frank. Mrs. Will Fahey is sweet on old Red Quinn."

Uncle Mickey didn't need to give my dad the customary Quinn slap on the back because he already looked like something had hit him.

"You're joshing me, Mickey."

"Don't worry, Frank. Your mom's virtue in not in danger. Red's probably just looking for an extra vote for Kennedy in that ward. And maybe she's looking for a little entertainment."

"Well then, they're both barking up the wrong tree."

I didn't like them laughing so loud if Mama was resting.

"Tell Rosie to call when she feels like having visitors, will you Frank? Tell her how glad we all are that she's back home."

"Will do, Mick. See you later."

"Well, well, Lucy," Dad said like he wasn't used to saying my name. Somehow it made me feel shy, too.

"Can I see Mama now?"

"Just a minute. Just a minute. I haven't seen you in a while. I thought we'd chat. What have you got here?" he said looking at the bowl on the counter, glad to have something to say to me.

"Dwight and Mamie."

"Oh yeah, who's who?"

"Uncle Red says Mamie's the one with the brains." Dad smirked at the fish bowl.

I didn't like him making that face at them. They kept me company at night in my room when sometimes there was nobody else. I liked imagining that my fish were making smirky faces back at Dad that I knew I couldn't get away with.

He put his hands in his pockets, but there was no change there to make his usual jingly sound. He had his concentrating look like when he poured Jameson's into a shot glass, careful not to use too much or too little or to spill any.

"Lucy, ah Luce, I want you to know that I knew you didn't want to go to your Grandma Fahey's, to stay for so long, I mean."

I hadn't.

"It was for the best overall, for everyone. And you have learned a lot, from what Grandma tells me."

I had.

"And, well," he smiled a bit, "you got these fine fish out of the deal."

"How come you didn't visit me or talk to me on the phone when I wanted to talk to you? It wasn't fair. And how come Jackie got to visit Mama and I didn't? And how come ..."

"Ah, Lucy, this was a hard time for everyone. I thought it would be easier, don't you see, easier for you, I mean, to focus on your studying. The comings and goings would have been hard on both of you, on all of us. I couldn't take care of everything."

I looked away from him. Dwight and Mamie seemed bored, too. I tapped on their bowl.

"Can I go see Mama? Is she upstairs?"

"She's in the yard, she's just looking over her garden. She looks ... well, she's been waiting for you. Your mother and I missed you, Luce. We're just glad you're back."

Mama was in her garden? That was good news. She must be feeling much better. When I thought of Mama among her flowers she was always on her knees planting and weeding and humming, her face tanned and content, her dark brown hair pulled back behind her ears by two combs. I ran as fast as I could through the house to the back door that led to the yard but was stopped cold by what I saw.

I wasn't expecting to see her as she was, even wispier than she had been when I saw her last. She was wearing her bedroom slippers and a pale yellow housecoat. She was more like a butterfly moving among the spent summer flowers than the mom who had been the free throw champion. She held her tortoise shell sunglasses in her left hand.

As the wind caught her long nylon sleeves, she looked even more like a winged visitor to her own garden, moving from plant to plant, touching the dried flowers that had passed her by this summer. All her daisies were drooped or gone. The tall, lacey purple plant that Jackie had begged for after he read *Riders of the Purple Sage* had overgrown many of her other favorites, but even its color was fading. She was back, but too late for the wild beauty of the season. No one, not even Mama could bring the summer back. A sound like "Mama" jumped from my throat and I ran to hug her.

"Luce!" She turned and called back to me, her arms outstretched. When I tried to tell her how much I missed her, I found out the tears that burn the most come from right above your heart and catch in your throat.

"There, there, Lucy, my brave girl."

The familiar housecoat billowed around us and I squeezed her tighter to make sure she was really there and not like the ghost she almost seemed.

"We are all home now. It's OK."

I wanted things to be as they had been before this summer. But they couldn't be and I knew it by her face. I couldn't say quite what had changed, what was missing. It was her left eye that she couldn't see out of anymore. It was the one I stared at now. A thought more like a sob washed over me: how could she have an eye that couldn't see me anymore?

I blinked and blinked until warm tears ran down my cheeks, and I looked harder at her face for an answer. Mama's left eye was not the same as the right one. The light on it was different; it was like a window that only reflected light so you couldn't see who was home.

I could see Mama inside her right eye. I wanted to say "I'm still me, too." Did she have to look harder to see me now?

She suddenly raised her right hand to her forehead. I thought she was starting the sign of the cross, but instead her hand fluttered over her left eye like a butterfly hovering above one of her flowers. Then she quickly put on her sunglasses.

"Rather bright, don't you think?" She smiled again at me from behind her dark lenses. "I took these off to see the colors better."

She took me by the hand and we walked toward her bed of mums.

"Just look at them, Luce." She waved one delicate wing-like arm over the mounds of bright yellow flowers. A single climbing rose next to the mums had made it on its own, too, this summer, and had dropped some red petals on the yellow.

"At least the late season color is coming into its own. And that rose. Look here, Lucy." Although she tenderly touched the rose, petals fell from it. "'The Last Rose of Summer,' just like in the old song."

I knew the one she meant. Daddy used to sing it.

"Ah, Luce," she pulled me close to her side. "But look," she insisted, "just look at these mums. This is their time of year. This is what I call glorious."

I knew she was trying to open up a space to let the color in where her absence had left a dark uncertain place in my chest. I sniffled and watched her as she studied the flowers like there were answers there.

"What do you think, Luce?"

To me each little bud was a pinch of yellow asking, "When? When? When?" The flowers completely opened were shouting, "Now! Now! Now!"

"You can always count on a mum in the fall. Guess they don't call 'em hardy for nothing, eh Luce?"

I was surprised by the way she was looking at me from behind her sunglasses, like she was waiting for an answer.

"Yessum."

Dad was watching us from the door to the back yard. She waved for him to come out, but he just waved back and walked away from the door.

"Have you seen Jackie yet?"

I shook my head. He even got to come home before I did.

"He's grounded already, I'm afraid."

That was OK with me. He wouldn't be running off to the Velvet Freeze with the Moggers to talk to seventh grade girls.

"Why don't you put your things away. Uncle Red left some things for you in your room. Run on now. And do try to be helpful to Daddy. He loves us all very much and he's doing what he thinks best. OK, Luce?"

I left Mama in a lawn chair that faced her garden and the western sky. She always liked to watch the clouds just over the horizon of the sloping field behind our house. I hoped we'd have a long Indian summer this year and Mama would get enough time in her garden after all.

I stood in my brother's doorway. He was stretched out on his bed with a real book, not a Classic Comic, in front of his face.

"Hey, Jackie."

He looked up as sullenly as if there had been actual bars on his door.

"Hiya, Luce."

His radio was playing from under his pillow. He hated being without it but that was a rule of being grounded, so he played it as softly as he could. Uncle Red said once Jackie looked like a refugee listening to Radio Free Europe when he saw him huddled in a corner with his ear to the radio so he wouldn't miss Dion and the Belmonts. I knew Jackie wasn't going to welcome me home officially or anything but I wanted to talk or hang out with him.

"Hey, Jackie. I got two fish."

"Yeah? Neat." He closed his book and sat up. "Where are they?"

I ran to the kitchen, proud to return with Dwight and Mamie.

"Here they are."

"Oh, these are just gold fish, Luce."

"Well, yeah."

"I thought maybe you had tropicals, like Deirdre Mannion. She has tropical fish in a big tank with a light and heater in it and everything. She lives in Mission Hills and her old man has a '58 T-Bird, a convertible."

I looked at poor Dwight and Mamie; they were not moving much, just sort of hanging out themselves, probably car sick from the ride over from Grandma Fahey's. I wondered if they'd need their own heater this winter. It would be just like that Deirdre Mannion to have prissy, spoiled fish.

"She has neon tetras and angel fish. Do you know what those are, Luce?"

"Sure I do. They're stupid fish." I'd never seen or heard of either.

He was in front of his mirror rubbing Brylcreme into his hair to make it come to a kind of peak in front. Then he shook his head from side to side just like Elvis in *Jail House Rock* to make it fall onto his forehead.

"I like my kind of fish much better."

"Yeah? Well, suit yourself." He was practicing raising his right upper lip at the corner and smiling back at Elvis in the mirror.

He used to treasure ordinary goldfish. Once I stood with him in the rain to dig a hole in the creek bank and say an Our Father and a Hail Mary when one of his had died. Dad had wanted to put it down the garbage disposal. Where had that brother gone?

I took Dwight and Mamie on down the hall to their new home, my bedroom. It seemed smaller, maybe because the space at the foot of my bed was taken up by something I never thought I'd see again: Grandma Keary's rocking chair. Uncle Red must have kept it for me. On the chair was a collection of some of her things, the mended vase from the Vale of Avoca, her blue enameled "Souvenir of Galway City" thimble, the candy dish shaped like a walnut shell and two knitting needles stuck in a ball of bright blue yarn still attached to a long, nearly finished scarf. Mama could tie off the end for me to wear it this winter.

She was in Heaven, her new home, and my home seemed different to me. The room was tidier than I left it, but the bed was not made my mom's cozy way, with the top sheet folded down over the comforter so you could slide right in after prayers. The sheets weren't starched and ironed either, as I had grown to expect they should be this summer at Grandma Fahey's.

I put Grandma Keary's vase on my shelf with my dinosaur and glow-in-the-dark saints, then curled up on my own bed for the first time since last May. I didn't know how much things, even little things, can grow so large in your heart if you have to leave them before you want to. I pulled my pillow from under the comforter to feel its coolness against my cheek.

I looked down at Grandma's Keary's rocker. The night of the *ceili* Uncle Red had said that Grandma Keary would always be around whenever the family got together. Well, here we all were again, Mama, Dad, Jackie and me. And Grandma's empty rocker. I thought it would be a while before I sat in it alone.

Maybe having her rocker was like the blanket from the Drumkeary ghost in Uncle Conny's story. He'd said that the Drumkeary ghost kept an eye out for our people. When I'd asked Uncle Red later if that story was true, he'd only asked me if I thought it was a good story.

"Heck, yeah. It is one of the best stories I ever heard. The ghost was her great grandfather and saved her life because she belonged to his family."

He'd said, "Well Lucy, did you know a good story is always a true one? In fact, the better the story is, the truer it becomes."

"Really Uncle Red? So, it's not, well, just a made up story then, about the ghost and the girl taking his blanket?"

"Did you also know, Lucy, that there's no such thing as a made up story? Not entirely anyway. Just like there's no such thing as a finished story. A story, if it's a good one, like your Drumkeary ghost for example, just sort of takes hold of you, becomes part of you. And you're real enough, aren't you Lucy?"

I had nodded like I understood.

"Well then, there's your answer."

He had seemed pleased as he'd puffed on his pipe.

"You know, Lucy, when you think about it," he was clicking the stem of his pipe on his teeth, "a good story is something you keep with you a while, and then pass on to somebody else who can use it, too."

He smiled and blew a smoke ring that floated over my head. I watched while it changed shape and disappeared.

Now, as I nestled deeper into my own pillow in my own bed at last, I thought maybe I no longer needed the Drumkeary ghost whose specialty, after all, was getting people home. I hadn't realized until now just how many stories I had been given this summer or how much I needed them. I heard them in the loneliest place, deep inside me where now a soft, steady comfort was making its way to the surface, almost like the harps that rose from the bogs so that our music would not be lost.

I didn't really want to give up any of the stories I heard this summer in St. Nat's, especially about the faeries. Where did they fit in between the visible and invisible in the *Credo*? I believed in the faeries this summer because believing in God was too far-fetched. I looked around my own simple room and realized that I might miss thinking about them anyway.

Or was it just Grandma Fahey that I was already starting to miss?

She was probably standing in my empty room now, dusting the picture of Uncle Natty and then the pictures in the hallway of Great Grandpa Regan and Our Lady of Perpetual Help as she did each week before her Legion meeting. She might even be thinking of *Tir Na N'Og,* The Land of the Young. I don't know if she believed that's where Uncle Natty was, instead of Heaven, because she always said that Heaven was packed to the gills with Jesuits. That worried me. Since I myself wasn't particularly good at poker, I didn't know how well I'd do there when the time came.

The story of *Tir Na N'Og* was one I didn't mind putting aside. Who would want to be a little kid forever? Not me. Especially if it would always be like this summer. But then I wasn't really Lucy *og*, the young one, as I had been at the beginning of the summer. Now I knew that everything changes, even the truth in stories. Besides, if Grandma Keary went to *Tir Na N'Og* how would I ever recognize her? I'd rather think of Grandma Keary in Heaven just as she was when I saw her last, laughing hard at something Uncle Red had heard down at Mr. Philsy Cannon's place.

I wondered if Uncle Red would miss me tonight waiting with him in his car, helping him with the crossword until Grandma's Legion of Mary meeting was over.

"Lucy, what's a seven letter word for a pair of ducks?"

"That says 'paradox,' Uncle Red. Not pair of ducks."

"Oh, it does indeed."

School would start back up in a few days and I'd be getting more homework about believing in the invisible God and all. Now that I was home again believing in Him was a lot easier. But all I really wanted to believe in was the visible, right in front of me. Mama in her garden watching clouds tumble across the horizon, Daddy rummaging in the garage trying to remember not to sound so angry with everyone, and Jackie in his room slicking fresh Brylcreme in his hair and singing "You Ain't Nothin' But a Hound Dog" at himself in the mirror. He thought I couldn't hear him.

When I heard piano music from downstairs, I had to remind myself that it was really Mama after such a long time of imagining I heard her voice or saw her in a crowd at church or on the downtown bus. I rolled over so my good ear was facing the door.

Mama was moving through a melody like she was trying to decide whether she wanted to play. It was one of the old songs she used to play and Daddy would sing. She only played the right hand, no harmonies. I knew she could make even that old upright that Uncle Red swiped from the AOH fill the house if she wanted to. But now she only played a few chords and then stopped and then picked up the melody again. It was like listening to only one part of a conversation, like when she used to stay on the phone with Grandma Keary for an hour.

The tune was one from Dad's college recital. I listened carefully for my dad's voice, as carefully as I had for the faeries to announce themselves in Grandma's yard. When I heard my dad's whistling, I ran to the top of the stairs, hoping he'd sing. Whatever they said to each other was muffled, but then Mama started to play with both hands, and Dad began to sing. I leaned over the banister to hear everything I could. Jackie stayed in his room, but turned off his radio as Dad began: "Believe me, if all those endearing young charms, which I gaze on so fondly today, were to change by tomorrow and flee from my arms, like faery gifts fading away."

Daddy's voice that always made me think of bells was becoming rubbery like it was after his brother died. I knew how he looked when his voice got that way. He'd be leaning forward, with a hand on the piano for support, his face kind of blotchy. He came to the end of the verse before Mama's accompaniment, like he was trying to say something before it was too late. "Thou would still be adored, as this moment thou art."

I worried how much longer Mama would get to keep the piano, if it was just a temporary gift as Uncle Red had said. But then I didn't think he'd let anyone, even the Ancient Order of Hibernians, take Mama's piano from her. He'd think of something, a story about where their piano had gone to so they wouldn't be expecting it back. Who knows, maybe someone at the AOH might even believe him if he said the faeries took it. I knew now that there was nothing, nothing at all, that couldn't be changed with a good story.

Epilogue: No Irish Need Apply

I'd passed my tests and so would go on to the next grade with my classmates. I didn't even mind going to school. What could they teach me that I didn't already know?

I think I surprised Sister Marie Francis, my new teacher, on the first day when she asked who knew the prayer of St. Francis. I raised my hand to ask would that be St. Francis of Assisi or St. Francis Xavier. When she asked me what I thought the difference between the two saints was, I reported that one was a Jesuit and the other was only a Franciscan. Everyone knew that the Jesuits were better than the Franciscans in the same way that the American League was better than the National League. Both good leagues, both played baseball, but one played to the home crowd in Kansas City.

I sat down, proud of myself for filling in the gaps in Sister's learning. Grandma Fahey would have been proud of me, too. But for my trouble I got assigned an extra report on St. Francis of Assisi and his best friend, St. Clare. If Jackie had given my answer to the question, somebody probably would have pinned another catechism medal on him.

I was kind of glad to be back at school. I could take it easy for about nine months. It would be a long time until next May to see if there was another note home about passing to the next grade.

Election day fell the day before my birthday. Uncle Red and Grandma Fahey and some other relatives came by that night to watch returns and to watch me open Grandma's present: a bright red blazer, with brass buttons and a beaded Mary of Gaels crest over the pocket.

"Try it on, Lucy," Mama smiled.

I didn't know if I was allowed. Only the older girls wore these with their uniforms.

Mama said how grown up I looked.

Grandma said that it is of the highest quality and there'd be room to let down the sleeves for next year. Dad said it fit me fine now. Uncle Red said I looked like a million. Jackie said that Deirdre Mannion had three different berets that matched each of her blazers. Mama said that my corduroy Mary of Gaels beanie would look just fine with mine.

After we had cake, everyone settled down in front of the TV set.

Uncle Conny, Uncle Mickey and Prof Ryan all stopped in, too. The election was turning out to be bigger than a Notre Dame game. Even Jackie hung around for a while. Grandma fell into lively conversation with Prof Ryan, although he seemed to be more interested in the card table where my dad and my great uncles and Uncle Mick were playing poker, gin rummy, then poker again.

No one bothered to look up when Kansas went early for Richard Nixon, but whenever any results from Illinois came up, everyone stopped what they were doing and looked up. Everyone but Grandma Fahey laughed when Uncle Red and Uncle Conny recited the litany of the dead Chicago relatives—Quinn, McKee, O'Fallon, Cavanaugh, and Skeffington—that still managed to vote for a Kennedy.

Grandma Fahey huffed, "Oh you, Red," when Uncle Red beamed that being a Democrat makes you bloody immortal in Cook County, Illinois. Then he called out, "What do you think, Lucy, your old pal Jack going to win this one?"

"Yes sir, Uncle Red." I knew by now that Illinois had more than three times the electoral votes that Kansas did.

Jackie rolled his eyes like he did every time Uncle Red asked my opinion on politics—which he did a lot since my conversation with the Kennedy boys last summer. But Jackie was just lucky I didn't tell everyone that Deirdre Mannion's dad was voting for the other side. Nobody'd be letting him out of the house tonight to do his homework at the Mannion's.

When I could keep my eyes open no longer Mom sent me off to bed, but I could hear the whistle of the teakettle and the pop and fizz of beer cans in my sleep.

A cold rush of air woke me up when the front door was opened for people to leave. The last thing I heard was Uncle Red saying it was still a squeaker and Grandma Fahey saying that it looked like snow. But even that exciting possibility couldn't keep me awake.

The next morning when my mother came in smiling, "Happy birthday, Lucy. Looks like we have a new President."

I knew from her chuckle that we were ahead. Senator Kennedy had a smile almost as bright as Mama's when she was happy as she was that morning. I had no way of knowing then how temporary, how like faery gifts, they would both be.

"It snowed last night, did you see, Lucy?" Mama hung the uniform blouse she had just ironed for me on the doorknob.

I sat up and looked out on the front yard; the world did look different to me, the sun made the snow glitter. I could scarcely believe my luck at both an early snow and the man who shook my hand winning his race.

When I came down to the kitchen, Uncle Red was already there, drinking tea that Mama had put out for Dad. Uncle Red was on long distance to Chicago. Mom poured tea in another cup for Dad saying that he had probably stayed up the latest of anyone.

Uncle Red put down the phone and yelled, "It's official. Our boy won." He laughed and shook his head and hugged Mama, and hesitated before slapping Dad on the back since his mouth was full of toast, but did it anyway.

"That skinny little Mick is President of the United States of America," Uncle Red boomed. "Jackie O'Robinson has just stolen home."

The phone rang. It was Uncle Conny. Uncle Red answered by humming "Hail to The Chief" into the receiver.

When he called Grandma Fahey he said, "Good morning, Maeve. I thought you'd like to know that they'll have to take down the No Irish Need Apply sign on 1600 Pennsylvania Avenue ... Yes I'm sure ... I don't give a damn for what *The Kansas City Star* says. I'm positive, Maeve."

Uncle Red then handed the phone to Dad. "Frank, she wants to talk to you."

"Well you're right, Mother. It would have just been a wasted vote in your precinct. I understand. I'll keep it under my hat."

When he got off the line, he looked at the faces turned to his and laughed, "My mother says she knew all along Kennedy would win, and that is why she didn't vote for Nixon."

"Grandma Fahey voted for Senator Kennedy?" I asked, concerned that Uncle Red was choking on his tea.

"No, Lucy. She just didn't vote," Dad laughed. "There's a difference."

Dad kissed Mom on the cheek and went out to dust the snow off his car.

Uncle Red sat down tired but happy at our kitchen table. He brushed his thick, white hair back from his forehead with his hand, but it only fell again. Then to me he said, "I almost forgot. Happy Birthday, Lucy. You're into double digits. You're official now, too."

He fished out a bright copper coin about the size of a fifty-cent piece from his pocket and carefully rolled it across the table to me.

"Gee thanks, Uncle Red."

"Rolling a new penny will change your luck."

I looked at the coin and back at him.

He continued, "To defy the wheel of fate, don't you see. My old granny always had us walk around the kitchen table backwards on New Year's Day. To change our luck."

"Did it work?" I asked.

"How would we ever know?" he mugged.

"How much is it worth?" I was already planning how I would spend it.

"It's a two pence in Ireland and you can't exactly spend it here, Lucy. But I'd say that after today it is the coin of the realm."

My new coin was like most Irish things, worth more if you knew their secret value like Uncle Red did. The coin in my hand made me feel warm and happy. Maybe this feeling was my luck changing. I looked at Uncle Red's shining tired face, and even my bare feet that dangled just above the cold linoleum floor felt warm.

"Uncle Red, do you think they'll give Senator Kennedy his own coin someday, like Roosevelt?"

"That's a dandy idea, Lucy, maybe you should take that up with him next time you see him."

I bet Jackie never felt this important even after he pitched his no hitter.

"It's a great day for the Irish, wouldn't you say, Lucy?"

By the light in Uncle Red's eyes I knew I didn't have to answer.

Jackie burst into the kitchen and yelled that he forgot he had to serve the 8:00 Mass and that he was going to be late. As he flew out the door, the black cassock and white lace surplice trailing behind him on a hanger over his shoulder made it look like he was being chased out of the kitchen by the ghost of a priest.

Mama looked up at the clock, "Oh, Lucy, look at the time. Hurry and get dressed now, too."

I was excited about heading off to school and into this first snow on my 10th birthday. My Irish coin clinked a new sound against the three dimes, all Roosevelts today, that I carried for lunch money in the pocket of my new red blazer. The snow was still lightly falling. I pulled the hood up on my uniform coat and ran across the open field behind our house.

There was more wind than real snow, although the ground and fallen leaves were covered with a fine powder. I wrapped Grandma Keary's scarf around my neck and held my hood closed against the wind. It might have been only the sound of the wind or the flannel lining of my hood brushing against my good ear, but I thought I heard someone call my name. I stopped and looked behind me, it had been that clear. No one was there. But I noticed how my footsteps had uncovered some leaves and the still-green grass under this early snow. The path of green footsteps I had made across the field led all the way back to our house.

I turned and looked ahead to the snowy field in front of me, the yet unformed path, and then once again behind me and smiled. I knew exactly where I was.

ABOUT THE AUTHOR

Suzanne Kelly was raised in suburban Kansas City and has long had an interest in the history of the Irish in America as reflected in songs and stories passed from generation to generation. In her travels she has been fascinated and amused by some of the commonalities among the Irish in America and those in Ireland, proving the truth of Gaelic lore that "one beetle recognizes another."

She comes from a large extended Irish family, one branch of which has been in Kansas City since an ancestor emigrated, fought for the Union in the Civil War, and settled there.

John F. Kennedy's race for the White House in 1960 galvanized Irish Americans in surprising ways that she features in her novel, set on the eve of his election.

Suzanne graduated from the University of Kansas with a BA in English and a law degree. She also holds an MA in English from Indiana University. Two Individual Artist Grants from the Montgomery (Ohio) County Arts and Cultural District have supported her work.

Having worked as an Assistant Ohio Attorney General and for an online legal publisher, Suzanne Kelly-Garrison currently enjoys her position as Lecturer of Law at Wright State University. She lives in Dayton, Ohio with her husband, poet David Garrison. This is her first novel.

RECENT BOOKS BY BOTTOM DOG PRESS

BOOKS IN THE HARMONY SERIES

Stolen Child: A Novel
By Suzanne Kelly, 338 pgs. $18
The Canary : A Novel
By Michael Loyd Gray, 196 pgs. $18
On the Flyleaf: Poems
By Herbert Woodward Martin, 106 pgs. $16
The Harmonist at Nightfall: Poems of Indiana
By Shari Wagner, 114 pgs. $16
Painting Bridges: A Novel
By Patricia Averbach, 234 pgs. $18
Ariadne & Other Poems
By Ingrid Swanberg, 120 pgs. $16
The Search for the Reason Why: New and Selected Poems
By Tom Kryss, 192 pgs. $16
Kenneth Patchen: Rebel Poet in America
By Larry Smith, Revised 2nd Edition, 326 pgs. Cloth $28
Selected Correspondence of Kenneth Patchen,
Edited with introduction by Allen Frost, Paper $18/ Cloth $28
Awash with Roses: Collected Love Poems of Kenneth Patchen
Eds. Laura Smith and Larry Smith
With introduction by Larry Smith, 200 pgs. $16

* * * *

HARMONY COLLECTIONS AND ANTHOLOGIES

d.a.levy and the mimeograph revolution
Eds. Ingrid Swanberg and Larry Smith, 276 pgs. $20
Come Together: Imagine Peace
Eds. Ann Smith, Larry Smith, Philip Metres, 204 pgs. $16
Evensong: Contemporary American Poets on Spirituality
Eds. Gerry LaFemina and Chad Prevost, 240 pgs. $16
America Zen: A Gathering of Poets
Eds. Ray McNiece and Larry Smith, 224 pgs. $16
Family Matters: Poems of Our Families
Eds. Ann Smith and Larry Smith, 232 pgs. $16

Bottom Dog Press, Inc.
PO Box 425/ Huron, Ohio 44839
Order Online at:
http://smithdocs.net/BirdDogy/BirdDogPage.html

RECENT BOOKS BY BOTTOM DOG PRESS

Sky Under the Roof: Poems By Hilda Downer, 126 pgs. $16.
Breathing the West: Great Basin Poems
By Liane Ellison Norman, 80 pgs. $16
Smoke: Poems By Jeanne Bryner, 96 pgs. $16
Maggot : A Novel By Robert Flanagan, 262 pgs. $18
Broken Collar: A Novel By Ron Mitchell, 234 pgs. $18
American Poet: A Novel By Jeff Vande Zande, 200 pgs. $18
The Pattern Maker's Daughter: Poems
By Sandee Gertz Umbach, 90 pages $16
The Way-Back Room: Memoir of a Detroit Childhood
By Mary Minock, 216 pgs. $18
The Free Farm: A Novel By Larry Smith, 306 pgs. $18
Sinners of Sanction County: Stories
By Charles Dodd White, 160 pgs. $17
Learning How: Stories, Yarns & Tales
By Richard Hague, 216 pgs. $18
Strangers in America: A Novel
By Erika Meyers, 140 pgs. $16
Riders on the Storm: A Novel
By Susan Streeter Carpenter, 404 pgs. $18
The Long River Home: A Novel
By Larry Smith, 230 pgs. Paper $16/ Cloth $22
Landscape with Fragmented Figures: A Novel
By Jeff Vande Zande, 232 pgs. $16
The Big Book of Daniel: Collected Poems
By Daniel Thompson, 340 pgs. Paper $18/ Cloth $22;
Reply to an Eviction Notice: Poems
By Robert Flanagan, 100 pgs. $15
An Unmistakable Shade of Red & The Obama Chronicles
By Mary E. Weems, 80 pgs. $15
Our Way of Life: Poems By Ray McNiece, 128 pgs. $15

Bottom Dog Press, Inc.
PO Box 425/ Huron, Ohio 44839
Order Online at:
http://smithdocs.net/BirdDogy/BirdDogPage.html

BOOKS BY
BIRD DOG PUBLISHING

Words Walk: Poems
By Ronald M. Ruble, 978-1-933964-71-3 168 pgs, $16
The Wonderful Stupid Man
By Allen Frost, 978-1-933964-64-5 190 pgs. $15
Dogs and Other Poems
By Paul S. Piper, 978-1-933-64-45-4 74 pgs. $15
The Mermaid Translations
By Allen Frost, 978-1-933964-40-9 136 pgs. $15
Home Recordings
By Allen Frost, 978-1-933964-24-9 124 pgs. $15
Faces and Voices: Tales
By Larry Smith, 1-933964-04-9 136 pgs. $15
Second Story Woman: A Memoir of Second Chances
By Carole Calladine, 978-1-933964-12-6 226 pgs. $16
256 Zones of Gray: Poems
By Rob Smith, 978-1-933964-16-4 80 pgs. $15
Another Life: Collected Poems
By Allen Frost, 978-1-933964-10-2 176 pgs. $15
Winter Apples: Poems
By Paul S. Piper, 978-1-933964-08-9 88 pgs. $15
Lake Effect: Poems
By Laura Treacy Bentley, 1-933964-05-7 108 pgs. $14
Depression Days on an Appalachian Farm: Poems
By Robert L. Tener, 1-933964-03-0 80 pgs. $15
120 Charles Street, The Village: Journals & Other Writings 1949-1950
By Holly Beye, 0-933087-99-3 240 pgs. $16

Bird Dog Publishing
A division of Bottom Dog Press, Inc.
PO Box 425/ Huron, Ohio 44839
Order Online at:
http://smithdocs.net/BirdDogy/BirdDogPage.html

CPSIA information can be obtained at www.ICGtesting.com
Printed in the USA
LVOW12s1930220913

353507LV00002B/4/P